W9-BVQ-834

BRIAR QUEEN

A Night and Nothing Novel

KATHERINE HARBOUR

HARPER Voyager

An Imprint of HarperCollins Publishers

This book is dedicated to my friends and family.

This book is a work of fiction. The characters, incidents, and dialogue are drawn from the author's imagination and are not to be construed as real. Any resemblance to actual events or persons, living or dead, is entirely coincidental.

BRIAR QUEEN. Copyright © 2015 by Katherine Harbour. All rights reserved. Printed in the United States of America. No part of this book may be used or reproduced in any manner whatsoever without written permission except in the case of brief quotations embodied in critical articles and reviews. For information address Harper-Collins Publishers, 195 Broadway, New York, NY 10007.

HarperCollins books may be purchased for educational, business, or sales promotional use. For information please e-mail the Special Markets Department at SPsales@harpercollins.com.

FIRST EDITION

Library of Congress Cataloging-in-Publication Data has been applied for.

ISBN 978-0-06-228676-5

15 16 17 18 19 OV/RRD 10 9 8 7 6 5 4 3 2 1

ACKNOWLEDGMENTS

Thank you to my editors at Harper Voyager—Diana Gill, who gave me my first chance, and Katherine Nintzel, who adopted the children of nothing and night and made *Briar Queen* a beautiful story. Without your guidance, this book never would have existed for all to read.

Thanks also to agent Thao Le of the Sandra Dijkstra Agency, for her unending support and suggestions. And thanks to Jessie Edwards, my publicist at Harper Voyager, for her enthusiasm and hard work.

Thanks all around to the team at Harper Voyager: To David Pomerico for his encouraging words. And to Margaux Weisman and Dana Trombley for their prompt responses to my questions. And many thanks to my copy editor, Laurie McGee.

To my coworkers at the Sarasota Barnes & Noble, especially Roberta Wells. To my manager Dom Rosenbloom, to Donna DeTeresa, Lisa Carter, and Jason Aragona, who helped with my first book's launch night. And thanks to Mike Little for the soundtrack and Arianna Westerfield for the book trailer. Thanks to Ellen Snyder, Christy Renshaw, and Ruth Nikolic.

Thanks to everyone who reviewed and tweeted about my first book and those kind enough to interview me on their sites.

And thank you to those who bought the first part of Finn's and Jack's stories and continue to read about them. This book in your hands wouldn't have existed without you.

PROLOGUE

Jack Hawthorn had begun to dread sleep. He dreamed now, and most of those dreams were nightmares. He wasn't used to fear: the drumming of his heart, the quickening of breath, the blood coursing through him.

In his apartment above the abandoned theater, sprawled on his bed beneath a film poster of Rudolph Valentino as the sheik, he traced his gaze across the ceiling's metal girders, down to the objects he'd collected over many, many years. Moonlight silvered the eyes of a taxidermy owl, a brass teakettle, an apple-green iPod, things he'd taken to prove that he was a part of the true world and not a phantom.

Now, he *was* a part of the true world, thanks to an annoyingly reckless girl with caramel-colored eyes.

He rolled off the bed. He dressed quickly and headed for the window. Shoving it open, he climbed onto the fire escape swirling with snow and dropped down into the parking lot.

In the Summerwoods, now barren with winter's descent, Jack passed the ruins of a chapel built by an English explorer named Drake and moved into a grove of birches, their paper-white bark blending with the snow to create an illusion of endlessness. Snowflakes dusted the dark brown hair falling around his face as he ventured farther into the woods.

At last, he crouched down beneath a rowan tree scored with five unsettling marks, to examine the frost-glimmering leaves. Because he was no longer a thing of the dark, he didn't see the murdered boy crouched nearby, hyacinth flowers drifting from a cavity in his chest. The boy, whose body should have been rotting beneath the sparkling leaves, said, "*Jack*."

Jack didn't hear. He picked a few things from the ground and stared at them, closed his fingers around them, and bowed his head.

The dead boy, once named Nathan Clare, didn't speak again. He'd seen the locket Jack had lifted from the leaves, the human tooth.

Jack rose and walked away.

Nathan Clare huddled in the snow, one hand curled against the hole in his chest. He couldn't tell Jack about the bloody horror of his death or warn him about what hid in the forest. Nathan would have to wait for *her* . . . the girl who had once tried to save him.

CHAPTER 1

Inanna was a goddess of light. Ereshkigal, her sister, was a goddess of darkness. Inanna missed her sister and went to the underworld to visit her. When she entered that place, at each gate she passed, she had to remove an article of clothing or jewelry. Soon, she had nothing left to protect her. When Inanna reached the underworld and moved toward her sister, the creatures of the underworld thought she was trying to take Ereshkigal back to the true world. They captured Inanna and made her one of the dead. But Ereshkigal helped her sister return to the light, and so remained in the dark forever.

—A Mesopotamian myth

He has teeth, and claws, and eyes that bite.

The voice of her sister, Lily Rose, was clear in Finn's head as Finn sat in a chair beneath the young oak that had once been a malevolent thing, its winter-bared branches now glowing with tiny stars that caused the snow around her to shimmer. She didn't know why she was here, but she felt she'd done some terrible thing.

Footprints suddenly appeared in the snow—something invisible was walking toward her. She whispered, "Go away . . . go away . . ."

Someone spoke her name. She reluctantly lifted her gaze.

A shadow in a scarlet gown stood before her, its dark hair writhing, veins glowing red beneath its charred, blackened skin. The air crackled.

"Reiko," Finn whispered. "I'm sorry."

The girl queen's venom-green eyes opened in her burning face. "Little mayfly. The Wolf is at the door."

❖ ❖ ❖

SOMETHING WAS KNOCKING TO GET IN.

Finn opened her eyes and heaved a breath. Cold crept beneath her bedcovers. Winter frosted the walls of her room, the floor, the mirror. One of the glass doors to the terrace had fallen open and was banging back and forth in a wood-smoke-scented wind.

She got up and shut the door. The bolt had come loose, so she secured it with a chair beneath the handle and stepped back, considering the whiteness drifting past the glass. It was the first snowfall she'd seen in a long time, and it was beautiful and menacing. As she listened to the heat rattling through the old radiators, she remembered a burning queen and what inhabited a certain abandoned hotel. She shivered. She looked around the tower room she'd made hers, with its cluttered bookshelves, her mom's watercolors, antique furniture she'd scavenged from other rooms in the house. No books flew across the room. Nothing shattered. She still wasn't sure if the occasional poltergeist in the house actually *was* her sister who had killed herself a year ago. "Lily?"

There was no answer.

"DOES HE HAVE TO BE THERE EVERY MORNING?"

"Yes, Da, he does." Finn had dressed quickly and applied a little of the dessert-themed makeup she'd taken a liking to, the chocolate eye shadow and strawberry-cupcake lip gloss. "He walks me to classes. He's a gentleman."

Her father looked annoyed. When they'd moved here a few months ago, they'd only had each other. Those few months in Fair Hollow had changed everything. Finn ventured, "So . . . are you going out with Miss Emory tonight?"

"It's not odd for you, is it? Me and Jane?"

"Well, she's my botany professor." Jane Emory was also part of a secret society who knew about Fair Hollow's supernatural residents, the Fatas—Finn hadn't told her father about the Fatas. She could never tell him about the Fatas.

Her father, who hadn't shaved or even combed his blond hair, glanced out the window again. He was always disorganized on Monday mornings. She'd set his thermos of coffee, his laptop, and his coat and car keys near the door.

"I've put all your stuff there." She shoved her unruly brown hair into a wool hat and, grabbing her scarf, nearly knocked down a random pile of books on the counter. That even the kitchen was cluttered with books was a testament to her and her father's reluctance to let go of anything they'd read and loved. "See you."

"You need to carry all those textbooks?"

"Ironic, that you should ask—don't we have shelves for these?" She poked at the pile of paperbacks on the counter. "I've got a lot to catch up on." She was, in fact, dangerously close to sending her approaching exams into a tailspin.

"Tell *him*—"

"His name's Jack."

"Tell Jack he's welcome to spend Christmas with us." Her da grimaced as if it hurt to say it. "If he'd like."

"Da . . . I'm *so* proud of you right now."

"Get out."

She grinned and stepped outside. The sunlight was already turning the snow to slush, but it was still sharply cold and her breath misted as it left her. She liked the cold. It cleared her head.

Jack Hawthorn stood at the bottom of the steps, waiting. In the day, he was a sight—dark hair falling around a regal, sharply boned face that belonged to another era. There always seemed to be a secret in his eyes. His anorak was lined with fake fur. He wore jeans and work boots. The tiny ruby glittering on one side of his aquiline nose had become a symbol of the blood that now ran through him where, before, his insides had been an alchemy of rose petals and Fata magic. She looked him over, skeptically. "You're not going to pass for ordinary, no matter how much you try."

"I'm used to attention." He smiled and crooked his arm. She slid hers through. As they began walking, her breath hitched.

His shadow was missing.

When they emerged from the darkness cast by a maple tree, his shadow had returned—maybe it had only been a trick of the light?

He caught one of her hands, drew off the glove, and kissed her cold fingers. His lips were warm and she felt as if a thread of electricity went straight from her fingers to her midriff. She didn't like displaying affection in front of other people, but, with him, she didn't mind. So she circled her arms around his neck while he held her as if afraid he might break her and kissed her with fierce caution. She always experienced a luscious peril when they kissed, as if she was practicing magic.

"We've got to get you to class." His voice was hoarse.

Reluctantly, she stepped back from him and pressed one hand over his heart. "Did it hurt?"

"Did what hurt? And if you say 'When you fell from heaven?' I'm going to be very disappointed in you."

"When your heart grew back?"

"Life was less complicated without it. But it wasn't really life."

"You look as if you haven't been getting a lot of sleep." She glanced at him as they began walking again. "You've been trying to find Nathan."

"One of Reiko's allies still hasn't been accounted for."

"You mean Caliban." She hated speaking the name of the killer whose true soul was that of a white hyena, his mortal mask an angelic-looking psycho. He had served Reiko Fata, the queen of a people who only mimicked being human. "So is every Fata in America an outcast or a criminal?"

"Not all. The native Fatas are lawful, but keep to themselves."

"What about Reiko's court? Are they all outcasts? And Phouka?" She thought of the punk-elegant girl now in charge of the Fatas.

"Renegades, outlaws, outcasts, all." Jack tucked a sheaf of hair behind one ear. "And Phouka is still a mystery to me."

"And Absalom Askew?"

"And him."

She knew Jack walked in the woods at night to meet with his friends. He still had his apartment above the abandoned cinema. He continued to work for Murray, the collector of antique automata and electronic games. Jack, stolen by the Fatas in the 1800s, had lived for nearly two hundred years among the ones who called themselves the children of night and nothing. They had tried to sacrifice him, and failed, and turned him into a Frankenstein creature, heartless and bloodless. He was flesh and blood now, as he'd wanted to be for two hundred years.

She didn't tell him about her dream of Reiko Fata, his burning queen of shadows.

JACK'S PRESENCE, AS USUAL, CAUSED FRICTION between Finn and her two best friends. As the four of them met on the grounds of Hallow-Heart College, in Origen Hall's snowy courtyard, Christie, his cheeks flushed and his dark red hair sticking out from beneath a woolen hat patterned with Celtic symbols, avoided looking at Jack. Sylvie watched Jack as if he were a lovely beast that might pounce. She toed the frosty leaves, twitched at her dark braids, and narrowed her eyes.

Christie spoke as if Jack wasn't standing right there. "I thought HallowHeart's core curriculum was to keep *his* kind away. He's going to classes now?"

"Not yet." Jack smiled.

Christie finally looked at him. "You nearly got Finn killed. And Sylvie. And me."

"But you're not dead, are you? Because, if you were, you'd notice."

"I still have nightmares about those doll-things with all the teeth. So does Sylvie. Right, Sylv?"

"Well, not real—"

"Phouka saved you from the Grindylow." Jack spoke patiently. "How is Phouka, by the way?"

"I wouldn't know. *You* would." Christie hunched up and returned to ignoring him.

"I don't think I know her as well as *you* do." Jack smiled again, and Finn wanted to pull his hair.

"Why is he still talking to me?" Christie pointedly addressed Sylvie, who slid to her feet and flashed a grin at Jack, who smiled back—this time, not like the devil. Sylvie said, "Walk with me, Jack?"

"It would be a pleasure, Sylvie Whitethorn."

As Jack strolled onward with her, the two of them chatting like old friends, Finn turned on Christie. "Why are you being such a—"

"He's antagonizing me."

"He's not. You're acting like a child."

"Compared to him, I *am* a child. So are you."

"Christie, stop."

He bowed his head and said, "What about Nathan Clare? And Angyll Weaver? And that psycho Caliban is still on the loose. People *died* because of Jack, Finn."

Finn's throat tightened when she thought of Nathan Clare, the boy Reiko Fata had tricked into a life meant for sacrifice. He'd been missing since Halloween night. His adoptive family—now led by Reiko's former lieutenant, Phouka—had spun it so that, to the general public, Reiko and Nathan had moved to Europe. "We don't know about Nathan."

"We *do* know, Finn. And the only thing that's different about Jack now is that he doesn't smell like a night forest full of roses anymore."

She stared at him. He said, "What?"

"Nothing. You're just very odd."

"*I'm* odd? Have you taken a look at your boyfriend lately?"

"Shall I sigh dreamily and say 'Every chance I can get'?"

"I'm sad for you, Finn. I really am."

JACK HAWTHORN CREATED A RIPPLE EFFECT in the corridors of Armitrage Hall. Walking beside him, Finn tried to ignore the stares of the other students. The rumor was he'd left his rich family to romantically survive on his own, even changing his name . . . all for Finn. There were a few who knew the truth, the privileged pretty boys and girls known as the blessed.

One of the blessed stepped into their path—Aubrey Drake held up a hand and smiled charmingly. His black hair was clubbed back, and his brown skin glowed as if he'd just returned from a tropical vacation. "Peace, Finn. Jack, I need to talk to you. There are some things happening."

"I don't recall"—Jack spoke in that idle tone that meant he was politely avoiding savagery—"needing your advice about anything."

Aubrey looked at Finn and lowered his voice. "You wasted one of their queens, and a *knight*. That's like . . . I mean, do you know what you've done?"

Two ancient beings had walked into a supernatural fire meant for her. Finn still had bad dreams about it.

"Reiko might have been an outlaw, but she had *allies*." Aubrey frowned at Jack. "You really didn't expect . . . I don't know—retribution?"

"What I didn't expect"—Jack's smile was a razor glint—"was you and your friends to be attending the sacrifice of an innocent girl."

Aubrey's expression became desperate. "We didn't know there was going to be an actual goddamn *sacrifice*. And we walked away."

"Instead of helping."

"Jack, what could we have done?"

Jack stepped close to the six-foot-tall football player and whispered with a terrible, leashed anger, "You left her to *burn to death*."

Finn didn't like the ugly turn this conversation had taken. "Jack."

Jack's eyes seemed to silver. He lowered his lashes and looked at Aubrey. "Good-bye, Aubrey."

Aubrey turned and trudged away as Sophia Avaline walked past. Lovely as a fashion model in high heels and a sleek dress, the history professor glanced at them but didn't say anything. Like Jane Emory, she was part of the cabal who knew about the Fatas. Unlike Jane Emory, Sophia Avaline had been there on Halloween night when Finn had nearly burned.

Finn frowned at Jack. "What is Aubrey talking about?"

He pushed his hands through his hair, and the bronze ring she'd once bound him with, two lions clasping a heart, glinted on one finger. "Someone—a Fata— will try for Reiko's place. It has nothing to do with you. With us."

"Jack, that has *everything* to do with us."

He whispered, "Not here. We'll talk later."

The Wolf at the door, Finn thought, remembering Reiko's words in her dream. "Okay. *Later.*"

"I'll pick you and Anna up. She wants to see *Swan Lake* for her birthday." He flashed a smile and she almost believed everything was going to be all right, that the world would remain normal.

"'THE ERL KING' BY Johann Wolfgang von Goethe." Professor Fairchild, as rumpled and charming as ever, stood at his desk. His British accent tended to make his words seem more interesting than they sometimes actually were. Gothic Literature was the official name of the course, not—as Christie called it—Defense Against Dark Faeries 101, although three of the poems they'd read in the past few weeks had been about malign spirits: Keats's "La Belle Dame Sans Merci," Robert Browning's "Childe Roland to the Dark Tower Came," and Christina Rossetti's "Goblin Market." It *did* seem as if Fairchild was trying to teach them something about defense against the Fatas.

Christie, who had recently taken up the course, was seated beside Finn, scrawling in the margins of his own copy of *Romantic Poets of the Victorian Age*. Finn looked down at the passage she'd read three times now, from "The Erl King."

> *"Father, my father, are you listening*
> *To what the Erl King is promising?"*

"Child, calm yourself, be calm, please.
It's just the wind rustling in the leaves."

Surrounded by invisible threads of electricity, by sunlight and whispered conversations, Finn felt the hair rise on the nape of her neck. Why didn't parents ever believe kids who claimed there was a monster under the bed or in the closet? Just because they couldn't see the monsters? In her experience, the monsters never showed themselves to anyone who had outgrown adolescence and its aftermath.

She looked up at Professor Fairchild, who had attended the Halloween ceremony that had nearly resulted in her death.

"The Erl King," Fairchild continued, "is an elemental, a thing of nature with unnatural intelligence. Why does he want the child?"

"Because," Finn spoke quietly, "he's a predator. And predators hunt the weak."

Fairchild blinked as if she'd pulled him out of a dream. He said, carefully, "The Erl King is one of the characters in poems of that time who symbolized primordial destruction."

"But that would mean *mindless* destruction." Finn realized they were talking about something else, something dark and secret. "And predators aren't mindless."

"Good answer, Finn, good answer." Christie applauded.

"Mr. Hart"—Professor Fairchild actually sounded stern—"this is not a game show."

"You're right, Professor. But I'd rather watch game shows than, say, human sacrifices."

Fairchild said, "Mr. Hart, stop wandering off topic. Now, interestingly enough"—he began to saunter around his own desk—"Mr. Hart's ancestor, Augusta Danegeld, was an accomplished poet whose works could be considered Gothic poetry."

Christie muttered, "Leave my ancestors out of this."

Finn gazed down at the poem again. *"Lovely, lovely child, come with me, such wondrous things you will see."*

FINN HAD FORGOTTEN the story of *Swan Lake*, of the wicked swan and the pure one, and the evil sorcerer who ruled both. The costumes were phantasmal, the swans in tatters of gossamer, feathers, and primitive half masks, the sorcerer a feral figure in black fur and plumes, a cross between an Aztec priest and a glamorous werewolf. When the curtains parted and the orchestra's music soared, Finn sat, enchanted, and didn't say a word. She'd been afraid the ballet might resurrect her grief for her ballerina sister, but she became lost in the gorgeous story and the music. Jack, who was from the Victorian era, when such productions were a luxury meant only for the wealthy, was reverentially quiet.

Anna Weaver, now fifteen—who still became silent and lost whenever her own murdered sister was mentioned—never took her attention from the stage.

Afterward, outside the Marlowe Theater, Anna asked if they could visit her sister. Finn looked frantically at Jack, who said gently, "Of course."

"Annie!" Someone moved from the theater crowds. Finn recognized Kevin Gilchriste, Fair Hollow's local celebrity, who had starred in a movie about wolves and winter and a girl in red. With his spiky brown hair and model cheekbones, he looked like he belonged in an Abercrombie ad.

"Kevin." Anna smiled shyly. "Did you like *Swan Lake*?"

"I did. I came with . . ." He glanced over his shoulder. "Well, she's still in there. Anyway, happy birthday. Hey, Finn, right? And Jack?"

"Hey." Finn watched warily as Kevin held out a hand to Jack. Jack gripped it and said, "I liked your movie."

"Thanks." Kevin stepped back, nodded to Anna. "I'll see you at the shop, Annie."

As he vanished into the crowd, Anna gazed longingly after him, and Finn thought, *Is that how I look at Jack? Like a little kid?* She turned her head to see Jack watching her with some amusement and said, rebellious, "Should we really be visiting a cemetery, knowing what we know about your family?"

"Phouka's regime is a lot less deathcentric—is that a word, 'deathcentric'? We'll be fine."

They drove to Soldiers' Gate. Although the sun had set, the gates were still open, revealing a Gothic and haphazard landscape of tombstones and mausoleums beneath snow and tree branches still crystallized in melting ice.

Anna led them to a simple granite headstone piled with bouquets of flowers, angel figurines, and trinkets. She bowed her head, her sun-gold hair gleaming. Finn glanced at the headstone carved with the name *Angyll Weaver.* Anna whispered, "I miss her."

"I miss my sister too."

"The girl who was named after flowers." Anna turned to Jack and frowned. "You're human now. They'll use that against you."

"I know."

"Who'll use it against you?" Finn's heart jumped. "Jack?"

Anna answered in her usual cryptic fashion, "I see their shadows in my dreams; even when I'm dreaming about stupid things like my mom's meat loaf, or gym class, I can see the shadows, running—"

A cell phone buzzed in Anna's coat. As she took the phone out and frowned at a text, Finn crouched down near Angyll's marker and righted a vase of chrysanthemums that had tipped over. "What shadows, Anna?"

"I don't know."

"*There* you are," came a voice from behind.

They whirled around.

Moving through the tombstones, the lamplight silvering his citrus-bright hair, Absalom Askew was a vivid figure in a jacket of red fur and jeans with embroidered Chinese dragons snaking up the sides.

"Absalom." Jack wryly greeted his friend. "Imagine meeting *you* here. In a graveyard."

"Jack. Finn." Absalom Askew's red Converses didn't make a sound on the crunchy snow and leaves. "Nice to see you out and about."

Finn carefully asked why he was there.

"I'll show you. Come, my children." Unusually solemn, Absalom led them to a tombstone engraved with a winged girl reading a book. Beneath this image were the words: *Here lies someone's child, one who was sweet and mild, one who, in our eyes, will, above all of us, rise.* The name *Mary Booke* was scripted into the marble.

Mary Booke had been Nathan Clare's true love, a human girl stolen by the Fatas, raised among them, and murdered by Caliban. As Jack sank to a crouch before the stone, his face solemn, Finn said, "Who had this made?"

"We did." Absalom looked at her. "No one in your world knew who she was."

Finn touched the tombstone as Jack spoke softly—*that*, Finn knew, was when he was at his most dangerous. "We were all just pawns to you, weren't we? To get rid of Reiko."

"You weren't *my* pawns."

"Were we Phouka's?"

"Did you know it was Anna's birthday?" Absalom, with that unsettling way he had of abruptly changing topics, turned to face Anna. He was, suddenly, holding a long gift box wrapped in pink satin ribbons, with a little porcelain doll's head in the center. Anna looked delighted.

Jack, rising, told Anna, "Don't accept tha—"

"Thank you, Absalom."

"Open it." Absalom glanced slyly at Jack as Anna unwrapped the package and lifted out . . . an umbrella. The handle and tip were made from wood painted white, and, when she snapped the umbrella open, an extraordinary painting from *Alice's Adventures in Wonderland* was revealed.

"How *lovely*," she whispered, eyes wide as she turned it.

"An umbrella?" Finn arched an eyebrow at Absalom.

"Now, it's just a *regular* umbrella—don't go trying to do a Mary Poppins off a roof or anything," Absalom said to Anna. Then he turned to address Jack, and shadows seemed to fall across his face. "We think the Wolf is here. Phouka believes he's been here since All Hallows' Eve."

Frost-glazed leaves skittered across the tombstones and snow as silence followed Absalom's words. Anna snapped shut the umbrella, looked from Jack to Finn, and said, "The shadows in my dreams are wolves."

"See?" Absalom regarded Jack, who remained grimly mute. "Talk to you later, Jack. I've got to be on my way."

"Wait." Finn stepped forward, but Absalom had already disappeared between one tree and the next. Finn turned on Jack. "*What is the Wolf?*"

He raised his eyes to hers and said, low, "Not in front of Anna."

"I'm not a kid." Anna's voice was calm. "And I'm not *slow*, like people think."

"No, of course you're not. But the Wolf is not a bedtime story for little girls."

"I'm *not* a little—"

"We're taking you home, Annie."

ANNA LIVED ON MAIN STREET, in a two-story apartment above Hecate's Attic, the shop her parents owned. Since the shop was just across from the park, Finn and Jack left the car and walked Anna home, then went for a stroll. As they wandered down the park path, Jack said, "Do you remember the Fata I told you about? The one I first worked for in Ireland? I thought Reiko was his wife?"

Finn tugged up the hood of her red wool coat. "He was a very bad man."

Jack gently corrected, "He was never a man."

Finn knew he was about to tell her about the Wolf and braced herself. "Go on."

"His name was Seth Lot. In 1800s Dublin, he was Reiko's lover, the one, I think, who made her what she was, cruel and reckless."

"What you're saying is—he's evil."

"There are levels of evil. I saw the worst kind in Seth Lot's house."

The winter night became threatening. Finn began to wish she was home.

"His house was like some of the abandoned mansions here in Fair Hollow, but it's older than any human residence. It was called Sombrus. And it could move, appear and disappear in and out of the world. Once, he and Reiko argued and she pinned his house in place. It took him and his pack a week to find the wand of sacred wood she'd staked into the roots of a tree in the courtyard, to hold the house down. For a while, he was stuck where he could do no harm." Jack looked down at his hands. "Then he and Reiko made up. They surrounded themselves with pretty young things, unfortunates who would eventually disappear. Reiko would never tell me what happened to them."

Finn could guess.

They were approaching the other end of the park, where a quaint white chapel stood for sale on the corner. There was a fire escape along the chapel's side, and a mass of fir trees darkened the street beyond. It was quiet here, free even of the sounds of traffic.

"Come on." She tugged him toward the building. The moonlight glittered on the snow, and the white chapel looked charming, not creepy.

"The chapel's closed."

"We're going to sit on the roof." She reached up and grabbed the handle of the fire escape to pull down the lower half. She felt a heady rush of fear and recklessness.

"Don't you think it'll be a bit icy?" He watched her, amused.

"It's all melted and the roof's flat." She was still trying to tug down the ladder. "Scared?"

"You'll break your wrists, doing that." He took hold of the bar and pulled the fire escape down with an ease that made her feel all warm inside.

They clambered onto the roof, which was damp but not icy. The view of Fair Hollow was magical. The moon was a crescent and the wind had that peculiar warmth that sometimes came during winter's beginning—she remembered that from Vermont, when her mom would take her and Lily onto the patio during a winter warming and make dinner on the grill.

As they selected a relatively dry space near the steeple, Finn said, "What do you think happened to the young people in the Wolf's house?"

In the moonlight, the colors of Jack's irises—one blue, one gray—was evident. He replied, "There was a rumor that Lot had once ruled La Bestia, the court of beasts in France."

He'd dodged her question. She didn't know whether to be awed or terrified that there were more Fatas: a reclusive nation here in America, and a court in France—she imagined decadent creatures in powdered wigs and punk-Regency clothing; then she pictured the things of tooth and claw that might hide beneath that glamour. She remembered reading about the eighteenth-century French writer George Sand, who claimed that she'd once glimpsed a gathering of were-wolves in Paris. "Okay. A court of beasts."

"The Fatas of France aren't actually beasts. Quite sophisticated, actually, and frivolous as hell, but it's a name that kept their enemies away."

"You haven't told me what happened to the boys and gir—"

"I'm getting to that." The ring she'd given him glinted. He'd once had a black Celtic cross tattooed on the back of that hand, but all those markings had faded when he'd been resurrected. "There is a history, in a certain region of France, of an animal that ravaged the countryside and slaughtered people during the 1700s. The Beast of Gevaudan."

"*No.*" Finn felt a nightmare world gaping around her—she'd read about Gevaudan in her father's books. "It *ate* people, Jack. *That's* Seth Lot? *That's what's here?* Will he know we were responsible for Reiko—"

"He'll blame Phouka and Absalom, and they can defend themselves."

"Caliban." She spat the name and all the hope drained from his eyes. She nodded. "*He'll* tell that monster."

"We have a small army at our backs."

"Do you think Phouka and her *family* care? They *used* us to get rid of Reiko and her boyfriend."

"Reiko was a danger to them with what she was doing."

Finn studied the pretty view and wished she didn't know what she did. She changed the subject. "Why do you think Absalom is giving Anna presents?"

"Typical. I tell you the Big Bad Wolf might be here and you're thinking of someone else's welfare. I've no idea. Absalom is crazy."

"You know he's not. He just wants people to *think* he's crazy. And I don't want to talk about your . . . ex-boss anymore." She paused. "What's it like? To live two hundred years?"

"Appalling. You get schizo after the first sixty."

She rested her head on his shoulder as he delicately said, "Finn. What do you want to do?"

"Go home and sleep and try not to think about wolves."

"I mean, what do you want to do with your *life*? After college?"

"So much pressure." She was glad he was distracting her from thinking about what might be lurking in Fair Hollow, waiting to avenge Reiko. "I don't know. Be a photographer? I want to see the world. And write about it. And find out things."

He clasped one of her hands, his grip firm and warm. "Then that's what you'll do."

She noticed that he said *you*, not *we*, and that troubled her.

FINN WOKE IN HER DARK ROOM—she'd fallen asleep in her T-shirt and jeans, with Jack beside her. He slept with one arm outstretched, moonlight etching his profile, the curve of his throat. She'd never seen him so vulnerable, even when he'd been about to die on Halloween night. She settled closer to his lean body and twined her fingers around one of his wrists.

His skin was icy.

His chest wasn't moving. His eyelashes didn't flutter. His breath didn't warm her skin. She sat up, panic stealing her ability to speak.

His eyes flew open and they were absolute black.

Then his irises returned to blue and gray, and he gazed at her drowsily. "Is it morning?"

She couldn't move, but her heart was trying to jackhammer its way out of her chest.

"No," she whispered, and she swallowed a sour rush of fear. "It's not morning."

"I shouldn't be here." He tugged her down against him. He wasn't cold now, as his arms went around her. She laid her head on his chest and listened to the beat of the heart he'd grown for her.

"Jack," she whispered, "what do *you* want to do?"

"I've done everything I've wanted to do." His voice was blurry. "It doesn't matter."

"It matters to me."

He didn't answer—sleep had stolen him from her once again.

CHAPTER 2

The Fairies went from the world, dear,
Because men's hearts grew cold:
And only the eyes of children see
What is hidden from the old . . .

—THE LITTLE GOOD PEOPLE: FOLK TALES OF IRELAND,
KATHLEEN FOYLE

The blizzard raged through the town as if caught in a snow globe, howling over roofs, banging at windows, hurtling branches and garbage bins through the streets. The holiday lights strung across the main avenue sizzled and went out. Even the raucous warehouse district was silent, its bars closed, its streets deserted.

The decrepit mansion that hid in the mountain forest, snow gusting past its broken windows, over the crumbling and unidentifiable stone animals guarding its cracked stairway, was a fantastic structure of medieval mixed with baroque and was surrounded by briars with hooked thorns. It hunched amid the snowdrifts and black alders in hungry silence.

Its windows suddenly blazed with golden light that spilled over the walls, the stone animals on the stair, across the exquisite carvings of briar roses. An enchantment glazed the mansion, which repaired itself in moments as the illumination from within kissed the snow around it into a dazzling landscape of diamonds.

The doors opened and a shadow emerged.

❖ ❖ ❖

THE BLIZZARD HAD SWATHED Fair Hollow in a blanket of velvety cold, so Finn and her father spent the morning unpacking Christmas decorations. In the late afternoon, Sylvie texted her:

Want 2 go sledding?

FINN HADN'T PLAYED IN THE SNOW since she was a kid. Christie and Sylvie had each brought a sled—Sylvie, an old-fashioned one from her dad's salvage shop and Christie, a modern piece of plastic. On the hills behind the park, as Christie and Sylvie, yelling and laughing, swerved down the snowy slopes, Finn pulled out her cell phone and checked for messages. Nothing from Jack.

As Christie and Sylvie trekked back up the hill, Christie, his cheeks flushed, called to Finn, "I'll race you."

Finn accepted the challenge along with Sylvie's sled and pushed off.

As the wooden sled veered down the slope, she gained a dizzying speed. She heard Christie whoop in the distance. Glancing over one shoulder, she realized she'd gone off in an entirely different direction. She turned her head back—

—and saw the horizontal slab of rock rising out of the snow before her.

Crack! The sled struck the rock and the impact knocked Finn, tumbling, into prickly blackberry bushes. Laughing, spitting snow from her mouth, she climbed to her feet and stared at the slab.

It was an *altar*. A pair of stag's antlers rose from a nest of ivy and pretty stones. Blue and green eggshells from wild birds were scattered around old beer bottles draped with cheap jewelry. Between a snake's skeleton and the skull of a small animal was a fan of black feathers. A stone head, androgynous and arrogant, had been crowned with red berries and leaves. The stag antlers and the snake vertebrae were a dead giveaway; this altar was a dedication to David Ryder and Reiko Fata, the Stag Knight—*Damh Ridire*—and the white serpent—*ban nathair*—who had died on Halloween night.

Finn scrutinized the shadows as fear whispered through her. It was early evening and the sun was already sinking, leaving only a cold gloom. She couldn't hear Christie and Sylvie. It was as if she'd been lured out of the world . . .

Fatas, she thought, and all she had for protection was a silver clover charm and Christie's iron bracelet.

She blinked and *they* were suddenly standing before the altar, three silhouettes scrawled like ink against the snow. She didn't want to run or call out or do anything that might instigate violence. So she calmly spoke the true names of her visitors, to at least bring them out of the dark: "Victor. Emily. Eammon."

The Rooks' eyes glinted silver as the darkness fell away from them. Their coats fluttered with ribbons, feathers, and talismans made from bits of old toys. Their skin matched the snow in color. Caught between life and death, as were all changelings taken by the Fatas, their appearance was horror movie disturbing.

"You think speaking our names gives you power over us?" The tall, dark-haired boy tilted his head to one side.

"No." She didn't move because that would suggest fear. "I'm just reminding you who you really are."

The girl sneered. Her plaited hair, black and blond, glittered with cheap barrettes. "We are the Rooks. That is who we really are."

"And those aren't our names." The youngest, a blond who looked as if he'd just stepped from a church window, gazed coldly at Finn. "I'm Bottle. My sister is Hip Hop. My brother is Trip. Don't use those other names again."

"Why not?" She needed to stall them until her friends found her. "They took you away from your mother and father and put dead things in your place—"

"Shut up!" Teeth bared, Hip Hop stepped toward Finn. Bottle caught her wrist, said, "No. *He'll* know."

Hip Hop smiled. "So? She deserves it, for what she did to our lady."

"I didn't do anything to Reiko." Finn's voice cracked.

"You did." Trip put his hands in his pockets. "You killed Reiko. Our queen. And you will pay for that, Serafina Sullivan. Someone's going to make you pay. He's been waiting. Watching. He'll get you."

Satisfied with his threat, Trip sauntered away, followed by his siblings, their boots soundless on the snow. The shadows beneath the trees swallowed their wicked, fairy-tale figures.

"Finn!"

Finn turned. Christie and Sylvie were running toward her. When Sylvie saw her face, she halted and said, "Someone else was here."

"The Rooks." Finn pointed to the altar. "This is their place."

Christie stared at the Rooks' footprints in the snow.

"They're not happy." Finn trudged toward the antique sled, which had splintered against the altar. "I owe you a sled, Sylv. Let's go home."

"What did they say?" Sylvie helped Finn untangle the sled. "Did they threaten you?"

"Of course they threatened her." Christie took the sled from Finn, watching her with concern. "It's what they do. It's their sole purpose. It's like they're *haunting* her."

"They're not dead." Finn didn't want to tell them about the Wolf. Not yet. The Rooks might have been lying. *He's been waiting. Watching.* "They're only frozen and changed—like they're becoming Fatas."

THE HARTS' BIG VICTORIAN was warm and cluttered, the family room's autumn-red walls hung with vintage sports posters and framed photographs of the Harts and their friends. The threadbare sectional was scattered with chew toys from the two wolfhounds and various portable electronica from Christie's six brothers, who ranged in ages from nineteen to twenty-four. Though the three oldest brothers had moved out, they visited often. The giant plasma TV was always tuned to a football game or a nature show. Heavy metal music thumped from the second floor. Two brothers were arguing amiably in the kitchen. Finn thought she heard one of them say: " . . . no such things as mermaids."

As Finn admired the seven-foot Christmas tree blazing with colored lights and boyish ornaments, Christie plucked a rubber squirrel and three remotes off the sectional sofa. "Sit. Sylvie's bringing food from the café near her apartment, because my mom's out and my brothers ate everything. There is *nothing* left but condiments."

Finn sprawled on the sectional. When the doorbell rang, Christie left to answer it. He returned with Sylvie, who sported a wool hat shaped like a fox's head, its tasseled flaps concealing her ears. Christie held two carry-out bags labeled CROOKED TREE CAFÉ. As Sylvie unpacked the lidded paper cups and the blintzes wrapped in wax paper, she said, "These are my treat. Where's Jack?"

There was a knock on the front door and Finn said, "That's him." She bounced up to answer it. Jack didn't like doorbells or bells of any kind; they were something he'd once avoided, like iron, salt, and blessed objects.

She stepped over a pile of boots in the hall and opened the door to reveal Jack, in a dark coat lined with fake fur, standing there, seeming distracted and tired. She looked at the basket he carried and her mouth quirked. "Have you just come from grandmother's house?"

"Phouka attempted to make cookies. Real ones. In an oven at the hotel. I think she magicked the oven. Not the gingerbread, which are burned on the bottom." He entered the hall and surveyed with amusement the mounds of coats and boots and backpacks. "I think she did it to unnerve all of us."

As they walked into the family room, Jack set down the basket. "Phouka sent some treats."

Christie walked over, peered into the basket, and drew out a deranged-looking gingerbread man, which he examined doubtfully.

From outside came the sound of glass breaking. They all glanced at the window. Past the blinds, Finn could see the empty house—now for sale—that neighbored Christie's.

"Maybe it's Mr. Redhawk's ghost," Christie suggested. "Not the ghost of Mr. Redhawk—I mean, the ghost he told me lived in his attic."

"There are no such things as ghosts," Jack said reasonably. "There are only the dead, who linger for all sorts of reasons."

Finn thought about Jack sleeping like the dead last night, and the cozy room suddenly didn't seem warm enough.

"Well, someone's been *lingering* in my neighbor's house for a while. I swear I heard someone moving stuff around in there when I was walking past, two nights ago."

Jack's eyelashes flickered, which meant he was interested in what Christie was telling him. "I'll have to investigate."

"Maybe it's one of your friends."

"Maybe it's a vagrant who used to be a liberal arts major."

Christie bit the head off one of Phouka's gingerbread men and went mutinously silent.

When they were ready to leave for the Lotus and Luna hangout, Christie and

Sylvie took Christie's Mustang, and Finn accompanied Jack in his sedan. The two cars began the half-hour drive into the mountains, along plowed roads that shimmered as if covered with white sequins.

It was Friday night, and Lotus and Luna, a restaurant that resembled a Buddhist-temple-turned-saloon, was packed. Seated at the corner table Jack had reserved were Hester Kierney and Ijio Valentine, two descendants of the families who had made a pact with Reiko and her tribe of immortal outlaws. Although referred to as the blessed, Finn saw no otherworldliness in Hester or in Ijio, only a secular glamour. Hester dressed like a 1920s starlet and wore expensive ornaments in her short, dark hair. Ijio was always in suits that seemed a bit stylish for a twenty-one-year-old. He was a philosophy major. Hester was deciding between physics and chemistry.

"You'd better get to the stage, Jack." Ijio checked his watch. "Now. Your lead singer is very tempestuous."

Jack bent and murmured into Finn's ear, "The *others* are here. Be careful."

And he was gone. Finn surveyed the crowd. She could tell who the "others" were. The regular people wore stylish winter gear, but the *others* wore fur and feathers and modern incarnations of Renaissance and Victorian clothing, what Sylvie called "neo-antique." *They* were as brightly marked as venomous snakes.

"Don't worry, Finn." Hester was watching her. "Phouka rules them now."

"It won't last." Ijio drank from a silver flask. "Not with that lot."

"What are you saying?" Finn folded her arms on the table. "Some new badass is going to come along and try to take over? Like what usually happens when a sheriff in a western dies? Anarchy?"

Christie leaned toward them with his own question. "You were both there on Halloween, to watch Finn burn. Let's not pretend you're actually friends, 'cause you're not."

"Christie, stop." Finn knew Hester had tried to call the police on Halloween.

"We didn't know it was going to be a *real* sacrifice," Ijio said, genuinely upset. "We thought it was just, I don't know, a dramatization. That bitch on wheels, Reiko, said nothing about fire and death."

"How does it work, exactly?" Christie pretended to be curious. "You clean up after the Fatas, keep their nasty secrets, ease their way into the world, and, when you're not interesting to them anymore—when you're official grown-ups—they make you forget they exist?"

Ijio smiled ruefully. "Pretty much."

"Huh. The whole 'My parents sold my soul to ancient devils to get rich' thing would really bother me."

Hester attempted to change the subject. "Where's Aubrey?"

"Did I hear my name?" Aubrey slid from the crowd. There was snow in his hair. He shook it out as he dropped into the booth beside Christie, shedding his jacket. "What are we talking about?"

The silence was awkward.

The trembling, sorrowing sound of a violin twined through the air and vanquished the canned music. Jack stepped from the shadows of the small stage, the violin cradled between his chin and shoulder, the bow a silvery twist as he drew several more mournful notes from the strings. The music, the beginning of "Greensleeves," went through Finn like a solar flare.

He winked at her before slashing into a mad rendition of a Pogues reel. The lights on the stage brightened as a drummer, a guitarist, and a bald and tattooed girl playing a fiddle appeared. Finn recognized them—they were Jack's Fata friends, the vagabonds. The crowd was soon shouting and stomping their feet.

"You were talking about Halloween, weren't you?" Aubrey looked at Finn. "There's a lot we didn't know. Not just the Teind. Phouka told me about how the Jacks and Jills were made, that they were"—he shuddered—"damn Frankensteins. I mean . . . what Reiko *did to Jack* . . ."

Christie suddenly stood. "Hester. Do you Riverdance?"

"A little." She rose and followed him. Sylvie, a bracelet of silver owls and acorns glinting on one wrist, grabbed Aubrey's hand and pulled him with her. She glanced back at Finn, her eyes dark.

As they left, Ijio tilted his head and blinked lazily at Finn. He said, "I don't dance. Wanna make out?"

"I don't think so. I'm going to get up now and watch Jack play. Don't come with me." She pushed up and moved through the crowd now enchanted by the quicksilver madness of Jack's music.

"Finn Sullivan?"

Turning, she met the summer-blue gaze of Kevin Gilchriste. He said, "I didn't recognize you with your hair up."

"Kevin." She smiled. Despite the movie star status, he was very nice and ordinary. "Hey."

They were practically yelling to be heard over the music, so he leaned close and said, in her ear, "He'll destroy you. It's what they do."

Then he was gone, leaving her stunned in the middle of the dancing crowd.

As the Fata musicians took over, Jack stepped down and took Finn's hand. On the stage, the bald Fata girl with the tattoos—Darling Ivy—was singing something pretty. Finn couldn't even smile as she and Jack spun.

He'll destroy you. It's what they do.

Kevin Gilchriste knew. Somehow, Kevin Gilchriste knew what Jack had been, what the Fatas were. And, despite his fortune and film career, Kevin wasn't one of the blessed. Which meant he was something else.

"Finn," Jack murmured into her ear after she told him about Kevin's remark, "there's no reason for anyone to come after us. And Caliban isn't an idiot. He's broken laws. If he returns to Fair Hollow, he'll be put down. As for Lot . . . he would have made his presence known long before this. And how does Kevin Gilchriste know?"

"*You* ask him." Finn didn't want to tell Jack she believed Kevin had been referring to *Jack* with that remark, not Caliban or Seth Lot.

Nothing out of the ordinary happened for the rest of the night. It was nice.

As Finn decided to let Jack know about the Rooks, Christie edged up to them. "It's ten o'clock. We need to get out of here. *Now.*"

"Why?" Finn said. "What happens at ten—"

Electronic dub music suddenly pulsed through the air, accompanied by a spinning rainbow of lights and someone dramatically introducing a DJ with a ridiculous name.

"House music!" Christie shouted, unnecessarily, as Sylvie began jumping up and down. He continued, "I'll get Sylvie. *Save yourselves.*"

Laughing, Finn went with Jack toward the exit.

AS JACK'S SEDAN SWERVED around the parking lot of a grocery store that had closed for the evening, Finn gripped the steering wheel and heard

Jack, in the passenger seat, swear. As she braked, the tires screeched. She parked, turned off the ignition. "Did you just shudder and close your eyes?"

"I'm beginning to remember what it's like to be mortal. No more lessons. Give me the keys."

"Well, it's *winter*. It's slippery, and I never had to learn in San Francisco." She grudgingly switched seats with him, stealing a kiss as she climbed over him. Settling into the passenger seat, she finally told him, "I went sledding today and ran into the Rooks."

"With the sled?" He pushed the key into the ignition.

"*No*. The sun went down and they were there. They'd built a little altar to their snake queen and David Ryder. They're not on the same page as Phouka and your Fata friends."

"Then I think I should have a talk with them."

"Don't bother. They don't scare me." She lied a little, with that last statement. "But I think they're expecting someone to come after us, too. They said he's been waiting, Jack, and watching. Is it Seth Lot?"

Jack was quiet as he drove.

He swore and slammed a foot on the brake, and Finn clutched the dashboard as the car jerked. He skidded to the side of a road made mysterious by snow and night and trees on either side. In a low voice, he said, "I thought I saw something run across the road."

"*What?*"

He opened the car door and stepped out.

"Jack, don't do that—"

As he bent down to look at her, the streetlight sharply defined his face, making him seem savagely feline. "Stay in the car."

Finn defiantly got out. Over the car's roof, he gave her an exasperated look, but she ignored it, peering down the road. It was a two-lane road, the forest cavernous and dark on either side. Jack whispered, "I thought I saw . . . *will* you get back in the car?"

"Was it a hyena? Caliban? Was it—" She didn't want to say *the Wolf*. She pressed her spine against the sedan and warily scanned the shadows.

Jack began walking farther up the road. As he crouched to examine a snowbank on one side, apprehension crept through Finn. She looked deep into the woods and felt as if something was staring back at her. Beneath the faint howling of the wind, she heard a rumbling growl. Not taking her gaze from the forest, she said, "Jack, I think we should get in the—"

Deep in the woods, a massive shadow moved.

Jack was suddenly standing before her, his eyes reflecting silver. "*Get in the car.*"

She slid in. He ducked behind the wheel and started the engine. She slammed down her lock and stared at that blotch of inky darkness in the trees. She blinked. It wasn't moving. She was just imagining . . .

In that mass of darkness, an elongated and misshapen head turned. She almost screamed.

The sedan roared to life and sped down the road. It was a moment before she could speak. "Were there animal prints in the snow?"

He didn't answer. She said, "Jack."

"There were prints." He kept his gaze on the road. "I don't know what kind they were."

He was lying, she realized, but she couldn't accuse him of that, and she didn't want her own terrifying theory to be confirmed. She took a deep breath. "I think I saw a grizzly bear in the woods. That's probably what it was."

"Probably not." He didn't look at her.

She got out her phone. "I'm calling Sylvie and telling her she and Christie had better take another way home."

FINN HAD JUST SETTLED into the warmth and light of her room, where giant forest beasts and the *crom cu* seemed like imaginary dilemmas, when her cell phone buzzed. She looked at the text:

Do u believe in ghosts? I'm outside.

She strode to the glass doors and saw Christie seated forlornly on one of the swings. He waved to her.

She opened the door and moved down the terrace stairs, crunching across the snow to the swing. "Ghosts?"

"Mr. Redhawk *did* have a ghost. I saw it. Tonight, as I was getting out of my car . . . a face, looking right out the attic window."

She peered through the trees at the silhouette of his dead neighbor's house against the gray sky. She thought of Nathan, still missing, and whispered, "What if it's Nathan?"

"We are *not* going into that house—"

"Why else are you here?"

He stood, too proud to back down from her challenge. "Remember what happened the last few times you wandered into 'empty' houses?"

"This is different. Mr. Redhawk's isn't a Fata house and we're prepared. And we're right near *your* place. Instead of running to your car and huddling in fear, we can run to your house and huddle *there* in fear."

"Sure. My mom can rescue us with knitting needles, my dad can use a hammer, and my brothers—"

"*Christie.*" Finn, her nerves crackling with adrenaline, thought about the Rooks and the thing she'd seen on the mountain road. Nathan Clare might be hiding in that house, injured or scared. How could she sleep, thinking about him? "We'll just look in the windows first."

He grimaced. "Let's go."

They walked through the small wood that separated Finn's backyard from Christie's street. Mr. Redhawk's house was a Tudor, with elms clustered around it and patches of brown lawn revealed through the snow. It looked as if its owner had only gone for a vacation.

"What if it's Caliban?" Christie whispered.

"It's not Caliban. He'd have come after us by—" She halted because, as they stood on Redhawk's lawn, a pale face appeared in the attic window and withdrew.

Christie said, solemn, "I told you."

"That's not a Fata, Christie. Or a ghost. That's a *person*."

"Let me get flashlights. Mr. Redhawk gave me the key to the back door, just in case he ever needed somebody to get in. Come on."

They walked the short distance to Christie's. Fidgety with nervous energy, Finn paced in the hall until he returned with the flashlights and the keys. She knew they should wait until morning, but the face in the window . . . she hadn't felt terror of it, or unease, and there'd been no buzzing in the air that usually signaled a bad Fata at work. Whoever was in Redhawk's house—that person was hiding, hurt, and scared. She *felt* it.

Christie led her to his neighbor's backyard, a cavern of tangled pines wreathed with mist and nettle bushes. The lawn was scattered with pale toadstools in a swamp of icy water like a pool of silvery star-melt. Finn whispered, "Weird."

"Did you hear that?"

"I don't hear anything." They had reached the back porch, where their flashlights lit up old crates and dead plants in pots. She trudged up the steps and Christie followed.

"Just a follow-up reminder—you *do* remember what happened the last time we went into a haunted house?"

"Nothing happened to us in Tirnagoth, Christie. They were just trying to scare us. Look at those toadstools . . . some are as big as my hand."

"Let's call the prince of darkness." He had his cell phone out.

"Don't bother Jack." She could imagine what Jack would have to say about this venture. "Just use the key, Christie, and stop being a chicken. I don't feel anything *evil* . . ."

"Okay. For Nathan." He unlocked the back door. As it creaked open, releasing the musty air of neglect, Finn said, "Are you wearing silver or iron?"

"Never without it. Do you have that fancy knife?"

"I have it."

He stepped past her and she slipped in after him. Their lights brushed old furniture, landscape paintings, and a moose head above the fireplace. Christie murmured, "I liked Mr. Redhawk. I remember this house all sunlit and smelling like bacon and coffee. He was kind of like a grandfather."

"I'm sorry." Finn glanced at him.

A furtive rustling came from behind a wooden door. Christie pointed his flashlight beam at it. "That's the study."

"I thought the ghost—person—was in the attic?"

"Maybe he wanted some reading material?" Christie nudged the door open with his foot. As they swept their flashlight beams over the cluttered office, he said, "Don't tell me *that's* natural."

The pale toadstools from the yard had gotten in and grown over bookshelves, the desk cluttered with papers, through cracks in the floorboards. The air was thick with a dust that scintillated in their light beams. Finn, reaching out, studied the shimmering stuff that fell over her hand. It wasn't dust—it was like pollen, or spores. It would have been almost magical if it wasn't so uncanny. "Christie—"

Something moved in the shadows behind the big desk, and Finn and Christie swerved their flashlight beams at the darkness there. When an eye blinked, Christie shouted and dropped his flashlight. Finn kept hers aimed at what huddled behind the desk—a naked figure smudged with dirt, arms over its head. For a luminous moment, she hoped . . . "Nathan?"

The figure's arms fell away and it raised its head into the light, revealing a tangled mane of pewter-pale hair and the stark, fine-boned face of a young man, a stranger. The pollen shimmered over him as he parted his lips. His eyes were green, the vivid color of summer leaves and dragonfly wings.

"Is he . . . ?" Christie picked up his flashlight.

"He's not a Fata." Finn twisted around, snatched a plaid blanket from an easy chair, and cautiously approached the young man, holding it out. "Here. We're not going to hurt you."

The stranger seemed dazed, as if he'd just woken from a long sleep, or a spell. As he accepted the blanket and wrapped it around his narrow hips, a bracelet of silver charms glinted around one of his wrists. Finn said carefully, "I'm Finn. This is—"

Christie murmured, "Should you be giving him our names?"

The young man rose, clutching the plaid blanket. He was taller than she'd expected. Slim muscles snaked beneath his skin. As he spoke, his cautious baritone had a British tartness to it. "Where am I?"

"In Mr. Redhawk's house. Did you know Mr. Redhawk?"

"No." He turned, looking around, and Finn sucked in a breath. Tattooed across his shoulder blades was a pair of amazingly detailed moth wings, in luminous silver and platinum hues. He continued, "I feel I've been here for a very long time."

"Do you remember your name?" Finn asked. He glanced at his hands and flexed them as if he hadn't seen them in a while. She had a sudden, sick feeling that in this house, he'd been something *else* for a very long time.

"No." He rubbed a hand across his face. He had another tattoo, on his upper right arm: a black, Celtic spiral that formed some kind of animal.

"Finn." Christie's car keys jangled as he took them from his pocket. "Go get my Mustang. We'll have to take him to the prince of darkness. I'll stay."

Finn backed away from the young man, who sank to a crouch, huddled in the plaid blanket, his hands—like Jack's hands had once been, crisscrossed with scars—knotted in his hair.

"I DON'T KNOW WHO HE IS. I don't know *what* he is."

Jack hunched forward on a chair in his tiny kitchen. Finn stood at the stove making tea, and Christie slouched in another rail-backed chair. The stranger sat in the main room, transfixed by a movie on Jack's small TV. He wore one of Jack's T-shirts and a pair of his jeans.

"You don't have any theories?" Finn brought three mugs to the table. As tired as she was, the mysterious young man with the moth tattoo fascinated her.

"I suspect he's some poor bastard who's been yanked out of his life to serve the Fatas. What he was doing in that house, I have no clue. Maybe he was enchanted into some sort of antique object Redhawk bought."

"This is going to be another weird conversation, isn't it?" Christie looked stern.

Jack said, "Yes, it is, Christopher—*don't touch that!*"

The stranger had begun wandering and his fingers were poised over the case holding Jack's Stradivarius. At Jack's reprimand, the young man looked up resentfully, tangled hair in his eyes, and said, "I wasn't going to."

"Jack. He'll have to stay with you." Finn watched the youth crouch down to gaze at Jack's cat, BlackJack Slade.

"Yes." Jack resignedly stirred his tea. "I realize that."

"What are we going to call him?" Finn watched the young man rise and continue to move around the apartment.

"I've no idea. I'll speak with Phouka tomorrow night, take him to Tirnagoth."

The young man spoke softly, gazing at two old-fashioned keys on a bookshelf, "'*By heart, you love her, because your heart cannot come by her; in heart you love her, because your heart is in love with her; and out of heart you love her, being out of heart that you cannot enjoy her.*'"

As he sank to a crouch, the keys in his hands, Jack stood and moved to him, squatted to face him. "Finn, would you fetch me one of those pins from the desk?"

Finn rose and selected a thumbtack, then walked to Jack. "Jack, I don't want him getting tetanus."

"Dip it in that bottle of rum then, please." His gaze never leaving the young man, Jack held out a hand. Finn dipped the thumbtack in a lid full of liquor—and didn't ask about why the rum was there—then dropped it into Jack's palm. "Thank you." To the stranger, Jack said, "I need to see if you bleed."

The young man held out a steady hand and didn't even flinch when Jack pushed the thumbtack into his skin. As blood welled, Jack sat back on his heels.

"Moth," Christie suddenly said and everyone looked at him where he stood in the kitchen doorway. "That quote he just recited . . . it's from Shakespeare's *Love's Labour's Lost*. That last bit was spoken by a character named Moth."

"Well." Finn sat on the sofa. "Should we call you Moth? It suits you. With that tattoo on your back."

"What about his other tattoo?" Christie indicated the Celtic design on Moth's upper left arm. "That looks kind of like a dog or something."

Finn glanced at Jack, who, along with "Moth," was staring at the dark tattoo banding their guest's arm.

Jack said, quietly, "It's a wolf."

BEFORE RETIRING FOR THE NIGHT, Jack called Finn to make sure Christie had gotten her safely home. His cipher of a guest had fallen asleep on the sofa. Jack hadn't recognized the stranger's moth wing tattoos, only Seth Lot's mark on his arm. Why had Jack never seen this young man in Lot's house? Was he dangerous or did he need to be protected?

Jack didn't think he'd be able to sleep—he tried not to. But, even after three cups of coffee, his eyelids drifted down.

He dreamed of a winter forest. A girl stood among the trees, head down, a black gown swirling around her. Her heavy dark hair was strung with pearls the color of a corpse's skin. She held a pair of tattered ballet shoes red and slick as blood. As she began to raise her head, he realized he didn't want to see what remained of her face—

The image jerked like an old film, into another scene.

Clotted gore streaked a wolf of white marble. Huddled nearby was a boy in jeans, his bronze curls crowned with autumn leaves and toadstools. Flower petals bled from a wound in his chest. It was Nathan Clare. He said, *"You mustn't save her. It will bring death to the world."*

Swift and silent and vicious, flashing tooth and claw, an enormous shadow glided through the forest behind Nathan.

Jack woke in a chilled sweat, whispered, "Nate . . ."

A shadow stood beside his bed, silver glinting in one hand. *Moth.*

Twisting up from the bed, Jack avoided the knife Moth slashed at him and slammed Moth into the wall. The young man fought with feral strength, wrestling Jack against a framed poster of *Frankenstein.* Glass shattered as Moth stabbed the knife into Bela Lugosi and reeled back.

Jack yanked the knife from the poster and turned on his guest.

"She told me . . ." Moth slid against the other wall. "She told me to . . ."

Jack tried not to be distracted by the alarming rate of his heartbeat. The knife was from his collection, a Renaissance blade fine enough to flay skin. He pointed it at his guest and fought an urge to slam it into Moth's heart. Hoarsely, Jack said, "Who told you to kill me?"

Moth looked up, miserable. "The girl with the dark hair . . ."

Jack whispered, *"Reiko."*

Moth turned and ran for the window. Jack leaped over the bed after him, but the young man was already over the sill. Scrambling onto the fire escape, Jack saw the other jump to the ground and run toward the woods.

Jack went after him, barefoot in the snow, and lost him in a mess of skeletal girders conquered by creepers and tree roots. As he sank against corroded metal, he shivered. What would he tell Finn? That the stranger they had tried to help was linked to dead Reiko, that the spiraling tattoo on Moth's arm meant he had once belonged to Seth Lot?

The wind sliced across his skin. He shivered and remembered that he was mortal.

FINN WOKE TO THE SOUND of breaking glass and, with disturbing words drifting through her sleep-dazed brain—*the devil is here*—sat up. Her room was dark and freezing. When she saw the glass glittering on her floor, the sweat on her skin iced over.

Again, one of the terrace doors was open, swinging gently in the wind—only, this time, several panes were shattered. Her hand crept to the silver dagger beneath her pillow. She thought, *Seth Lot.*

She reached instead for her cell phone on the nightstand and scrolled to Jack's number.

When she looked up, someone was crouched on the stone wall of her terrace.

She dropped the phone and grabbed the dagger. She swung her bare feet to the floor and said with faltering bravado, "You can't come in."

The shadowy figure raised its head and she inhaled sharply when light fell over the face of the young man they had named Moth. His eyes seemed even greener in the glow of the winter night. He said hoarsely, "The crooked dog came for you. I stopped it."

Finn couldn't move. Her hand was sweaty on the grip of the knife.

He jumped from the terrace wall, and vanished.

She lunged forward. "Moth!"

She halted on the threshold. The snow on her terrace was cut with claw marks from a large animal. She backed away. She carefully closed the broken door, uselessly locked it, and sat on the floor with the knife, to finish calling Jack.

He silently arrived an impossible fifteen minutes later. When she saw him on her terrace, she jumped up and said, "Caliban was here."

"I noticed the prints." He wrapped his arms around her. He smelled like winter and evergreen. He whispered, "What drove the *crom cu* away?"

"Moth."

"Ah. A complicated person, that Moth. He tried to kill me tonight."

CHAPTER 3

I hid my heart in a nest of roses,
Out of the sun's way, hidden apart;
In a softer bed than the soft white snow's is,
Under the roses, I hid my heart.

—"A Ballad of Dreamland," Algernon Charles
Swinburne

After the Caliban/Moth incident, Finn wanted a nice, normal day during which she could pretend the Fata world didn't exist. Jack had remained with her through the night and they'd talked, stretched on her bed, until she'd finally slept. When she woke, he was there with coffee he'd gotten from Main Street because he hadn't dared go through the house to the kitchen and risk encountering her father. He'd left after a hungry kiss that he'd reluctantly broken away from. She'd slumped back with a groan and curled around her pillow.

Sylvie, who was unnervingly intuitive, addressed the issue as they drank coffee fraps in Origen's courtyard. "You're such a lucky bastard. Not only is he enchanting on the eyes, but he's got to be somewhat brilliant."

"Yeah." Finn didn't mean to sound wistful. "We talk a lot."

Sylvie whispered, "Ohh . . ."

"It's as if he's afraid he'll infect me with darkness or something. Or snap me in half." She didn't tell Sylvie that she herself was partly to blame for Jack's reluctance, because she was still afraid of what he'd been.

"Maybe he's really, really Catholic."

"It's like prom night all over again." Finn clenched the straw between her teeth, remembering her first boyfriend, Daniel Osborne, blond and shy. "My sister followed me and knocked on the window of my boyfriend's car when things were getting interesting . . . he ended up sneaking into my room one summer afternoon. Afterwards, we had Popsicles."

"He climbed into your room? Is that a thing with you?"

"Obviously."

"Aubrey was my first. In his family's beach cottage. There's something sexy about summer, isn't there? I felt like a real grown-up. Then I screwed things up when I kissed his brother, who's two years younger than me."

"You cougar, you."

"Speaking of wild animals . . ." Sylvie's voice hushed. "Do you really think that was Caliban last night? And you find this naked and stunned Moth person in Mr. Redhawk's house, and it doesn't occur to you that he might be a double agent or something?"

That morning, on the walk to HallowHeart, Finn had told Christie and Sylvie about Caliban's visit and Moth's true nature. They were quiet afterward, which meant they were upset. *And I haven't even told them about Seth Lot.*

"I don't know, Sylv. I hope not. On both counts."

ON THE STAIRWAY of Armitrage Hall later that afternoon, Christie proved he still hadn't grown as a person as he, Finn, and Sylvie watched Jack striding toward them. "Here comes the prince of darkness."

"*Will* you stop calling him that?"

"I still say you're a lucky bastard." Sylvie ignored Christie's narrow-eyed glance in her direction.

Jack looked as fine as ever in his greatcoat and windswept regality, and, as usual, the sight of him made Finn feel as if her world had righted itself. He nodded to Sylvie and Christie before saying, to Finn, "I'm going to Tirnagoth tonight."

She heard her named called and turned. Hester Kierney, stylish in a cashmere coat of electric blue, was walking in their direction. She extended a glittering, white envelope toward Finn. "For you and your friends. An invite to my winter party."

"Hester." Jack nodded once.

"Jack."

"Don't take it," Christie warned Finn. "You never know what happens at those things . . . human sacrifices and so on."

"You'll notice"—Hester didn't look at Christie and her smile didn't falter—"I didn't give the invitation to *you*, Christie Hart. Hello, Sylvie."

"Hey, Hester."

"Thank you." Finn considered the envelope.

"It'll be fun. I promise. An oasis amid the stress of midterm exams."

"And will any Fatas be attending this oasis, Hester?" Christie smiled.

"Yes, Christie, they will." Hester strode away. Then she paused, and turned, and walking backward, said, "Bring your skates, if you've got any. And Christie . . . try to be fun again."

"Smack*down*." Sylvie looked at Christie, who ruefully murmured, "She's never forgiven me for breaking up with her when we were seven. So. Jack. Who's going to take Caliban down? I don't really care about Moth. I mean, he only tried to kill *you*, so . . ."

"Christie." Finn cast a stern glance at him. "When Moth tried to kill Jack, he said a dark-haired girl had sent him."

Christie went pale. "Reiko?"

"No." Sylvie frowned. "Reiko's dead. She *burned*."

Christie glanced at Jack. "You said there are no human ghosts. What about Fata ones?"

"It's not Reiko. There might be more than one dark-haired girl who wants me dead. And Fatas don't become ghosts. Finn, I'll walk you home after I've spoke to Cruithnear and you're done with class?"

"You can walk me to work." Finn tried not to let the idea of a ghost Reiko trouble her—she had enough to worry about.

"MISTLETOE." PROFESSOR JANE EMORY MOVED among the lab tables. Every student had in front of him or her some sort of winter plant with a little card describing it: poinsettias, holly, ivy, miniature fir trees, and the mistletoe. Finn had gotten black hellebore.

"Each plant symbolizes life in winter, breath beneath the snow, existence continuing in a hostile environment. The mistletoe. *Viscum album*. Family: Loranthaceae." Miss Emory lifted Christie's plant and smiled as a few students whistled. Christie sprawled back in his chair. He'd dropped one of his courses for botany because he claimed it seemed more exciting. Finn suspected he just had a crush on golden Jane Emory.

Professor Emory waved a chiding forefinger at them. "The mistletoe is a vampire, feeding on the life of its host—a tree—making the tree's vital energy its own. How does it do this? It grows on old trees, apples and hawthorns mostly. When a threadlike root pierces the bark, it feeds off the tree's juices. The wood of the mistletoe has been found to have twice as much potash and phosphoric acid as the host tree."

She set the mistletoe back down in front of Christie, who widened his eyes at Finn across the aisle. He said, "Maybe the tree thinks it's romantic . . . the brooding *sexy* mistletoe *sucking* at its energy."

Jane Emory leaned against her desk. "Maybe that's the nature of parasites—to be appealing until it's too late for the host. Now, to the black hellebore. *Helleborus niger*. Family: Ranunculaceae . . ."

As the class ended, Miss Emory called out, "There'll be an exam tomorrow, on the differences between plant families, tribes, and species. And it'll be based on the genus of each example given."

Oh hell. Finn glumly knew she couldn't pack that much detail into her brain.

Christie moved to Finn. "*Not* subtle. Comparing you to a tree and the prince of darkness to mistletoe—"

"Who said she was doing that?" Finn felt defensive; she suspected that was exactly what Jane Emory had been doing.

"*I* say she was doing that." Christie saluted Miss Emory as he strode out the door.

"Finn," Jane Emory called before Finn could slip out. She was seated on her desk, looking casually angelic. "Could I speak to you?"

"Sure."

"I wasn't alluding to you and Jack just now."

"But you were alluding to *something*."

"Well. Yes. I suppose I was. Not deliberately."

"The Fatas."

"Finn, at some point, we need to talk . . ."

Finn thought about the HallowHeart teachers who had attended the Fatas' sacrifice, the ones who called themselves guardians, protectors of Fair Hollow's residents. Jane Emory, who was one of those guardians, had not been there. But she had known about the Teind.

"We do need to talk," Finn said quietly, "but not now."

"Finn—"

"Later, Jane. Maybe." Finn turned and walked out.

FINN STILL WORKED EVENINGS at BrambleBerry Books, but not alone. As she watched the new hire skillfully park his Chevy between a Honda and a florist's delivery van, the sun began to set behind a bank of clouds and snow was already beginning to drift past the silent, gargoyle-decorated nightclub across the street.

As he entered, Micah Govannon—a true native of Fair Hollow with that name—shook snow from the long, tawny hair that fell over his face and smiled shyly at Finn. Slender in a dark blue sweater and tartan trousers, he wore black-rimmed glasses. There was a thin scar on his nose, and one on his neck, more on his hands, but Finn didn't dare ask about them. He was Christie's friend and Christie had told her Micah had been in a terrible car accident. He also played the cello, attended Saint John's U., not HallowHeart, and was addicted to coffee.

"Is there coffee?" He unwound his scarf, which she recognized as one of Charisma Hart's creations—Christie's mom was a serial knitter. "Because I really need coffee."

"In the back, but it's instant. Mrs. Browning didn't get to the Crooked Tree this morning."

"It'll do." He strode toward the back, followed by the shop's two resident cats. "I just finished playing a bar mitzvah."

He returned a few seconds later, coffee in hand, to lean against the counter and look down at the book of poetry Finn was reading. "Is that interesting?"

"It's by Augusta Danegeld." She showed him the cover with its illustration of a black wolf tangled in briars. "Christie's great-grandmother. Anyway, she wrote really sexy poems about mysterious, otherworldly men in Victorian times."

"Are the poems scandalous?"

"Like *Fifty Shades* with button-up boots and high collars."

A flash of reflected light made her glance out the window. A silver Rolls-Royce had pulled up in front of the Dead Kings nightclub. As music and lights glowed from beneath the building's black shutters, the Dead Kings' patrons, some of whom seemed to be nothing more in the dark than a drifting hand, silver eyes, luminous skin, a flicker of old jewelry, began to appear.

Micah had followed her gaze. "That's a popular place."

"Don't ever go there."

"Christie said the same thing."

They watched as a taxi double-parked to release a young man in a pale suit and a girl in a coat of crimson velvet, her face shadowed by its wide hood. As they glided toward the Dead Kings, the young man in the white suit glanced over his shoulder.

Finn gasped, so sharply it made Micah look at her.

"Micah, I'll be right back." Before he could say anything, she pushed out the door and ran across the street.

At the entrance to the Dead Kings, Mr. Wyatt, HallowHeart's metalworking instructor and the Dead Kings' bouncer, politely stepped in her way. His dreadlocks glittered with snow. "No."

"Mr. Wyatt, someone I know is in there. Please—"

"Perhaps, Miss Sullivan"—his voice was gentle—"you were mistaken."

"I wasn't *mistaken*." Her voice shook. "I'll wait outside all night if you don't let me in."

He raised a charcoal-colored cell phone. "I have your father's number. From Professor Avaline. Shall I call him?"

Defeated, she stepped away. She trudged back toward the bookshop, where a concerned Micah stood in the doorway. He said quietly, "You just told me not to go in there."

"I know." Inside the shop, she dug her cell phone from her backpack and pushed Jack's number. He answered. She said, "Could you come to the bookstore?"

Jack arrived shortly, sweeping into the shop with snow flecking his navy greatcoat. He shook Micah's hand when Finn introduced him, before turning to her, his eyes dark, and asking, "What happened?"

She pointed to the Dead Kings. "I need to get in there."

"Why?"

"Can I tell you later?"

He frowned at her. Then he headed for the door. "I'll ask again as soon as we're in."

Finn grabbed her coat. "I'm sorry, Micah. I've got to leave an hour early—Mrs. Browning'll be back soon."

"Go on." He accompanied them to the door. "Good luck with whatever you're doing, because I'm not going to ask."

She hurried after Jack, across the street, and caught up to him in front of the Dead Kings, where Mr. Wyatt eyed them with a wry cynicism that told her he'd expected this.

"Wyatt." Jack inclined his head. The metalsmith did the same—they were like two samurai about to unsheathe their swords. Jack continued, "A wrong was done to Finn Sullivan on Halloween night. Phouka says she is to be given what she wants."

"Well, if the *Banríon* says . . ." Mr. Wyatt pushed open the door and mockingly ushered them through.

As they strode down the crimson hall toward the inner doors painted with an image of a fairy knight, Jack, without looking at Finn, said, "I'm asking now."

"I saw my sister's boyfriend come in here with a Fata girl."

"Leander Cyrus." His mouth a grim line, Jack shoved open the doors.

"Yeah. You remembered his name."

Dub music with a Celtic influence pulsed around them as they stepped into the crowded club, where blue-green light smeared the faces of dancers and the skin of those lingering at the glass bar. Lining a wall painted with a mural of an art nouveau king and queen were shelves of exotic liqueurs in fantastically shaped bottles. Finn kept close to Jack, her face shadowed by the cowl of her Renaissance-styled hoodie. She said in his ear, "You don't know what Leander looks like."

"I've seen photos of him, in your room." He scanned the crowd. "There are some bad people here tonight."

Finn ducked her head as a young man in black moved past them. His eyes glinted white, not silver. A girl with blue hair and a blue band painted around the bottom half of her face glided past Jack, her lips parting as she looked him over. On the stage set up for live music, a bare-chested youth with cropped hair and spirals painted beneath his eyes grabbed the microphone. Accompanied by drums and an electric guitar, his voice was a howl that sent splinters into Finn's already raw nerves.

"The Unseelie," Jack said. "No wonder Wyatt didn't want us in here."

"*Leander* is here. There!" She'd caught sight of a flash of golden hair in the eerie light near the stage. She grabbed Jack's hand and pulled him with her.

One of the dancers jostled her and she lost her grip on Jack, then turned to see him gazing after a female figure in a hooded coat of crimson velvet. Finn remembered the girl Leander had come with and pushed toward her, glimpsing the girl's face, strangely familiar—

Someone seized Finn's other hand. She whirled to face a grinning young man with bleached hair and ram horns strapped to his head. His bare chest glistened with green spirals. "Well, hello, pretty pretty. However did a thing like you get past the guard dog?"

"Let go of me." She tugged, but his grip was like steel. His nails, painted green, were sharp. She looked up into silver eyes with rectangular pupils and began to feel that strange buzzing in her ears . . .

Then Jack was between them like a slice of dark murder and the Fata had let go of her hand and was backing away, saying, "Sorry. I didn't know . . ."

Finn had spotted the golden-haired figure in the pale suit moving up a flight of stairs. She broke free from Jack and wove through the Fatas, heard Jack swear violently as he plunged after her. She ran up the stairs and he followed. Pushing through a stained-glass door, she stepped onto the roof.

The figure in the pale suit stood with his back to them, his head bowed. Hoarsely, he said, "Why are you following me?"

"Leander." Finn moved forward. "It's me . . . Finn."

Jack stood in the doorway. In a voice like a knife, he said, "Cyrus. Turn around, face her, and tell her what you are."

Leander Cyrus shuddered and turned, shoving his hands through his hair. When Finn saw all the rings he wore, a slow horror crawled through her. She walked across the rooftop and reached out to touch his wrist, carefully wrapping her fingers around it. She breathed out in relief when she felt his pulse. "Leander—"

"Why," he whispered, lifting a dark gaze to hers, "why are you *here*? With *him*?"

Jack. He meant Jack. As if he knew what Jack had been. She said, "My da and I moved here a few months ago. Why are *you* here?"

His hand in hers was cold and his fingernails were dirty. His hair didn't look too clean either. His suit was expensive, but threadbare. He whispered, "I came here to kill a wolf."

He raised his head, and she stepped back with a small cry—his eyes glinted the mercury silver of a Fata's and the scent of oceans and flowers came so strongly from him, it made her choke. She recognized the flower smell, spicy and delicate—morning glories, which had once grown outside of her window in San Francisco.

"Finn." Jack's voice was soft. "I hoped I would never have to tell you."

"You knew? You *knew* what happened to him? *Jack*."

"I recognized the name when you first spoke it."

"Recognized the . . ."

She looked back at Leander, the kind, familiar young man who had been an older brother to her younger self, the one who'd taught her how to use a camera, who had taken her to old movies, and who'd comforted her whenever she'd cried over a cruel remark from Lily.

Leander Cyrus was a Jack. He had always been a Jack.

"You never saw him in the day, Finn. You never noticed because you were a child, and to a child, a Jack's habits would not seem so odd."

Leander stepped back. "I'm sorry. I'm so sorry, Finn."

She flew at him, pummeling him, and he didn't try to defend himself as she shouted, *"What did you do to my sister!* What did you *do?"*

Then Jack's arms were around her, pulling her away.

"Finn," Jack said calmly, "he's bleeding."

She saw the blood on Leander's mouth where one of her flailing fists had struck. Her eyes wide, she whispered, "Leander . . ."

He backed away.

"Why are you bleeding if you're a Jack?" She reached out, gripping his hand—

—and was knocked out of herself . . . as if someone had snatched her soul from her body and flung it above a winter forest from which rose a mansion of leprous marble, with stone wolves on the cloven stairway and shadows moving behind windows that were nothing more than shards of glass. It was a phantom house and, as the sun set, it glowed with light, transforming . . .

Then she was *inside* the house and knew she could never leave it as she walked its corridors, a gown of smoke and belladonna petals billowing around her legs. When she halted before a colossal mirror of tarnished glass, she saw a ghost, its dark hair snarled with lilies, its face in shadow. Soon, *he* would come, to lay his fine, jeweled hands upon her—

She was jarred back to herself, on her knees, with Jack crouched before her, gripping her shoulders, speaking her name over and over again. She retched, gasped, "I'm okay."

"You didn't tell her?" Leander's voice was wild.

"Tell her what?" Jack snarled.

Leander shook his head. "Just keep her away from *them* . . ."

He turned and stepped up onto the low wall of the roof. Finn screamed, "Leander!"

He jumped.

She staggered up and ran to the wall with Jack. There was no sign of anyone in the alley below.

"I recognized him in the photographs you showed me, the ones of your sister." Jack slid down, his back against the wall, and sat there. She dropped down beside him as he continued, "I should have told you. I just couldn't."

She tracked her memories of Leander, of day-bright San Francisco, of carp in sun-drenched water, of bicycling through hilly streets, of walks in Golden Gate Park . . . she couldn't place Leander in a single one of those sunlit memories. Why had she never noticed how strange it was that Lily only saw him at night? "All that time with Lily, he was a Jack. How could I not *know*?"

He twined his fingers around her wrists, pressed his thumbs gently against her pulse points. "You were a child."

"You said you recognized him. From where? Who does he belong to?"

Jack hesitated. "Seth Lot."

She closed her eyes as her stomach heaved. She saw the ghost girl walking barefoot in the hall of a house with stone wolves guarding a split stairway. "Leander was bleeding. Why do Jacks bleed?"

Warily, he said, "Finn . . ."

"He had a *pulse*." She pulled herself to her feet.

"Finn." Jack stood up, alarm in his voice. "I know what you're thinking. Don't. Please don't."

"He's *in love*. If the person a Jack loves dies, does a Jack return to what he was? Or does the heart and blood remain? Why is he still bleeding, Jack, if Lily is dead?"

"I don't know." His voice was ragged.

"It *wouldn't* remain." She was amazed by her own calm. "When I left you, you began to go all hollow again. Whatever Leander was"—she gripped the low wall as a terrifying hope soared through her—"he loved my sister and loves her still."

"Finn. *Stop*."

"They take people and put dead things in their place, all fixed up to look like the ones they stole away." She remembered what Reiko had said on Halloween: *I can bring back your sister.*

"Finn, please don't think like this."

Reiko had said, *Do you want this world of absolutes and accidents? Of hopelessness and ugly deaths?* "Jack . . ."

He looked away and said nothing more.

FINN CLAMBERED UP JACK'S FIRE ESCAPE, following him. Not once on the drive here had she mentioned Lily Rose.

As they climbed into his apartment, he paused as if listening to a distant sound. He bent to draw a knife from one boot, then glided toward the bathroom, yanked the door open.

Moth was crouched between the sink and the toilet, his arms over his head. He still wore the clothes Jack had given him, but he was barefoot, surrounded by pieces of glass from the mirror that had hung over the sink. He whispered, "I've no reflection. I'm not real. I'm not really here."

Finn knelt before him. "Of course you're here. I'm speaking to you, aren't I? Why did you try to kill Jack?"

"The dark-haired girl," he said faintly, "told me to."

Finn pressed on, "Does the name Reiko Fata mean anything to you?"

He continued, "'*If she be made of white and red, her faults will ne'er be known.*'"

"This," Jack said, crouching beside Finn, "is getting weird."

Finn took out her phone and tapped at it. Jack said, "What are you doing?"

"Calling for reinforcements."

CHRISTIE AND SYLVIE ARRIVED dressed for battle in silver and holly. As they hauled themselves over the windowsill into Jack's apartment, Moth rose from his place on the bathroom floor and stared at them.

"Is *that* Moth?" Sylvie was apple cheeked from the chill. A Laplander hat was snug on her braided hair.

Moth backed away until he came up against the sink. Finn winced as glass crunched beneath his bare feet. He whispered again, this time in English, "*Dragonfly*. Why would you let *her* into your house?" He pointed at Christie. "And I remember *you* now, the one who found me . . . the *Sionnach Ri* . . . trickster . . ."

"They're not whoever you're mistaking them for." Jack leaned in the doorway of his kitchen. "What a hell of a night. I'm going to make tea. Moth, you're probably bleeding all over my floor. Sit down. Hello, Christopher. Sylvie."

Moth walked to the sofa. As he sat, warily watching Christie and Sylvie, Finn didn't see any blood on his feet. She said, "You're lucky. You didn't get cut. You've met Christie and that's Sylvie."

"I thought . . ." Moth shook his head and hunched over again, his thumbs pressed to his temples. "I have misremembered . . . what were those names I said?"

"You forgot them already?"

"Great." Christie stared at Moth. "Someone else who's lost his mind."

An hour later, Christie and Sylvie had learned all about Leander Cyrus, Moth, and Seth Lot. Moth listened without speaking, his hands clenched together.

"So," Christie spoke carefully, hunched up, "your sister's boyfriend, all this time, was a Frankenstein?"

Sylvie was watching Moth. She whispered, "And Leander worked for this Seth Lot? What does that mean?"

"It means"—Christie sounded desolate—"the Big Bad Wolf knows about Finn. I wonder if he knows we all helped perish his ex-girlfriend?"

The silence that followed was broken by Moth. "I don't remember a man who is a wolf. Why can't I remember him?"

Christie asked Jack, "How is the fairy mob handling this grim turn of events?"

"Christopher," Jack spoke idly, "that fairy mob might be the only thing standing between you and the *Madadh aillaid*."

"Is that the Big Bad Wolf's fancy name?"

Jack looked at Moth. "You don't remember the Wolf king, Moth, only a dark-haired girl. You tried to kill me because the dark-haired girl told you to. You protected Finn from the *crom cu*. So my guess is that you have left Seth Lot's services and now work for another—only you don't remember who that is. You've been enchanted. Or cursed."

Moth's bracelet of silver charms caught the light and Finn could make out the charms' individual shapes—a bee, a seahorse, an owl . . . an octopus with a tentacle missing. Her stomach somersaulted. "Moth, where did you get that bracelet?"

He stared at it as if he'd never seen it before. He took it off, held it out to her. "It was hers . . . the dark-haired girl's."

With one trembling hand, she accepted the charm bracelet. There was the butterfly she had bought at a thrift shop in San Francisco, the skull with garnet eyes, the guitar, the octopus . . . The air in the room seemed to crack. She met Moth's green gaze and whispered, "Who is the dark-haired girl who sent you?"

No one spoke. No one moved.

She pulled out her cell phone, tapped it to a picture, and raised it before Moth. "Is this her?"

His face changed. Light dawned behind his eyes. He whispered, "Lily Rose."

AS MOTH SPRAWLED BACK ON THE SOFA, his gaze opaque, Finn gazed down at her sister's picture. Sylvie was sitting at the edge of her chair, nibbling on a thumbnail and watching Finn. Christie turned a battered Rubik's Cube he'd found on a shelf over and over in his hands, but his attention was also on Finn. Jack was leaning forward in his chair, feet apart, hands clasped between his knees, his face sober.

"I don't remember things in order anymore." Moth spoke as if the memories restored by Lily's photo hurt him. "Sometimes, I remember the Wolf's house . . . sometimes, it was a ruin, other times, like the home of a lord. I ran away, once, and stone wolves chased me, brought me down." He continued softly, "I came to

No longer property of
Marion Carnegie Library

MARION CARNEGIE LIBRARY
206 South Market
Marion, IL 62959

that house a long time ago. Before that, I traveled with a company in England. Actors. We were actors. Someone—a red-haired girl—I made her angry. Then I was . . . not me. The wing tattoos on my back . . . they're a curse." He looked up at Finn. "When I was me again, I was in that house, the one with the stone wolves. And so was the dark-haired girl. Lily Rose."

"But"—Sylvie frowned at Finn—"you saw your sister fall. She was in the *hospital*."

"It wasn't her." Finn didn't take her gaze from Moth. "It wasn't Lily who fell or Lily in that hospital bed. It was one of their tricks. Moth, is she alive? Lily Rose?"

"Finn," Jack said urgently.

"I think we were friends." Moth seemed to not have heard her question. "All the others in that house were cold things, cruel. But Lily Rose spoke to me. She was kind." He lifted his head. "I don't remember when I left, or how. I think she helped me escape, sent me to protect you. Then a sharp, dark man caught me. He made me sleep, and I woke up in the attic of the house you found me in."

"*Moth.*" Finn leaned forward. "*Where is Lily Rose?*"

Moth slid his gaze to Jack, his body suddenly taut. "She wanted me to protect you from dangerous things."

"Jack isn't dangerous to me." Finn wanted to shake him. "Where is my sister?"

"I'm to protect you. I remember what *he* used to be." He pointed at Jack. "I saw him, in the house of the Wolf."

"I don't recall meeting you." Jack narrowed his eyes.

"Please." Finn's composure cracked. "*Tell me where my sister is.*"

Moth lowered his head. "I dare not. I'm to keep you safe." He shivered as if shaking something from himself and said, "Fifteen ninety-five. Lily Rose would tell me that whenever I began to forget. It was the year I was stolen away. He'd taken my name. Fifteen ninety-five, she would say, and I would almost be myself again."

"Finn." Jack stood. "Let's go outside for a minute."

As Finn climbed out onto the fire escape, Jack came after. She gazed out over the snowy parking lot as that terrible night replayed in her head . . . her sister, shattered in blood and glass. She felt the poisonous sleepiness return, fought it with clenched teeth. "I thought she was dead. Seth Lot took her."

Jack gently said, "I'll have Moth tell me where she is. Then I'll go search for her."

"I'm coming with you."

"Where Lot has taken your sister—if what Moth has said is true—it isn't a safe place. And . . . this concerns me—that bracelet is made of silver. Where Moth has come from . . . silver and iron decay or transform."

Her stomach twisted. Where *was* Lily Rose? "You'll take me with you or I'll find a way to go alone. I'll find Leander. And if any of your Fata friends even *attempt* to make me or *my* friends forget you, my sister, or anything else, I've got things written and hidden, files on several computers, and little reminders scrawled on some of my everyday stuff."

He stared at her, his brows knit. Then he bent his head and kissed her.

She hadn't expected such a tactic and knew that he was trying to distract her. She got a little angry, so the kiss wasn't delicate, but heated and fierce. She stood on her toes, wrapped her arms around his neck, and pushed her hands through his hair. She dragged his lean-muscled body close as her blood became fiery butterflies . . .

She pulled away and steeled herself from winding her arms around him again as he leaned back against the railing, one boot heel pressed against it, his hair in his eyes as he watched her. They were both breathing quickly.

She pointed at him. "I mean it, Jack. Do you think Moth's telling the truth? He doesn't even know his real name."

"Lot"—Jack was studying her from beneath his lashes, which meant he was scheming—"will have taken that from him. Moth is a changeling, a stolen-away. From Elizabethan England. He's probably lost his mind more than a few times. As for Leander, he seems like a fugitive as well." Jack settled against the railing beside her and she could feel him sheltering her from the cold. "Leander called himself 'Cyrus' when I met him in San Francisco, when Reiko was visiting Lot, who'd made a temporary den in Muir Woods. Cyrus went to Seth Lot because he'd lost whoever had made him a Jack. He was rootless, as I once was."

Finn hated to think of Jack as he'd been, someone who'd caught the attention of a creature who had murdered him and brought him back to life stitched full of magical roses that kept him immortal. In the beginning, Jack had lured Finn to him like the elf knight in an old ballad, with no good intentions. And, dull with grief, she'd fallen for him. Was that how it had been with her sister and Leander? She carefully set her hands on the railing. "It wasn't just Norn, the Fata my sister met when she was little. It was Leander, too, who told Lily some of those things in her journal. Leander loves her. He bleeds for her. *My sister is still alive.*"

"We need to remember that Leander and Moth once belonged to the Wolf. Go home, Finn. I'll take Moth to a safe place after I've talked to him."

"Remember our deal, Jack. Find out where my sister is and *take me with you.* And don't try to trick me."

His mouth curved, but his eyes were troubled. "I wouldn't dream of it."

AS FINN ENTERED THE LAMP-LIT HALL of her house in a jangling of keys and elation, her father called from the parlor. "Finn."

She ducked her head around the corner.

"Come. Sit." He patted the sofa next to him. She sauntered in and dropped beside him, glad Jane Emory wasn't there. As he handed her a cold cherry Coke, she squinted at him. "How did you know I'd be exactly on time?"

"After Halloween, I didn't think you'd want to terrify me again."

She'd vowed to never tell him what had actually happened that night. Now, she had another secret, one she *wanted* to tell him, but didn't dare, not until she knew Lily was really alive. It didn't feel real, that remote possibility, but she would keep it in a death grip until she found out.

As her father handed her a plate stacked with nachos, melted cheese, salsa, and his famous guacamole, her mouth watered. He said casually, "How's Jack?"

She bit into a nacho and noticed a book on gardening laid facedown on the table. It was winter. Her da didn't have any indoor plants. She sighed and looked at her da, saw how the shadows had left his eyes and he was smiling more. "Fine. So are Sylvie and Christie. How is Jane Emory?"

"She's the one who suggested I invite Jack for Christmas." He switched on the TV. "Want to watch a movie? Something scary, or an action movie, seeing as you don't like romance or comedy."

"You know what? Let's watch something funny."

CHAPTER 4

It is true we shall be monsters, cut off from all the world: but on that account we shall be more attached to one another.

—*FRANKENSTEIN*, MARY SHELLEY

Sylvie and Christie had signed up for phys ed activities that complemented HallowHeart's posh, old-fashioned, and eccentric vibe. Sylvie took archery and Christie had fencing class, which he'd convinced Finn to try, but she wasn't very good at it. Still, it beat soccer.

As they'd walked toward McKinley Hall, with its Doric columns and the face of the sun god Apollo carved in granite over its doors, Christie had quietly asked Finn if she knew for certain if her sister was alive. She'd told him she wasn't sure, but she needed find out. And Jack would help her. Christie hadn't said anything else to her since. Now, in the fencing studio, he was pretending to be busy with his gear, ignoring her, and she was tempted to poke him with her foil.

When Jack arrived after class had ended, Christie scowled and began slamming his equipment onto a bench.

"Finn." Jack leaned in the doorway. "Christopher."

"Christopher isn't talking to me, so he won't be engaging you in conversation either."

"Have you ever used one of these, Jack?" Christie straightened and twirled his foil. "I mean, in your abnormally long life, you must have."

"I've done so."

Christie tossed Jack a foil. Jack caught it with one hand and stepped forward. With a flick of the wrist, he neatly disarmed Christie, caught Christie's foil, and tapped Christie three times—"Tierce, quarte, septime—"

—before sliding both foils into their holders. "I won't fight you, Christopher."

"You can't take her." Christie's voice startled them both—it was in pieces. "You can't take her, Jack, to find her sister. Finn, you don't even know if she's alive or where the hell she *is*. What if it's a trap?"

Jack said, "Do you think I haven't thought of that?" He reached out a hand to Finn, who clasped it. "I can't change her mind."

Finn looked at Christie. "What if it was one of your brothers?"

Christie grabbed his backpack. "He's going to get you killed," he said, before he stalked out of the room.

When he'd gone, Finn turned to Jack. His eyes, one of which was always darker than the other, now seemed inky with secrets. "Did Moth tell you? Where Lily is?"

He said softly, "She's in the betwixt and between. Neither here nor there, second star to the right and straight on till morning. Down the rabbit hole. She's in the Ghostlands, Finn."

She whispered, "I was afraid you'd say something like that."

"CHRISTIE'S A VERY PASSIONATE PERSON." Sylvie wandered around Finn's room after Finn told her about the incident in fencing class. Sylvie grinned. "I feel fiendish, tricking Christie and Jack like that. What do you think they'll do when we don't show up for dinner?"

Finn looked up from her laptop. "Christie wanted to poke Jack with a sharp stick today. Maybe putting them at a table with pointy utensils wasn't such a good idea. But they *will* be in public."

Sylvie's impish mood faded. "Finn . . . where *is* Jack taking you?"

"I don't know what that . . . place is, Sylv. There are a lot of different names for it, in every myth I've read. Only it's real. And I'm going. Because that's where Lily is . . . the birthplace of Seth Lot and Reiko Fata."

Sylvie frowned down at her stockinged feet. "Do you ever think of Reiko? Like, wonder what she was before she became the queen of hell?"

On Halloween night, Reiko Fata had followed her consort David Ryder into the sacrificial fire, not only because he carried the heart she'd grown for love of Jack, but because that heart—even cut out of her—that heart had made her *human*. And David Ryder, a cold and soulless elf knight, had loved her, had bled for her. At the last moment of their long lives, two terrifying rulers of faery had become human and died for each other. And Finn *did* feel guilt, and angrily thought that she shouldn't—Reiko Fata had no right to get that from her. "Sometimes," Finn said, "I wonder if Reiko was ever a real girl, like us."

"She murdered Jack to keep him. And she was going to *kill* you. Burning to death was too easy an end for her. So don't you feel bad about it."

"I don't," Finn lied, and she thought again of the words Reiko had spoken on Halloween night: *I can bring back your sister.* "Sylv, I think Reiko knew Lily was still alive."

"Of course she knew. Let us go with you, me and Christie."

"*No.* Jack said he'll have a hard enough time keeping *me* safe, let alone two others."

"Is that gorgeous train wreck you call Moth going with you?"

"I don't know."

"How will you get your sister away? You told us Seth Lot's a killer, and I've got the feeling you left out some of his story. He's a real monster, isn't he?" Sylvie's voice was small. "Aren't you scared?"

"I'm scared . . . beyond scared. But if he took Lily, I'm going to get her back." Her hands curled into fists against her rib cage. *No matter what.*

Sylvie gazed at a framed photograph on one wall. "Your sister was so pretty. Is that Leander—"

The photograph flew from the wall and struck the floor. Glass shattered.

Sylvie's mouth fell open.

Finn jumped up and strode to the photo in its mosaic of broken glass. Shot in stylish black-and-white, Lily and Leander smiled up at her. She murmured, "I meant to tell you. I have a ghost. I thought it was Lily."

Sylvie's voice dropped to a whisper. "You think your sister is haunting you?"

Finn picked up the black-and-white photograph and the pieces of glass. "I don't think it's Lily anymore. I don't know *what's* doing this."

Sylvie stood up. "Do you have a Ouija board?"

Finn stared at her. Then she walked to the closet, opened the door, and stood on tiptoe to reach the shelf stacked with board games. She pulled down a rectangular box, turned, and offered it to Sylvie. "I've got this."

Sylvie came over and looked doubtfully at the box. "I didn't even know they made 'Hello Kitty' Ouija boards."

"It was a gift," Finn said defensively.

"Well." Sylvie accepted the box, opened it, and unfolded the board on Finn's bed. "It's a very *Gothic* 'Hello Kitty,' so I suppose it'll work."

Finn hesitated, watching Sylvie place the pink planchette on the board decorated with pink and black letters.

"She's your sister, Finn." Sylvie patted the bed. "Come on. Let's talk to her. She might be communicating from wherever *they've* taken her."

Finn pictured Lily lying broken and bleeding in glass shards on a night street sluiced with rain, saw Lily in the hospital, connected to plastic breathing tubes. She felt the poisonous sleepiness begin to return—

She sat on the bed, placed her hand on the planchette. Sylvie laid one hand over hers and whispered, "Okay. Ask the name first."

"How do you know about this?"

"My gran is Shinto. And her gran was a *yamabushi*, someone who speaks to spirits. I learned some stuff."

"What about your mom—"

Sylvie shrugged. "My mom is an actress, nothing else."

Finn sidestepped that one. "I just ask a name? All right . . . *who is here?*"

The planchette jerked. Sylvie breathed out. Finn watched the piece of plastic slide to the letter *D*, not what she'd expected. The planchette circled, pushing toward the *E*, before veering sharply to the *A*.

"Finn." Sylvie's voice shook a little. "Maybe it *isn't* your sis—"

The planchette shot across the board, became airborne, and hit one of the photos on Finn's desk. Finn scrambled back as the plastic thing ricocheted against another photograph on the wall, before dropping to the floor.

Finn grabbed the framed photo the planchette had knocked over on her desk. In the photo, Lily Rose and Leander grinned into the camera he was holding. Turning, Finn studied the photograph on the wall, its glass cracked by the planchette: Lily and Leander, elegantly dressed and seated on a divan of red velvet. She felt a horrible ache in her throat, for Leander, who'd once been human and who had been transformed into a stitched-together creature that couldn't endure the sun. She whispered, "Whoever it is, Sylv, this ghost . . . whoever it is knows what Leander is. Help me take these photos down, would you?"

WHEN CHRISTIE ARRIVED at the Antlered Moon Pub and was shown to the booth where he expected Finn and Sylvie, he instead found only the prince of darkness hunched over a cup of coffee. Jack looked up at him and said, "The ladies aren't coming. We've been set up. You might as well sit down."

"I'm not going to."

"They've already ordered and paid, Christopher. Dinner's on its way." Jack pushed a coffeepot across the table. "Coffee?"

Christie slouched opposite him. "I already had my five cups. Is there any liquor on the bill?"

"I wish."

Christie leaned forward, squinting. "Are you ever gonna age?"

"It's inevitable, isn't it?" Jack sat back as their plates arrived. Sylvie knew Christie well; she'd ordered a giant venison burger and sweet potato fries. The same for Jack.

"Is it inevitable, Jack?" Christie poured ketchup on his burger. "Because it doesn't seem inevitable, around you, that Finn will ever turn nineteen."

"Christopher. This world holds as many bad things as the world of the Fatas."

"I'd say *your* bad things are worse. Take Caliban, for example. And that . . . kelpie that was in our well. And the Rooks, threatening Finn. And there's even worse on its way, isn't there?"

"Phouka and Absalom will deal with what's coming. As for the Rooks, their allegiance has idiotically switched to someone else."

"You sure those three scavengers haven't switched to the winning team?"

"Don't underestimate Phouka and Absalom."

"I don't trust them and I don't trust you, because you're two hundred years old and there's no way you're not messed up in the head."

"What happened to the poetry, Christopher?"

"You think her sister's really alive?"

"I think the evidence is distressingly clear. And Lily Rose fits the profile of what Seth Lot prefers."

"Shit," Christie said raggedly. "Where are you taking Finn?"

"It's a place—places—hidden from the true world."

"Another dimension?"

"Another *perception*. And if I don't take her, she'll find a way on her own. You *know* her, Christopher, how stubborn she is . . . reckless, headstrong . . ."

"I know she would die for her sister. And I've read enough mythology to know she can't bring Lily Rose back from wherever she is without a sacrifice. A *sacrifice*, Jack."

"She won't be making any sacrifices," Jack said evenly.

"How do you—" Christie broke off as he met Jack's gaze. Suddenly, grudgingly, he felt admiration, and hated it.

JACK CAME FOR FINN IN THE LATE AFTERNOON. She couldn't help but smile when she saw him. With his dark hair tucked behind his ears and his hands in the pockets of a parka lined with fake fur, he looked so beautifully ordinary. He said in that voice that made her skin warm, "Are you and Sylvie proud of your little trick?"

At first, she thought he meant the Ouija board, then realized he was talking about the peace dinner she and Sylvie had set up. "Did it go well? Christie's still alive?"

"We're going to run away together. Let's walk to LeafStruck."

As they began strolling down the street, Finn considered Jack: valiant, self-possessed, mysterious. "You know, you'd be a pretty sexy old guy."

He glanced at her with amusement. "Your trains of thought completely escape me sometimes."

"Only sometimes?"

The sun began to set. She watched her boots kick up dirty snow. Jack had delivered Moth to Colleen Olive, the Fata girl who haunted the neglected Leaf Struck Mansion like the spooky old bride in Dickens's *Great Expectations*. If Moth went off the rails, Colleen Olive could take care of herself. Jack said, "I've been dreaming about Nathan."

Finn's stomach dropped when she thought of Nathan Clare, the innocent boy who'd once shared LeafStruck with Jack and Colleen Olive. "Okay."

"I went looking for him a few nights ago." He handed her a pewter locket shaped like a book. With unsteady fingers, she opened it and found a picture of a girl with dandelion hair and a freckled face.

"Mary Booke," she whispered. "This was Nathan's."

"There were other things near it." Jack didn't look at her.

She gripped the locket so tightly, its edges bit into her skin. She felt the ache of grief in her throat. "You think Caliban . . . killed him?"

"Caliban," he said in a low voice scarier than a snarl, "has a lot to answer for."

They reached LeafStruck Mansion on its hill. Even winter-bared, the elder trees around it seemed to create a dark cavern. As they trudged up the steep stairway toward the house, Finn thought of the other mansions in Fair Hollow, abandoned, closed up, and utilized by the Fatas.

"Jack"—she looked at him as they stood before the front door—"do you need to have that knife in your hand?"

"It's a misericorde, beloved, and, yes, I need it. I'm feeling very vulnerable right now." He pushed open the door and entered. She followed, breathing in the clotted, sepia warmth of the hall. A lamp of orange glass glowed on top of a black wardrobe. LeafStruck's interior reminded her of taxidermy and sinister grandmothers.

"Colleen?" Jack moved to the staircase that led to the second floor. "*Cailleach Oidche!*"

No one answered. He glanced back at Finn, who pulled from her backpack the silver dagger Eve Avaline had given her. He frowned at it. She said, "It's a knife, beloved."

"Put that away before you fall on it."

"I don't think so."

As he led her up the stairs, she glanced at the portraits of yellow-eyed, elaborately costumed people on the walls. When they reached the upper hall with its velvet wallpaper and clunky furniture, they found it illuminated only by a beam of light from a door left ajar. The other doors were shut. Jack motioned for Finn to wait as he approached the open door cautiously. He stepped into the room. She heard him speak to someone before he opened the door all the way. "It's okay."

She moved into the room, which looked the same as before, cluttered with ornamental eggs of wood, metal, glass, and clay. There was a bed in the alcove now, an oversized thing draped with gossamer and covered with Pier 1 pillows.

The owl girl, veiled as usual, sat in a chair, her hands gloved in pale satin, her ivory cocktail dress a little more fashionable than the gauzy tea gown she'd worn the last time Finn had seen her.

Colleen Olive's voice was a husk: "Moth the lovely has gone down to make coffee and fetch the cakes."

"We didn't see him. How are you?" Jack dropped onto a dusty love seat. Finn sat beside him and didn't take her attention from the figure the Fatas called the *Cailleach Oidche*. She'd read up on her Celtic mythology and knew what owl girls were capable of.

"I am well. And you, Jack? How are the pains and pleasures of being mortal?"

"It's because of Finn that I'm not one of the shadows any longer."

The veiled head and its blurred face slowly turned toward Finn, who had to brace herself against the uneasiness that spidered up her backbone. "Serafina Sullivan. Braveheart. I cannot thank you enough for ridding us of the white snake."

"You mean Reiko—"

The owl girl raised a hand. "Don't speak that name in my house. Moth has told me what he can remember. He has told me about your sister, the stolen-away. It was a vile thing done. The white serpent did a vile thing to me, once." Colleen Olive's voice had grown stronger. Before Finn could avert her gaze, the Fata reached up and pulled the veil from her face.

It wasn't the ghoulish horror Finn had expected. Colleen Olive seemed as young as Finn. Tangled brown hair streaked with white fell around her face dissected by a scar that slashed between her golden eyes, down her nose and mouth. "I will tell you about the Wolf, Serafina. The *Madadh aillaid* feeds off the young of your people and corrupts the innocent of mine. He is cast out because he is a killer of Fatas and mortals. He is one of the oldest. And he was the white serpent's lover. I see Jack has told you these things, in a gentler way, perhaps. Has he described the place where the Wolf keeps your sister?"

Finn looked at Jack, who was watching Colleen Olive as if he'd wronged her in some way. He said, "I haven't told her much about the Ghostlands. I don't know what to tell her, because there's very little I remember."

Colleen Olive's eyes were an elemental gold, not the ghost-light silver of most

Fata gazes. She said to Finn, "Jack cannot go alone to find her. You must accompany him, to claim her. It is the blood in you that will be your most powerful weapon. Mortal blood can influence things in the *Taibhse na Tir*."

Someone was running up the stairs. They all turned their heads, expecting Moth. The doorway remained dark as an unearthly chill snaked through the room. Colleen Olive said, "That was not Moth."

Jack moved to his feet and Finn rose with him. Colleen Olive also stood, the veil drifting from one hand. *"Something else is here."*

Jack bent down, slid the Renaissance misericorde from one boot, and moved toward the door. As Finn followed, he said, "No."

"I'm coming with you."

"Why do you have to be so—never mind." He stepped into the hall. The single lamp on a rolltop desk couldn't keep the shadows at bay. She whispered, "What is it—"

There was a thump from downstairs.

Jack motioned at her to remain where she was and began to glide down the stairs. She followed—and saw the front door wide open, snow drifting over the floor from the night beyond. She was halfway down the stairs when he called out, "Moth! If you're down here, answer—"

There was a shriek from the floor above, followed by banging and the sounds of things breaking.

Jack bolted past Finn, back up the stairs. She raced after.

In the upper hall, he halted and cursed. The door to the *Cailleach Oidche*'s room was wide open and slashed.

"Are those claw marks?" Finn put her back against a wall.

Jack reached out and shoved the door all the way open. The ornamental eggs had been smashed, the furniture overturned. Feathers from the pillows were scattered everywhere. Finn gripped the hilt of her silver dagger and looked at the windows, all open, curtains fluttering.

Jack backed away. "Don't worry about Colleen. *We* need to get out."

Finn turned, shouted, and clapped a hand over her mouth. Clawed into the wall was the stylized image of a wolf. She whispered, "You said it wasn't *him*—"

"It's not." He grabbed her hand and they ran into the hall—

At the top of the stair stood a tall, spindly figure in a long black coat, all its face but for one golden eye veiled by scarlet hair. It didn't move, its hands at its sides, its nails long and sharp and black.

Jack spoke with unnerving calm. "Don't look away from it."

He needn't have said that—Finn couldn't take her gaze from the still, doll-like figure with its horrible sense of *awareness*. Animal fear almost paralyzed her.

"Don't even bat an eyelash until we're past it, understand?" He led her toward it. "When we're past, run like hell."

She wanted to scream as they came within two feet of the doll. She could see the seams in its jointed fingers, the perfection of its alabaster face. It was an artificial man, but it was *alive*.

The toe of her sneaker bumped against one of the antiques strewn through the hall—as if someone had deliberately created an obstacle course. She staggered against Jack, who caught her, his gaze on her and hers on him—

—then two black-nailed hands were around her throat and the doll-thing was so close, she could see the details of its face through the red hair, the lips baring canine teeth, the goat eyes made of glass and their malevolent intelligence. Even as she struggled to breathe, she didn't drop her gaze from it—

Jack's arm slid, snake swift, over her shoulder, the misericorde glinting in one hand. She closed her eyes before she could see the blade pierce one of the creature's glass optics.

As the Grindylow released her, Jack hauled her up, urging her to run. They clattered down the stairs, turning their backs on the thing they weren't supposed to look away from.

Something leaped over them, dragging Jack into the dark below. Finn nearly fell down the rest of the stairs. At the bottom, she pulled herself up and found Jack kneeling in the hall below. The doll-thing had one hand in his hair and the other around his throat. An inky substance drooled from its shattered eye.

"Finn," Jack spoke tautly, "it's a Grindylow. It will kill me if you look away from it. It will move and kill me. Don't look away from it."

Clutching Eve's silver dagger in one shaking hand, she whispered, "What do I do?"

"I'm trying to get free—don't come at it with that knife—that'll set it off, a defense mechanism, and it'll move even with you watching it. Hold on." He carefully pulled his hair from the Grindylow's frozen grasp, avoiding its claws at his throat. "When I tell you to, drop that knife and kick it toward me."

"Okay." Wide-eyed, her eyes burning, she waited. She wondered if the Grindylow understood what they were attempting.

"Now!"

She let the dagger fall, kicked it—

The Grindylow moved, hissing, as Jack twisted free and caught the dagger—

—the doll-man suddenly stood before Finn, its smile vicious, the hollow of its eye socket still oozing black ichor. It had one hand stretched toward her—its other hand, with its razor nails, had clawed across Jack's chest. As Jack looked down and slid to his knees, Finn's gaze, for a moment, dropped from the Grindylow—

She was flung away and hit the floor. She scrambled up, swayed on her feet. Jack was struggling to stand. The Grindylow was gone.

She winced, felt as if bones had broken. *"Where is it?"*

Something stood in the shadows behind Jack. Finn stumbled, glanced away for one second, and the Grindylow *moved*—

Then Jack was lifting himself from the blood-smeared floor and *Moth* was gripping the Grindylow by the throat with both hands, his expression savage. His arms trembled, but his gaze never left the creature as he said, "Get a mirror!"

Finn twisted around, frantically searching. Down the shadowy hall that led to the kitchen, she saw something pale moving, like a ghost—

She ducked as a white barn owl sailed over her head, out the door.

There was a glint at the end of the hallway. She ran toward her own reflection, grabbed the mirror from the wall, and raced back to where Moth held the seemingly lifeless Grindylow and Jack didn't dare approach with the silver dagger.

Jack gave her back the dagger and took the mirror from her. He raised it behind Moth so the Grindylow could see its reflection. The monster in Moth's grasp made a sound. Its skin began to harden. The awareness within its one remaining eye began to dim as reality asserted itself.

Finn took a swaying step forward, forgetting about the dagger still in her hand.

That motion triggered the Grindylow's self-defense mechanism. Even with their gazes upon it, the Grindylow shrieked and came to life, knocking Moth aside and leaping at Finn. Jack let go of the mirror, which smashed to pieces as it hit the floor. He lunged, the misericorde back in his hand.

Finn froze with the dagger, as the Grindylow twisted toward the other armed and moving threat—Jack.

Jack slammed his misericorde into its throat. The Grindylow collapsed, its alabaster shell cracking, revealing a mass of writhing vegetation and a black snake curled in the rotting flowers of its skull. As Moth stomped the snake and smashed the Grindylow's skull beneath his boot heel, Finn reeled back with a hand over her mouth. She sank down and Jack squatted beside her. "You're fine."

She studied him. "You're not."

"Surface wounds." He smiled, then winced. "I may need a booster shot."

"I remember these things." Moth pointed at the remains of the Grindylow. "That is an antique scourge, sent to hunt me. The *Madadh aillaid* knows I'm here."

Jack looked at Finn and said, "We need to take him to Tirnagoth."

Finn hadn't wanted this yet—take Moth to Phouka and Phouka would find out about Lily Rose. She didn't quite trust Phouka and didn't know if she ever would, because Phouka had once been Reiko Fata's lieutenant.

She caught the glimmer of something yellow and glassy in a corner, realized it was the Grindylow's second eye, and decided they might need Phouka after all. She stood up. "Let's go."

She staggered. Jack caught her, gently smoothing her hair from her face.

"Perhaps," he ventured as Moth returned to the kitchen and began rummaging in the drawers for defensive cutlery, "I should take you home."

"No, you shouldn't. I'm getting used to this sort of thing." She kept telling herself not to fall down.

Jack said, "That's what I'm afraid of."

CHAPTER 5

"There are some upon this earth of yours," returned the spirit, "who lay claim to know us, and who do their deeds of passion, pride, ill-will, hatred, envy, bigotry, and selfishness in our name; who are as strange to us and all our kith and kin as if they had never lived."

—*A Christmas Carol*, Charles Dickens

The abandoned Tirnagoth Hotel had once been Reiko Fata's headquarters and, at night, its sinister elegance whispered of fine things decaying. The gates, tangled with withered vines, opened slowly as Jack's sedan approached.

In the circular drive, Jack, Finn, and Moth got out of the sedan. Finn still felt the unease-bordering-on-dread that the Fatas' proximity caused. Shaky and exhausted from fighting the Grindylow, she felt as if she'd just recovered from a brutal virus and desperately wanted to go home. "It's quiet."

"Not really." As Jack undid the metal gates, the music and voices of a revel blasted from the courtyard. Climbing the stairs after him, Finn gazed up at the words etched in stone above the impressive entry of medieval-looking doors.

"*'The unseen is here and calleth to thee,'*" Jack explained.

Moth studied the hotel. Remembering how he'd fought the Grindylow, Finn wondered exactly what he'd done for Seth Lot as he whispered, "What is this place?"

Tirnagoth's doors swung open and a slim figure emerged, brilliant hair falling around a pretty face with the eyes of a devil. "The entrance to Fairyland."

"Absalom," Jack spoke wearily.

Absalom Askew, who appeared to be a teenager but who was probably as old as rocks, assessed their condition with one sweeping gaze. He blinked rapidly when he saw Moth, who stood with his hands in the pockets of the fur-lined coat he'd borrowed from Jack.

"Jack. Serafina. Who is this charming young man you've brought with you?"

"I'm Moth." Moth frowned. "That's what I'm called."

"What you're called." Absalom stepped back, gesturing inward. He wore a dark suit with an orange silk tie and tiger eye cuff links. "Welcome to Tirna-goth."

Jack, stepping in, looked Absalom over. "Nice suit."

"Oh, this old thing." Absalom straightened one cuff. "It's just for the celebration. To which you were invited. Did you forget?"

"Yes." By his tone, Jack obviously hadn't.

Absalom led them into the lobby where bronze lamps shaped into ivy tendrils and a chandelier of pink glass splintered light across black velvet furniture, a chessboard floor, and white taxidermy animals.

"It seems different in here," Finn said. As they passed a display with mice frozen in the act of pulling a miniature coach made from a pumpkin, Jack met Finn's gaze with a wide-eyed look.

"Phouka's into shabby chic with just a *smidge* of Dracula. I find it stimulating." Absalom led them down a windowed hall. Beyond the windows was the inner courtyard, bright with lights and moving silhouettes. There was a pulse of drums, skirling fiddle music, shouts, and laughter.

"What's the celebration?" Finn ventured as Jack's fingers twined with hers.

"The queen's coronation." Absalom flung open a set of glass doors stained with images of poisonous-looking flowers, and they entered an office with antique photographs on green walls and a giant fireplace of white marble containing blazing candles.

Phouka sat on a desk that had been constructed from birch trees, images of birds, leaves, and insects carved into the wood. Her auburn hair was coiled up with pearl stars. She wore a white suit with flared trousers and a bodice like chain mail. She was painting her toenails silver and didn't look up when they entered.

"My queen." Absalom gestured to Finn, Jack, and Moth. "We've guests who've come from a battle."

Phouka raised her head. She moved off the desk. "Absalom, fetch the first-aid basket from the kitchens—and I'm not a queen. I'm only regent."

"Shall I fetch Lazuli—oops. Never mind." As Absalom left, Finn glanced at Jack, who'd stiffened at the mention of the gentle, pale-haired Fata. She looked at Phouka. "What happened to Lazuli?"

"He was murdered on All Hallows." Phouka didn't drop her gaze from Jack's.

"I didn't kill Lazuli." His voice was low. "He told me what I wanted to know and I left him."

"I didn't think slitting throats was your style. Who did that artwork on your chest?"

"A Grindylow. Sent after *him*." Jack nodded to Moth.

Phouka's attention settled on Moth. "And you are . . . ?"

"I'm called Moth." He was squinting at her. "I've seen you before."

"I've no doubt." She tilted her head and asked Jack the question with her eyes.

"He was Seth Lot's. He escaped. His memory's shot." Facing off against Phouka's immaculate sophistication, Jack, bruised and bleeding, was very human.

Phouka walked slowly around Moth while he stood as if afraid to move. "He's not a *sluagh*. Not a Jack. I smell blood, but . . ." She frowned as she halted before Moth. "Changeling. But he's been one for a very long time."

"He's from Elizabethan England."

"Oh." Phouka stepped back. "*Aisling* then."

Absalom returned with a basket of first-aid supplies and a black bottle of wine. He handed the basket to Finn, who'd remained silent during the preemptive conversation, and said, "Jack's *your* knight. You may tend to his wounds."

Jack removed his coat and stripped off the torn T-shirt, muscles moving beneath the velvety skin of arms and shoulders. The scars and the tattoo that had marked him as Reiko's had vanished with his resurrection. As he sat on Phouka's desk, Finn delicately swabbed the shallow scratches across his chest and didn't mind the blood—they had fought hard for *that*. He didn't even wince. When she placed one hand over his heart—*her* heart—just to feel its pulse, he said, smiling at her, "Finn, the natives are staring."

Phouka, Absalom, and Moth were watching. Moth's gaze was enigmatic. Absalom, drinking from the bottle of wine, winked at her. Phouka's eyes were pure silver.

Phouka graciously turned to Moth. "So, no memory? That's troubling, especially since you were in the house of the Wolf."

Moth hunched miserably in his chair. "Why can't I recall? I don't have a reflection. Sometimes I bleed. Sometimes I don't."

"What a quandary." Absalom leaned forward. "Lot's last mortal queen was plucked from sixteenth-century Norway. That daffodil-haired boy he had as his assassin was from Renaissance Venice."

Moth continued, "I remember bits and pieces of my life—but the memories of Lot's house are jumbled. You . . . do I know you?"

"I doubt it, *aisling*." Absalom drank from the bottle again; he seemed to want to get wasted.

"Absalom," Phouka warned, "you're wandering."

"What"—Moth dragged his hands through his hair—"is an *aisling*?"

"A human stolen out of time and kept immortal," Jack said. "The oldest Fatas have that power." He pulled his coat back on, winced.

Finn looked at Phouka. "Seth Lot has my sister."

"Your sister?" Phouka seemed startled. "Your *dead* sister?"

"She isn't dead," Moth told her. "I spoke to her, often, in Lot's house. I don't remember how she came to be there, but she was the only good thing . . . the only good thing . . ."

"So you haven't asked us if Seth Lot's in town." Absalom sounded as if he was merely talking about an eccentric relative. "He is."

Finn gripped the edges of her seat and exchanged a quick look with Jack. He was stone-faced as Phouka rose and said, "I would like to speak to Finn alone, please."

Absalom, still holding the wine bottle, sauntered toward the door. "Come along, gentlemen. We shall retire to the salon and smoke cigars and chat about the stock market and, possibly, our mistresses."

Jack whispered, "Careful," to Finn, before following Absalom from the room. Moth drifted after.

When the door had closed, Phouka settled into the chair opposite Finn and leaned forward. "Let me tell you why what you're planning is a *bad idea*. That boy Moth is not only unreliable, he's unstable. I don't know who sent him here, but if he was Seth Lot's, he's not to be trusted."

Finn pulled back her coat sleeve to reveal Lily's bracelet of silver charms. "Moth had this. It was my sister's. It even has the octopus charm I broke when I borrowed it." She hesitated. "My sister's boyfriend was named Leander Cyrus. I saw him here in Fair Hollow—and Jack recognized him as being one of Seth Lot's Jacks. All that time he was with my sister, Leander was a Jack."

"Now I'm very unhappy."

Finn continued, "My sister wrote things about a wolf-eyed man in San Francisco."

Phouka watched her, the light reflecting uncannily from her eyes. "So. Lot plotted to get your sister, while Reiko plotted to get you. And what a mistake that was. It killed her."

"It was an accident," Finn said quietly.

"Finn. A sacrifice has to *mean* something to work. Something of value must be offered. Reiko should have sacrificed Jack, whom she loved, not plotted to end *you*. You never would have brought her Fatas one hundred years."

"Why *did* it work? With her and David Ryder?"

"Because David Ryder offered himself when he saw things going south. And Reiko may have lunged for him to retrieve her heart, her power, but I believe she genuinely wanted to rescue him."

"Will you do it when the time comes? Will you offer death a Teind?"

"I will sacrifice something I love if I need to."

Finn wondered what she meant. She told Phouka: "The first day I met Jack, I was just a kid, and my mom had died, and I said something wrong to a girl in red—she tried to drown me that day."

Sympathy seemed to flicker in Phouka's alien gaze as she said, "Reiko. You see why, Finn Sullivan, it's not so good to know us."

"Jack says I need your permission to get my sister out of the Ghost—"

"Not only *my* permission. Has he told you what the Ghostlands are? A hidden world kept from the eyes of mortals, only seen by those who are blessed, or cursed. The Ghostlands are the Wild West, the realm where our kings and queens battle to learn who's strongest. It's where forgotten places and things end up. It's where Fata changelings are born and human changelings die. It won't drive you mad, but you'll never be the same if you survive. Tonight, you encountered a Grindylow—that's only a fragment of what waits for you in the Ghostlands."

Terror clawed Finn's breath away as she considered what she would really have to do, where she would have to *go*.

The lights flickered out. For a moment, it became very cold, and Finn was reminded that what sat opposite her was a shadow creature wearing a young woman's form. Then the warmth and the lamplight stabilized as Fata reality returned and Finn said, steadily, "Do you think I'm the same now as I was before Jack? I can do this."

Phouka glanced out the window, at the silhouettes of the revelers in the courtyard. Her voice was calm. "And Jack. Let's discuss the circumstances surrounding Jack's resurrection. None of us know how he survived the divine fire, how he became temporarily mortal—and, yes, I mean temporary, because he's already changing back—and that makes him dangerous to *us*."

"Changing back?" *No*, Finn thought, but she had seen him lose his shadow, felt his heart and breath stop.

"If you go into the Ghostlands, you may lose him to what he once was. You might not find your sister, or succeed in rescuing her. You dislike me for saying these things, but I'm warning you—the *Madadh aillaid*, Seth Lot, was *held at bay* by Reiko and David Ryder. He's the thing in the dark, the beast in the forest. He is the Erl King."

"And Caliban works for him. Caliban came to my house . . . I think. There were animal prints in the snow. And Moth . . . Moth was out there and fought him off."

"Then Moth is more than he seems. Did you see this happen?"

"No."

"And Leander Cyrus? Have you had contact with him?"

"A little."

"I don't like any of this." Phouka rose and began to pace. Finn, who had never seen the cool Fata girl nervous, found it alarming.

"Leander *bleeds*." Finn stood to face her. "I think he still loves my sister. You know I'll find a way to get there."

"For us, there are many ways into the *Taibhse na Tir*. It's our element. I've shut most of those ways. For your kind, there's only one entrance now."

"Okay. A bargain then—"

"No." Phouka's eyes darkened and she almost seemed like the girl she might once have been. "You poor mortals, with all your heartweaving and unraveling.

There'll be no bargain. I'll help you because you already did me a good turn on All Hallows' Eve."

PHOUKA WANTED TO SPEAK TO JACK ALONE, so Finn and Moth stepped onto a terrace overlooking the revel in the courtyard, where bonfires roared in stone urns and lanterns of colored glass hung from the trees. A young man in a floor-length dark coat was playing a fiddle while a wiry man with black-and-gold hair beat at drums. Finn recognized the fiddler as Farouche the love-talker, one of Jack's friends, the one who had lured Sylvie into Reiko's spell. She still didn't understand Fata allegiances—they seemed to be loyal to no one but themselves.

Moth frowned down at the revelers, all of whom were either masked, tattooed, or wearing elaborate face paint. Finn, who had finally stopped feeling the effects from the encounter with the Grindylow, suspected the adrenaline spike now keeping her alert would also prevent her from sleeping. "I'm sorry, Moth, for what happened to you."

He raised his head and looked at her. "Finn—"

A girl in a sleeveless black gown moved up the terrace stairs, her hair the color of the marigolds wreathing it. She smiled. "Serafina Sullivan. Hullo—I'm Aurora Sae, one of Jack's friends. We haven't met properly."

"Hello." Finn reluctantly clasped the Fata girl's hand.

"I'm glad"—Aurora Sae smiled—"that you had a better trick than Reiko."

The fiddler in the long coat was swaggering toward the terrace, blood-red hair sweeping over his face in the snowy wind. He bounded up the stairs, bowed briefly, and said, "No hard feelings, serpent slayer?"

"No hard feelings?" Finn felt snarly. "You terrorized one friend and handed both to the Grindylow."

"Farouche!" Aurora Sae pushed at him, seeming genuinely angry.

"It was the Teind and Reiko was my queen." Farouche shook his hair back from a face that would have been beautiful if he wasn't what he was. "I couldn't *not* do what she wanted." He smiled at Moth. "Who is your sullen friend?"

Moth leaned against a wall painted with a mural of a winged boy burning a butterfly. He didn't answer. If he didn't recognize Farouche, he recognized what he was.

"We're not all like Farouche." Aurora Sae slid an arm through Finn's. "Come meet the others."

"I'd rather not," Finn began, but Aurora Sae whispered, "You must make friends among us. We *do* understand friendship, Finn Sullivan."

With Moth following, Finn allowed the Fata girl to introduce her to Jack's vagabonds, who were as stunningly attractive as other Fatas but less alien in their nature—or better at hiding it: the wiry drummer, Atheno; the dark-haired boy called Black Apple; Darling Ivy, the girl with the shaven head. Dogrose was dressed in old velvet, with glitter dusting his brown skin. Pretty, tawny-haired Wren's Knot leaned against Dogrose's knee, holding a staff topped with a doll's head.

Finn soon found herself seated at the base of a winged statue with Aurora Sae, who began weaving violets into Finn's hair. The drummer Atheno brought Finn a slice of wedding cake, and the boy called Black Apple offered her a cup of dark wine, which Moth seized and dumped.

Black Apple frowned. *"Rude."*

As the Fata boy drifted back among the revelers with Aurora Sae, to dance, Moth hunkered down beside the statue and, for a moment, he reminded Finn of Jack when he'd been a Jack. As Moth disdainfully watched the Fatas, Finn said faintly, "It must be nice."

Moth's eyes narrowed. "Nice? They've no purpose. No history. Just this. Just now. And they are as thoughtlessly cruel as rabid cats."

Finn considered the Fatas. "They're acting like the Winkie guards after Dorothy killed the Wicked Witch."

"Pardon?"

"Never mind." She saw Jack and Phouka step onto the terrace and it looked as though they were arguing. She met Moth's gaze. "Tell me about my sister."

Moth bowed his head, hesitated, before speaking softly, "He cannot touch Lily, the Wolf. She's innocent and strong. To him, she's like the sun. His court is filled with criminals and outcasts—"

"So was Reiko's."

"Lot's Fatas are not like these. Lot's tribe are blood drinkers, ghouls, elf knights, corrupting spirits, goblins, gorgons . . ."

Finn felt fear whip through her. "Lily . . ."

"There is one among them who became Lily Rose's armor, who kept her from any mischief, a boy who was once mortal."

"You mean Leander." She remembered what Leander had shown her—Lily Rose in that decaying mansion.

"Cyrus didn't know, when he met Lily, what Lot was planning for her."

"What about you? Were you Lily's friend?"

"Lot was never concerned about me and Lily Rose in his house. But when he found out about Leander's visits to Lily—Leander had to run. Yes, I think Lily Rose and I were friends."

He stood and looked down at her, and his tangled hair shone. "Your sister won't break. But you need to get her out of there. There are things I'm remembering. I remember the inside of the Wolf's house, if Jack has forgotten. I'll lead you to her."

Finn smiled. "I know you will."

MOTH REMAINED AT TIRNAGOTH and Jack drove Finn home. As they got out of the car, she gripped his hand, worried about the darkness in his eyes. "You're staying, aren't you? I don't want you to be in that apartment alone."

Jack's voice bled exhaustion. "Let Moth and me fetch your sister. Live your life. Be happy. If we succeed, you'll be happier."

"And if you don't succeed? What then? I just live my *happy* life without you? Without a sister I could have saved? Waiting for that bastard to come after me? No. You can't change my mind, so why are you trying?" She stalked toward her house.

He caught up to her. "I've stolen away enough of your days and nights."

She frowned. "'*Stolen my days . . . ?*' Don't you ever say anything like that to me again."

His voice was low. "You could have died tonight."

"I didn't. How are your wounds?"

"And who asks their boyfriend questions like: 'How are your wounds?' That isn't normal, Finn."

"Well, what if you were really into football or skateboarding or extreme sports?"

"I wouldn't have *wounds*," he gently explained. "I'd have injuries."

"How are your *injuries*?"

"They hurt."

"Come on. My da's out. I'll fix you up."

His smile was wicked. "Are we going to play doctor?"

"Maybe." She unlocked the door and pulled him into the house, which was still drafty despite the heat rattling the radiators. The hall lamp had been left on. They trudged up the stairs.

The instant he shut the door to her room, he dragged her against him and she wound her arms around his neck as his mouth slid over hers. The wanton gentleness of the kiss sent sparks through her and he smelled so good. Their coats landed on the floor. She needed only this, his salty skin and his mouth, this fragile desire—

"Ouch," he said and she pulled back. He smiled ruefully and she noticed, now, the split in his lip.

"I thought I tasted blood." She tenderly touched his mouth. "Do you hate it?"

"Hate what?"

"Being . . . you know . . . breakable."

"Well, if you can do it, so can I." He grinned, winced again.

When someone rapped gently at her terrace doors, Jack sighed. "It's Absalom."

She saw, beyond the glass, the youth with the orange hair. When he winked, she scowled and wondered how long he'd been there. She stepped away from Jack, rubbing the back of her neck.

Jack opened the doors and Absalom, looking like a harmless waif in a down coat, said, "May I come in?"

"Finn?" Jack glanced at her.

"He's *your* friend."

"But this is *your* house."

"Absalom may come in. *Only* Absalom."

"There's only me." Absalom stepped over the threshold. He carried a Bruce Lee lunchbox, which he opened to reveal a piece of brass shaped like a heart with a compass in it. Jack, gazing down at it, said, "What is that?"

"The Grindylow's heart." Absalom held it out to Jack, who tentatively accepted it. "Phouka sent me to LeafStruck to clean up the Grindylow and check on Miss Olive. So I took this as a souvenir. It's a compass. It guides the Grindylow back to its owner."

Jack nodded once. "The Wolf. This will lead us to the Wolf's house?"

"I've tinkered with it. It'll send you in any direction you want." Absalom moved into the room, peered at the Cheshire Cat clock on the wall. "Do you know why a raven's like a writing desk?"

Irritated by Absalom's verbal wandering, Finn planted herself in front of him. "Did you come here to help us or talk a lot of crazy?"

Absalom gently told her, "If the Wolf sent a Grindylow after that boy you call Moth, he knows Moth has escaped him. And then there's Leander Cyrus . . . Phouka doesn't trust either one of them."

"I want Moth with us." Finn sat on the edge of her bed. "He says he remembers the *inside* of Seth Lot's house—and we can't find Leander."

"Seth Lot's house." Absalom sat in the rocking chair, picked up a *National Geographic* magazine, and began leafing through it. "Do you understand the nature of how we travel? Has Jack told you?"

Finn looked at Jack, who dropped with a sigh into her red plush chair as Absalom continued, "To prevent mortals crossing into the Ghostlands, a skeleton key was created—get it? A skelet—never mind. Reiko used the seven abandoned houses of the blessed: LeafStruck, MoonGlass, etc.; Phouka sealed all those. Now there's only one Way into the Ghostlands—for mortals—and one key, divided between Phouka and Rowan Cruithnear. Phouka will give you her half of the key." He hunched forward in his chair. "The Wolf stole his domicile from a creature of dreams. The house travels. You must get your sister out while his house is in the Ghostlands, because there you can pin his house in place. The house will cease to exist, in either world, until he finds whatever pinned it. You'll then be able to escape."

"How do we pin his house?" Finn leaned forward.

"I don't know how, Finn Sullivan. With iron, I suppose. But you won't find iron there, and you can't bring it . . . iron transforms into something else in the Ghostlands."

"Sacred wood," Jack said. "Reiko once used sacred wood to hold Lot's house down."

"There you go then." Absalom tucked the *National Geographic* into his coat, stood up, and began sauntering toward the glass doors. "One more thing: Lot's house . . . it hoards dreams, memories, phantasms. If you get in, be careful."

Jack was gazing at Absalom with dark skepticism. As the Fata opened the glass doors, Finn got to her feet and strode after him, onto the terrace. Jack remained in the chair, examining the Grindylow's heart.

Finn shivered in the winter night. "Absalom, what will the Ghostlands do to Jack?"

"He already died, technically, so don't worry about it."

"*Absalom—*"

"Finn, you're very young." He turned to her and his voice was gentle. "You believe you've lived your entire short life to find love. Life is more than that. Do you understand that Jack is still immortal, that his every molecule now mimicking human is really still 'other'? He wasn't transformed by that divine fire—he was offered a form, and he chose the form of something he'd always wanted to be—a mortal. It's an *illusion*."

"He's real, Absalom. He has a *soul*."

"Have you ever heard of the *Tamasgi'po*, Finn? No? 'Spirit in a kiss,' a lethal poison to our kind because it infects us with memories. And we are *old*, some of us. What are memories but the cellular structure of a soul?"

"Absalom," Finn hesitated, "do *you* have a soul?"

"Oh, we don't believe in souls." Absalom began moving down the stone stairs. "Which is why we try so very hard not to die."

CHAPTER 6

May their backs be towards us, their faces turned away from us, and may God save us from harm.

—Old Irish saying

Since Finn needed to meet with the HallowHeart professors to ask for their half of the skeleton key into the Ghostlands, she went to the one professor she grudgingly knew better than the others—Jane Emory.

Jane Emory's cottage was located at the end of a woodsy, residential road, and it was exactly what Finn had expected—a charming oasis of wind chimes, stone sun faces, and clay cherubs. The garden was now veiled beneath snow. Attached to the kitchen was a small greenhouse.

As Finn stepped into the kitchen, Miss Emory opened the fridge and drew out plates of neat little sandwiches and a pasta salad. "Would you like tea or this green juice I blended? I forgot what I put in it . . . kale, garlic—"

"I'll take the tea, thanks, Miss Emory." Finn, draping her coat over a chair, noticed the alarming amount of rabbit figurines in the kitchen—not cuddly ones either. Some were primitive totems; others, disturbing hybrids of human and animal.

"Please call me Jane." As Jane lifted the plastic wrap from the tea sandwiches, she said, "I wanted to talk to you about Halloween night."

"Why weren't you there?"

"Sophia Avaline wanted me to look after your father while she and the others went to watch over you and your friends. I think Sophia suspected something terrible was going to happen. I think she put safeties in place."

Finn sat down and remembered Sophia Avaline's white face the moment Reiko had announced Finn was to be the sacrifice. "What about Dean Cruithnear?"

Jane hesitated. "I honestly believe he didn't suspect it would be you. It would have been *helpful* if he'd told us about the sacrifice in the first place . . . Perhaps he thought it was none of our business because Nathan Clare had agreed to it."

"Professor Avaline said, that night, the sacrifice is something that must be done, to keep the peace. *She* didn't seem surprised."

"Of course she said that—Reiko needed to believe we were harmless, that we'd accept whatever she threw at us." Jane looked at her. "They all had knives, you know, and Wyatt had a revolver filled with silver bullets. If any of the Fatas had even *suspected* that Wyatt and the others were armed . . ."

Finn's eyes widened as she imagined what would have happened if the professors had gone to war with the Fatas.

Jane sighed. "When I saw you in your kitchen on Halloween night . . . I knew. I just knew something had gone wrong. And then I glimpsed Absalom Askew behind you. He winked at me."

"Absalom."

Jane turned to put the kettle on. "From what we've noticed, Absalom is an unstable element."

"You think? And you mean an unstable *elemental*." As Finn selected one of the sandwiches, Jane continued, "Before Halloween, Absalom told James Wyatt that Jack would be the death of you."

Finn frowned at the sandwich. The sunlit kitchen suddenly seemed to darken as if a cloud had passed over the sun.

"Sophia Avaline believed it was a warning." Jane sat down. "So they all brought iron or silver, sharp things hidden in their clothes, because who would suspect a bunch of college professors to be armed? Before all hell broke loose, Sophia, Hobson, Wyatt, Charlotte Perangelo, and yes, even Edmund Fairchild, were all prepared to battle through that ring of malevolence to free you, armed with nothing more than old-timey kitchen implements and fancy silverware and Wyatt's Colt." Jane rose to lift the whistling kettle from the stove. "But you and Jack pretty much allowed us to remain neutral. Halloween . . . well, that was a game changer."

"Despite what Sophia Avaline said that night, about allowing me to be sacrificed to keep the peace, you don't intend to *ever* let the Fatas take another life, do you?"

Jane set two mugs down on the table. "We've failed at that, haven't we? Angyll Weaver was murdered. And Nathan . . . no one knows what happened to Nathan."

Finn bit into her sandwich even as her stomach convulsed.

"Finn, the Fatas are like earth, fire, water, and air. They can either help or harm—and Reiko's Fatas seemed intent on harm."

"You allowed her to get away with so much."

"We didn't *allow* it." Jane's voice was filled with sorrow. "We couldn't *stop* it."

"How did you find out about the Fatas? I mean, you, personally?"

"Each of us encountered them in our teens—not Reiko's Fatas, but others. And we kept our memories of them even after we got older. That's not common. It was Rowan Cruithnear and Sophia Avaline who found each of us and organized us, and Rowan Cruithnear who gave us jobs in this very haunted town."

"So there are probably others like you? In the country? The world?"

"It would be nice if we knew that. Rowan had to stop searching after a while. But you asked how *I* found out about the Fatas." Jane chose a sandwich. "I was eighteen. In Virginia Beach, at dusk, I met a boy on the seashore. He was lovely and charming and he had hair as red as reef coral. No one else ever saw him. He was my secret."

Finn wished she hadn't guessed where this story was going.

Jane stirred cream into her tea. "I began to get sick. I was tired all the time."

"You weren't . . . ?"

"No, I wasn't pregnant. But I learned, after my parents took me to a doctor, that I'd lost a lot of blood."

"Oh." Finn sat back.

"He was what they call, in Irish mythology, a ganconer, a love-talker. In Greece, he would be an incubus. He was bleeding me and taking away the memory of it. He was also a creature of the sea tribes, the water Fatas, who are in no way friendly to us."

"How did you know it was him? The red-haired boy?"

"I did some research. I wrapped up an old iron spoon and went to meet him. But it's as if he knew. He never showed up. I never saw him again. After that, though, I could tell . . . I noticed others."

"So he was like a mermaid love-talker?"

"He didn't have a tail." Jane smiled wryly.

"My sister once did a drawing of a mermaid, with starfish and crabs in her hair. She looked like a shark. It was creepy—it wasn't a *nice* mermaid. Then Lily started to read about mermaids, *a lot*. Whenever we went to the beach, she wouldn't go in the water. I knew something was wrong. Like she was going crazy. But it wasn't that . . . someone had *told* her about mermaids."

"Before she met Leander Cyrus?"

"She had an imaginary friend she called Norn."

"Did she?" Jane sounded troubled. Delicately, she continued, "Finn, do you think Jack knew about Lil—"

"No."

"I understand how you feel about him. But he's been badly hurt—manipulated, traumatized. I can't even imagine what he's *seen*—"

"And I'm only an eighteen-year-old girl who can't possibly understand those things."

"Don't get defensive. Just be careful."

Finn ruthlessly changed the subject. "I've seen Sophia Avaline's sister. Eve."

Jane became startled and wary.

"Her name was Eve, right? She's dead. I mean, well, she's a spirit, I think. And I think Professor Avaline knows. I think she blames Jack."

"Finn." Jane sat back in her chair. "*Did* he . . . ?"

"Jack didn't kill Eve. It was Reiko." Finn gazed down into her tea. "Jack thought he loved Eve."

Jane was quiet, so Finn filled in the silence: "My sister might be alive, Jane."

Jane lifted her head, her eyes widening, and Finn told her about Moth, Seth Lot, Lily's charm bracelet, and Leander Cyrus. Jane looked dumbfounded, then horrified, as Finn told her that she needed the key to the Ghostlands. "Finn, you *can't*."

"If you don't help me, I'll find another way."

"Your father—"

"Won't know. And have you heard him when he talks about my sister? No. Because he still *can't*. Phouka told me no time will pass here while we're gone, as long as we return the way we came."

"Damn her."

Finn leaned forward and calmly said, "My sister, Lily Rose, is a monster's prisoner. If you don't help me—"

"You don't know this is *true*, Finn."

"Leander loved her and he's a Jack. He *bleeds*. Jane, you have to—"

"Stop." Jane's voice was strained. "I know what I have to do."

AS JACK ENTERED MURRAY'S ARCADE, he surveyed the throngs of teenagers until he saw Absalom disguised as one of them, standing with a plastic gun and shooting at monsters on a screen.

"Jack." Murray, a Scotsman in his late fifties, approached Jack. The owner of the arcade wore a tracksuit as if he'd just returned from jogging. "A word with you please?"

"About what?"

"Don't be confrontational. Just"—Murray nodded to the exit door—"come join me on the patio."

THE "PATIO" WAS A CEMENT BLOCK with a railing, a view of the alley, and an expensive outdoor grill, all garishly illuminated by Christmas lights strung from the eaves. After brushing snow from one of the plastic chairs, Jack sat and regarded the grill with amusement. "Aren't you afraid someone's going to steal that?"

"Oh, the someones know better." Murray settled into the other chair and glanced around. "I should have brought beer. Would you like me to fetch some Killian's? You are of an age, aren't you?"

Jack was suddenly on edge. "I am."

"And how long have you been that particular age?"

Jack's new heart rocketed. He was on his feet in an instant.

"Now, now." Murray held up both hands. "I'm Scottish—you think I'd *not* notice the damn fairy folk in my own backyard?"

Jack sat back down. "Do all Scots have this sort of radar?"

"Only the ones with superstitious grandmothers. And you *did* obtain some antique pieces for me that seemed impossible to acquire. Also, you're always gloomy and ghost-eyed, I never saw you until after sunset, and, as for your 'family'—"

"Okay." Jack settled back, calmer now. "You've got the sight."

"Ah, yes, I've got me '*the shining*.' I'm not the only one who noticed your tribe . . . Clive Redhawk had an idea the Fata family was otherworldly. I heard him muttering 'goddamn skinwalkers' one night when we were in BrambleBerry Books and you lot got out of a Mercedes. *Skinwalkers*, Jack. How unpleasant is that?"

"Redhawk—*Christie's neighbor?*"

"God rest his soul." Murray looked at his hands as if missing that bottle of Killian's. "He was full-blood Iroquois. This whole town is haunted, isn't it?"

"Somewhat. Murray, don't tell anyone about them."

"Do I seem eager to spend time in the cuckoo's nest? Or, if *they* find out, twisted up like a pretzel? Now, tell me"—Murray leaned forward—"are they a danger to us?"

"Like fire. Like wind or earth or water, if it turns against you."

"How absolutely terrifying. I've already got horseshoes hung all over my doors and iron nails in the window frames."

"A wise precaution, if a bit dated. Electricity and goodwill usually keep the Unseelie at bay. Or silver. Elder wood. Not steel though. Only pure iron."

"I've got friends here, Jack."

"And family in Scotland? You should worry more about them. The Scottish court is a bit hostile toward mortals."

"What a bloody comfort you are. And what about the little girl you're running around with?"

"Finn?" Jack felt wary. "I won't let anything happen to her."

"And Clive Redhawk? Was that a natural death?"

"As far as I know."

"Jack, if *we've* noticed, don't think there aren't others who haven't also clued in on what's going on. And don't think *that tribe* doesn't have mortal enemies who could be just as dangerous. Look at how hard-core the Puritans were about the supernatural—"

"Are you trying to tell me something in a roundabout sort of way? Because I get enough of that from my 'family.'"

"I'm just saying . . . be careful. Now, have you come to talk to that redheaded devil playing *Zombie House* and pretending to be a boy?"

THE DEVIL PRETENDING TO BE A BOY didn't look up from shooting zombies on the screen as Jack approached. Jack leaned against the game console and said, "You forgot to change out of that nice suit."

Absalom shrugged and grinned. "I thought I'd start a decent fashion trend."

Jack glanced around at the other teenagers in the arcade. He shouldn't be here, pretending to be one of them. Casually, he said, "You recognized Moth."

Absalom shot an on-screen ghoul, point-blank. "You and I have known each other too long, if you can read me like that."

"*Who is Moth?*"

Absalom slammed his hand on a button to begin another game. "He was an actor in one of Shakespeare's companies. I was a girl at the time."

"Of course you were." Jack folded his arms, still leaning against the console. "Go on."

"He betrayed me. I cursed him—damn, I did *not* see that zombie coming. Did you see it?"

"How," Jack spoke slowly, "did you curse him? In what way, exactly?"

"I've done it to so many people, I've kind of forgotten. I suppose that's how Lot found Moth in his travels—sensed a bit of magic, undid it, and had a pretty soldier for his army. I imagine Moth was grateful enough, in the beginning."

"What was Moth's name before you wrecked his life?"

Absalom set the plastic gun down. "I don't recall. The curse I set on Moth won't fade. Lot probably fractured it, a little. But it's still there. I can smell it, like gunpowder and molten metal."

"I wonder how Moth ended up in a dead man's attic?"

"Oh. Well, do you remember that key that helped Finn last month? Got her into all sorts of Fata things?"

"The one," Jack said softly, dangerously, "shaped like a *moth*?"

"*I* didn't turn Moth into a bloody key, but, because of my curse, whatever it was, Moth became transmutable, changeable. Someone else turned him into a handy-dandy gadget and left him for our fearless Finn."

Jack didn't flinch. "Who did it then?"

"Who seems to have an affinity for keys and insects?"

"The Black Scissors. But he's not Fata. He can't—"

"The ability to change mortals' shapes is a sin. It's what Reiko did because she was an awful person. It was her talent. The Black Scissors, being a twisted-up mortal, should not be able to mutate people."

"But you think he did."

"He *was* Reiko's crush, for a time. She taught him all sorts of forbidden knowledge."

Jack remembered something Moth had said: *The sharp, dark man.* "Of bloody course."

A teenage boy and girl passing by looked in their direction and Jack smiled at them. The girl blushed. So did the boy. Jack turned back to Absalom. "*You're* the one who changed Moth in the first place."

"What can I say? I'm a sinner. And I was quite awful, once."

"Maybe that gave Seth Lot and the Scissors a way to shape Moth, the poor bastard. Moth didn't seem to recognize *you*."

"His memories are in pieces. Curses—and life with us—do that."

"He's to be our guide in Lot's house. I need to know I can trust him, Absalom."

"Oh, you can't trust him. I'm on your side, Jack. You helped me with my snake problem, and you and Finn, I've no doubt, will cause all sorts of delightful trouble for the Wolf. Wreaking havoc on Fata rulers seems to be Finn Sullivan's calling. I'm half in love with her already."

"You want Lot dead, but you won't come with us. Like Phouka, you don't want to get your hands dirty."

"Fatas can't kill each other, you know that. We use mortals or *sluagh* or Grindylow. That's why Phouka won't involve herself. As for me, when I go to the Ghostlands . . . I become a terror. I'm better here. Better for all of us."

Jack mightily wished he could unhear that last part.

"You know"—Absalom's innocent mask cracked, just a little—"you'll have to slay the Wolf."

Jack turned and walked away. "I'd no intention of letting him live."

AS JACK CLIMBED OVER THE WINDOWSILL and into his apartment, he was so distracted by what he'd learned that he didn't sense he had a visitor until the coldness of the otherworld struck him like a glacier. He went still, aware of Ambrose Cassandro's misericorde in his left boot, of the Indonesian *kris* dagger sheathed in one sleeve.

A lamp blinked on.

Sprawled in one of his chairs was a young man who resembled an angel statue, his silver gaze all malice, his scars testimony to a violent life. His fur-lined coat was a gray pelt that brushed the floor.

"Jack." Caliban Ariel'Pan tilted his head. "How you've changed. What's it like, being a lump of blood and tears?"

"Let's skip the courtship." Jack sat on the windowsill, which brought one hand closer to the misericorde in his boot. "You here to threaten or kill?"

"I'm not here to kill you, Jack. He wants you and the schoolgirl in the Ghost-lands. You're curiosities to him. Aren't you lucky—*don't*." Caliban leaned forward, his gaze fastened on Jack's left hand, which was sliding toward the boot and the weapon. "Right now, boy, I'm better and faster than you."

Jack straightened. In a casual tone, he asked, "What did you do to Nathan?"

"We did to him what we do to all traitors." Caliban stood. "Are you going to let me out of that window, now that I've threatened you?"

"Is that all then? Empty threats? Like visiting Finn's house the other night and getting kicked in the teeth by an *aisling* boy?"

Caliban sauntered toward him. "You might want to be careful of that pretty boy with the moth wings—he's insane. And he's more than an *aisling*."

Jack rose and stepped aside. As the *crom cu* swept past, Jack said, "It doesn't matter what I am. I'll find a way to end you."

Caliban smiled and the beast crept through his voice. "I expected you to say that."

His fist slammed so brutally into Jack's chest, Jack almost went out the window. He caught himself against the frame, coughed as agony shot through him. He dodged the second blow and kicked out. Caliban glided back, laughed, and lunged. Jack twisted away. He was smashed against the wall, not the window, but his head struck plaster and he nearly fell to the floor as dizziness overwhelmed him. He retched, struggled as Caliban's hands folded almost gently around his throat.

Caliban released him and rose. "It's no fun hurting you when you're breakable—well, it *is*, but not as much fun as it'll be taking you apart when you come to the Ghostlands. See you, Jack, you and your girl."

Caliban vanished over the sill. Jack sagged down against the wall.

The apartment was freezing—one of the mirrors in the parlor had cracked. As Jack staggered up, he glimpsed a small, dark form on his bed. His heart constricting, he strode over to find BlackJack Slade, curled and stiff, his eyes glazed with frost; the loyal cat had frozen to death from the supernatural cold Caliban had brought with him.

Jack gently wrapped the cat's body in a quilt and bent his head until his brow touched the fabric.

IT WAS EIGHT IN THE EVENING when Christie and Sylvie picked Finn up at her house, to take her to Hester Kierney's skating party. She hadn't wanted to go, but they had guilted her into it.

As Christie drove, he said, "How exactly are you going to get your sister away from a werewolf?"

"I don't know. And Seth Lot isn't a *werewolf*."

"Does Jack know how to find your sister?"

Finn frowned at Christie. "We've been given some things to help us locate the Wolf's house."

Christie met Finn's gaze in the rearview mirror. Finn had dressed for Hester's party in a red Renaissance-style hoodie, jeans, and a white wool hat and scarf that had been Lily's.

"You look like mistletoe: white, red, and poisonous."

"Mistletoe isn't a threat to anything supernatural, is it? Turn here, Christie." Sylvie pointed.

"Only a Nordic god named Baldur," Finn said as the Mustang curved up the drive toward an art deco house, its run-down state and age becoming apparent the closer they got—the windows, decorated with languid, stained-glass women, were grimy. The circular front stair had cracked in half. A tree was growing through one wall, but the grounds were lit up like the holidays, with colored lights spattering the snow and music pulsing. There were cars parked everywhere on the front lawn.

"Is that another one of *their* houses?" Finn leaned forward, intrigued. She wished she had her Leica camera.

"It was called MoonGlass by the former owners, the Kierneys, Hester's great-grandparents." Sylvie hauled her skates from the car floor.

"They just gave it up? A house like that?" The Fatas' temporal power always amazed Finn.

"They probably don't even remember why. I bet the Fatas haunted the hell out of it until nobody wanted it anymore. Like paranormal termites."

"Remember what you told me? What your mom said, Christie?" Finn studied the forlorn mansion. "The spirits used to have places in the world, caves and wells and forest groves . . ."

"Now they've got real estate." Christie parked between a Prius and a Lexus on the snowy lawn. Grimly, he said, "Let's go have fun."

They followed a plowed, lantern-lined path to the back, where a maze of tall hedges held a galaxy of tiny lights. Christie, his skates slung over one shoulder, said, "The party's on the other side."

Music and laughter threaded from beyond the hedges, so they wove through the maze, which ended at an iced-over pond glimmering with the blades of skaters and the reflections of a bonfire around which HallowHeart's elite lounged—Aubrey Drake was sprawled in a deck chair and talking to the exquisitely dressed Ijio Valentine. In a sky-blue pavilion, guests clustered around tables of treats. A generator provided power to heaters and two giant speakers. Christie indicated the DJ, a tall boy in a Dr. Seuss hat. "Is that Ricky O'Dell? You'd think, with her connections, Hester could've gotten a professional DJ."

The last time Finn had gone skating had been with her mom and Lily, on the pond near their house in Vermont. Lily had accidentally spun Finn into a tree. Finn smiled and hope roared through her. *Lily was alive.*

"Skate first. Food later." Sylvie sat on a bench to wrestle with her devil-red skates. She looked fashionably punk in plaid trousers and a black turtleneck. She'd streaked her hair with red. Christie, dropping down beside her, said, "Is that Victoria Tudor over there?"

Sylvie glanced at Finn. "I've counted four of Christie's exes so far. Vic Tudor is one of them. Sit, Finn, put on your skates."

"You go ahead. I'll come after."

Hester Kierney, pretty and sleek in ice blue, crossed to them from the bonfire. "I'm glad you came, Finn. Sylvie. Christie."

Christie smiled at her. "For you, Hester, I'll try to be fun again. Maybe you and I—"

"It'll never happen," Hester said, before slipping an arm through Finn's. "Let me introduce you to the rest of us."

Christie and Sylvie were already trudging toward the pond. *Traitors*, Finn thought, before the heat of the bonfire blasted her and she reeled back—

"Finn?" Hester's eyes went wide with horror and regret. *"I'm sorry."*

"Nice, Hester." A curvy blonde in pink rolled her eyes and gently guided Finn to a deck chair. "Did you forget about her nearly getting barbecued on Halloween night?"

"We, uh, promised not to talk about that." A boy with brown hair swept over one eye looked over his shoulder. "Vic, get her a cocoa. You like marshmallows, Finn?"

Finn felt prickly, surrounded by the blessed, the ones even Reiko Fata hadn't dared touch. She straightened in her chair and tried to ignore the bonfire and the unpleasant memories that surfaced. "I like marshmallows."

A willowy girl who resembled the brown-haired boy handed Finn a paper cup of marshmallow-frothed chocolate. "I'm Victoria. That's Nick, my brother."

"She's met everyone else." Ijio Valentine's eyes glittered in the firelight.

"Not me." The curvy blonde sat next to Finn. "I'm Claudette Tredescant. And we want you to know, we are *beyond* sorry about that night."

Her stomach suddenly sour, Finn set down the untouched cocoa. "Aubrey already apologized. No hard feelings."

Then Aubrey asked, "Where's Jack?"

"On his way." Finn began to take off her boots. If she could get her skates on, she could escape to the pond.

Aubrey rose and grabbed his skates. "We're sort of afraid of him."

Finn experienced a moment of hilarious disbelief. "Afraid of *Jack*?"

"Yes." Hester smiled, but her eyes were dark.

Finn straightened. "You think Jack's going to start killing you off for revenge or something?"

"The good-looking ones always die first." Ijio poured something from a flask into his cocoa.

"You had *Reiko Fata* lording it over you. She was a sociopath. And *Caliban* was her pet." Finn's phone hummed in her pocket. She took it out—and it instantly went dead.

Ijio shrugged. "Oh, we were terrified of Reiko. At least we knew what to expect from her. We never saw Caliban." The lights flickered for a moment, the music stopped, before everything buzzed back to life. "There are Fatas here, Finn, so electricity and batteries are kind of iffy."

Finn scowled at her phone and stood, balancing on her skates. "Jack is not going to kill you." She wondered if they knew about Seth Lot and decided she'd better let Phouka handle that. "'Hey, Jude' is playing. I'm going to skate to the Beatles."

Aubrey gallantly extended one hand, snow glittering in his clubbed-back hair. "Come on. I'll get you onto the ice."

She gripped his hand. They trudged across the snow-crusted ground and he walked in his skates like a pro. As she stepped onto the ice, she glanced back and saw a slender figure speaking with Hester Kierney. Her heart jumped when she recognized Phouka Fata—now Phouka Banríon—all wintery, flower-child elegance, her auburn hair coiled up with sparkling flowers.

Aubrey gripped Finn's hands and gently spun her. She laughed when she found her balance so easily. "I haven't done this in years."

"It's just like riding a bike. You know, I've never ridden a bike."

Christie was weaving in and out among the skaters. Sylvie was spinning with a pretty boy—Black Apple, one of Jack's Fata friends. A willowy figure wearing a rabbit mask swerved past them. A bald girl in black fur spun, ribbons fluttering on her sleeves. Finn recognized her as Darling Ivy.

"Oh, hell," Aubrey murmured. "*They're* here. Jack's friends."

"Well, you can't *not* invite the fairies to the ball." Finn was actually a bit relieved to see Jack's crew.

"You're a very brave girl for using that word." Aubrey glided backward. A blonde in a clinging dress of green silk—Aurora Sae—caught his hand and drew him away.

Finn felt someone grab her wrist, and spun, expecting Jack.

It was Moth, in jeans and a black hoodie, his pewter-colored hair tousled beneath the jacket's hood, his face shadowed. His gaze in the firelight reminded her of phosphorous. With the shadows sharp in his face, he looked completely otherworldly.

"Finn Sullivan," he said in his low, British voice, his fingers twining firmly with hers as they glided in a circle, "you should not have come. Keep skating."

"Why?" she whispered. The air began to buzz as if a thousand invisible flies had just descended. Something pricked at her brain, and she felt the first drop of blood slip from one nostril.

"Because the Wolf is no longer at the door—he's come through it." He gently turned her so that she could see the blessed had stepped back from the bonfire and Phouka stood before it, facing away from the pond, her posture that of a warrior about to defend her castle. Some of the Fata skaters were halting near Finn, forming a protective semicircle. The other guests, the normals who hadn't noticed anything, continued to frolic.

The world spun around Finn.

Christie and Sylvie slid to her side. Christie whispered, "What the *hell* is going on?"

"Don't you see?" Sylvie's voice was faint, her gaze fixed on the activity near the bonfire. "He's here."

Here is your enemy, Finn thought. *Here is the one who took Lily away.*

Tall shadows moved from the hedge maze, bleeding across the snow, unseen as yet by the gathering of HallowHeart's oblivious, frivolous students. The shadows became strangers in fur coats and clothes with a punk, belle epoque flair. Old jewelry flashed on their fingers and throats. Their faces were young, beautiful, their brutal aristocracy meant to inspire terror.

One figure separated from the pack and approached Phouka. His hair was mahogany brown, his face that of a Brontë antihero with a thin scar across one cheekbone. He wore an expensive suit beneath a fur-lined greatcoat and he carried a walking stick like a weapon.

Phouka walked toward him and greeted him.

"No," Finn breathed, her stomach knotting up at the betrayal.

"Finn." It was Aubrey behind her. "You've got to trust her."

Finn thought, *Where is Jack?* And was glad a moment later that he wasn't here, because the Wolf was strolling past Phouka, approaching the pond, followed by his pack, and the Wolf knew Jack.

Watching Seth Lot walk toward her, Finn felt a dazzling terror that was almost ecstasy.

Seth Lot halted on the snowy shore with only a few inches of ice separating him from Finn and her protectors. He appeared exactly as he had in Finn's memory: a young man with an exotic, black-rimmed gaze the blue of tundra skies. Those eyes reflected the firelight as he tilted his head and studied Finn, who met his gaze only because she had no choice. Confused by his attractiveness and his gentle manner—she hadn't expected a *soulful* evil—she remained very still.

"Serafina Sullivan." His eyes didn't silver and he didn't smile, but his voice was amiable, a young man's voice. "I've been looking forward to meeting you."

He extended one hand, its fingers scabbed with rings that looked as if they could have belonged to pharaohs or Russian kings. "Please, don't be afraid."

This was the wolf-eyed man who had seduced Lily, who had kissed Lily's wrist and left a mark. Finn glided forward on her skates, defiant, even as Christie tried to catch her and Sylvie whispered her name. She approached the Wolf to show him she wasn't going to let fear rule her, and said, "Seth Lot," holding out the hand adorned with her sister's bracelet.

His cool, strong fingers grasped hers. Although his nails were short and manicured, she could imagine claws as he said, "You've heard things about me that may have been exaggerations." He looked past her, at Moth, and softly said, "Hello, traitor."

Finn realized Lot had stepped onto the ice. His hands firm around hers, he turned her in a circle as his gangsters prowled forward. Gently, he said, "I've heard things about *you*, Serafina Sullivan, how you caused the death of Reiko."

"I didn't"—her voice shook a little—"kill Reiko."

"I think you did." He smiled.

My, what big teeth you have. He didn't, but a threat was implicit in that smile. Finn's eyelashes fluttered as a poisonous drowsiness crept over her. The Wolf leaned down and, scented with winter and expensive cologne, whispered in her ear, "You know that your sister lives." He stepped back, releasing her so suddenly, she staggered. He said, "Come for her. I'll give you seven days in my world. If you don't find my house by the seventh day, I come find you. Your sister dies. Your Jack dies."

Finn felt as if something else were speaking through her, past her terror. "And what happens when I do find your house?"

"Then I give you a fair, fighting chance to win Lily back."

Jack's vagabonds, in their tatterdemalion finery, now surrounded the wolves on the ice. The Fata called Atheno, who bore an uncanny resemblance to Iggy Pop, grinned and stretched out his arms. "Why does the *Madadh aillaid* come to a gathering of mortal children, to threaten a braveheart who only defended herself from one who did her wrong?"

The scarlet-haired fiddler, Farouche, stepped to Atheno's side, his face remote with caution. "Careful, Atheno. It isn't like the old days."

"No, it isn't." Seth Lot continued, almost lovingly. "In the old days, we would have torn all of you apart and bitten the bones."

The blessed, and the other students—aware now of the standoff—stood like deer in headlights, fascinated and confused. As Seth Lot and his pack faced Atheno and the vagabonds, Phouka, fierce in her punk fairy-tale glamour, moved toward the Wolf. More Fatas were arriving from the hedge maze, striding across the snow—Phouka had called in reinforcements. Finn hoped things weren't about to get ugly as Lot's words jumbled around in her brain.

"This is my court, *Madadh aillaid*." Phouka spoke in a voice that could have cut steel. "And you are not welcome here."

Seth Lot's gaze scathed the small army behind Phouka. He said something low and vicious. Finn stepped back and felt Christie grip her elbow as Sylvie flung an arm around her. Then Seth Lot continued, "By the Law of Tooth and Claw, I am entitled to the lives of the queen killers."

Phouka replied, "We don't follow La Bestia's rules here. This isn't the French court or the wolf tribe. You've no right in this land to claim anything."

Seth Lot's attention returned to Finn, and his blue eyes seemed to glow. Fear almost shattered Finn's composure.

Then a voice carried through the vagabonds, "I'm here, Wolf."

"Jack," Finn whispered, turning her head.

Jack, in a navy greatcoat, moved carefully through the Fatas to place himself between Seth Lot and Finn.

"Jack." Seth Lot smiled. The two of them seemed like young men, not antique spirits. "My favorite and best *sluagh*. Regardless of what your false monarch says"—he nodded to Phouka—"I expect you and your *muirneach* to come find me. If you do not, I'll rip through every one of these pretty children"—he gracefully indicated the blessed and the students, who were, fortunately, too far away to hear his threat—except for Aubrey, who swore breathlessly—"until you do. Do you understand me, Jack Fata?"

The tension in the air crackled like gunpowder. Finn whispered, "His name is Jack Hawthorn."

Seth Lot's gaze fell upon her and she continued faintly, "He is mine and I am his. Until the end of the world."

"Is that so, Serafina Sullivan?" Seth Lot spoke intimately, as if it were only the two of them. "Then I look forward to ending your world."

He turned and, followed by his pack, strode past Phouka and the other Fatas, toward the hedge maze.

When the wolves had gone, Finn felt all the strength leave her. Jack's body shored hers up and one of his arms braced her. He said hoarsely, "What were you *thinking*? Challenging him like that?"

She wrapped her arms around him, breathing in his scent, pressing her face against his chest and the drum of his heart. "He knows we're coming after Lily. It's what he wants."

FINN AND JACK ENTERED HER ROOM through the terrace doors. Christie and Sylvie had driven home with a Fata escort from Phouka. Moth had remained with the Fatas.

As Finn switched on the lights, the malicious resonance of Seth Lot's voice echoed in her head. She said to Jack, "Are you going to tell me why you're all bruised and banged up?"

"Caliban came to visit." Jack lowered himself onto the pink sofa, wincing a little. "He killed my cat."

"BlackJack Slade?" She sat beside him. "Jack, I'm *so* sorry . . ."

Then she asked, "Do you wish—"

His mouth curved at one corner and he rested his arms on the back of the sofa, legs apart. "If you're asking if I wish I'd never been made human, shame on you."

She settled beside him, into the curve of his arm. "Ouch." She slipped a hand into an inside pocket of his coat and drew out the dagger that had poked her shoulder blade. "How many of these do you *have*?"

"As many as I need." He smiled rakishly as she drew her legs beneath her and frowned at him. She was much more afraid for him than she was for herself. The way Lot had said Jack's name—it had been like an old lover who wanted to tear the other's throat out.

"I *am* sorry about BlackJack." She slid a hand into one of his and his lashes lowered briefly. A muscle twitched in his jaw. He said, "I think our main concern should be the Wolf."

"He's not lying about Lily."

"Finn—"

"Why would he lie? He could just *tell* us to go to the Ghostlands or he'll kill our friends and family . . . my friends and . . . I mean . . ."

"I know what you mean." He met her gaze, his own warm. "And you're right—he doesn't need to lie."

A shiver convulsed her as her mind conjured an eternal sentience, a freak of nature that had willed itself into a solid form—the Wolf.

"We can take him," she whispered fiercely. "*You* can take him."

"No need to stroke my ego. And you sound like a gangster's moll."

She slid onto his lap and folded her arms around him. She pressed her brow against his. "Jack. We'll be okay."

He shifted a little, winced again. "It hurts, doesn't it? Being mortal. I forgot how much it hurts."

TONIGHT, JACK WALKED IN A GARDEN with a girl in a red dress. As she turned, her skin split and fell away and a charred creature of fire and ashes said, "*Jack . . . don't you love me?*"

He woke with Reiko's name clotted in his throat and an unearthly cold in his bones. His heart was like a stone. He was dead again. He breathed out an anguished, "No . . ."

Beside him, Finn stirred in her sleep, tightened her hand around his, her white sweater rucked up around her midriff. Clad only in his jeans, he shivered in the cold room. He could feel things now—chill and warmth, the drum of his heartbeat, the heaviness of the blood through his body. Tonight, he felt a breathless terror of the inevitable, of his heart stopping, of the blood pouring from him, of *mortality*.

His heart beat once, twice, and continued its steady pulse. The blood moved sluggishly through his veins.

It's only temporary, he thought, closing his eyes, *this*.

He tenderly touched Finn's warm, tangled hair with trembling fingers. To protect her, he might have to give up all that he was and once again become the otherworldly monster he had been.

CHAPTER 7

*There are more of the Sheogue in America than what there are here, and more of the
other sort of spirits.*

—*Visions and Beliefs in the West of Ireland*,
Lady Gregory

As Jane Emory steered her VW Bug around a corner, Finn said, "What will
I do if your friends don't let us have the other half of the key?"

Jane kept her eyes on the street. "I don't know, Finn."

"Is it a vote?"

"The decision needs to be unanimous, yes." Jane parked her yellow Bug opposite a well-kept brownstone apartment building. The branches of a large
elm—Finn was getting quite good at identifying trees thanks to Jane's class—
concealed the building's upper windows, and the setting sun burnished the brick
exterior, glinting red across the glass. "This is it. Rowan Cruithnear's domain."

"It's very like him."

"I *hate* this. If you go, Finn . . . if you go *there* . . . God, I don't want you to go."

"My sister is alive, and when I come back with her, it'll make everything all
right." As they got out of the car, Finn tried not to sound as jittery as she felt.
"I'm not going to ask you about your vote, so you can stop being all tense."

"Honestly? I haven't decided yet. The Ghostlands . . . and then there's your
father . . ."

" . . . Who can't know and wouldn't believe it even if he did."

They were buzzed into the building's pale green hall and ascended a flight of stairs that seemed to curve up forever. By the time they'd reached the top landing and a door as green as wood moss, Jane's doubts had reasserted themselves; she turned to Finn. "Are you sure—"

"Jane, Leander Cyrus, a Jack, loved Lily. He bleeds and has a pulse. That's how I know my sister's alive, not just because of the bracelet from Moth or what Moth has said." Or because of Seth Lot's terrifying challenge. "Would it ease your conscience if I told you I'd find a way into the Ghostlands no matter what any of you say?"

They heard the downstairs door slam. As familiar voices echoed up to them, Jane rapped on the green door.

Sylvie and Christie appeared on the stairs, followed by Jack, who moved to Finn. His gaze was dark. "Are you ready?"

She nodded.

Christie was looking around. "Have you ever seen *Rosemary's Baby*, Miss Emory?"

As Jane regarded Christie with fond exasperation, the door opened and Rowan Cruithnear, dressed as usual in a suit finer than any college dean should be able to afford, greeted each of them before leading them into an apartment that was as Spartan and elegant as he was. There were neat bookshelves everywhere, little bonsai trees on the sills, and furniture that seemed a hybrid of Ikea and ancient Rome.

Sophia Avaline was seated on the sofa, legs crossed, black hair in a knot. Mr. Wyatt crouched near the fireplace while Professor Fairchild leaned beside a window, an open book in one hand—even out of class, Fairchild looked like an eighteenth-century poet. Miss Perangelo stood beside him. Hobson, the red-bearded math professor, was pouring coffee into several china cups on a tray.

"Serafina." Sophia Avaline gestured to an unoccupied love seat and Finn sat with her friends as Jack settled in the chair beside them. Avaline continued, "Tell us."

Jack's fingers twined with Finn's as Finn spoke with quiet savagery. "I thought my sister, Lily Rose, had killed herself. She didn't. Her boyfriend was a Jack who served a Fata named Seth Lot. Seth Lot took her. He's given me seven days to come find her in the Ghostlands. Or he'll kill her. I need to get into the Ghostlands."

"Madadh aillaid." Mr. Wyatt, a neutral figure Finn didn't quite trust, seemed shocked. "Do you have any witnesses, Miss Sullivan? That the Wolf would be *here . . ."*

"The witness is on his way," Jack said. "Phouka Banríon is bringing him."

Sophia Avaline had become coolly angry. "Do you realize what you're asking us to do? You're asking us to allow you, with this damaged young man—my apologies, Jack—to enter a place most people only glimpse through drugs or a psychotic break from reality. The *Taibhse na Tir."*

That breathy, alien word seemed to convey all sorts of unpleasant possibilities, and Finn felt goose bumps break out over her skin. Being here, speaking to adults who knew about the Fatas . . . this made what she was about to do a cold reality. For one horrifying moment, she thought she might blurt out that she couldn't go.

Then Jack said, in that calm voice that always made her brave, "I believe Finn's entire time in Fair Hollow has been a psychotic break from reality."

"Thank you," Christie said.

"I'm sorry"—Finn looked soulfully at Christie and Sylvie—"about all of this."

"You're sorry?" Sylvie leaned forward. "For opening our eyes? Who knows what might have happened if we didn't know about—"

The door buzzer went off. Rowan Cruithnear walked out of the room and returned a few moments later—to a profound silence—with Phouka and Moth. Phouka, radiating casual regality, said, "Has the tribunal begun without us?"

"Madame." Rowan Cruithnear inclined his head. "Could you introduce your companion?"

"This is Moth, one of Seth Lot's victims."

"Not a victim." Moth pulled back his hood. "An accomplice, once, before I knew there was a world beyond the Wolf's."

Professor Fairchild, intrigued, asked, "What changed your mind? About the Wolf?"

"I don't remember much more than scattered things, horrors. In Seth Lot's house, a girl named Lily Rose befriended me, helped me escape, and sent me to watch over her sister. I . . . remember the inside of that house. *That* I remember."

"When was your sister taken?" As Miss Perangelo spoke to Finn, she watched Moth.

"It doesn't matter. She's *alive*." Finn hated that her voice shook.

"We aren't prepared to deal with other Fatas," Professor Fairchild murmured, "outside of Reiko's court. And the *Wolf*—"

"Are you kidding?" Christie glared around the room. "Angyll Weaver was *murdered* by one of Reiko's monsters. So was Nathan Clare. What does it take to activate you people?"

"First of all," Mr. Wyatt said in his casual baritone, "we're not Transformers, so there's no *activating* us. Second"—he looked around at his fellow teachers—"you're not seriously considering allowing this *child* into the Ghostlands? With two unreliable Fata creatures?"

Jack said, his voice low, "Seth Lot and his pack made a surprise appearance at Hester Kierney's party. He's going to begin ripping through Fair Hollow unless Finn and I come after him in the Ghostlands. Are you prepared to deal with it now?"

Avaline glanced at Phouka. *"Why didn't you tell us Seth Lot was here?"*

Phouka's eyes mirrored the lamplight. "Why worry you? It's not as if you're of much use anyway."

"We can't fight Seth Lot." Rowan Cruithnear straightened, his demeanor stony. "Not here. There is only controlling the damage he does."

"There's also Caliban." Jack's pronouncement was met with uneasy silence.

Professor Avaline once again addressed Phouka. "I thought your kind had that situation under control?"

Phouka's demeanor matched Sophia Avaline's in coolness. "The *crom cu* returned to his master. Like you, I cannot afford to declare war on the Wolf. Finn Sullivan has no choice but to go to the Ghostlands and you've no choice but to let her. The Wolf has taken all choice from us. Here, she will die and so will others. Here, there's only so many ways we can protect her. As you say, we would only be controlling the damage."

"What we are *doing* is sacrificing her, yet again." Sophia Avaline's anger was startling. "For *convenience*, this time. And we can't follow her into the Ghostlands with kitchen knives and handguns. She'll only have Jack and those Fatas allied with Phouka Fata—I'm sorry . . . Phouka *Banríon*."

Phouka's silver eyes narrowed. "It's always been *Banríon*. And the moment the Wolf took Lily Rose Sullivan, Serafina's fate was sealed. She'll have to journey into the Ghostlands now, where there will be *options* that are not available here."

"She's a *child*," Avaline said. Jane remained silent, Finn noticed.

Rowan Cruithnear moved to the center of the room. "We are straying from the topic of this meeting, which is to decide if we give Finn Sullivan half of a key that will take her into the Ghostlands."

Finn sat very still, not daring to speak, afraid any wrong word would tilt the balance out of her favor.

"Yes." Jane's voice was anguished. "Because I know she will not give up."

"No." Mr. Wyatt folded his arms. "I vote 'no.'"

Miss Perangelo frowned. "No."

"Of course *yes*." Professor Fairchild looked at Miss Perangelo. "Blood calls to blood. She *must* bring her sister home."

Professor Hobson glared at Wyatt and Perangelo. His red hair was almost bristling. It seemed he was about to say yes, when his shoulders slumped. "No—I can't send a child there."

It was Sophia Avaline's turn. "We've never entered the Ghostlands. With a few exceptions—such as Rowan—adults can't. The Way never opens for us. But we've had to deal with the young people who've returned from there, and we've had to put them back together again. So I say no."

Finn looked pleadingly at Rowan Cruithnear, who bowed his head. "Serafina, if this is a trap set by the Wolf, I am condemning you."

"If you say no," Finn managed past the ache in her throat, "you're condemning my sister. You're thinking it's too late, she's been with that monster for a year, that she's lost. But Lily is strong. She'll keep herself . . . somewhere. The way Reiko removed her own heart and put it in a box, my sister will hide her soul so that the Wolf doesn't get it. *I can't leave here there*."

"May I speak?" Jack's voice sliced the resulting silence like a finely honed blade. "I don't want this for Finn. But she is *not* a child, and she doesn't belong to me or any of *you*. And she has made this decision because it is the only one true to her heart. If you had any genuine affection or concern for her, you'd allow her to do this."

Wyatt muttered, "Fatas and their damn warrior ethic."

As Sylvie gripped one of Finn's hands and Christie glanced at Jack with sober respect, Finn felt as if a brilliant sun warmed her through.

Rowan Cruithnear regarded the other professors and the years seemed to age him. "I am sorry, Miss Sullivan. We cannot, in good conscience, allow you into the Ghostlands. If the Wolf comes for the children of Fair Hollow, we'll deal with him."

FINN FELT AS IF she was losing Lily all over again. Too broken to speak to Jack, Christie, or Sylvie, she asked Jane to drive her home.

In her room, in the dark, she curled on her bed and reached for her sister's journal. She skimmed through it using the flashlight app on her phone, until she came to the passage she remembered: *The* Madadh aillaid, *the Wolf king. I should never have let him kiss my wrist and leave that mark. I've let him into my world now.* Finn remembered Seth Lot in Golden Gate Park, a young man with wolf-blue eyes—even then, he'd had them in his sights.

She heard the doorbell ring, then her father's voice and a woman's.

Moments later, there was a knock at her bedroom door. She called out and her da stuck his head in. "Jane's here, Finn. She needs to talk to you. About the argument you two had earlier—you argued?"

Jane stepped into the room and switched on the lamp near the door. She held out a small box of black velvet. "I brought you a gift."

"I'll leave you two to talk then?"

"Yes, Da, thank you. I'd like to speak to Miss—Jane—alone."

He began to close the door. "Don't stay angry at each other." Then he was gone.

Finn hadn't taken her gaze from the box in Jane's hand. She whispered, "What is it?"

Jane walked over, sat on the end of Finn's bed, and opened the box. Finn stared at a spiral of silver with a silver skull in the center. "Is that—"

"Yes. Rowan didn't want to give it to you in front of the others, because he suspects one of them of being a traitor. Rowan has . . . let's call it a medieval psyche. He believes in honor and sacrifice and all those other philosophies. And then there's this, what he found fluttering on his desk." Jane took a box of transparent plastic from her purse. The box had airholes, and flickering inside of it was a monarch butterfly the color of daisies.

"I don't understand."

"Look closely at the black markings on the wings."

Finn squinted and thought she was seeing things; scrawled blackly across the orange wings, repeatedly, were the words: *Lily Rose is alive*.

"Who sent it?" she whispered, awestruck.

"Well, there's no signature, but we couldn't ignore it even if it's a trick. If there's even a possibility your sister is . . . well, we can't abandon her."

Finn carefully took possession of the second half of the Ghostlands key. "Dean Cruithnear thinks one of the professors works for Seth Lot?"

"Let's just say that certain things have occurred to make Rowan believe one of the others is serving the interests of the unknown."

"What about you? Why does he trust *you*?"

"Well, I'm sort of his great-and-then-some granddaughter."

Finn kicked back the covers. "I *knew* he was older than he looked! Was he cursed, like the Black Scissors?"

"Sort of. Only it wasn't supposed to be a curse. That's a story for another time. Now, you'll be going to Lulu's tonight, with Jack and Moth, to leave for . . . that place."

"Lulu's *Emporium*?"

In a small voice, Jane said, "What will I do if you don't come back? I don't think I could . . ."

Finn was not the hugging type, but she got on her knees and slid her arms around the woman. "Thank you, Jane. *Thank you*."

"You can thank me"—Jane hugged her back—"by returning with your sister. You and Jack will be going to Rowan Cruithnear's house in the Ghostlands, where Rowan can protect you and prepare you. He can provide you with guides and guards and a witch who will lead you to the Wolf's house. He can't come with you right now, because he thinks it'll lead Seth Lot to you."

Finn sat back. "When I return, Phouka said no time will have passed."

"Not if you do it right. Finn . . . what will I tell your father if something happens to you?"

"I'll be back before he realizes I'm gone. And nothing will happen to me."

BY ELEVEN O'CLOCK, Finn was ready. She'd packed a leather backpack with Eve Avaline's silver dagger, Slim Jims, apples, three cans of espresso, two bottles of iced water, and a gift for Jack. She was dressed for travel in boot-cut jeans and a black sweater, her red coat, and Doc Martens.

As she slid a good-bye letter to her da beneath her pillow—just in case—she looked around the room and said to her ghost, "If I don't come back, make sure he gets that."

A flash from the antique Leica camera on her desk made her flinch. She slowly walked toward it. The camera clicked and flashed again.

"*Okay.*" She grabbed the camera and shoved it into her backpack. As she did so, she heard a clatter and turned to see that the first photograph she'd taken of her and Jack in the sunlight had fallen to the floor. She bent down and picked it up. The glass over the photo hadn't even cracked. She traced Jack's image. He watched every sunrise, every sunset, and lingered at each as he hadn't been able to before—as if expecting that fragile humanity he'd stubbornly longed for to vanish at any moment. She glanced at her sister's journal on a nearby table. Lily had always been there for her after their mom died. Lily had championed Finn, encouraged her, and enraged her. And then Lily had abandoned her.

Finn pushed her hands through her hair as the anguished realization that she was choosing Lily's welfare over Jack's overwhelmed her.

Then Jack was knocking at the glass doors.

She stood, walked to them, and opened them. Dressed in a Victorian greatcoat of black suede, his hair tied back, he looked like some kind of nineteenth-century assassin. He had a backpack flung over one shoulder. "Ready?"

"Very." She slid her own small backpack on and smiled to prove she wasn't scared.

As they strode to Jack's sedan at the curb, Jack said, "Phouka and Cruithnear conspired on this. Phouka and Moth will meet us at Christopher's. Sylvie's there too—you'd best call her and tell her we're on our way."

AS FINN GOT OUT OF JACK'S SEDAN in front of Christie's house, Sylvie ran down, threw her arms around her, and whispered, "I knew the HallowHeart professors would come through."

"It was Cruithnear and Jane Emory, actually."

Christie sauntered up, hands in his coat pockets, his dark red curls sticking out from his knit hat. He said, "So you're going."

"You," Finn said steadily, "are the best friends I've ever had."

"I suppose *he'll* protect you, being a killer and all." Christie meant Jack. His voice was stripped raw. "Just don't forget where you belong. No matter what that place is like—and I'm imagining some seriously messed-up American McGee version of Disneyland—it isn't your world. *This* is."

"Okay, Christie."

"Take this." Christie took a small book from his back pocket. "Famous poems. Words are weapons against them."

"And this." Sylvie pressed into Finn's other hand a silver compact mirror decorated with a pretty geisha. "My good luck charm against Grindylow."

Then Phouka stepped forward with Moth and handed a wooden dagger to Finn, another to Jack. Both were made of polished wood and inscribed with symbols. Phouka's silver eyes seemed to convey all the strangeness of the Fata world as she said, "Made of winter wood. They won't decay in the Ghostlands, as silver and iron will. And"—she took from her coat a scabbard made from the same wood—"this is for your silver dagger, Serafina. It fits? Good. Don't draw that silver until you absolutely must, or it'll rot. This scabbard will protect the blade until then. The only way I know of to kill a Fata such as Lot is to strike as he is riding the shadow, in the midst of a change—that's when he'll be vulnerable. The wooden weapons are for defense. Your silver knife is to kill him. Strike once. Strike true."

Finn wanted to say she wasn't sure if she could do that—until she thought about what Lot had taken from her.

"Finn," Jack spoke gently, "we need to go."

Moth nodded once to Sylvie and Christie before striding toward Jack's sedan. Finn hugged her friends one more time before turning and following Jack. She glanced through the trees, at her home. Her father was probably working on his students' papers, drinking tea and believing she was safe in bed. With any luck—well, with an insane amount of luck—she'd be back in that bed before the sun rose. And Lily would be home.

Jack drove onto Main Street, which was beautiful with its banks of snow, the Christmas lights, and shop displays. It was busier than usual, with most of the shops cordially remaining open until midnight, nearly every pedestrian carrying a shopping bag. As the sedan turned onto a narrow avenue, Finn glanced at Moth in the backseat. "Are you sure you're ready to return?"

"Lily somehow got me free of that place. I'm not going to leave her there."

A few streets later, Jack parked the sedan in front of Lulu's Emporium, an old church that had been renovated into a fancy Chinese restaurant. Moth and Finn shouldered their small backpacks as Jack led them through the doors into a sophisticated dining room with red lamps and votive candles illuminating statues of scarlet dragons and manga-style paintings of saints.

"Lulu." Jack inclined his head to the curvy woman sauntering toward them, her pale hair wreathed with jasmine, her black silk dress and high heels patterned with the same flower. She wasn't a Fata, but Finn sensed she wasn't all that ordinary, either.

"Hello, Jack." She arched an eyebrow. "Introduce me to your friends?"

"This is Finn Sullivan. This is Moth. This is Lulu. And Lulu is—"

"—a guardian of the betwixt and between." Lulu's eyes, for a moment, pooled to an unsettling black before she smiled like a movie star.

"Witch," Moth muttered.

"The polite term is *ban dorchadas*. Woman of darkness." Lulu winked at Moth.

Jack turned on him. "Exactly what have you got against witches?"

"The polite term is 'woman of darkness,'" Finn reminded him.

"I don't trust them," Moth said, defiant.

"That may be a problem where you're going." Lulu led them through a pair of scarlet doors, into a courtyard shimmering with snow and scattered with slender trees. In the center was a stone arch carved into images of eyes, hands, and feet tangled in vines, flowers, and fruit. There was a black door in the center with a golden lock-plate, but no handle. Finn, gazing at the door, felt a breathless anticipation.

"Isn't it pretty?" Lulu smiled. "Phouka's idea, to center it in that, after she shut up all those wonderful old houses."

"Lulu, Moth," Jack said, "I need to speak with Finn alone."

As Jack drew Finn a little ways down the path, he took from his coat pocket a tiny box of carved wood. "Merry Holidays."

She fumbled in her backpack, produced his gift wrapped in gold paper. "Same here."

He unwrapped it as she lifted the lid of the box, revealing a pendant—two lions clasping a ruby heart. It matched the ring she'd given him, only it was made of white gold.

"For my lionheart," he told her, lifting from his box a small golden phoenix on a leather thong. His teeth flashed. "I'd rather be a phoenix than a jackal."

"Merry Christmas." She kissed him, quick, because Moth and Lulu were watching.

Wearing their gifts, they walked, hand in hand, back to the door to the Ghost-lands. Finn wasn't scared anymore, which was probably crazy. As Jack fit to-gether the pieces of the key and a butterfly-winged woman with a skull head formed, Finn was a little disappointed at the lack of special effects.

Lulu said, "After you pass through the arch, you'll be at the train station near Rowan Cruithnear's home. Rowan will send someone for you."

"Train station?" Finn's eyes widened as Lulu continued, "Rowan plans to get the elixir—which loses its potency here—from the Blue Lady while you wait, safely, in his house."

Finn said, "What 'elixir'?"

Lulu explained: "Phouka told you your blood will be like a beacon to the Un-seelie. The elixir will make you seem like one of us. Jack may need to take it, too." She looked at Moth. "I don't know about you."

"We'll see." Moth was watching her. "After Rowan Cruithnear, what then?"

"Rowan wants you to have guides—Fata ones—and the Grindylow heart, the compass Absalom Askew gave you, can be used if you're ever lost. Remember, the roads in the Ghostlands will run parallel to those in the true world. Some-times, the true world breaks through. You're not to interact with such breaks, because it will take you out of the Ghostlands and you'll end up somewhere in Tennessee or Alaska or something."

She stepped forward. "Now for the rules. Rule one: Don't eat or drink any-thing that isn't from the true world—that includes fruit you haven't picked your-self. Two: In the Ghostlands, beauty often conceals danger. Three: Poetry can be a weapon—*beka*—spells in the voice. Four: You're going to drink an elixir . . . take one dose only, no matter how tempted you might be to take more. As for your tech—your cell phones—don't bother. They won't work. And Fata me-chanicals can only be operated by Fatas. Spirit energy."

Finn's eyes grew wider with each warning cited. Beyond the arch and the door she could see the streets of Fair Hollow and the winking lights of an electric tower —it didn't seem possible that there was another reality. She said, "Is that all?"

"That's all." Lulu stepped back and saluted. "Good luck."

Jack inserted the key into the lock and the door fell open.

CHAPTER 8

For neither Death nor Change comes near us,
And all listless hours fear us,
And we fear no dawning morrow,
Nor the grey wandering osprey Sorrow.

—*The Wanderings of Oisin*, W. B. Yeats

As Finn stepped into the Ghostlands, it was as if she'd passed through an electric current. Her breath was swept away and her entire body tingled and went numb. She thought she was falling—

When she opened her eyes, staggering a little, she saw a field without snow, without power lines or electric towers, only a cascade of stars across a sapphire-black sky. The silence around her was alien. Her first breath shot adrenaline to her brain. As terror sheared her nerves, she realized she wasn't holding hands with anyone. She whirled in a panic. "*Jack!*"

"Here. I'm here." He stepped before her.

"Where's Moth—"

He pointed to something that fluttered around them—a large, pale-winged insect, a luna moth. "There."

"That *can't* be . . . We *need* him."

"He'll change back. The Way through must have triggered the curse. Back in Shakespeare's day, he pissed off Absalom."

"*Absalom* did that to him?" She reached out a hand to the insect, which continued to frantically circle them. It was so fragile—and it contained all of that brooding young man, condensed. Did he understand what had happened? "What a nightmare, for him."

"Absalom, being Absalom, has forgotten how he cursed Moth. I think we've found out how."

"We can't *leave* him like this."

"We don't have a choice. We must catch that train, Finn. We need to get the elixir from Cruithnear before we encounter the bad sort of Fatas."

The moth was the size of her hand, and it was white with silver markings—she peered closer. "Do those look like death's head markings on its wings?"

"Don't think about it. You'll make yourself sick." As Jack turned away, his eyes seemed to silver. "Right now, we've other things to worry about: that is *not* the right station."

"What do you mean, it's not the right—" Her voice shook. The building before them had been created in the '40s art deco style. On either side of its circular stair were two green marble statues of goddesses draped with crimson ivy that had run riot. Within the leaves, Finn saw angular faces of green stone with hollow eyes and open mouths, weatherworn green men wreathed in thorns. Like most Fata places, the railroad station exuded an ominous sentience.

"This isn't the right station. I've never been to this one. I've no idea where we are."

She breathed deep. "Let's find out then."

He looked at her as if not sure whether to be impressed or worried, then indicated her wrist. "Your sister's bracelet—it's not falling apart. Remember? Silver rots here."

She glanced at the bracelet, and the silver charms winked in the starlight. "It must be magic."

They walked to the station. Beyond the broken windows, a chandelier of orange crystals lighted a deserted lobby and a wall scrawled with sparkling graffiti, like runes. Phosphorescent toadstools scabbed another wall shattered by a cadaverous tree fruiting with apples. On the platform was a sign with names and times:

Blackwing . . . Midnight

Phantom Queen . . . Three o'clock

Chimera Blue . . . Anytime

"Do things here run on—dare I say it again—magic?"

"If you want to call it that."

She sank down onto a bench, her backpack between her feet. She shivered. She couldn't hear any insects, and the air carried the scents of alien flora. "What are we going to do?"

"Wait for the next train. We'll just be taking the circular route to Cruithnear."

That was somewhat reassuring, but she was still shaking a little. "Tell me more about *him*." She didn't say Seth Lot's name out loud as the moth glided around them.

Jack settled beside her. "I was sixteen. I was starving, desperate, and phenomenally stupid. My dad—the exorcist—had warned me about them. Lured by a beautiful face, I walked right into their lair."

"Reiko." Finn imagined Seth Lot in his fur coat, all fin de siècle wolfishness, cupping the face of a young and pretty Jack and smiling at him like a king about to grant knighthood. She imagined that same king whispering into the ear of a Jack with scars and cold eyes and no hope of being anything other than a killer. Her voice broke a little as she said, "Reiko took you to him. Even though people disappeared in his house."

Jack's voice had a low intensity as he continued, "He mutilated some of his Jacks and Jills until they didn't look human anymore. He smashed one boy's skull into another shape. He broke one girl's bones and reset them until she was a *thing*. And what else did they have after that? Serve him or die. I think many of them wanted to die."

Finn watched a slight tremor begin in his hands as his eyelashes flickered. She hurt for him.

"Fatas don't murder mortals, Finn. But Lot has learned how. As for killing Fatas—he'd do that without a thought, using his Jacks and Jills, the Grindylow. He's a criminal of his kind, an outcast for that reason. The face he wears is a mask over the beast he has become after centuries of riding the shadow."

Jack had once explained to her that *riding the shadow* was a term the Fatas used to describe the process of changing their shapes, a rare thing. Shapes were very important to the Fatas, and Finn suspected they didn't retain memories or personalities very well without some definite, long-term form. They were spirits, after all.

She looked around, reaching out to touch a satiny-red rose that blossomed from a bush clawing up one wall.

The moth fluttered into her face as Jack's hand closed over hers. "Remember rule two? Beauty conceals danger—that rosebush might have once been a person. Don't pull anything off it."

Finn remembered what had happened to Christie and Sylvie, what Reiko had done to them. "That was Reiko's hobby, wasn't it—changing people into *things*. And Seth Lot's hobby . . . we'll have to kill him, won't we?"

Jack's eyes were dark. "Yes." He didn't elaborate.

The forlorn whistle of a train disturbed the air—it was a startling sound in this still, starlit place. Finn had liked that sound while nestling in her bed late at night, in Vermont—now, it made her taut with excitement and dread. "What train do we take?"

"The first to come our way."

She stood up. "What's the train made of, if not iron?"

"Something you might call organic metal."

The locomotive that came hurtling up the tracks was of a dark metal that seemed to have *grown* into the forms of roses, thorns, and ravens. Its windows, tinted red, smoldered with interior light. As the train slowed to a gliding halt, Finn marveled at its lavish details. When the doors slid open, Jack stepped up, turned, and held out a hand. He pulled her in, and the moth fluttered past her.

The train car's interior was a luxury of rose-red leather, brass lamps shaped like Greek harpies, and black lacquer. Finn asked, "Where are the other passengers?"

"Hopefully, there aren't any. We haven't gotten you the elixir yet."

After they'd settled into a seat, the train lurched forward. As an alien night flashed beyond the windows, and Finn began to experience a stomach-churning dread, Jack told her, "If we're ever separated, ask the way to Orsini's Books in Crossroads. You'll be safe there. Everyone knows Orsini and he's a friend of mine. And one more thing—let's not ever get separated." He slid the Grindylow's heart compass from his pocket and frowned at it.

Finn asked, "Why do you think the key didn't take us to the right station?"

"That's a good question."

She was about to demand an *answer* to the question, when a man entered their car. He wore a black-and-red conductor's uniform, and his long hair was the same rosy hue as the car's interior. He bowed to them, his eyes flashing. Finn's skin crawled when he spoke. "Payment?"

Jack held out a little tin box. The conductor accepted it, tilted the box's contents—two ivory objects—into his palm. When he smiled, his teeth glinted silver. "Very good, sir. As you can see, there's been a change of plan. Cruithnear's precaution."

"At the last minute. I see. And where are we going, if not Cruithnear's?"

"To the *Ban Gorm*, for the elixir. A driver will meet you in Darkside, at the clock tower."

As the conductor turned and walked out of the car, Finn slouched in her seat, somewhat relieved they now knew where they were going. "Well, that answers my question. Why did you give him teeth?"

"Don't ask."

"Where did you get them from?"

"And so she asks." Jack glanced out the window. The train sped past moss-draped trees, a rusting tractor, and a chapel of white, rotting wood. They might have been traveling through any midwestern or southern state. "You really want to know?"

"No. I don't. Why did Rowan Cruithnear mess with the plan, d'you think?"

"Maybe to deceive the traitor he suspects."

"Who is the *Ban Gorm*?"

"The Blue Lady, purveyor of things from the true world."

"Like what kinds of things?"

"Curiosities and worldly objects. Art. Books. Music—record players work here. Typewriters. Clocks—"

"Got it." A swarm of flickering lights shot past the window. *Fireflies*, she hoped, and she began to study objects in the car. Gazing into one of the lamps ebbing with a jellyfish glow, she whispered, "I'm sorry I brought you back here."

"Don't be an idiot." He leaned close and his mouth blossomed over hers in a kiss as intoxicating, as sweet, as blackberry wine. She didn't feel like a girl when he kissed her, but like fire in a girl's form, burning and hungry. It was he who pulled away this time and breathlessly said, "We'll have to not do that so much."

"It *is* distracting." Feverish now, she curled her hands in her pockets to keep from touching him again.

The door to their car slid open to admit a Fata dressed in a green coat brocaded with roses, her yellow hair wound into plaits. She carried a basket of black wicker. As she sat near the front, turned away from them, Jack met Finn's gaze and shook his head in warning. Finn stared at the Fata woman, who made a curious sound, as if she were breathing in a scent—

Jack broke a tiny crystalline sphere between his fingers. As it crumbled like sugar in his hand, the fragrances of honey and fire blossomed through the car, and Finn realized he was disguising the scent of her *blood*.

"It'll be all right," he said calmly. "Go on and sleep. We've a ways to go."

Not wanting to sleep, not with a blood-scenting Fata on the train, Finn nevertheless closed her eyes and let exhaustion overpower her.

THE TRAIN HALTED and Finn immediately awoke. The scent of fire and honey from the tiny globe Jack had broken had faded.

Jack murmured, "Another one."

A young man had entered their car. His silvery-white coat matched the pale hair sleeked down his back. A violin case of ivory leather was slung over one shoulder. Cold air followed him as he moved down the aisle. Finn didn't dare look at his face.

Jack pressed one hand over hers. A dagger slid from his right sleeve, into his other hand. It wasn't the same knife he kept in his boot—this knife was black, its handle shaped like a jackal's head. She shuddered at the idea of violence, so early.

The Fata sat in the back, where he could watch them without being seen.

"Narcissus." The Fata woman in front spoke casually.

"Yes, Greta?" the white-haired musician answered.

"Do you scent red? Do you see a shadow cast upon the floor?"

Finn saw her own shadow stretching from her boots and realized no one else in the car—including Jack—had one.

The musician replied, "I do."

The yellow-haired Fata turned her head and met Finn's gaze, her own shining silver. Finn slowly looked over one shoulder and found the Fata called Narcissus staring at her. She could almost feel every muscle in Jack's body tense. There was a moment of silence and a pressure in her head. A drop of blood fell from her nose, onto her wrist. Light-headed from fear, she flinched and quickly raised a hand over the lower half of her face. The moth fluttered against her cheek.

Jack said in a careless tone, "You will leave us be, *Narcissus and Greta*, because I'm Jack Daw, and I don't have a shadow, and the blood within me has turned to venom. I have dealt with far worse Fata than a *ban sidhe* and a ganconer."

Greta turned away, her back stiff. Narcissus laughed once and looked out the window.

The pressure in Finn's head vanished. She wondered what, exactly, Jack had been before she'd known him.

When the train stopped again, Narcissus disembarked. There was no station—he walked toward a twisted wooden arch that led into a forest flickering with ghostly blue lights and vanished.

The train continued on, past boarded-up houses, a stone church with windows glowing ivy green, a cemetery behind a spiky fence. Finn glimpsed a hooded figure in scarlet moving among the tombstones and quickly looked away. *Just deal with it*, she told herself. *Because this is real.*

"Our stop is next." Jack again folded a hand over one of hers.

A few minutes later, the train pulled into a station of shiny black stone that might have come from an old Hollywood set. Lamps of purple glass hung from red, lantern-shaped roofs. The windows were screened with parchment. On the platform stood a girl in a black frock, holding an ebony parasol.

As Jack and Finn passed Greta to exit the car, the Fata woman sweetly called, "Good luck, little girl."

Jack tightened his grip on Finn's hand as they stepped onto the platform. The girl with the parasol, her eyes dark hollows, watched them. Finn whispered, "What will my sister be like, after being in *this* place for a year?"

"If she's anything like you, she'll be just fine." They moved toward a forested slope divided by a mammoth stairway of moss-splotched stone.

Finn forgot what she'd wanted to ask next, breathing out, "Are we climbing *that*?"

"The Stair of the Fox Spirits." A few old-fashioned lamps lit the way, but there were sections banded by darkness. As Finn gazed up, Jack reassured her, "We'll eventually get there. Dusk and night are the only times here. There is no sun. No moon."

"There are stars." She gazed up at the night sky and its canopy of constellations that seemed brighter than the ones at home. A shivering anticipation almost made her smile. "Let's go."

As they climbed, Jack didn't even breathe hard, but Finn eventually felt as if her lungs had been filled with acid. When he offered to carry her, she snarled softly and he smiled. After what seemed like an hour—her feet were dragging by then—she raised her head and saw a metal arch contorted into vines and stylized eyes. Beyond the arch was a town that seemed salvaged from rust-belt America, its street lined with birches, their silver leaves drifting through the air, their roots snarling the blacktop. There were buildings and shops, some with lit windows, but the lighting wasn't electric; it was natural and luminous, as if it came from fireflies or deep sea creatures.

"Like bioluminescence." Finn couldn't conceal her awe as she studied one streetlamp glowing jellyfish blue. "Like the ones on the train."

"Don't be fooled by the pretty." Jack led her down the street, past a shop displaying antique-looking metal arms and legs. In a boutique swirling with live butterflies, a girl surrounded by ball gowns on broken mannequins was pinning the insects into her hair. As they passed a granite bank building pulsing with lights and eerie music, a red-haired Fata boy in a black sailor uniform stepped out and lit up a cigarette. His eyes flashed a savage silver when he saw Finn— Jack looked at him and he glanced away.

As they continued walking, Jack told her, "Darkside was called something else when it was a human place. Before it was abandoned. A whole town—villages, streets, structures, vehicles . . . anything forgotten, lost, the Ghostlands claim. I know a mermaid who rules from the wreckage of a famous ship, and a changeling girl who's made her home in a lost plane. Don't stare."

Finn quickly skewed her gaze away from an androgynous Fata in a white coat, who was walking a black pig on a leash. After the sharp terror on the train, she was beginning to feel a dreamy acceptance. "You sure know a lot of girls, Jack."

"That was the old me." His voice was sultry. He led her toward a fountain choked with dead leaves, where water gurgled from the mouth of a stone sea serpent. There was a clock tower at the end of the street. The clock, a gigantic thing of intricately carved wood that reminded her of an octopus, had thirteen numbers on its face.

A blue roadster came roaring around a corner, its headlights phantom green. Jack turned, squinting.

The car halted at the fountain, its hood ornament revealed to be a fish-bodied horse—and the driver was Atheno, one of Jack's vagabond friends. Finn smiled as Jack said, "Well."

Atheno jumped out, looking like a rock star, a necklace of green pearls gleaming against his bare chest. He bowed. "Jack. Miss Sullivan. I'm to be your driver. I was here, visiting, when I learned you'd be arriving. I volunteered."

"See?" Finn looked at Jack. "We'll be fine."

"I never said we wouldn't."

As they eased into the back of the car, Atheno continued, "Rowan Cruithnear's going to be delayed crossing over, so I'm to take you directly to the Blue Lady."

"I don't like it when plans change, Atheno."

"It's for your own good, Jack. We'll get you and your girl that elixir right away."

ATHENO STEERED THE ROADSTER up the steep curve of a road lined with old warehouses and oak trees cascading with moss and ivy that seemed to have overtaken anything made of concrete or metal. One building, its yard scattered with derelict vehicles, was painted with the words BOSTON AUTO PARTS.

Finn, catching her reflection in the rearview mirror, saw an unfamiliar creature with tangled hair, eyes rimmed in shadow, lips of bitten red. She said, "Tell me about the Blue Lady."

"The Blue Lady"—Atheno met her gaze in the rearview—"deals in the betwixt and between—mortal things for Fata desires. Is that a moth in your hair, Finn Sullivan?"

"It's a moth."

The roadster curved into a driveway lined with trees blossoming white roses. At the drive's end, on a hill covered with bluebells, was a majestic Queen Anne house painted oceanic blue. Jack murmured, "Bluebells . . . an exceptionally malevolent flower. Why is Cruithnear delayed?"

As Atheno halted the roadster in front of the house and Finn was reassured by the lights glowing in the first-floor windows, Atheno said, "Just last-minute stuff. Go on, children. I'll wait. The lady and I are having a disagreement at the moment, so I won't be going in."

Finn and Jack got out of the car and moved up the steps to the veranda, where bits of broken mirrors on ribbons glinted, hanging from the rafters. Remembering shattered glass and her sister lying in it, breathing as if everything inside of her had broken, Finn halted. *That was a lie.*

"Protective charms, of sorts," Jack told her as he knocked on the Blue Lady's door and it swung open.

"Jack, if she has protective charms all over her porch, why would she leave her door open?"

"Good question." He warily peered into a hall painted pale blue. There were holes in the walls, a shattered vase on the floor.

Finn whispered, "Here's another question—why does it look as if she's been robbed?"

"Atheno!" Jack turned. "We need—"

The roadster was empty.

"Maybe he went around to check the back?" Finn flinched as the moth flew past her, into the house. "Should we—"

"We're going in. Don't leave my side. We need that elixir. And, yes, Atheno's probably checking the back." Jack didn't sound convinced. They moved down the wrecked hall toward a parlor of blue and white, where they found more broken and overturned furniture, and water on the floor and watery footprints leading to the fireplace, where a mural of a shirtless boy holding a rooster and a hoop had been painted above the mantelpiece. On the mantelpiece was an ivory box with a white card propped against it. Jack avoided the water on the floor and moved toward the fireplace. He reached for the card propped against the box, read it silently. He looked at the box. As he took it down and carefully raised the lid, Finn said, "Are you going to tell me what's in it?"

"I'd rather not."

"What does the card say?"

"Someone sent the Blue Lady an invitation." He tucked the card into a back pocket and surveyed the parlor. "Come on. We've got to get out of here."

"What about the elixir?"

"We'll have to find Atheno first."

As she followed him into the hall, she snatched the card from his pocket, saw words scrawled in black ink—*The Mockingbirds invite you to evening tea. Any evening*—before he plucked the card from her hand

"Who are the Mockingbirds?" She halted as he stepped out onto the veranda. "What was in the box, Jack?"

"A piece of the Blue Lady."

"Oh . . ." She was about to ask him *what* piece when she heard a gurgling sound from within the house and turned her head.

At the end of the hall, Atheno knelt, clutching his throat.

"*Jack!*" Horror and instinct had her running back into the house to help Atheno, who had defended her from the Wolf.

Jack shouted and lunged after her.

The door slammed shut between them.

As Atheno pitched forward and Jack hit the door, yelling, Finn heard a familiar, low laugh that curdled her nerves. She turned.

A figure in a black coat stepped in front of the door. Caliban Ariel'Pan smiled at Finn, silver eyes like death-light behind a veil of platinum hair.

She backed away, slipped in something wet, looked down to see that Atheno's body was gone; only a knot of weeds and ivory wands remained. Nausea spasmed through her.

"He was water tribe. Like the Blue Lady." Caliban didn't seem concerned by Jack slamming himself against the door. "He's reverted to his element."

"You." Finn felt a flickering anger beneath the gut-twisting terror. "You *murdered* him."

"The lady of the house and the kelpie were going to hand you over to me. Trust me when I say he deserved it—"

A stone garden ornament shattered a window. Caliban spun around.

Finn almost shouted for joy as Jack, feral and dangerous, vaulted over the sill.

Caliban stepped back and glanced at Jack's right hand, which bled from a glass-edged cut. "Still bleeding, Jack? Mortality isn't so wonderful then?"

The *crom cu* leaped, smashing Jack against the wall. As Jack hit the plaster with a crack, Caliban taunted, "Why'd you bring her here, Jack? Getting tired of being a *real* boy? I see your shadow keeps slipping away. Maybe you don't love her as much as you think."

Lifting his head, Jack bashed a fist at the *crom cu*'s throat. Caliban feinted, caught one of Jack's wrists, and flung him halfway up the stairs.

"*Jack!*" Finn clutched the banister as Caliban whirled and came at her.

She backed away.

He grabbed her and knocked her against the banister. Her head struck the wood. Explosions of light and pain blinding her, she slid to the floor.

"On the other hand"—Caliban's fingers knotted in her hair—"the Wolf won't mind you having a few bruises and broken bones."

She heard Jack attempting to drag himself up as Caliban hauled her away. When the *crom cu* dropped her on the kitchen floor, she scrambled back against a cabinet and whispered, "I dreamed of Reiko."

He halted, and an almost human expression of loss crossed his perfect face. He crouched before her like an angel gangster in his black suit and coat. Amiably, he said, "I don't dream. What did she say?"

"Nothing," Finn hissed. "She just *burned*."

He bared his teeth and slammed his hands against the cabinet on either side of her head. "*You* should have burned."

Then the moth glided between them, across Finn's lips, and away.

Caliban blinked. "What—"

Finn pushed back against the cabinet as his malevolent attention returned to her, his eyes narrowing. He didn't see Moth, human again, rising up behind him. Caliban said, "Jack is still mortal. I'm going to break him into pieces."

"Seth Lot doesn't want you to hurt us."

"I'm not going to *hurt* you, darling. I'm just—"

Moth smashed a chair over his head.

The *crom cu* twisted around in a hail of wooden splinters and launched himself at Moth.

As they struggled, Jack appeared. He'd lost his weapons, so Finn snatched the wooden dagger Phouka had given her and slid it across the floor. He grabbed the dagger, lunged, and slammed it into Caliban's shoulder before falling to one knee.

Caliban tore the dagger out and dropped it, staggering. "*Elder wood?*"

As Moth rose, the *crom cu* turned and vanished into the dark.

Finn, crazy with adrenaline, looked at Moth, who had two scratches down one cheek, but seemed otherwise unharmed. She pushed herself up, grabbed the elder wood dagger, limped to Jack, and helped him to stand. She said, to Moth, "How'd you change back?"

"No idea." He shook his head. "You've got a shadow again, Jack."

"Of course." Jack grimaced. "Just when I'd rather *not* be mortal."

Shaking, Finn touched Jack's bruised jaw, the scratches on his throat. "Are you okay?"

"Aside from a concussion, yes. Are you?"

"Aside from a concussion, yes. You think he's gone?"

Jack was watching Moth. "Something made him leave."

Moth shrugged. "I think he was afraid of the elder wood."

Jack turned to Finn. He examined her skull with gentle fingers and peered into her eyes. "You sure you're all right? You'll have a lump on your head."

"Bruises, that's all." And a mighty headache, but she didn't want to complain. "I've got Motrin, if you need any."

He lowered his head and his warm hands dropped from her, leaving her cold. "We need to search this house for that elixir and leave before Caliban recovers."

THEIR SEARCH ENDED at a glass and metal cabinet, its drawers filled with tiny bottles. "Most of these are perfume," Jack said. "But—" He selected a dark blue one shaped like a mermaid and sniffed it. "Mermaid venom. It'll disguise your blood scent for a while."

Finn gazed doubtfully at the stuff. "I don't have to drink it, do I?"

"No. Don't get it on your skin either. Here." He carefully doused her clothes with the liquid, which smelled like patchouli and ocean air. "Moth. You, too. Just in case."

"Where will we go now, for the elixir?" Moth grimaced as the mermaid venom contacted his clothing.

Jack selected a few more bottles and dropped them into his backpack. Then he walked to the pool of bones and water weeds that had been his friend Atheno. He bowed his head for a moment, before gathering the necklace of green pearls from the mess and draping it around his neck. He straightened, his face in shadow. "Scarborough Fair. It's always here at winter's beginning. That's where we'll get the elixir."

"I remember that place." Moth shouldered his backpack, and Finn realized the backpack must have transformed with him, like his clothes. "It'll be a bloody unsafe trek—and the *crom cu* will know that's where we're going."

"It's closer than Cruithnear and we can't risk another train ride without the elixir." Jack sheathed the black *kris* in one sleeve and the Renaissance blade in his left boot. "May I see the compass, Finn?"

As Jack studied the Grindylow compass and Moth paced, Finn plucked an object from the Blue Lady's collection of bottled potions—a small glass vial shaped like a female sphinx. It was labeled *Tamasgi'po*, and the words *Spirit in a Kiss* were written beneath the name. Absalom had mentioned something called *Tamasgi'po* while warning her and Jack about Seth Lot's house. She tucked the sphinx vial into a coat pocket.

She didn't look back at Atheno's remains as they left the *Ban Gorm*'s house, but grief nipped at her. *Had* the amiable Fata betrayed them? Or had Caliban lied?

CHAPTER 9

There is a queen in every house of them. It is of those they steal away, and make queens of for as long as they live or that they are satisfied with them.

—*Visions and Beliefs in the West of Ireland,*
Lady Gregory

As Sylvie unlocked the door to her father's shop, she knew her stepmom would be at Pilates and her dad at the Antlered Moon Pub's poker night. She'd once liked the thrill of being alone in the apartment at night—not anymore. Since it was nice and warm in the recently closed shop, she switched on the banker's lamp and the old stereo in the alcove office. Listening to the comforting sound of a DJ chatting about the weather, she glanced out the front window at the snow-swept street where traffic lights swung in the wind and the occasional car glided past.

She began rummaging through the office closet. When she found what she was looking for, she grabbed the rectangular wooden box that held the Ouija board she'd bought at a garage sale and sat on the floor. The board, made in Italy, was illustrated with beautiful images of Renaissance people. She set the black planchette beneath letters shaped like mythical creatures and gnawed at her bottom lip before placing one hand on the piece of wood. "Spirit who haunts Finn Sullivan's house . . . I call thee to me, answer by the count of three."

She counted swiftly, waited.

The planchette twitched, slid jerkily to the letter *B*, its image a bear.

" 'B' . . . 'E' . . . 'T' . . ." It finished spelling *Betrayal.*

The air hummed. Sylvie blinked and shivered. The shadows in the shop seemed to alter, the moonlit spaces folding into a landscape of snow, the salvaged objects becoming a forest. The front door blurred into a stone arch, and beneath that arch stood a figure in a blue T-shirt and bell-bottom jeans, his feet bare. Long, dark hair eddied around his face. He spoke as if from a great distance. "*Sylvie Whitethorn. The Dubh Deamhais . . .*"

Sylvie stood, the sweat cold on her skin. She took an unsteady step forward. "Thomas Luneht. You *can't* be the one haunting Finn—"

" *. . . warn you.*" His voice became static. " *. . . not here . . . go to Sphinx . . .* Betrayal."

Thomas Luneht and the otherworldly landscape vanished.

Sylvie sank down onto a voyage trunk, staring blankly at a carved door reclaimed from an old mansion in Albany.

The bells above the entrance to the shop began to jingle, stopped as if frozen by an invisible hand. A glacial breath snaked through the heated air. She reached out and, fumbling, switched on another lamp.

There was a rustling near the grand piano her father had obtained from a composer's estate. Something giggled.

Sylvie scrambled up and stretched out the hand on which she wore two silver rings. She'd been such an idiot—she'd used a spirit board in a place filled with things salvaged from the dead. And her parents weren't home. She backed toward the stair that led up to the apartment.

The white-wigged mannequin in the corner, the one in an eighteenth-century ball gown, rocked slightly. Sylvie nearly fell over a bicycle. She staggered up.

The mannequin began to glide across the floor, the gown's fabric rustling like desiccated leaves. Sylvie told herself she'd faced worse than some stupid piece of plastic. She pulled herself up, grabbed the bicycle, and flung it at the mannequin.

The bicycle hit and snapped off the mannequin's nose and two fingers. The mannequin staggered but continued sailing toward her.

It stopped a few inches away and the shadows veiling it vanished in tatters, revealing a flesh-and-blood woman in a powdered wig and ball gown, her eyes black, her teeth red and sharp. Crystals glittered on her eyelashes. In a staticky voice, the Unseelie said, "You . . . play with the dead."

Sylvie backed away, but the creature followed like some undead Marie Antoinette. Sylvie's lungs hurt from the supernatural cold. Her breath misted as she exhaled. When her spine struck the office desk, she fumbled through the papers, seeking something she'd seen earlier. "What *are* you?"

The creature bared its red teeth and whispered, "I am Cold Jenny and I am your dea—"

Driven beyond fear into mania, Sylvie slammed her father's silver letter opener into the Unseelie's left eye. As the blade sank into plastic, she let go of the handle and watched, her mouth open in an unvoiced scream, as the mannequin tumbled to the floor, the letter opener sticking from a painted eye. One of its hands fell off and rolled beneath the piano.

Sylvie grabbed a shovel propped near the back door, strode over, and slammed it down on the mannequin's neck, separating its head from its body.

EVER SINCE THAT HORRIFYING NIGHT when a monster had risen from a bathtub in his house, Christie had been a light sleeper. The kelpie had come from the old well in the basement. Mr. Wyatt had helped seal that well by advising Christie's dad to fill it with concrete. When it was done, Wyatt had etched a symbol of protection in the concrete, before laying the boards back over it.

Christie hated going down into that basement, but he did it every evening, to check.

Tonight, afterward, he stepped onto the porch to gaze at Finn's house through the trees.

"Aren't you cold?"

He was always tense and only jumped a little when Phouka came out of the dark, her pale skin competing with the new-fallen snow. She looked deceptively girlish in tartan trousers and a jacket of mauve fur opened to reveal a black T-shirt with the silhouette of a white cat on it. Her auburn hair was swept into a fur hat with earflaps. She made him breathless and hot all at the same time.

"Not as cold as *you*." He stepped to the middle of the porch as if that could stop her from coming up the stairs.

Her lavender-gray gaze drifted over him. "Christie Hart, speak something of a poem to me."

He said, "'*She came to Envy's house, a black abode, ill-kept, stained with dark gore, a hidden home in a deep valley, where no sunshine comes, where no wind blows, gloomy, and full of cold.'*"

"Ovid." Her eyes glinted the silver of Fata anger. Sweetly, she continued, "And not very flattering. May I come in and get warm?"

"My family's in there." He lifted his chin, defying her.

"Why would I cause thee and thine harm, Christie? Now, may I come in?"

He backed away. "I don't think so." He turned and hurried into his house, then shut and locked the door. He loped up the stairs, avoiding a skateboard, a pair of ski boots, and a dog toy.

He stepped into his room—and found Phouka lounging in the leather armchair he'd inherited from his grandfather.

"*How*—"

She recited something in Irish, and he recognized the Gaelic welcome from the plaque his mother had hung over the front door. He'd completely forgotten to take it down. He slumped against the wall. "You came through the window?"

"It's tradition. Haven't you read *Peter Pan*?" She moved to her feet. "I like what you've done to your door."

His door was Sharpied with lines from his favorite poems. He watched her out of the corner of one eye as she wandered around his room, her fingers gliding over his collection of old albums, the taxidermy fox he'd bought in a junk shop.

"Why are you here? I don't want you here. Good-bye." He opened his door and didn't look at her again.

"Would you look at me if all I was wearing was this fur hat?"

He sucked in a breath through clenched teeth and told himself *not to fall for it.* He didn't turn.

"Can I prick you?" he suddenly said as he plucked a thumbtack from the bulletin board near the door. He swung around to face her, a little disappointed to see she still had her clothes on.

She held out a hand. He took hold of it. Her skin was cool. He gently stabbed the ball of her thumb. When no blood welled, he felt an idiotic betrayal and lifted his gaze to hers, glimpsed what he might have mistaken for sorrow if he'd been stupid. He stepped back. "That's what I thought."

Her eyes darkened. "Christie . . . when Rowan Cruithnear tried to go through the Way, we discovered a hex scratched onto Cruithnear's half of the key."

"What does that mean?"

"It means there's a traitor among the professors and the key malfunctioned. We don't know what happened to Finn and Jack and no one can use the Way until the key is fixed. Including Rowan Cruithnear."

"Why are you telling me this?" He wondered if there was a type of hysteria that made a person numb. Maybe it was just shock.

"Because Finn is your friend and I thought you should know."

"Thanks. Really." He wanted to swear at her. "Tell me what you're going to do to help her."

"We need to fix the key. I've shut all the Ways and can't open them again. Not so soon."

"Meanwhile, Finn and Jack are stranded?" He pushed his hands over his face. "Please . . . just leave."

She was close in the blink of an eye and whispered into his ear, "*'And even with such-like valor, men hang and drown their proper selves. You fools . . . I and my fellows are ministers of fate: the elements of whom your swords are temper'd.'* Every queen needs a wise man, Christie Hart. You'd better learn to become one."

As her lips brushed his, he felt as if dew-shimmering cobwebs grazed his skin. In the second he realized what a bad mistake he'd made offending her, she was gone.

SYLVIE'S DAD AND STEPMOM WERE HOME NOW—it was past midnight—and she was about to do something very reckless. Her father always seemed to hear her bedroom door open, or her feet creaking the stair. Ever since she'd fallen off her bike—and into Reiko Fata's bad spell—he'd become less easygoing about her nocturnal activities.

I should just move into the dorm, she thought, gliding down the back stairway in her socks and trying not to breathe. *I'm eighteen. I should be going wild.* The entity called Cold Jenny had made her afraid enough—and brave enough—to seek supernatural help.

She was out of breath by the time she'd biked up the lane leading to the abandoned house called the Sphinx with its Egyptian sculptures and windows like dark pools. She left her bike at the foot of the steep stairway and began to climb. This had been Thomas Luneht's house. This was where his spirit had directed her to go.

On the narrow porch, she opened her backpack and pulled out a store-bought book on witchcraft, adjusted her silver bracelets, touched the iron nail in one pocket, and removed a blue candle and a piece of blue chalk. She drew the symbol from the book, and lit the candle, wishing her hands would stop trembling. She set the old photograph she'd brought in the center of the symbol and recited the words she'd memorized, from Edgar Allan Poe:

> " '*By a route obscure and lonely,*
> *Haunted by ill angels only,*
> *Where an eidolon named NIGHT,*
> *On a black throne reigns upright . . .*' "

A chill skittered across the back of her neck as her breath became vapor. The branches of the nearby trees rattled. Snow whispered.

The soft voice from behind her frightened her more than any sepulchral words. "*Sylvie . . . Whitethorn . . .*"

"Can I look at you?" she asked cautiously.

"*No.*"

She closed her eyes and pictured Thomas Luneht. She tried not to think: *He's dead.*

" *. . . betrayal . . .*"

"What *betrayal*? Thomas"—she swallowed the sour taste of fear—"is it Finn and Jack . . . ?"

"*He's here . . .*"

Thomas Luneht's presence was snuffed out with a sound like electricity popping, and she pressed a hand over her mouth. Someone else stood behind her. Terror gripped her limbs as a voice, cool, masculine, and amused, reached her.

"Speaking to the dead, Sylvie Whitethorn, is never a safe endeavor. Believe me—I know." Something had used Thomas Luneht to lure her here. She tensed to run, her muscles so taut she thought they might snap. She said, "*Who are you?*"

"You know who I am, Sylvie Whitethorn." As he crouched beside her, leather creaked and she could smell winter and wood smoke. She turned her head. He wore a long coat and a hat like a Spanish cowboy's, its brim shadowing the upper half of his face. He was smiling.

"Black Scissors." Her mouth went dry. Several ebony moths with ghostly markings fluttered around them.

"That is one of my names."

"I don't think I should be talking to you. What happened to Thomas Luneht?"

"Thomas"—the Black Scissors looked out over the street—"was my apprentice, one of the blessed who decided to rebel against the devils. He's dead. The crooked dog mutilated and killed him. He remains, waiting to be freed."

Sylvie pressed a thumbnail against her teeth. "You hate them, the Fatas."

"Isn't that obvious, considering what they did to me? How would you like to become a force to be reckoned with?"

"No thanks. I'd just like the basics in life: to look pretty, eat chocolate, and go to the dance with the handsomest and most popular boy. And the Fatas aren't *all* devils."

"You and your kind are nothing to them but playthings. They *gut* adolescents and stuff them with flowers and make them into the living dead." The anger in his voice had replaced the slinky menace. "Your friends have been betrayed."

A chill stabbed into Sylvie's stomach. "How do you know?"

"Rowan Cruithnear has not gone to the Ghostlands. Something is wrong with Phouka Banríon's Way. Or her key. Thomas Luneht has told me, as much as he is able, that there was some interference."

Sylvie felt panic quicken her breathing and tried to calm it. "What does that mean?"

"Your friends are abandoned in the Ghostlands without Cruithnear. So, Sylvie Whitethorn, again I ask: Do you want to become a force to be reckoned with?"

She met his dark gaze and didn't see an old thing there, but a young man, merciless and determined. She said, "Tell me your true name."

"I was once William Harrow."

She held out a hand. "Nice to meet you, William Harrow."

His hand, strong and scarred, clasped hers. She didn't say anything about his missing pinkie. Then he held up a pewter key in the shape of an elaborate dragonfly. "Do you want it?"

"Why would I want it?" She began to understand why mortals never liked dealing with otherworldly people.

"Why, to enter the Ghostlands and give it to Finn and Jack."

"The Ghostlands . . ." Sylvie became breathless with the possibilities.

"The key will open anything." The key vanished with a flick of his fingers. "You can have it if you promise me something."

She warily said, "What is it you want me to promise you?"

"Become my apprentice."

"And what would I do as your apprentice?"

"Not witch things. You are not a witch. I'll teach you how to defend yourself from the Fatas and Fata malice."

She said, with conviction. "I'll do it. How do I help Finn and Jack?"

"I've been communicating with a friend in the Ghostlands. And we've a theory that ancient Fatas like Seth Lot cannot be killed with the mere stab of a silver knife."

She wanted to scream at him: *Why didn't you tell us this before?* But she knew why—he wanted something else. "What do you want for *that* information?"

"Nothing." He smiled. "All communication with my friend has been cut off, but I *have* learned the Wolf can only be killed by poisoning, pinning, and decapitation. A trinity death."

"All three of those things?" Sylvie felt all hope fall away.

"All three. And if you steal something for me, I'll give you a weapon that'll decapitate a wolf."

She bypassed the "steal" part of his sentence and said, "How will we find Finn and Jack . . . if we go, to take them your key and your weapon?"

"*We*, Sylvie Whitethorn? I can't go with you."

Sylvie realized she was thinking of Christie, of entering the forbidden Ghostlands with *Christie*. It was a terrifying, exhilarating idea.

The Black Scissors continued, "In the Ghostlands, the dragonfly key will lead you to a witch named Sylph Dragonfly—she'll take you to your friends. I also advise you to seek out Jill Scarlet, who hunts monsters. She may try to meet you at the place where you enter, but I can't guarantee it."

Monsters. Sylvie took a deep breath. "What do you want stolen? And from whom? And who is your mysterious friend in the Ghostlands?"

"I want a book stolen. I want it stolen from Phouka Banríon. And my friend in the Ghostlands is Lily Rose Sullivan."

CHRISTIE, SITTING IN HIS MUSTANG in front of the gates to the Tirnagoth Hotel, was relieved—and nervous—when the gates creaked open, shedding snow and withered ivy. As he steered his car up the overgrown road, the hotel continued its masquerade as a boarded-up shell tangled in ancient trees, ivy, and briars. The instant his headlights hit it, the Tirnagoth became its notorious and sophisticated alternate, glowing with lamps and as stylish and new as it had been when it had first opened in the 1920s. It was a terrifying transformation that almost made him swerve into a tree.

Sylvie had called him and told him everything . . . including what the Black Scissors wanted him to say—a charm to bring the Black Scissors's sought-after item to Christie, who would steal it from the Tirnagoth Fatas, from Phouka, to save Finn.

He parked his Mustang in the drive and sat there, gathering his courage. And every second he hesitated, Finn might be in peril.

When something jumped onto the hood of his car, he flinched and swore. A boy with long black hair crouched there, his face white against the plumage of his coat collar. His eyes were an unholy silver. Trip Rook.

"Get off my car!" Christie shouted.

Trip Rook slid off, sauntered to the driver's side, and knocked on the window. Christie tried to ignore him, but the Rook didn't leave. Finally, Christie rolled down the window and Trip leaned close with a nasty grin. "Her majesty sent me out to fetch you."

Wondering why Phouka had sent this psychopath, Christie sighed and got out of the Mustang. As he followed the Rook toward the gates leading into the courtyard, he said, "So, Trip, does she know you threatened Finn?"

"We didn't threaten her. We just told her what's what."

"Yeah. Why don't I tell Phouka what you said?"

Trip laughed harshly. "Go ahead. It's not like she trusts us anyway."

"Trip. Be nice." Standing between the hotel doors was a girl in a black gown, her golden hair knotted with flowers, a pair of fake butterfly wings strapped to her back. A blond boy in red was draped against the door frame beside her.

"I know you." Devon Valentine, whom Christie recognized as the dancer who had slit his wrists nearly one hundred years ago, smiled and bowed. "My apologies for All Hallows. Trip, go away."

Trip gave him a single-finger salute and vanished into the shadows. Christie remained at the bottom of the stairs, staring up at the dead boy who had given him to the Grindylow on Halloween night. "I came to see Phouka."

"I'll take you to her." The girl cast a flirty glance at Christie as he moved up the stairs. "I'm Aurora Sae. And you are . . . ?"

"Not dead." And Christie's hard grin was meant for Devon Valentine.

A silhouette appeared in the doorway. "You two. Get lost."

Aurora Sae and Devon Valentine moved gracefully back into the hotel's light as Phouka came forward, regal in a white coat and boot-cut jeans, her autumn hair tucked into a fur cap. "Christie Hart. What brings you to Tirnagoth?"

He had to remind himself that her freckles and autumn hair were a disguise. She wasn't letting her gray eyes silver, either. He said, "I'm sorry. For accusing you earlier."

"Come inside then. I'm *inviting* you." She turned and sauntered back into Tirnagoth. The last time he'd been here, he and Sylvie had fought for their lives against the Grindylow. And Phouka had saved them. He resentfully followed her.

The lobby had undergone a renovation of pink, black, and white. He heard harp music. A girl and a boy playing chess with some funky-looking pieces sat on the lobby desk, its pale wood carved into images of lizards and ivy. Their only source of light was a Tiffany lamp shaped like pink toadstools.

"Did you redecorate?" Christie took off his knit hat and ran a hand through his curls.

"A bit, here and there."

"I like it. It's very *Alice in Wonderland* meets Japanese horror movie."

"Just the look I was going for." Phouka led him into a glass-walled room scattered with ornamental trees in urns and fancy furniture in various shades of yellow and ivory. A painting was hung over a mantelpiece of yellow marble. As Phouka shed her coat and sat, arms draped over the back of the sofa, Christie took the chair opposite and studied the painting—a creepy mermaid with bone-tangled hair and a vampire mouth. He said, carefully, "Did you know about Finn's sister being taken by the wolf man?"

"I did not. And he's not a man. He's a thing wearing a man's shape."

"Did you tell Finn and Jack about the trinity death?"

"What are you talking about?"

"The trinity death." He spoke slowly, accusing. "The only way to kill Seth Lot."

"Your anger is giving me a headache. You've been drinking a lot of coffee, have you? It's made you frisky. The only death I know for the Wolf is stabbing him with silver as he's riding the shadow—who told you about the other way?"

"Seth Lot can only be killed by three things at once—poisoning, pinning, and decapitation. Right?"

She leaned forward, intent. "Where have you gotten this information from? I didn't *know*."

"The Black Scissors—who said he got it from Lily Rose Sullivan."

She sat back. "You can't trust him."

"Can I trust *you*? You people don't care about anything. Why did you send Finn and Jack to the Ghostlands?"

Quietly, she said, "We wade through rivers of your blood. We become your dreams, your nightmares. We're scarcely able to think properly, what with the lot of you constantly battering us with your emotions. We're elemental and free and because—with a few exceptions—we don't flaunt our passions to the world, you think we're cold. I don't care for your accusations or your attitude."

He bowed his head. Then he looked up, desperate. "Do you think Finn'll die in the Ghostlands?"

"I don't know, Christie. As soon as the key is fixed, Rowan Cruithnear will get the Black Scissors's information to Finn and Jack."

Christie hunched over and put his hands over his face. He said through his fingers, "Could I get something to drink?"

"I'll fetch you some water." She stood and left the room.

Christie raised his head. With shaking hands, he took the crumpled paper from his pocket. He rose. He began to recite the words Sylvie had given him.

A small object flew in from the hallway. He gaped as it circled him like a surreal bird—it was a hand-sized book with an ivory leather cover, its pages fluttering. It dropped to the floor at his feet and shut. The book had a lock—a tiny porcelain hand.

He snatched up the little ivory book and tucked it into his jacket.

When Phouka returned with a glass of water, Christie accepted it and drank it down. He said, "I'm going home now. Because I don't think you can help me."

He walked out, his heart jackhammering. Her gaze remained upon him until the door closed.

❖ ❖ ❖

IT HAD STOOD NEGLECTED in the woods for years, a birdcage-shaped structure of glass, a conservatory with metal doors and a sign of Egyptian art deco elegance that read STARDUST STUDIOS. Its parking lot was shattered by roots and weeds. Vandals had scarcely touched its tempting shell, and there were only a few breaks and cracks in the glass. The debris of leaves and rotting branches had fallen from its domed roof as if repelled, smearing and staining the exterior. Beyond the dirty glass were the silhouettes of old-fashioned furniture and film equipment. No one had ever broken in. Attempts had been few. It was as if the structure repelled people, as well.

But other things were drawn to its humming power; nested within the glass shell were four lost souls who could sometimes be glimpsed as a ghostly face, a filmy gown, the shine of an eye. These others kept themselves hidden from the sinister figure who walked the borders, the one who communed with the dead, the Black Scissors, whose spy, a spirit once named Thomas Luneht, trailed him like a dragonfly glimmer.

These spirits, waiting within StarDust, wanted revenge.

IT WAS NEARLY TWO IN THE MORNING when Sylvie and Christie, wearing small backpacks, trudged through the woods with flashlights.

"There." Sylvie aimed her light through the trees to reveal the glass birdcage shape of StarDust Studios.

"*That's* the Black Scissors' door to the otherworld? The film studio Tirnagoth gave to his wife? Are you having any second thoughts, Cherry Blossom?"

"Are *you*, Christopher Robin?"

"Hells no." He plunged forward and she grinned and followed.

When the tall figure of the Black Scissors emerged from the surrounding darkness, Sylvie felt Christie tense beside her. As the Black Scissors tilted his head, waiting, Christie said, with desperate bravado, "You show us yours. We'll show you ours."

The Black Scissors smiled, the upper half of his face shadowed by the brim of his hat. He lifted something strapped to his back—a walking stick of dark wood with a grip shaped like the head of an Egyptian jackal. "In this is sheathed an iron and silver sword. The wood sheathing it is from an elder tree beneath which Lot buried his victims. The sheath will prevent the iron from decay in the Ghostlands."

Christie took the ivory book from his jacket.

"Two exchanges." The Black Scissors held up an ornate key shaped like a dragonfly. He offered it to Sylvie. "Yours."

She accepted the key. She was as nervous as if she'd just made a deal with the devil—but he was a devil who expected her to get through this, to make it back out of the Ghostlands.

Christie reluctantly held out the little ivory book he'd taken from Phouka. He looked guilt-ridden. "What is it? Some sort of collection of magic spells? Her diary?"

The Black Scissors said nothing, offering him the jackal walking stick. Christie grudgingly took it, and the Black Scissors tucked the ivory book into his coat. He said, "The sword can only be drawn once, because the elder wood protects the silver and iron. When you enter StarDust in the Ghostlands, I've left something for you, on the table near the door. A bottle. It's an elixir that'll disguise your mortal blood. Only one drop each. And one more thing—" The Black Scissors continued gently, "Serafina cannot take her sister from the Ghostlands. She can free Lily Rose from the Wolf's house, but she can't bring her to the true world. Seth Lot's house hoards memories, dreams, phantoms."

"You expect us to tell Finn to leave her sister *there*?" Christie's voice became tight with disbelief. "No. *No*—"

"Christie." Sylvie spoke softly. "He's telling us something."

Christie shook his head and glanced desperately at Sylvie. "Lily Rose *can't be a ghost*. Sylv—"

The Black Scissors had vanished. His voice drifted to them, "If you bring Lily Rose to the true world, there will be terrible consequences. I'll see you soon, Sylvie Whitethorn."

Christie and Sylvie turned toward StarDust and Sylvie whispered, "We have to tell Finn."

"First." Christie was pale with anger and fear. "We have to find her."

"Let me see that." Sylvie took the jackal walking stick from him. She carefully gripped the handle as she held it horizontally before her. When something clicked beneath her thumb, she partially drew a sword that almost glowed in the night. She and Christie regarded it with awe. She noted, "It's so *thin*."

A dead leaf drifted from StarDust's snow-dusted roof, onto the blade's edge, and was neatly sliced in half. Christie's eyes widened. "And so sharp."

Sylvie sheathed the blade, hooked the walking stick on its strap over one shoulder, and stomped toward StarDust. "Let's go."

As their lights brushed across the metal door, a muffled laugh erupted from the trees. Sylvie's light speared through the night, but Christie knocked her flashlight aside and quickly turned his off. She did the same. They waited.

Whatever came crashing through the woods made Christie say, "That sounds like drunk people."

As the first figures appeared, Christie and Sylvie snapped on their lights.

"Shit!" Aubrey Drake flung a hand over his eyes. "Hey! Who's there?"

The girl with him—Claudette Tredescant—snorted. "It's Christie and Sylvie."

The other five blessed came from the trees, carrying bottles and reeking of something that wasn't nicotine. Christie waved his flashlight. "Aubrey, what are you doing here?"

"This is where we hang out for stress relief." Aubrey unsteadily extended one arm and made a gesture as if he was an emperor indicating his empire.

"And to get stoned," Ijio added, one arm around Nicholas Tudor. Victoria Tudor was watching Sylvie and Christie. Claudette Tredescant was giggling. Hester Kierney, the voice of reason, said, "We can go somewhere else."

Sylvie and Christie looked at each other. Sylvie aimed her light back at the blessed. "You're really coming out into the woods to get high when there's a Very Bad Man—Wolf—prowling around? You *saw* him at Hester's party."

"That's basically why we're getting high," Aubrey said, " 'cause there's nothing else we can do."

"Guys." Hester Kierney seemed to catch on to something. "Let's go to Drake's Chapel. I think Christie and Sylvie want to be alone."

"Wait—ow!" Sylvie glared at Christie, who had hit her with his flashlight.

"Okay." Aubrey looked doubtful. He ruefully glanced back at Sylvie as he and his friends trudged away, and murmured, "Why would they want to make out in that scary-ass place?"

When they'd gone, Sylvie turned to Christie. "They think we're *on* each other."

"And that's what worries you? We're about to step into another freaking dimension and you care about a bunch of sellouts thinking we're a thing?"

Sylvie breathed deep and turned to face the door, which was made of dark metal, not glass like the rest of the structure, and engraved with images of eyes, hands, and feet tangled in ivy and stars. There was an old-fashioned brass lock. The whole building had a look that reminded Sylvie of old Hollywood. And it seemed to be *waiting*.

"You ready to do this?" Christie asked as she gripped the dragonfly key like a weapon.

"It's an adventure," she whispered, and she shoved the key into the lock.

Christie clasped her hand as the door swung open.

SYLVIE FELT CHRISTIE'S HAND SLIP from hers the moment they stepped through the door into the rosy glow of twilight. She gazed in wonder at the studio before her—it was still abandoned and creepy, and the dusky light, though reassuring, was a shock, because they'd entered at night. She was surrounded by skeletal film equipment and furniture gone to rust and ruin. Lichen and rotting leaves streaked the glass walls and caused unsettling shadows. Beyond the glass doors at the back were a forest and a red sky—there was no snow, only green grass and green trees.

She became aware of a lack of presence behind her, a coldness at the nape of her neck.

She twisted around and found herself alone.

And she didn't have the dragonfly key. She stared at her empty hands as if expecting it to appear.

"Christie!" She flung herself at the front door. When it wouldn't open, she backed away and turned to confront the abandoned studio. Panic made her mouth dry. She wove through the room, moving quickly to the rear doors.

She laughed with relief when they opened, and she called out Christie's name as she ran around to the front of the building. She circled the studio, twice, before she realized he wasn't there.

She sank down against one glass wall, hugging her backpack and staring at the path of white sand that led from StarDust Studios through the alien woods.

Phone. Her hands shook as she fumbled her cell phone from a pocket, only to find it dead. Why had she thought it would work here? She huddled in a tight knot against the glass wall and cursed her naive confidence.

She looked up and saw lights dancing in the trees. The lights whirled playfully closer—they were orbs, some as tiny as dimes, others as big as golf balls. She smiled, charmed, as the Tinkerbells scattered in a sort of dance.

Then the bigger ones suddenly grew shadowy tentacles. They spiked into grotesque silhouettes that began crawling toward her. She scrambled to her feet as the air became heavy with the reek of old blood. When she saw something like a large, shadowy eel writhing toward her, she realized she had two options—fight or flee.

She fled.

CHRISTIE FELT SYLVIE'S HAND YANKED from his as he stumbled into electric light.

Stunned, he looked around a luxurious, lamp-lit interior scattered with gleaming, old-timey film equipment. Faux animal skins were flung over leather furniture. There was a stage made up to look like a ballroom, with a fancy chandelier and red and white tiles. Behind it was a painted backdrop that made the false room seem larger. Everything looked new—as if the studio was waiting for the return of its inhabitants.

He whispered, *"Sylvie?"*

He flung the front door open, saw the night woods they'd left—only without snow. The branches rustled with leaves. There was green everywhere beneath a dark sky slated with stars. He slowly turned his head and scanned the lit studio, whispered again, *"Sylvie?"*

A dense, girl-shaped shadow stood on the stage. It wasn't Sylvie. He *knew* it wasn't Sylvie. Because it stood in a pool of water, softly chanting, *"'Jack be nimble, Jack be quick . . .'"*

Christie backed away, felt something crunch beneath his boots, and looked down to see glass littering the floor. He continued walking backward out of the building. The door slammed shut before him, leaving him in the dark woods. Alone.

He turned in place. *"Sylvie!"*

He raised a hand to bang at the door engraved with eyes and vines—and saw the first scrawl of poetry, his own poetry—inked across his wrist. Slowly, he pushed up his sleeves, his shirt. He saw more words on his arms, his chest.

Phouka. He suspected the poetry was a spell, something to protect him. He sank to a crouch, unable to stop the panic that almost blinded him. He realized how very alone he was.

A tiny scroll of wet paper clung to his left boot. He pulled it off, opened it, and saw the words *Drink Me.*

The world spun, went dark.

"BEATRICE."

"Abigail."

"He's so pretty, isn't he, Eve?"

"Stop it. What have you done?"

The whispers jarred Christie back to consciousness. He swore and scrambled up—he'd been placed on a divan in StarDust Studios. The lamps were still lit. The place remained empty, waiting.

A girl giggled. He turned. "Syl—"

Two shadows waltzed together on the stage. Both wore flowing dresses. The air was so cold, his breath was vapor. He braced himself and walked toward the stage.

The shadows spun to face him, and two rotting corpse girls smiled at him.

He bolted out the doors, into the forest.

HESTER KIERNEY, FOLLOWING HER FRIENDS through the woods, heard Christie call her name. Curious, she slipped back along the path. Pushing her hair farther up into her newsboy cap, she looked around. "Christie?"

Still a little drunk, she approached the grimy glass building known as Star-Dust. She didn't see Christie or Sylvie. But there was something in the snow, in front of the door. She walked to it and bent down to pick up an old-fashioned key shaped like a dragonfly.

"Huh." She turned and gazed at the metal door engraved with unseen people tangled in ivy. She pushed the key into the lock and, when the door opened, her eyes widened.

CHAPTER 10

Are you going to Scarborough Fair?
Parsley, Sage, Rosemary, and Thyme;
Remember me to one who lives there,
For once she was a true love of mine.

—"Scarborough Fair," a Yorkshire ballad

Someone betrayed us." Jack's voice was hard. He hadn't been able to start Atheno's roadster, so he, Finn, and Moth were walking along a street lined with tall hedges on one side and a field scattered with trees and boarded-up houses on the other.

"Rowan Cruithnear thinks someone's a traitor." Finn ached all over from the fight with Caliban and kept glancing over her shoulder, expecting to see the evil form of a white hyena behind them. Jack had told her, while swabbing her cuts, that being stabbed with elder wood would put Caliban out of commission for a while.

"Well, you practically had to ask everyone in your little town for permission." Moth also kept glancing around.

"Only Phouka and Cruithnear knew our exact route." Jack scanned the night sky as if seeking direction from the stars. "We were to go to Cruithnear's—that plan shouldn't have changed."

"Jack . . ." Finn hesitated. She was fighting a terror of the strange world around her and surprised by how calm she sounded. "Caliban told me Atheno and the Blue Lady were going to give us to the Wolf."

Jack knotted his fingers in the necklace of green pearls he'd taken from Atheno's remains. He said, low, "Someone, aside from Caliban with the Wolf's directive, had been to visit the Blue Lady first."

"The ones who left the invitation. You still haven't told me who the Mockingbirds are and why they killed the Blue Lady." Finn checked that the silver dagger was still in her coat pocket.

"The Mockingbirds?" Moth halted. "They're ghouls, as I remember them. What was the invitation for?"

Ghouls. Finn's stomach twisted. "The invite was for tea."

A black Rolls-Royce glided slowly, silently past. They all had their hoods up, and ducked their heads until it had gone. Jack began walking again. "The Mockingbirds are not friends with the Wolf."

"It doesn't matter—I don't want to meet them." Finn glanced at the hedges to their left and noticed tiny lights flickering among the leaves. The lights were so pretty, like a miniature universe of stars, but she was wary of them. When Moth murmured, "Don't look at them," she tried not to.

Out of the corner of one eye, she saw a tiny orb of light darken and expand into a shadow that capered on the pavement before vanishing.

"Keep walking," Jack ordered. "They're only curious, for now."

"What are they?" Finn tried not to look again. "Pixies?"

"Dangerous." Moth swatted away a dancing light that had come too close.

The street suddenly ended. A field stretched before them, an abandoned factory, all smokestacks and dulled metal, looming in the distance. More of the lights flocked in the dark, like fireflies.

One of the orbs came toward them, spiraling playfully before slanting into a spindly shadow that remained low to the ground. When it began crawling along the pavement, Finn pulled the Leica camera from her backpack, raised it, and clicked a picture. Several orbs flinched back. The crawling shadow curled in on itself like those firecracker worms she and Lily had used to light on the Fourth of July.

"Finn, my love," Jack said as they stood with their backs to each other in the center of the dancing lights, "what are you doing?"

"Light and shadow. What cancels both out better than a flash?" Her hands shaking, she took more pictures as she, Jack, and Moth backed away. "Jack? Is Scarborough Fair beyond that factory?"

"It is."

"Then I think"—she lowered the camera as adrenaline surged through her—"we should run for it."

"Don't let any of the shadows touch you," he commanded. "But the lights can't hurt you. And keep that camera handy."

Moth's gaze was flicking from one shadow to another. "*Now!*"

They flung themselves across the field, which was knee-high with skin-ripping briars. As Finn ran between Jack and Moth, dodging the frantic, hunting orbs and shadowy tentacles, she saw, beyond the factory, a tall archway made of wood and withy strung with stained-glass lanterns. A green banner embroidered with the words SCARBOROUGH FAIR stretched above it.

She stumbled and cursed, and Jack caught her. Moth cut at the shadows with a wooden dagger and stayed by her side. She hated feeling helpless and struggled to keep up as they ran again.

Something tangled in her hair, chittering. She cried out and swatted at the air. Her hand hit something solid. Moth swore as a large shadow swept down toward them like a big wasp.

Jack flung a blade. It glittered in an arc and struck the shadow wasp, slicing it in half. The creature fell apart in strands of gossamer darkness. Jack snatched up the knife as they continued running.

They reached the arch. She looked back to see that the orbs hadn't followed, and she breathed out a relieved laugh, watching them hover and spiral, keeping their distance, as if held at bay by an invisible barrier.

Jack turned to her and his eyes were silver. "Don't make eye contact with anyone. Don't accept any gifts. Don't wander off. I'll repeat that: *Don't wander off.* Even though the fair doesn't move until season's end, I don't trust it."

"It *moves*?" She studied the landscape of quaint lanterns and striped pavilions beyond that archway.

"Not until winter's end."

"How exactly does this whole place move?" She imagined a magic tornado sweeping everything up and setting it neatly down in another location.

"Not the way things usually do." Jack tugged the hood of her red coat up over her hair. "Whatever possessed you to bring that old camera?"

She shrugged. "It just seemed appropriate, to bring something like an artifact. Like a good luck charm."

As they walked toward the archway, she felt excitement overwhelm dread. A Ferris wheel glittered, spiky and sinister, against the night sky. Lanterns strung between the pavilions lit banners proclaiming FREAK SHOW, SPELLS AND INCANTATIONS, TREATS OR TRICKS, and WONDERS OF THE TRUE WORLD. A top-hatted man on stilts lurched around, handing out advertisements. Finn ducked her head as he loomed over them before moving on. A muscular man tattooed with eyes held a large hammer and shouted challenges to strike a black metal dragon. When a silver-haired boy accepted the hammer and struck, lights flamed in the dragon's eyes and its mouth opened to drop a glass apple into the winner's hand. A carousel of mythical animals—a golden gryphon, a silver sphinx, a manticore, and a unicorn—rotated in a circle of lights and music that sounded like the lullaby "Hush, Little Baby." The old-fashioned exhibits of taxidermy creatures, the steampunk mechanisms of the rides, and the Fatas themselves in their neo-antique fashions, created a dream-dark atmosphere. Some of the Fatas seemed to shift in and out of shadow and light.

Fairies, she thought as they passed a makeshift stage where a young man in jeans, tattoos, and a headdress of ram horns was performing a sword-swallowing act. She shivered.

Jack said, his voice low, "Need I remind you to pretend as if you've seen all this before?"

"I have." Moth frowned as they approached a vine-covered stall where two black-haired men with gold hoops in their ears were selling fruit from crates and baskets. The fragrance of the fruit—tart, sweet, fresh—went right up Finn's nose. Her mouth watered. Her stomach felt as if it had grown teeth and was eating its way out of her. She reached for a peach—

Jack's hand covered hers. He bent his head.

He kissed her with lush deliberation. When he let her go, she wobbled a little, but the ferocity of that unexpected kiss had burned away the desire for the fruit. She wished he'd stop using that strategy. She scowled as whistles and good-natured laughter came from some of the Fatas. One of the rakish fruit sellers, his thumbs in his jeans pockets, said, "Well, that's one way to satisfy a young girl's appetite."

"Better than *your* way," Moth retorted.

The fruit seller winked and grinned. His teeth were sharp.

Jack murmured in Finn's ear, "You still wear the silver?"

She pulled back her coat cuffs, revealing her sister's charm bracelet. It hadn't even tarnished. "Maybe it's not real silver, if it should have rotted here."

"Nevertheless, don't brush up against anyone."

She squinted at him. "Someday, that kissing thing isn't going to work."

"Then I'll have to think of something else." He swaggered onward with a grin.

They passed three young men in red bowler hats, slouched against a gypsy wagon painted black. Within the wagon were birdcages, all of them empty. Finn turned in place when a girl in an aviator's cap and leather dress strolled past, her silver eyes as reflective as a cat's.

"Most of those who come here are changelings," Jack told Finn. "Or *aisling*s. Mortals, stolen away, who've become strange and inhuman. This is a place to purchase Fata things that delight or terrorize, help or harm."

"Jack," Moth whispered, "we need to keep out of the light. Finn's shadow . . ."

Finn noticed the darkness stretching from the toes of her Doc Martens to the nearest lamp. She glanced up and around at the Fatas, none of whom had shadows. She swore softly.

As Jack and Moth steered her among pavilions less well lit, Jack said, "This'll sound like odd advice—but don't touch your dagger or any weapon unless you need to. Contact with weapons *invites* violence, in this place."

Finn slid her hand from the silver dagger in her coat as Jack gently tugged her toward a ribboned pavilion that stood beneath a birch tree strung with blue lanterns. A young black man sat on a thronelike chair beneath it, surrounded by a collection of ornamental bottles in jeweled hues. As Jack, Finn, and Moth approached, he leaned forward. Jack drew back his hood and the black youth said in a jovial tone, "Jack Daw. Where *have* you been? And who are your charming companions?"

"I've been elsewhere. And let's call my companions Kate and John. Kate and John, this is Teig Lark—alchemist, moonshiner, and medicine man."

"Also, poisoner." Teig Lark's smile glittered. His snow-bright hair hung in thick braids. He wore white jeans and rings on his bare toes. "But not so much now that monarchy is dead. So, Jack, are you here to trade for something? Apple Love perfume for your lady? A DragonSteel potion to fight an enemy?"

"The elixir."

Teig Lark's smile vanished. "Then I shall need to speak with you privately."

"No. She doesn't leave my—"

"Jack." Teig Lark became somber. "I deal in secrets. You don't want some of the things you know to reach other ears. I'll leave the flap open, and you'll be able to see your companions." He rose and slipped into the pavilion.

"And just what kind of secrets aren't we supposed to know?" Moth demanded.

"If I told you, they wouldn't be secrets." Jack ducked into the star-patterned pavilion and he and Teig Lark began speaking in low voices, Jack keeping his gaze on Finn.

Moth slouched against the birch. Finn sank to the ground beneath it, rummaging in her backpack for a Slim Jim and a can of espresso. "Do you want some?"

Moth looked disdainful. "No."

"Moth . . . that fruit, back there—"

"That was goblin fruit—spells encased in things made to look like fruit. Those Fata men would have gotten more from you than teeth or blood or a kiss." He looked impatient. "I believe there's a poem about goblin fruit. Haven't you read it?"

"Maybe. Get some food." She gestured to the fair and decided she wouldn't be sampling any fruit here. "You're a changeling, so you can eat, right? I can hear your stomach growling and you're getting grouchy."

"There's a girl selling soup—" He nodded to a Fata girl spooning soup into wooden bowls. Dressed in striped tights and an Elizabethan corset, she looked like she belonged in a modern Shakespeare play.

"What will *she* ask for?"

"I suppose I shall find out." Since Moth rarely smiled, it was startling when he did. He called out, "Hey! Soup Girl!"

Incredibly, the soup girl answered this uncivilized summons and sauntered over. She looked Moth up and down, from his tousled pewter hair, to his battered boots. "And what would you like?"

"How much for—"

The Fata girl stepped forward and kissed him. As light and shadow rayed out around him, Finn jumped up, grabbed her backpack, and swung it at the Fata girl.

Someone blew shimmering pollen into Finn's face. She inhaled, stumbled back, and raised an arm to shield herself.

"JACK." TEIG LARK SPOKE the moment they were in the pavilion. "I don't want anything—I owe *you*. That pretty boy with you? He isn't whatever he's pretending to be. He stole the hearts from two Fatas, both of whom came looking for him."

"*Moth?*"

Outside, Finn cried out and raised an arm as if shielding herself. Jack started toward her. "Finn!"

"Jack!" Teig Lark tossed an object to him.

Jack caught the tiny bottle and dove out of the pavilion—

Something hit him hard in the face. He fell back, stunned. He heard Teig Lark yell and stumbled up, his vision sparking.

Someone grabbed his shoulder. He whirled, striking out.

A pretty Jill in a sundress—and he knew she was a Jill from the glint of death in her eyes—smiled at him.

He avoided the blade in her hand, twisted, kicked out, and caught her in the ribs. She fell, rolled up. He slammed a hand into her head. She collapsed, her dagger spiking into the grass.

When Jack realized Finn and Moth were gone, he stood very still.

He had lost her.

FINN GROGGILY LIFTED HER HEAD and saw lamps of yellow glass dangling in front of black drapes patterned with gold suns. She was in a pavilion. A human-sized doll made from wax was seated in a chair. A large wooden harp formed into a girl stood in a corner. There was a sentience to the doll and the harp that made her skin crawl—

"Fairy dust," she said through her teeth, remembering the flung glitter and falling asleep. She struggled to rise.

Someone grabbed her. As she was hauled out of the pavilion, she lashed out. She was released. She staggered back and stared at a golden-haired figure in a white suit. "*Leander?*"

"That"—Leander pointed to the pavilion—"belongs to Lot's lieutenant. She's here with Caliban."

"Caliban already attacked us."

"Go back to Jack, Finn. I can't help you." He began walking.

She strode alongside him. "Did you help Seth Lot steal Lily? *Did you?*"

"You shouldn't have come."

"I saw you *bleed*. You still love her! What did you expect me to do, Leander? Forget her? Pretend she was really dead? Seth Lot came to me and told me to find him or he'd kill Lily. Seven days, Leander. I have *seven* days."

Leander stepped back, whispered, "No . . ."

"Just *tell* me how to get Lily out of the Wolf's house. And where it is."

"I don't know where it is and you can't get her out. I'll find your sister. But I won't give you to the Wolf in exchange." He leaned close to her and whispered, "They're watching me, Finn. I can't help you. Return to Jack before *they* get him."

He backed away and vanished among the pavilions. She started after him, realized he might be leading *them*, the enemy, away.

She turned and ran through the fair, terror for Jack causing her to shove past Fatas, to ignore anything that might be following.

A fist slammed into her stomach. She fell to the ground, blood filling her mouth as she bit through her lip and curled around *pain*.

Then she was being dragged through the shadows, away from the fair, into the field. She spat blood and yelled, attempting to clutch at grass, weeds, dandelions, until her hands were streaked with green. When she was finally released, she heard a voice that made her flinch. "Well. That was easy."

She raised her head to see Caliban walking around her. "Do you know who's going to gut your Jack? David Ryder's Jill. You remember the Stag Knight, don't you? The one who *burned*? His Jill is with the Wolf. And she doesn't like *you*."

Fighting the pain in her skull, Finn bit her lip against a whimper. *Don't let him know how scared you are.*

A summery breeze drifted through her hair. She smelled flowers. She focused on something not far away, a blur of yellow. Daisies, her mom's namesake. She remembered her mom making daisy chains in the spring. *Protection from the fairies*, she'd say.

Finn scrambled up, reeling, and lunged.

Caliban snarled, "Oh, *no*, you don't."

She rolled into the circle of daisies, where she lay, staring up at the night sky. She waited breathlessly, her stomach clenched, hands curled at her sides.

AS JACK HUNTED FOR FINN, anger and fear tearing him to pieces, he ripped open pavilions and pushed into stalls and wagons.

Then he saw Leander striding toward him.

"Where is she?" He stalked toward Leander, who backed away. "I don't know, Jack. She didn't go back to y—"

There was an immense rustling, like the leaves of a thousand trees being struck by the wind. Jack's body iced.

He stared around at the cavernous forest that now surrounded the pavilions and glittering rides. Scarborough Fair, which had not been scheduled to leave until winter's end, had moved and taken him with it.

AS CALIBAN CROUCHED outside of the daisy circle, Finn sat up and slid as far away from him as the border of flowers would allow.

"Lucky you," he said. "And clever. Daisies . . . bloody stinking things. But you can't stay in there forever."

She was exhausted—she'd been running from this psycho all night and it had been a very long night. Her voice scraped out of her. "The Wolf sent you to separate me and Jack, didn't he? It's part of his game . . . a trick . . ."

Caliban shrugged, his predatory gaze fastened on her.

"Calib—"

"Don't," he hissed. *"Don't* say my name. *You took her away from me."*

The fair looked miles away. Jack didn't know where she was. She had to stall. She said, "Reiko never loved you—she loved *Jack.* That's why she died. And you never loved her—you don't bleed. You really *are* nothing—"

He leaped at her.

He fell back, choking. When he scrambled up, there were cinder marks on his skin—as if the daisy pollen had burned him.

Finn continued with shaky bravado, "Are daisies like napalm to you people?"

"My people"—he rose to prowl the circle and she stood also, teetering a little and pressing one hand against her sore midriff—"are harder to kill. Not fragile, like you lot, with all your bits and pieces that come off so *easily*."

"You were once one of us," she whispered.

"I should slap your mouth for saying that." His voice was ugly.

She stumbled on something, caught herself, glanced down to see Christie's book of poetry spilled from her backpack and open on the grass. A breeze ruffled the pages.

"You can't stay in there forever, *leannan*."

"You said that already." Finn waited until the book's pages settled. "Jack and Moth will find me."

"Is that what he's calling himself? *Moth*? Lot's fancy *aisling*. Let me tell you, darling, some things about Jack and *Moth*, because I knew them, way back when—"

"*'It is bitterness to my heart, to see my father's place forlorn.'*"

He took a step back.

She continued reading from the poetry book that had drifted open to that particular poem, "*'No hounds, no packs of dogs.'*"

He growled. Jack had once told her that Caliban, long ago, had been a Celtic chieftain's son who'd been tricked away by the Fatas and had returned to his home, years later, only to find his loved ones aged to dust and bones. She read on, relentlessly, "*'No women and no valiant kings.'*"

"*Stop*. Where did you—" His gaze dropped to the book. He snarled, looked up, past her. Then he smiled and said, "You're on your own."

He vanished into the night.

She stood, turning toward Scarborough Fair.

It was gone.

The lights and noise had been replaced by silence. The empty field with the abandoned factory rising in the middle was dark but for the flickering of those menacing orbs. Jack had said, *It moves*, and so Scarborough Fair had.

Finn stood, cold and alone, in the dark.

The orbs swarmed and came at her.

❖ ❖ ❖

JACK AND LEANDER FOUND David Ryder's Jill still unconscious and hauled her into the pavilion with the harp and the wax doll. When her eyes opened, Jack gently asked her where Finn was. She laughed and told him that Caliban had taken her.

Jack didn't kill her. He turned and walked out and Leander followed.

"Jack, he won't hurt her. Lot doesn't want that."

"No. He wants to play games with the lives of two girls." If Jack thought about all the things that could happen to Finn in the Ghostlands, he would lose his mind. The presence of David Ryder's former Jill couldn't be a coincidence, either—she'd been lying in wait.

"There's a train station near. We can go back to where Scarborough was—"

"What town is this?" Jack asked.

"King's Highway."

"The way back is too far. I have a friend who lives near here. Maybe he can help us."

THE TRAIN THAT JACK AND LEANDER BOARDED was red as rusted metal and sporting bullet scars. It was blessedly free of any sinister Fatas. As Jack and Leander settled into a car furnished in Old West decor, Leander said, with desperate anger, "Why did you bring her?"

Jack gazed out of the window. "You know Finn. Do you think I could keep her away?"

Leander was silent for a moment. Then: "I didn't betray Lily Rose to Seth Lot—if that's what you think."

"Lily Rose is in the house of the Wolf and you're his Jack."

"Not anymore." Leander drew back his white blazer and Jack saw a holster and a brass flintlock pistol engraved with sea serpents, a weapon made to kill Fatas. "I traded for this at the *Ban Gorm*'s—"

"The Blue Lady? You were there? How curious. Her left hand is now missing a body."

"Jack. *Lot* knew the Blue Lady traded in mortal things, like the elixir. Why did you go *there*?"

Jack rested his head back against the seat. "Our original plans were sidetracked. What are you going to do with that gun?"

"Find the Wolf's house and get Lily. The bullets are coated with a special poison. My friend—"

"Finn told you the ultimatum Lot gave her?"

Leander whispered, "Yes."

"Why were you in Fair Hollow?"

"To meet a friend who would bring me into the Ghostlands. She gave me the poison for the bullets."

"Phouka had all the Ways shut, except for the one at Lulu's."

"There's another."

As dusk began to streak the sky, signaling a new day, the train halted at a crossroads where old row houses and cottages the colors of Easter eggs were tangled with prehistoric yew trees. A tower with a clock face overlooked a pond blazing red in the twilight—the place resembled a resort town gone to seed. Jack and Leander exited the train and strode quickly to a purple Victorian, where a weathered sign above the door read ORSINI'S BOOKS.

Inside the shop, books had overrun the interior, tumbling from tables, towering in piles, stuffed in crates and on shelves crammed with unusual objects collected from the true world . . . an old typewriter, a stone Celtic cross, a stuffed owl. The wooden floor creaked beneath their boots as they searched. Leander murmured, "Jack, the chances of her being here . . ."

"When I want your opinion, I'll be sure and ask for it."

Leander halted and Jack followed his gaze to the back door, which was open and half off its hinges.

"*Orsini.*" Jack ran out the door.

In the courtyard, he fell to his knees beside a pile of black fur and earth . . . it was all that remained of his old friend. With one shaking hand, he tenderly touched a bear-shaped brooch in the fur. When he swallowed a howl of anguish, it was as if he'd inhaled a ball of thorns. "Tell me, Cyrus"—he didn't look at Leander—"what terrible things have *you* done for the Wolf?"

Leander crouched beside Jack. The Celtic knot and wolf tattoo on the side of his neck was visible as his golden hair fell back. He said, carefully, "Not as many as you have, with Reiko."

"I'm not the one who caused an innocent girl to be taken from her family."

"Not yet."

Jack thought of Finn out there, alone—or, worse, with Caliban—and wanted to rip someone apart.

Leander bowed his head. "I never should have spoken to Lily when I saw her. All of this . . . it's my fault."

Jack relented. "Reiko has had her claws in that family since Finn was a child. But you might have prevented her sister's fate."

Leander shouted, "I've tried everything to free Lily! I will do anything for her!"

"What do you mean, exactly?"

Leander's expression was desolate. "I will die for her." He hesitated. "Jack . . . Caliban and Lot are tracking you by your blood—because of what happened to you on Halloween. The elixir won't work on you. You've been marked from the beginning."

"Atheno betrayed us."

"Well, he *was* a kelpie. Are you really surprised? You need to disguise your mortality if you're going to move through the 'lands. You need to be what you once were."

"And how do you propose I do that?"

"I know a witch."

"Do you now?" Jack felt a glittering darkness stir within him.

"She can help you."

"And what about Finn?"

"You'll have to risk the witch scrying for her—and that might alert Lot's spies. I've led them on for a bit . . ." Leander rose, digging into his blazer pocket. He took out an amulet and held it toward Jack. "Take it. You need this more than I do."

Jack gazed at the amulet, a dragonfly made of brass and crimson glass. "Where did you get this?"

"I stole it from the Wolf. It's something I was supposed to return to its owner, in exchange for information. But I've since learned what I need to."

"Why is it shaped like a dragonfly?"

"Because the witch is *called* the Dragonfly. She lives near the Green Mill."

Jack accepted the amulet and met Leander's gaze. "You know where the Wolf's house is, don't you?"

Leander backed out the door. "Lily can't be taken out of the Ghostlands, Jack. I'll save her before the seven days are up. I'll kill Lot."

Then he was gone.

"Leander!" Jack felt the brass and glass dragonfly move in his hand. He unfolded his fingers and the amulet, now a mechanical insect, rose, twitching and clicking, from his palm to hover before him.

Jack said, hoarsely, "When I'm done burying my friend, take me to your witch."

AFTERWARD, BEFORE HE LEFT, Jack took the phoenix pendant Finn had given him from around his neck and reluctantly slid it into a cup of tea, leaving only the leather thong exposed.

"Clever girl. If you find your way here . . ."

CHAPTER 11

And Christabel awoke and spied
The same who lay down by her side—
O rather say, the same whom she
Raised up beneath the old oak tree.

—*The Rime of the Ancient Mariner*, Samuel Taylor
Coleridge

Finn fled into the forest, away from the swarming lights. When she glanced back, she saw the branches twist like wooden snakes to form a barrier behind her. The orbs broke into a glowing wall at the forest border and didn't follow.

She turned to face the forest. Mist crept across the ground. The trees were black oaks and firs, coiled together, mammoth, like towers. Toadstools as big as her hands and as richly colored as jewels—emerald, crimson, jet black—spilled over roots and slabs of rock. Only the whisper of wind-brushed leaves broke the silence.

Shivering and fighting a desire to collapse, Finn pushed forward, shoving at branches draped with moss, swatting aside creepers as thick as her wrists. When she accidentally snapped a branch, sap as warm as blood spattered her and she cried out, remembering how Reiko Fata had once turned Sylvie into a tree.

What sounded like a woman laughing in the darkness made her halt as a mind-wrenching terror shook her.

The laughter descended into a sobbing shriek and a death rattle groan. Finn pulled herself up into a tree and huddled there, felt the old enchantment, the desire to sleep, creeping up. But she couldn't sleep, not here, and despairingly fought it as her eyelids grew heavy. She was so cold, her body kept convulsing, but the tree was warm, its bulk sheltering her from whatever prowled the forest.

As she touched a sticky clot of blood where she'd scraped her forehead on a branch, she saw electric lights glowing through the leaves.

She stood up in the tree and nearly yelled with joy when she saw the neon sign of a Shell gas station beyond the forest. There was a busy highway in front of the gas station—*the true world*. Warmth, shelter, and safety.

After only a moment, Finn slid back down into the crook of the tree. If she walked out of this forest to that gas station, she would never get back to the Ghostlands. She would lose Lily.

She curled beneath the canopy of leaves, with the dark murk beneath her. Somewhere in this nightmare place, her sister walked the halls of the Wolf's house. *Lily. Are you really here?* She thought she might cry herself to sleep, but exhaustion hit her like a train.

A crack of wood shot through the silence, echoing. Sucking in a breath, Finn lifted her head and watched a massive shadow step out of the trees.

It was a prehistoric stag, as big as a car, its antlers hung with objects—a tiny china-doll head; a baby spoon; keys and jewelry. The stag glided majestically past her tree, into the dark, and, as it did, its form seemed to curl upright—until it walked as an antlered man, away from her. Her stunned gaze followed it.

Quelling an instinctive fear of the uncanny, something now familiar to her, she climbed down from the tree and prowled after the antlered shadow as it became a stag again.

Something brushed against her lips.

A large luna moth appeared from the dark. Dismay and joy tangled through her when she recognized the silvery death's head markings on its white wings. "*Moth!*"

She couldn't see the sky, but starlight permeated the forest as she and the moth followed the stag. The leaves rustled like ghost voices. The moth was a comforting luminary. As the stag led her through a blueberry thicket in a meadow frosted by starlight, she began to notice, in the trunks of some trees, knots that resembled twisted faces. She spotted the corroding hulk of a jeep near the stump of an oak.

She stepped on something that cracked and, startled, looked down to see a metal helmet like something out of World War I. As she continued on, she saw more helmets in tufts of moss and leaves, an old rifle disintegrating in the roots of a tree, a gas mask circled by red toadstools like little worshippers around an idol.

When the stag passed through a giant briar arch and vanished into the shadows, Finn hitched up her backpack. Arches here, she was beginning to realize, signified doors. So she stepped through.

Beyond a cluster of elms was a chain-link fence surrounding a black house that resembled an Italianate villa. In the front courtyard, ebony statues glistened, wreathed with blackberry briars. A red Cadillac rusted in the drive. It wasn't a scary house, but, rather, one that seemed to hold its secrets close.

The doors opened and something moved onto the porch.

A young woman emerged into the light. She was wearing a white dress and button-up boots. Her hair was short and scarlet. She clutched a plush toy—a black rabbit. A young man stepped to her side, his face wreathed with crimson curls. He was dressed in an old-fashioned suit and held a walking stick. The pair was as pale as bloodless things and, for a stomach-wrenching moment, Finn thought they didn't have eyes, until starlight glinted across them.

"Is it her?" The young woman nodded as if deciding something. "Yes. It must be her."

Finn began to back away. Remembering Jack's warning, she didn't reach for her silver dagger. Instead, she fumbled in her backpack for the Leica camera.

"We were sleeping." The young man had a deep voice. "I'm Roland. This is Ellen. We won't speak your name—there are eyes and ears in this forest, and although most are friendly, one must be cautious."

Finn pulled the Leica camera from her backpack and pressed the button. The young man flinched at the flash and said, "Stop that."

"Come in for tea." Ellen held open the door, revealing a cozy parlor with a fireplace and lamps. It didn't look like a bad fairy's house, but, then, none of them ever did, did they? "And shelter. The forest told us you were coming."

Still armed with the Leica, Finn moved cautiously toward the house. She trudged up the creaking stairs and the moth followed. Neither of the strangers said anything about the moth.

Ellen and Roland led her into a salon scattered with claw-footed furniture, old books, and toys that looked as if they'd come from the Edwardian era. As Ellen sat on a green velvet sofa, Roland clattered around in an antique kitchen Finn could see through glass doors smeared with lichen. She gingerly settled into an armchair that reeked of cigar smoke and kept the camera in her lap.

"You're bleeding." Ellen gently set aside the rabbit toy. "You can't do that here."

Finn touched the cut on her brow. She whispered, "What are you?"

Ellen sat primly, hands folded in her lap. "What a rude question."

"Sorry." Finn's fear ebbed. "I need to find . . . a place. Can you help me?"

The young woman's eyes were burgundy brown. Her skin breathed cold, but Finn had learned to not recoil from anything that looked human but wasn't. "Look, I need to get to Orsini's Books, at Crossroads."

"That's very far." Roland returned with a tarnished pewter tray full of tea things and some unsavory-looking muffins. As he set the tray down, he said, "Worldly food. It's old, but it's all we've got."

The tea looked fine, but the muffins had mold on them. As Finn held the teacup just to warm her numb hands, the moth settled on the cup's rim. "Do you know how I can get there?"

"The train." Roland sat beside Ellen and hunched forward, studying Finn. He took up the walking stick and twisted the handle shaped into the head of a horse. As the handle snapped off, he tilted down the staff and a tiny vial slipped into his hand. He lifted it to the light, revealing a liquid so purple it was almost black. He tossed the vial to Finn, who caught it and frowned down at the bottle swirled into an artwork of skeletons and fruiting vines with a brass skull for a lid. She whispered, "It's the elixir, isn't it? To conceal my blood."

"We bought it from the Blue Lady a long time ago. When we were different. One drop will make you as the Fatas are. It will mask your mortal scent." Ellen folded her hands in her lap. "If you take more, it'll change you, poison you."

Holding the vial as if it was a grenade—she wasn't about to drink anything given to her by strangers—Finn whispered, "How do I get to the train?"

"You'll have to go through Maraville to reach the train station."

The moth suddenly swirled up from the tea and flew across Finn's mouth.

"Look away," Roland said quietly, "from the moth."

Finn skewed her glance to a taxidermy wolverine on a nearby table.

The air cracked. Out of the corner of one eye, she saw a burst of light and shadow. A second later, she heard a British baritone shivering with breath. "Finn."

She turned her head to find Moth standing there, his eyes wide in the firelight, his dark hoodie and jeans making his skin seem paler. She moved to her feet and almost hugged him, but settled for a smile. "What *happened*?"

"A kiss. The girl selling soup at the fair asked for a kiss, and I changed the instant I did it. Twice now, I've brushed against your lips and become myself again."

"A kiss? So, in the forest, when you kept sweeping against me—but it didn't work."

"The Black Forest doesn't like transformations." Ellen looked out the window. "It won't allow that sort of thing. It used to be an army of mortal men, and they were enchanted by a *ban dorchadas*."

"A *ban dorchadas* is a witch," Moth reminded Finn, who, recalling the World War I helmets and rifles in the forest, shivered.

"You need to go to Harvest Station," Roland said. "There are maps in our attic, in a cigar box, I believe. We drew them. Do I know you?"

The question was directed at Moth, who squinted. "I don't remember."

Finn was gazing down at the elixir and wondering what it would do to her. She whispered, "What is Maraville?"

"A town. A rotted-out place. You need to trust us and drink that." Roland pointed to the vial.

Moth held out a hand. "Let me see that?"

She gave him the vial. He uncapped it, sniffed it, let a drop fall onto one thumb, and tasted it. He nodded and returned it to her. "It's safe. Go on. You'll need it. One drop."

"How do you—never mind." She thought of Jack searching for her, how he would worry. Could she trust Moth? She didn't have a choice. She tilted her head back and let one drop of the elixir fall onto her tongue.

She'd expected a kick—and got one; the elixir tasted of lightning and champagne, mist and berries. It made her insides warm like a blush and her eyes water. As she slid toward the floor, Moth caught her, and said, "Don't fight it."

She hunched over as her stomach heaved and closed her eyes.

When she opened them, the world had become one of exquisite details and colors so vivid they didn't seem real. She could see the patterns in Moth's irises, the strands of gold in his pewter hair. Ellen and Roland seemed as luminous as lamps, their hair so red it was like crimson velvet against their gloomy surroundings. She straightened and felt every muscle glide beneath her skin. Her exhaustion had vanished. Strength coiled through her.

Moth pointed a finger at her. "*Don't* get used to it."

She moved around the salon, touching things—a porcelain figurine, a bottle of dried figs, a selection of rusting metal keys. She could see the most delicate details. Everything had a scent and seemed to have a secret; the world had become hyperreal. She heard Roland say, "In the attic, there are trunks of other people's belongings. You may find things you can use."

Finn turned. "Why are there other people's things in your attic?"

"Seth Lot used to bring his captives here." Ellen reached for Roland's hand, clasped it. "It's called stitchery, what he does, to make Jacks and Jills."

Finn flinched. "You mean, he *murdered* them here?"

"He murdered *us* here."

With these words, Ellen and Roland vanished. The parlor descended into dusky shadows. The red light from a new morning bled over the rotting furniture and the button eyes of the toy rabbit on the floor. Cold and dust drifted through the room. Finn couldn't move. She wondered if she'd ever be warm again with the elixir frosting her blood.

She felt Moth's hand close over hers. "Finn."

She wanted to go home. She tucked the vial of elixir into her backpack. "Let's go to the attic and find some useful things."

As she walked into the hall, a disturbingly familiar perfume that reminded her of nightshade and snakes drifted over her.

She and Moth stepped into a high-ceilinged chamber shaped like an octagon, its art deco furniture shrouded beneath cobwebs. The black floor, patterned with crimson spades, was littered with leaves, the red walls hung with large paintings of ruins in the wilderness. A stairway curved up in the chamber's center.

Finn glimpsed her reflection in a large mirror framed by pewter leaves—she'd become a shadowy-eyed girl with tangled hair and a feral face. When she tilted her head, her eyes glinted oddly. She looked around, realized she could see *in the dark*. "Moth, can you see?"

"Of course. It's the elixir."

The elixir. She walked toward a huge fireplace and tried not to think about exactly what that stuff was doing to her. On the fireplace's mantelpiece was a clock with thirteen numbers, its hands turning backward. Above it was a painting of a Victorian coach and horses plunging through a forest.

Moth began trudging up the rotting stairs—she reluctantly followed. They ascended to a black hallway with waxy vines tentacling over the walls. At the hall's end was a large room, its glass ceiling blossoming with dusky light. They entered the glass-ceilinged chamber. Moth opened a porcelain cabinet shaped like a girl to reveal a collection of gleaming knives. He whistled. Finn, moving past him, said, "Won't weapons invite danger?"

"Nevertheless . . ." He began selecting a few.

Finn walked toward a bed hung with sooty velvet and surrounded by furniture shaped like grotesque animals. Glimpsing a shadowy figure seated in a chair, she flinched before realizing the figure was made of wax, with silk hair and glass eyes. She remembered the wax doll in the Scarborough pavilion, the one that had belonged to Seth Lot's Jill, and whispered, "Moth."

He sauntered to the doll, leaned toward it. "There's a tag."

"What kind of tag?"

"A label tag." He read it: "'This is Adonyss, who used to lure youths to dark places and drink their blood.' Sounds like a pervy bastard."

Finn skewed her gaze from the wax doll. "That used to be *alive*?"

"He was a Fata."

She bumped into a chair, and flinched, because the chair was carved into the realistic image of a seated man, his eyes closed. There was a tag hanging from one arm. Nearby was a bronze lamp shaped like a girl. The lamp also had a label. Finn's skin crawled. "Were they all *alive*?"

"I'm thinking they were."

She looked at the bed—the looming headboard consisted of several curled male and female figures. She swerved her gaze upward, to the portrait hung above it.

Her breath caught in her throat.

The painting was of a young man in Victorian clothes, one booted leg slung over an arm of the chair in which he was sprawled. He held a jackal-headed walking stick in a jeweled hand and long, dark hair set off a princely profile, familiar, yet alien to her.

Lily had once told Finn that her favorite god in mythology was Dionysus—not the mad, dark wine-god Dionysus, the wildling who drove girls and boys crazy, but the gentle god who defended girls by revealing to them their strengths, the one who led people away from crazy. That was who Jack reminded her of, in his portrait above the grotesque bed.

She turned and found, on the opposite wall, a framed poster of a young woman with black bangs above electric-green eyes: Reiko Fata as a '60s Biba girl.

"This place"—her heart crashed—"belonged to Jack and Reiko."

Moth glanced up from studying another chair. He frowned.

Jack, she thought, *this is part of your past, this terrible place.* "Where's the attic? We need to find Ellen and Roland's maps and get out of here."

THE ATTIC OF THE BLACK HOUSE was a robbers' den. Moth flung open the lids of steamer trunks and crates and started raiding.

"How long has he been taking people?" Finn looked around at the opened trunks, the coats and boots and jewelry and weapons. She felt sick at the thought of Jack being here while the Wolf murdered.

"Judging by the age of some of these things, quite a long time." Moth was crouched near a trunk, studying an antique pistol in his hands.

"You're really taking that?"

"No. No bullets or gunpowder."

She glanced again at the sad, discarded clothes and objects: a leather book titled *Animals of the Western Hemisphere*, a tin of cigarettes, an artist's paintbrush, a . . . tooth nestled in a black velvet jewelry box.

"The cigar box!" She grabbed it from a shelf beneath a round window and found, inside of it, a book of red leather with a butterfly embossed in black on its cover. She opened the book to find its pages illustrated with maps stained by age and spilled coffee. Two names were scrawled on the cover page: *Ellen Byrd* and *Roland Childe*. It was a journal—and there were photographs that looked as though they'd been taken in the 1930s. In one of them, Ellen and Roland, in aviator caps and jackets, crouched before a small plane. "They were *explorers . . .*"

"They got lost and they were found by Lot. Let's see the maps."

She handed the book to Moth. Experiencing a bitter anger at the fate of Ellen and Roland, she began searching for things that might be used as weapons against the Fatas. No silver. No iron. Those things decayed here.

"Here's Maraville." Moth was studying one of the maps. "It's not far."

THEY LEFT THE HOUSE and Moth led her back into the forest, where Finn felt safe amid the oaks and pines and dark earth scents. They stayed on the road, passing a few decrepit farmhouses, a gas station nested with bats, and two trashed cars.

When they pushed through a curtain of ivy and saw the glisten of metal in the trees, Finn halted. Beside her, Moth also regarded the small airplane molded into the branches of an enormous oak. He said softly, "Betwixt and between. They must have flown through one of the spots where the Ghostlands and the true world cross."

Finn thought of Ellen and Roland, aviators, explorers who had found an uncharted place that had killed them. She thought of girls and boys like Moth and Nathan, stolen out of their lives. "How do you bear it?"

"I think of the place I came from. There were good things, familiar things. Then I think, if I'd lived out my life, back then, I would have died of plague or starvation. Or, more likely, murder. I realize that now is not so bad. And I'm one of the lucky ones."

"But you're still broken."

"But your sister put me back together."

The road soon narrowed to a lane winding through a wood of gnarled trees draped with cobwebs and creepers. The toadstools underfoot were luminous, producing small puffs of spores when stepped on. Finn kept a hand over her mouth and nose until they'd cleared the fungi. As they passed beneath a vast, glittering spiderweb, she wondered what Ghostlands spiders looked like, shuddered, and attempted another conversation, "Who turned you into a moth? Was it Absalom?"

"I don't know."

They halted, staring across a field of red flowers at a sprawling building surrounded by dead trees, its windows boarded up, its bricks splotched with lichen and strange graffiti. A giant crack ran up the middle of its stairway, where a figure lay. Beyond the building, surrounded by a forest of firs and pines, was a town that looked as though it had expired from urban blight.

"I don't like the look of that school." Finn, thumbs crooked in the straps of her backpack, wondered if the elixir was making her insanely brave. The field, she realized, the red flowers, were poppies.

"And that must be Maraville. Harvest Station should be straight down that road. Past those houses. You did notice the figure on the stairs?"

Finn had seen it. "Let's go."

The school's shadow seemed to slime their skin as they approached. The sudden gloom cut into Finn's courage a little. The boarded windows and the huge doors made her uneasy. She could smell mold and dead things.

When she recognized the body on the stairs, she began to run, her boots tearing at poppies as a name ripped from her throat. "Sylvie? *Sylvie!*"

She reached the figure on the stairs and knelt beside her friend, pushing the black braids away from Sylvie's pale face. Moth, crouching near, said, "She's breathing. How did she *get* here?"

Finn couldn't answer. "Sylvie. Please *wake up*."

Sylvie opened her eyes and croaked, "Finn?"

Finn heaved a sigh and sat back on her heels. A world without impetuous, optimistic Sylvie was unthinkable.

"I found you." Sylvie let her head fall back. "I can't believe I found you."

"*What are you doing here?*" Finn helped her sit up. The other girl was dressed for winter in tartan trousers and a coat lined with fake fur. Her eyes and nose were red, as if she'd been crying. She hugged Finn. "We sort of got a key."

"*We?* There's no 'we,' Sylvie. You're the only one here."

"*Christie.*" Sylvie scrambled up.

"*Christie?*" Finn stood with her friend as Sylvie looked frantically around and said, "Christie! He came with me—I let go of his hand . . . oh, *Finn.*" Sylvie began stomping in a circle, pushing her fingers through her braids. "I let go of his hand when we came through—it was like we were pulled apart. I walked so far to find him . . ."

"Sylvie, *how did you get here?*" Finn wanted to grab her and shake her as terror for Christie made her almost crazy.

"The Black Scissors. He sent us. He wanted me to tell you about Seth Lot . . .

how he can die—poisoning, pinning, and decapitation. Those three, together, are the only way to kill an ancient Fata." She unslung the walking stick and handed it to Finn, who carefully accepted it. Sylvie said, "It's a sword, inside. Don't draw it until you're ready to kill Seth Lot."

"I'm not here to kill Seth Lot." Finn stood very still—the idea was nightmarish. She was selfishly glad to see Sylvie but, at the same time, furious at her friend's recklessness.

Sylvie glanced around. "Finn—where's Jack?"

"We've lost him. It's a long story. We're on our way to him now. Why did you bring your bow and arrows?" She didn't let herself think of Christie, alone.

Sylvie shouldered her little backpack and the aluminum quiver of arrows, her bow. "The Black Scissors told me to bring weapons. How are we going to find Christie?"

Moth was gazing at the school. "We need to leave here before nightfall."

"Why?"

"Something is nesting in that building."

"*Christie* might be in there." Sylvie took a step toward it, but Moth grabbed her wrist. "No. There is no mortal blood in that place." He glanced at Sylvie. "And *your* blood will be obvious to whatever hides in there."

Another chill swept over them as the swings on the school's playground began to sway, creaking. The field of poppies rustled. Sylvie backed away. "What is that smell? Roadkill?"

"Ladies," Moth said, "we need to depart *now*."

They all looked toward Maraville, the collection of houses sunk in rot and neglect. Finn said, "Christie might be *there*."

She strode toward the town. Sylvie and Moth followed, plunging into the field of poppies, occasionally glancing over their shoulders at the school, which seemed to be darkening as evening prowled across the sky. They entered the town through a lot of towering pines and dense firs that would have been beautiful if it weren't for the menace of the nearby school and the hollow and vine-knotted houses without tenants. When they reached a blacktop road littered with crimson leaves and shattered by tree roots, they trudged past more colonial-style houses claimed by the wild.

"Finn," Sylvie whispered, " . . . your eyes . . . they just went silver."

"I took something that disguised my blood," Finn explained, and she tried not to seem startled—Jack hadn't told her about any side effects from the elixir, such as seeing in the dark and her eyes turning a different color.

"*'Drink me.'*" Sylvie halted. "The Black Scissors said to drink something when we crossed over . . . I didn't see anything, because Christie was gone . . . I for-got—"

"Here." Finn rummaged in her backpack and drew out the bottle of elixir.

A rock shattered the bottle in her hand.

They whirled, frantically looking around for whatever had flung the rock. A weird whistle, as if someone was pretending to be a bird, came from within the forest.

Finn dragged Sylvie against her as Moth ducked into the doorway of a little building, its glass window painted with the words DETROIT'S BEST COFFEE. She looked around at the shadows between the houses and tensely said, "What is it?"

"I don't know. We're going *there*." Moth pointed to a rusting school bus parked on the side of the road.

They dashed toward the bus. Moth pushed open the doors and practically shoved Finn and Sylvie into the vehicle before leaping up and shutting the doors tight. He looked around. "It's iron. Sometimes iron remains before the Ghost-lands changes it—"

Sylvie screamed.

Finn nearly did the same when she saw the flower-wreathed skeleton, like some kind of grotesque altarpiece, at the back of the bus. She dragged her gaze from it as Moth walked toward it, to examine it. She didn't feel any less horrified when he said, "It's not real bone. It's coral. These are Fata remains."

"Fata? How did it get past iron?"

"Well, it's dead. There are only two things here that can get past iron—changelings and *sluagh*."

"You think *changelings* dragged it in here? Or dead—"

Something crashed onto the roof of the school bus. They drew together, away from the broken windows. Outside, a shadow glided past. Something laughed like a deranged schoolboy, and the reek of roadkill drifted in with the fragrance of flowers.

Moth slid two blades from within his jacket. Sylvie glanced admiringly at them before swinging the bow from her shoulder and drawing an arrow from the quiver. Her hands were shaking.

Then a girl's voice—it had something wrong with it—prowled around the bus, "Come out, come out, from the big yellow bus. Come out, come out, and get eaten by us."

The taunt was followed by one of the most terrifying silences of Finn's life.

Something began to breathe, brokenly, beneath one of the windows. Sylvie, her eyes wide, aimed her bow and drawn arrow at that window. A figure wearing a plastic possum mask peered in, ducked down.

When several figures in masks began clambering through the windows, regardless of the jagged glass, Finn shouted, "*Bail!*"

Finn and Sylvie ran toward the exit. Moth slammed one hand on the doors' mechanism. As the doors fell open, Finn and Sylvie lunged out, past two more figures in plastic masks. Finn heard Moth shout, "Keep running!" as she and Sylvie raced toward an ivy-clotted alley between two boarded-up houses. She glanced back to see Moth heading in another direction, followed by several of the masked creatures.

As Sylvie hauled herself over a fence, Finn heard running steps behind her and a piercing whistle from the pine trees surrounding the houses. She glanced over her shoulder to see a figure in a suit and plastic crow mask loping after them.

She and Sylvie fled across a yard, toward a cottage in a cavern of weeds and creepers. Sylvie grabbed Finn's hand, pulling her into the creepers, and they slid along the paint-peeling exterior of the house, to the cottage's back door. Sylvie indicated a window to the left, which was open.

They heard more whistling.

Finn pulled herself over the windowsill, and Sylvie followed. They dashed through a kitchen where yellow wallpaper peeled from the walls, and an old refrigerator covered with souvenir magnets and faded photos was open to reveal rotting food in a slant of sulfurous light.

When another whistle came from outside, Finn and Sylvie dove to the linoleum and crawled toward a closet door. Finn reached up, grasped the knob, and winced as the door creaked. As they crept into the closet and shut the door, she could clearly see Sylvie's white face in the dark. Finn pressed her brow against her drawn-up knees.

The cottage door crashed open. She reached out to grip Sylvie's hand.

Something heavy hit the floor. There came the sickening sound of a blade being driven into flesh, a pained cry. The second time they heard the noise, Finn drew the silver dagger. Sylvie, who had lost her bow, pulled two arrows from the aluminum quiver and held them like knives.

There was a murmur, a cough, a gargling voice. It was unbearable—

The closet door flew open.

Finn shouted as she was dragged out, the dagger wrenched from her hand. She heard Sylvie scream.

Moth was crouched near the door, his hands pinned to the floor by two blades. He despairingly met her gaze through a tangle of hair. Standing around him were several figures in stained and torn school uniforms, each wearing a plastic mask representing an animal—an alligator, a crow, a fox, a rabbit, a possum.

The rabbit—a girl—sauntered forward as Finn rose unsteadily, keeping her back to the wall. Sylvie, on the floor, scrambled across it until she was against Finn's legs. They'd taken away Sylvie's arrows. There were scratches on her cheek.

"Well," Rabbit Girl said, eyes shining in the hollows of the mask. "I smell blood."

As terror spiraled into an insane anger, Finn found her voice. "What do you want?"

Rabbit Girl came closer. There were old bloodstains on her blouse and kilt. Her dirty blond braids were knotted with ribbons and plastic charms. She smelled like poppies and something dead.

"What do we want?" The girl leaned forward, and Finn looked away from eyes that glinted like beetles. "Well, we're hungry."

Sylvie lunged up, slamming the arrow she'd hidden into Rabbit Girl's chest. As the girl staggered back, Sylvie and Finn launched themselves past her, toward Moth.

The animal-masked figures blocked the door, but Finn and Sylvie managed to yank the kitchen knives from Moth's hands before pulling him up between them. This time, he bled.

"You should have kept running." His voice scraped out. The muscles in his arm were steely against the back of Finn's neck. "I could have kept them away."

Rabbit Girl plucked the arrow from her chest. The point of the weapon dripped papery-red petals as more petals slid from the tear in her skin.

"You're a Jill." Moth straightened, sliding his arms from around Finn's and Sylvie's shoulders and standing on his own. He looked around at the masked creatures. "You're all bloody Jacks and Jills."

"That's not what we're called." The boy wearing the alligator mask gestured gracefully to his companions. "We are the dead. And you are in our territory."

"So"—there was a smile in Rabbit Girl's voice as she twirled the arrow in one grubby hand—"you're our evening's entertainment."

Finn spotted her backpack nearby, along with the jackal-headed walking stick. As the Jacks and Jills closed in, she began sliding along the wall. Moth tensed. Sylvie was whispering a prayer in Japanese.

Something caught the light on Rabbit Girl's wrist—a pewter spoon twisted into a bracelet, like something made in an arts and crafts class. The crow wore battered Nikes. The alligator had on a Star Wars watch.

All the little details clicked. They were kids, teenagers transformed into these horrors, probably by the Fata whose coral skeleton decorated the interior of the school bus.

Moth began to whisper and she recognized the words from Ovid, one of Christie's favorite classical writers: "'*She came to Envy's house, a black abode. Ill-kept, stained with dark gore, a hidden home.*'"

The masked figures halted. Rabbit Girl tilted her head as Moth continued, "'*In a deep valley where no sunshine comes, where no wind blows, gloaming and full of cold.*'"

The creatures, listening, didn't move as Moth said to them, "There was a queen who took each of you, wasn't there?"

Finn reached for the jackal-headed walking stick and her backpack—

—a gloved hand gripped her throat and pushed her against the wall.

The point of Eve Avaline's silver dagger glittered before her eyes as Caliban smiled beyond its length. "Hullo again, darling. I rode the shadow all the way here, just to be with you."

Sylvie grabbed Moth's arm as he lunged at Caliban.

"Children." Caliban slowly turned his head, his hair shifting like white satin. "Children, I am disappointed. I thought you'd have taken them apart by now—although this morsel belongs to the *Madadh aillaid*." He smiled at Finn, who clawed at his wrist in a frantic attempt to get his hand away so that she could breathe. He said, "Know how I found you? I caught a scent when I left Scarborough—*her* blood." He nodded at Sylvie.

Moth stepped forward, but Rabbit Girl and Alligator pointed butcher knives at him. He halted.

Caliban looked Moth up and down. "You've been brought low, haven't you?"

The *crom cu* flipped Eve's dagger, slid it into its elder wood scabbard, and tucked it into the pocket of Finn's coat. When he released her from the stranglehold, she collapsed to the floor, rasping in lungfuls of air. He'd put the dagger in her coat as a tease, hoping she'd reach for it so he could hurt her again.

Without taking his gaze from her, Caliban said, "I remember who you are, Moth. Lot told me what was done to you. Move again and I take one of her eyes."

Sylvie tugged Moth back as Caliban told Finn, "The Wolf didn't expect you to call in allies, darling."

Finn pointed at the silent Jacks and Jills. "Why don't you tell *them* what I did to make your master angry?"

"Glad to." Caliban turned to face the Jacks and Jills in their animal masks and ruined uniforms. "She is a queen killer. She killed the *ban nathair*. Reiko."

"It was *her*?" The possum stared at Finn as the others whispered among themselves—admiringly.

This wasn't the reaction Caliban had expected. He spoke as if he were addressing idiots. "She murdered a *queen*. *Your* queen. You were her subjects. Now you are nothing."

Rabbit Girl stepped forward. "We are nothing because of that Fata bitch in the school bus, the one who lured us into a lake, drowned us, and gave us to the Wolf so that he could stitch us up. Was *your* queen like that?" The rabbit mask tilted malevolently.

Caliban evidently hadn't expected *that* reaction. He slid a dagger from his coat and snarled, "Cursed *sluagh* . . ."

Ignoring Moth and Sylvie now, the masked teenagers moved forward, their attention fixed on Caliban. The *crom cu*'s voice twisted, "I'll take each of you apart and gnaw the bones."

As the *sluagh* circled him, his coat began to writhe with shadows.

Finn, edging toward the door, grabbed her backpack and the walking stick.

Alligator lunged and slammed a rusty steak knife into Caliban's shoulder. The *crom cu*'s yell descended into an animal howl as Finn, Sylvie, and Moth dashed out of the cottage, into the pine forest.

FINN COLLAPSED beneath a giant fir's downward-sweeping branches. Moth dropped to his knees beside her. Sylvie leaned against the tree, her breath like sobs. Finn reached up and pulled her down and they huddled together. As Finn met Moth's gaze over her friend's head, he raised his hands. The knife wounds were gone.

Finn let her head fall back against the tree. "How will we get to Orsini's?"

"Finn." Sylvie's voice was soft with wonder. "What is that, through the trees?"

Finn followed her gaze to a platform and a brick building with a quaint air of '60s Britain. By the time she realized what it was, the mournful whistle of a train was echoing through the air.

CHAPTER 12

I shall grow up, but never grow old,
I shall always, always be very cold,
I shall never come back again.

—"THE CHANGELING," CHARLOTTE MEW

The dragonfly of brass and crimson glass that was Jack's guide paused in its arrowing flight, as grief for Orsini, who had been like a father to Jack, crashed over him and he slid down against a tree. Then he thought of Finn with Caliban, and adrenaline—that lovely, mortal elixir—shot through him. He pushed to his feet.

The insect led him past a railroad track to a derelict station. After mounting the station's steps and finding no signs of life in the carved, wooden building, he pressed his brow against the door and thought, *Finn. I should never have brought you here.*

The dragonfly led him down the tracks, into a grove of willow trees, their fronds veiling a lichen-scummed pond gleaming green in the fulvous light. A deteriorating mill house shadowed the water, its giant wheel sinking, its exterior slimy with algae and rippling scallops of fungi. A yew to one side curled over the building, its branches clutching. Moving among the willows, Jack noticed bones scattered in the tree roots, in the mud around the pond. Whatever had taken up residence in the mill hadn't been here long—there were only a few bones. There was also a blinged-out Chevy pickup truck in the dirt driveway. *That* made Jack cautious.

He turned to the dragonfly, which clicked as it hovered in place. "I'm guessing your witch wants me to put an end to something here? She knows I'm not Jack Daw anymore, right?"

A terrified cry from the mill house made him curse—it had been a human voice. He prowled toward the sounds of splashing in the darkness between the mill wheel and the pond. Then he saw the mill's resident.

The Fata seemed to be a giant shadow, its true form—monstrous and horse-headed—blurring as it moved shoulder-deep in the water, its teeth bared, its eyes like pearls. Fish slid from its tangled mane. Its body coiled over the victim frantically paddling to keep his head above the water.

Jack drew the jackal-headed *kris* from his coat. "*Uisce!*"

The Fata in the water became a pattern of shadow and light, glided back into the darkness beneath the mill wheel, and reemerged as a smiling, black-haired man waist-deep in the water. Green runes glistened around his muscled arms and torso. He wore a necklace of human teeth and smiled as if he and Jack had just met in the local pub. "*Jack?* Jack *Daw?* When did you get back?"

When he recognized the Fata, Jack didn't let his dismay show, but smiled back, comrade-like, "Not long ago, Ivan Vodyanoi. What are you doing eating veal? I thought you liked a fight?"

"I do. And these boys *fight*. They step right into my pond, thanks to that Way over there." He gestured in the general direction of the train station Jack had found abandoned. "Straight from the true world. This one"—he pointed at his flailing victim—"is covered in scrawlings. I couldn't quite sink my teeth into him, so, if you don't mind . . ." He began wading through the deep water as if he were walking.

The victim yelled out, splashing in the shallows at Jack's feet. Keeping his gaze on Vodyanoi, Jack reached down. A wet hand gripped his. Jack pulled the victim out, heard him sputter, "*Jack?*"

His astonished gaze dropped to the boy spitting up water and shuddering. "*Christopher Hart?*"

"Gentlemen." Vodyanoi was in the shallows before them now, his smile broad, his arms stretched to either side. "I'm hungry. If you'll leave, Jack Daw, I'd be grateful, since I never interrupted any of *your* kills."

"I'm not Jack Daw anymore."

Ivan Vodyanoi's black eyes narrowed. He said, "You are Jack Daw. The one I taught how to play the violin like a devil. The one I taught how to kill in the water."

Jack had a creeping memory of sitting near Orsini's pond while this creature showed him how to play an instrument of bone, and he experienced a bizarre affection for Vodyanoi. He said, "I am Jack Hawthorn now."

"Jack. *Jack*." Vodyanoi's smile returned. "Do you really think a name change is going to make you any less of a predator than the rest of us?"

"I am not"—Jack spoke in a low voice—"like you."

"No." Vodyanoi's smile grew until the entire lower half of his face seemed all curved teeth. "You are not. You'll come apart easily now."

Darkness slid over Vodyanoi as he began to ride the shadow. He vanished within it.

Christie shouted. Jack grabbed him and yanked him away.

Then Vodyanoi collapsed into a smoky pool drifting on the water. Jack stepped back. "Christopher, I want you to run when I say—follow the dragonfly—"

Darkness swept up from the pond. Jack was slammed against the ground so hard, he felt as if his brain had been struck loose. He clenched his teeth and tried to move as, beside him, Vodyanoi's black mass settled back into the form of the man with the dark hair. Ivan waved a forefinger at Jack as if he'd been naughty, before rising and walking toward Christie, who was trying to crawl away.

Jack hated that the resurrected mortality he'd sought for so long was a weakness here. He hauled himself to his feet as Ivan gazed down at Christie, who, with a sob, had given up, his face in the grass. Vodyanoi said, "Well, maybe I'll take your eyes out first, Jack. You can always hear the boy scream—"

As Ivan turned, Jack launched himself at the water Fata, the misericorde in one hand, the *kris* in the other.

"WHAT IS IT WITH YOU and water monsters?" Jack sat with Christie on the bank of the mill pond as what was left of Ivan Vodyanoi—a sludge of putrefying water plants, bones, and human teeth—sank into the earth.

"Both eyes." Christie was blank with shock. Every now and then, he would shudder. There were pond weeds in his hair. "You got him in both eyes, with one move. And you're not even a Jack anymore."

Jack had checked himself for injuries, found only minor cuts and bruises. He grabbed the cuff of Christie's coat, pulled up one sleeve, frowned at the words scrawled in black ink over the boy' s skin—his arms, throat, hands—everywhere but his face. Jack felt something else at work, then, and hope, a rare thing for him, sparked.

"The marks just appeared when I got here." Christie spasmed again. "I think Phouka did it to protect me, back home."

"Didn't work, did it? And how did you *get* here?"

"A dragonfly key from the Black Scissors. We stuck it in StarDust Studio's door, me and Sylvie."

"Where is Sylvie now?"

"I don't *know*." Christie put his head in his hands, his voice breaking. "We were together when we stepped through. Something pulled us apart."

"You lost her."

When Christie looked up, his eyes were rimmed with red. "Where is Finn?"

"I lost her. Am I going to hear it from you? No? Good."

"Jack, what are we going to *do*?" Christie abruptly hunched over and was sick in the grass.

Jack glanced at the artificial dragonfly hovering in the branches above. "We're going to find Finn and Sylvie."

The sudden buzzing of cicadas made him climb to his feet. When a drop of blood fell onto his sleeve, he raised a hand to his ear, felt more blood leaking from it. He wanted to move and couldn't. "Christopher. Something—"

The buzzing faded into the sweetest sound he'd ever heard—his mother's voice singing an Irish lullaby. A languorous peace hazed over the horror of the past hour. He moved in the direction of the song—

Someone shouted his name before tackling him into the grass. The warmth ran from him like blood. The world became a chilly patch of willows and water—green ivy was twisted around his wrists and legs, was creeping toward his throat. He didn't see his mother, but a woman made of ivy, one mad green eye watching him as she bared human teeth in the skull of her head.

Jack had seen some bad things on his visits to the Ghostlands, but never anything like this. One rarely saw her kind, because most were dead by the time they realized what had gotten hold of them.

Christie, who had tackled him, hurdled toward the creature, a wooden dagger in one hand. He slammed it into the green woman's skull. The creature's scream nearly deafened Jack, who pressed his hands over his ears and watched as the green woman disintegrated into a tattered drift of dead vegetation and withered ivy. Her skull fell at Christie's feet.

"Siren." Jack pulled himself up. "Ivan's lover was a bloody siren."

"You nearly got taken out by that monster's girlfriend?" Christie was still holding the wooden dagger that had cracked open the siren's skull. He began to sway a little. Jack hoped he wouldn't faint. Or vomit again. They needed to leave. What if there was a brood?

Then Jack looked at the boy, wondering. "You didn't hear it. The siren. Why didn't it affect you?"

"Don't know. I've got implants." He gathered his hair back from one ear to reveal a small metal disk. "I got them when I was a kid. Hearing impairment."

Jack said carefully, "Technology shouldn't work here, but you didn't register the siren's voice because of those. Interesting."

Christie stared down at the siren's skull and began to turn a greenish color. "What would have happened if I'd heard her, too?"

"Well." Jack sauntered to Ivan Vodyanoi's remains. "She would have wrapped us up nice and tight. She would have drained us of our bodily fluids. Within a few days, we would have been two mummified corpses."

"I wish I hadn't asked—what are you doing?"

Jack was crouched beside Vodyanoi's bits and was picking out the human teeth. "Human teeth are valuable in the Ghostlands."

"That's so horribly wrong." Christie was staring nervously at the siren's skull, as if expecting it to jump at him.

"Why don't you smash the teeth out of that?" Jack gestured to the skull.

Christie's voice was faint. "I'm not touching it."

Jack tossed the Indonesian *kris* to him and said, "Keep that. Try not to fall on it. Get the teeth from that skull, Christopher. We may need to bribe some people to save Finn and Sylvie."

Christie glanced down at the skull, muttered, "You really are a psychopath. I think I'm going to be sick again. That guy was going to *eat* me."

"Well, there's no accounting for other people's tastes."

❖ ❖ ❖

CHRISTIE WAS IN HELL.

They were following a metal bug, which, when he stared at it long enough, seemed to become a tiny winged woman of brass and glass. He kept picturing Sylvie caught by something worse than Ivan Vodyanoi and thought of Finn stalked by that terrifying Fata man with the wolf-blue eyes. He regretted the loss of his backpack, which had had clothes, food, the useless phone, and a switchblade in it. They hadn't been able take Ivan Vodyanoi's truck because Jack said only Fatas could work vehicles here. More damn fairy magic.

"Is Tinkerbell leading us in a *helpful* direction?"

"Yes. What did the Black Scissors tell you?"

"The Black Scissors told Sylvie how that bastard Lot can be killed, since you can't shove him into a sacrificial green fire. He said you need to do three things: poison him, stab him, and cut off his head. Is that dragonfly a *fairy*?"

"You'll need to cease using that word if you appreciate breathing. It's stopped." Jack indicated the dragonfly, which had darted up into a tree and appeared to be sulking. "There now—you've insulted it with the 'f' word."

Christie wished he could stop shivering. "How can you be so calm?"

Jack turned, his eyes shadowy. "I believe this Dragonfly witch is allied with the Black Scissors. The dragonfly seems to be a popular motif with our coconspirators."

"The dragonfly key . . . the Black Scissors said it would lead us to a witch who would help us . . ." Christie went quiet, imagining Sylvie alone in this place of horrors. She'd always been a beacon of common sense to him, and she'd talked him down from some crazy things—like running away with Victoria Tudor when he was twelve years old. What if Sylvie was dead? When his mind ventured in that direction, he felt breathless and dizzy, as if the ground was moving. He groaned and sank to a crouch.

He heard Jack walking back to him, leaves crackling beneath his boots, then Jack's calm voice. "Breathe deep, head between your knees. Don't pass out. I won't be carrying you."

"Okay. Okay, I'm good. Sylvie isn't dead. And Finn is safe. How did you lose Finn?"

"Caliban took her."

"Oh *God* . . ."

Jack looked up at the dragonfly and snapped his fingers. "Get down here and do your job. The *crom cu* won't hurt her—the Wolf isn't done playing."

As the steampunk dragonfly swept onward, Christie stood. Jack said, "What else did you have to tell me?"

Christie breathed out. "Sylv has the sword the Black Scissors gave us to kill the Wolf. It's special iron sheathed in elder wood. Phouka never told you about how to kill Lot?"

Jack was grim. "No. What else?"

Christie hunched his shoulders and whispered, "The Black Scissors said Lily Rose can leave the Wolf's house, but not the Ghostlands. Something bad will happen."

"If Lily Rose is here, we're not leaving her." Jack turned away and they followed the dragonfly to a stairway of mossy, root-tangled wood that sloped up into a darker forest.

Christie tentatively asked, "So who suggested visiting this witch?"

"Leander Cyrus."

"The guy who tricked Finn's sister?"

"Cyrus was a pawn."

"And what if Caliban's delivered Finn to the Wolf? What are we going to do—"

"The Wolf doesn't have Finn. Finn is clever. She's resourceful." Jack glanced back at Christie. "And I believe in her."

JACK HALTED and watched the tinkered dragonfly glide toward a thicket of elder trees through which very little light entered. He could smell, in that gloom, the tang of baneberry and belladonna, the sharpness of crowfoot and nightshade, the earthy venom of wormwood and Death Angel mushrooms. As the metal dragonfly flickered in that darkness exuding the noxious perfume of earthborn poisons, Jack turned to Christie, who looked wretched and fragile. He sloughed his coat and tossed it to the boy. When Christie caught it, Jack said, "There's a bottle in the left pocket. You need to drink a drop of what's in it before we go near any sort of *ban dorchadas*."

Christie gratefully tugged on the coat and pulled out the precious bottle of elixir. "What is a ban dork—"

"A witch." Jack pointed at the bottle. "One drop."

"What'll it do?"

"It'll disguise the smell of your blood. It was meant for Finn." Jack's voice broke on her name. He hated himself for having left her for even those few minutes with Moth, and he felt a surge of the ugly violence that had ruled his life for so long.

Christie reluctantly took one drop of the elixir, froze, and appeared stunned. A hint of silver shone in his dark eyes as he gaped at Jack. "This is . . . all these *colors*." He turned in a circle. "I feel like I just got shot up with adrenaline. Is this what you felt as a Jack?"

"Somewhat. Only hollow and cold and without remorse."

As Jack began walking, Christie trudged after him, still gazing around in wonder. "So this witch'll find Finn and Sylv?"

"And give me something to keep Seth Lot's pack from tracking me—at the moment, my blood is like the damn aurora borealis and that elixir won't do the trick."

"Is it because of what happened to you? That whole zombie-corpse-resurrection thing?"

Jack cast him a stern look. "We need to be quiet now."

They prowled through the twisting trees, which grew so close he and Christie sometimes had to step sideways. When they came to a rusting sign that read STORYBOOKVILLE, Christie halted. Draped by kudzu and weeds, the sign was accompanied by a metal statue of a knight on a horse. The paint was peeling from the horse's panoply. The knight's lance was broken, and there was an old bird's nest on his head.

They continued on along a root-entwined path. They passed a decrepit concession stand that creaked in the occasional wind ghosting among the trees. As they drew near a pink, miniature castle stained with dead leaves, one of its towers coiled with an oak, Christie wondered out loud what kind of amusement park Storybookville had been. Jack said, "Evidently not a very popular one."

They stepped into a clearing surrounded by a garden of wild plants and found a pretty cottage painted black, its door and roof tiles scarlet. Wind chimes shaped like insects hung from crooked apple trees. Roses the same ruby hue as the apples latticed lamp-lit windows. They could hear music crackling from some archaic device within.

In fairy tales and in Jack's world, cottages were often deceptively charming domiciles that housed blood and horror. Jack didn't move as the dragonfly skirled to the door, where it dropped and hit the stone path and became a metal amulet.

As Christie studied the cottage with the appropriate apprehension, Jack moved forward and picked up the dragonfly amulet.

The red door opened.

Sylvie Whitethorn stood on the threshold.

"Sylvie!" Christie ran forward, but he was stopped by Jack's arm as Jack said quietly, "That's not Sylvie."

They drew back. The girl's gown was a silky gossamer darkness that clung to curves Sylvie Whitethorn didn't have. Her hair, a fall of licorice black, was knotted with tiny braids and talismans. When she tilted her head, her kohl-rimmed eyes were revealed to be ghost silver. The otherworldliness that breathed from her rattled Jack's nerves.

"Who are you?" The replica of Sylvie Whitethorn leaned in the doorway, her smile a shadowy thing, her voice and face so familiar, even Jack felt the deceptive comfort of trust.

"Why don't you tell us *your* name?" Jack smiled like the wicked thing he'd once been.

The Sylvie replica's unsettling gaze fell upon Christie and a dark power purred through her voice. "Why don't *you* tell me *yours*."

CHRISTIE'S THROAT CLOSED as the Sylvie look-alike gazed at him. "I'm not supposed to tell you my name. Miss."

She gestured. "How is it, lovely boy, that you don't have a shadow?"

He twisted around, trying to find his shadow in the dusky light.

"I'll confess I know *you*, Jack Daw," the witch continued.

"It's Jack Hawthorn now."

"My garden is a dangerous place for mortals, Jack Hawthorn."

"Jack." The alarm was peaking in Christie. *"Why don't I have a shadow?"*

"The elixir changes you, mortal boy." The witch drifted toward Christie, who took another step back as she reached out to brush short black nails across his neck, one fingertip following a scrawl of ink on his collarbone. Her face was exactly like Sylvie's, her lips red as if she'd just eaten strawberries. A necklace of green and blue beads glistened across the swell of white skin above her bodice.

"Witch." Jack's voice knocked Christie's head up. "Stop that. You can sense that he's mortal? Even with the elixir in him?"

The witch smiled sweetly at Christie. She leaned close and whispered, "You're different from most mortal boys. Do you even know what you are?" She twirled and sauntered back to the cottage, her gown's hem drifting around her bare feet. "You may enter if you can guess my true name."

Christie looked at Jack. "Do we want to—"

"*Tarbh-naith irach,*" Jack said. "Dragonfly."

She shook her head and paused before her door. "You'll never get what you need from me with *that* lack of imagination. My garden is hungry, so you'd best move quickly."

Christie gazed around at the statues tangled in vines and shady-looking plants. A marble girl reaching for an apple had lost her arm. A stone man crouched in a cave of briars, his broken hands outstretched. As the leaves rustled, sounding like the voices of lost souls, Christie swallowed. "*Were these peop—*"

"You were meant to be a changeling," Jack said to the witch, not seeming at all concerned by the growing sentience of the vegetation around them, "to replace a girl named Sylvie Whitethorn. Only something in the true world prevented that, so you survived betwixt and between."

"She was going to replace Sylvie?" Christie now had his back against an apple tree.

"Do you know her?" The witch's smile vanished. "My original?"

Christie, staring at her, whispered words that came to him like a protective prayer, "*She never walks, but glides. A shadow of blue and green. A lovely flicker to the eye. And, in her heart, a queen.*"

The witch's eyes went from unholy silver to a delighted sapphire blue and she tilted her head to one side and said, "Drat. You *gave* me that poem. I shall have to give you something in return. Come on then. You may call me Sylph."

She turned and moved into the cottage.

Christie, who hadn't meant the poem as a gift, who barely understood why he'd spoken it, glanced at Jack, who strode toward the cottage. Realizing he'd be left alone in the whispering garden, Christie hurried after him.

THE HOME OF SYLPH DRAGONFLY wasn't what Christie had expected. A fire crackled in a brick hearth. The two large rooms were cozy and cluttered with fantastically shaped bottles, trinkets, fossils, weird dolls, and plants grown wild on the sills of the latticed windows. There was an old-fashioned Sears sewing machine in one corner and a battered record player of Barbie-pink plastic on a corner table surrounded by vinyl albums. The forest-green walls were covered with photographs of people who didn't look quite human. Christie peered at a sepia-tinted picture of a young man with pale, tangled hair. The youth was smiling, one hand resting on the shoulder of the girl who was now humming softly as she opened cabinets in the kitchen.

Christie turned to Jack, who was examining a bowl of apples. "Is that Moth in this pic—"

An invisible force slammed Christie against the wall.

Jack shouted. Christie shook his head and staggered upright, staring at Sylph Dragonfly, who pointed at the photograph and hissed, "*How do you know him?*"

Jack stepped between Christie and the witch and said, "We call him Moth. Please don't swat the boy again—he's very fragile."

Shaking and bruised, Christie sank down into a chair near the table. His vision was weirdly vivid, and he was beginning to feel a rush that could have come from a hundred energy drinks.

Sylph frowned at the photograph of her and Moth. In it, she wore a black frock, and Moth was dressed in a ribboned jacket. "He is not a friend. He is a mad bastard and a liar and an agent of the Wolf."

Jack bit into the apple he'd selected. "Break your heart, did he?"

"I don't have a heart." Sylph Dragonfly sounded defiant. "That *aisling* boy was charming. He stole things from me."

"Things?" Jack's look was provocative. He set the apple's core on the table. "So what did he call himself?"

"He called himself Alexander Nightshade. It wasn't his true name."

"The Black Scissors." Jack studied the witch. "You know him. What did he promise you for helping us with the Wolf?"

"What do you think, Jack Daw?"

"He promised you Moth. I need to find someone, and I believe your Moth is with her. So, you see, we can help each other."

She held out a hand. "Give me the amulet."

Jack handed the dragonfly amulet to her. She frowned at it, then tenderly set it in a tiny golden cage that she locked with a key she tucked into her bodice. "That's what Alexander Nightshade—Moth, you call him—stole from me."

"Miss Dragonfly." Jack began with dangerous patience.

She suddenly stabbed him in the hand with a large pin. He flinched.

She grabbed his bleeding hand and gazed down at it. "That's how the Wolf and his *crom cu* are tracking you. That blood is not like any in this land."

"I need to be changed," Jack said calmly. "Temporarily."

Not liking the sound of that, Christie slid to his feet. "Can't you take a potion like I did?"

"None would work." The witch was watching Jack. "Do you know what needs to be done?"

"It needs to be convincing, the full stitchery."

"What is stitch—" Christie broke off, his stomach churning. "Jack, is she going to *shapechange* you?"

"You must believe it, Jack Daw." Sylph Dragonfly's serious expression made Christie wonder exactly what it was Jack wanted. "For it to be real to *them*, *you* must believe you are a Jack again."

HUDDLED ON A BENCH IN THE WITCH'S GARDEN, Christie waited while Sylph Dragonfly worked her dark magic on Jack inside the cottage. The tension in the air was as murky as a threatening thunderstorm.

He cautiously studied the statues, which the Dragonfly had reassured him were only statues and served as scarecrows to keep unwanted visitors out of her garden. His dry clothes were from the witch—a gray T-shirt and jeans, a fur-lined coat with a hood. His boots had dried by the fire.

He put his hands over his face, shivering when he heard Jack yell from within the cottage. He closed his eyes and pretended he was home, that Finn was safe, that Sylvie did not have a terrifying double, that no one was lost in this sinister Wonderland.

When he opened his eyes, Sylph Dragonfly stood before him. Her eyes seemed shadowy, not silvered, as she said, "It is done."

"I don't want to know what you did." He actually felt sorry for Jack. "What's so important about the amulet Moth stole from you?"

She sat beside him. Her skin was luminous. He felt a horrifying twist of desire and wrestled with it as she said, "It was my heart. Then Leander Cyrus stole it from the Wolf. You and Jack returned it."

He frowned at the primitive skin drum she held out to him. Symbols were inked across its surface. She set a small box on the bench between them, opened it. "To find your friends, I need you to strike this drum three times for each girl lost."

"Shouldn't Jack—"

"He can't, at the moment." She set a jeweled talisman—a dragonfly—on the drum and handed him an ivory stick. "Three times. For each."

He reluctantly struck the drum. The dragonfly pointer slid over a symbol. He hit the drum again. Another symbol. And four more times, the talisman jumping to four more symbols, which, he began to realize, formed a map. He looked at Sylph Dragonfly. "Do you know where they are, just from this?"

"I cannot give you that information. Not without receiving something in return."

He wanted to break the drum. Instead, he gave her his sexiest smile, one that had resulted in phone numbers and naughty texts in the sane world. "What do you want in exchange—and I'm not giving you my soul or my firstborn."

"Whatever would I do with those?" She traced the ink-scrawled poetry on his hands. When she touched the words on his throat, he realized how very unlike Sylvie she was. She whispered, "Someone placed a protective heka on you."

"Hek—"

"A spell. Magic. Usually spoken with words. Only the words are written on you. How curious."

"Even more curious—they're my own words. Miss Dragonfly, where are Sylvie and Finn?"

"Kiss me and I'll tell you."

Every instinct within him screamed *Don't kiss her.*

He leaned forward and kissed the witch.

CHAPTER 13

I lay at earth in Battle Wood
While Domesday Book was written
Whatever harm he did to man
I owe him pure affection.

—"Fox-Hunting," Rudyard Kipling

Finn hoped Caliban was dead, that the undead Jacks and Jills that had taken him down wouldn't follow. The frustration and dread resulting from the encounter had caused her to throw up the meager bit of food she'd eaten before they reached the train station.

The station was deserted but for a sharp-looking young man in a dark blue suit, who tipped his fedora at them and frowned at Sylvie before returning to the book he'd been reading. The train that arrived was a lovely thing of night-blue steel sculpted into swirling art nouveau women with molten eyes. As they boarded, a female conductor in crimson leather accepted a small velvet bag Moth handed to her. Sylvie asked as they walked to their seats, "What was in that bag?"

Moth said, "Teeth." He looked at Finn. "I found them in Roland and Ellen's attic. The conductor said we should be at Crossroads by evening's end."

Finn had decided they would wait at Orsini's Books, as Jack had told her to. Maybe Jack was already there . . .

As they moved down the aisle, past a youth wearing a brown fur coat, the youth lifted his head and sniffed. The gesture made Finn's blood run cold. Moth took a tiny bottle from his backpack and spilled it over Sylvie's coat, a liquid that smelled like grass and toadstools. Sylvie said, "Hey—"

Moth put a finger against his lips.

The boy in brown fur wrinkled his nose and looked out the window.

"What was in the bottle?" Finn kept her voice low as they chose a seat in the back.

Moth said, "I found it in the Blue Lady's house. It's Essence of Earth. It'll disguise Sylvie until we can find more elixir."

Finn slouched in her seat as the train glided past a boarded-up church in the woods, over a bridge that seemed to be made mostly of trees. She watched the boy—the Fata—in brown fur as he combed leaves from his hair. His nails were short and sharp. He appeared to be grooming himself. Like a cat.

"Freaky," Sylvie observed, and then she fell into an exhausted stupor against Finn's shoulder.

Finn felt sleep creeping up on her and didn't fight it.

WHEN THE TRAIN pulled into another antiquated station, a Romanesque building of pale green marble with lion sculptures, Finn was awake and ready. They filed onto the platform and before them the train tracks crossed the main street of a town consisting of cottages and Victorian houses in various stages of pastel-hued deterioration—it could have been any small town in the true world. Finn spotted the sign that read orsini's books hung above the door of a Victorian painted a Gothic purple.

The door to the bookshop opened at Moth's touch. They entered a huge establishment, where shelves of books reached up to the ceiling and more books cluttered tables and towered in piles on the floor. Wooden cubbies were stuffed with crumbling, crackling tomes. The hazy light pouring through the high windows shimmered on dust-powdered furniture bulky enough to have been made for a small giant. Finn called out, but there was no answer.

"Hey, look." Sylvie peered through an arch into a cathedral-ceilinged parlor. Finn flipped a wall switch and stained-glass lamps glowed. The parlor's atmosphere was scholarly and cozy. More shelves overflowed with books, and the walls were covered with glass display frames containing pinned insects, folding fans, ammonite fossils, pieces of painted pottery, and bits of parchment scrawled with writing.

"There's an upstairs." Moth moved toward a staircase draped in shadows and piled with more books. "I'll go up."

Finn turned. "Moth—"

He was already gone. She listened to his footsteps creak the floorboards above as she began exploring the parlor scattered with furniture that looked as though it had come from a seventeenth-century grandmother's garage sale. She frowned at a painting of a big, bearded man in a fur coat, hung above a black metal fireplace shaped like a dragon's head. "I wonder if that's Orsini."

"Finn." Sylvie sounded desolate. "Jack isn't here."

"We'll wait." Finn wandered to a desk. She saw a cup of tea with a leather thong draped over the cup's rim. Carefully, she reached in and drew out the phoenix pendant she'd given to Jack. She clutched it to make sure it was real. "He's been here. I gave this pendant to him—no one would know but me . . ."

"So where is he now?" Moth had come back down the stairs. He began moving around the parlor, putting items in his pockets. Finn, fastening Jack's pendant around her neck, scowled. "Are you pillaging again? This is Jack's *friend*."

"Well, he's not here, is he?" Moth took something down from a shelf and walked back, held it out to Finn. "It's got jackals on it. Maybe he left another clue."

It was an ebony box decorated with running jackals painted gold. As Finn accepted the box and set it tenderly in her lap, Sylvie sat up straight.

With tender reverence, Finn opened the box. Inside was a girl's embroidered glove, a ring of garnets shaped like hearts, a small leather-bound book of poetry, and other things. She lifted out a chain of dried daisies that crumbled in her fingers. "It's Jack's."

"A box of mementos?" Sylvie leaned close.

Finn touched a pocket watch with rust on it, the silvered photo of a girl in a gray gown.

"Those aren't mementos." Moth was expressionless. "Those are trophies."

Finn opened a locket and gazed at a painting of a young man with a face similar to hers. She knew his name—Ambrose Cassandro, the Jack who'd been her

Jack's friend, and her ancestor, the Jack brutally murdered by Seth Lot. "Some of these *are* mementos. I think this was a safe place for Jack, a way to escape Reiko. I wonder if Seth Lot knew about Orsini . . ."

As Moth strode from the room, he said, "I'm going to finish checking out the upstairs. Don't open those doors to anyone."

"He must think we're idiots." Sylvie scowled.

"No, he just thinks we're girls. He's old-fashioned."

"Jack's old-fashioned and *he's* not a jerk."

An antique rotary phone on one shelf suddenly rang, startling both girls, who stared at it as if it were a deadly insect, its black carapace glistening as it vibrated. Finn rose and reached for the receiver. Sylvie said, "Finn, don't—"

"What if it's . . ." Finn lifted the receiver and a familiar and dreaded voice came from it.

Caliban.

"So you've reached Orsini's, pretty girls? If you're wondering, Rose Red and Snow White, where your fox boy is, his belongings were found near a pond where a beast lived."

Sylvie's voice crumpled, "*Christie* . . ."

Finn said, tautly, "Caliban . . . *where is Christie?*"

"Probably in bits and pieces in Ivan Vodyanoi's stomach. You know what a Vodyanoi is, don't you, clever girl?" Laughter prowled beneath Caliban's voice. "I'll have to ride the shadow again and come find you and cut Sylvie and Moth out of your life. Literally. Isn't Orsini dead—"

Finn hung up the phone and stared down at it.

"He's a liar," Sylvie whispered. "We know he's a liar. *Christie isn't dead.*"

Finn blinked away the sting of tears. She thought, *Not Christie . . .*

Then: *It's my fault.*

"What's a Vod . . . Vod—"

"A water monster." Finn swallowed. "A bad one."

Sylvie sounded as if she was trying not to cry. "Caliban knows where we are."

Finn stumbled to her feet as Caliban's last taunt cut through her grief. "He implied that Orsini's dead. If Jack found . . ." She ran through the shop. Sylvie followed. They stopped at the splintered back door leading to a courtyard.

Finn walked out to a pile of upturned earth and the stone laid over it. As she crouched down and lifted the stone, Sylvie knelt beside her. They stared at what had been left under the stone—a picture of a dragonfly torn from a book.

"What does it mean?" Sylvie sobbed once. "Finn, what if Christie's *dead*—"

The silence was suddenly shattered by a riot of roaring engines from the street. Finn and Sylvie hurried back inside, and Moth came loping down the stairs. He unnecessarily said, "We've got company."

Sylvie stepped back. "How could Caliban get here so *fast*?"

"Caliban?" Moth turned on her as the shop was suddenly bright with skirling lights from outside. A silhouette appeared in the door's window and, when someone knocked, they all flinched. The dark shadow outside turned its big, animal-shaped head. There were two more polite knocks, then a friendly voice: "Finn Sullivan? Jack sent me."

Sylvie drew back. "It's a *trick*."

"Why don't they just break in then? They will eventually." Almost lunatic with fury and sick with fear for Christie, Finn strode toward the door. She said to the visitor, while trying not to think about Christie, "Prove Jack sent you. What sign did he leave me?"

The voice answered, "A dragonfly—because he's gone to a witch called the Dragonfly. He also told me to tell you: *'Thou art mine and I am thine. 'Til the sinking of the world.'*"

Finn opened the door a crack. Blinding light haloed a figure in a brass helmet cast into the form of a fox's head. He was plainly dressed in jeans, a red hoodie with ribbons fluttering on the sleeves, and buckled boots. At the curb were two more figures seated on motorcycles shaped into sleek animals. The fox smiled beneath the muzzle of his helmet. "Hello, Finn Sullivan."

"Show me your face."

He was looking past her. Softly, in a voice that was almost familiar, he said, "What fair companions you have, Finn Sullivan. What are their names?"

"Not until I see your face."

He removed the helmet and Christie smiled at her.

"*Christie!*" Sylvie lunged forward, but Finn stopped her as the Ghostlands night became a breathing, menacing mockery of all that she cared about. Her stomach twisted. She said to the Christie look-alike, "You have *no right* to wear that face."

"Sorry. I was born with it." As his gaze slid to Sylvie, it flickered silver. "*You* look familiar."

Sylvie drew back, her eyes enormous. She whispered, "Not Christie?"

"And you don't remember me." The replica looked at Moth. Though he had Christie's face and dark russet curls, he wore a gold hoop in each earlobe and he moved like something that slinked in forests. "Never mind. I'm Sionnach Ri. I'm here to escort you to Jack. You're not safe here."

Moth said, "I don't trust him."

"Only trust me when I say that relying on *him*"—Sionnach Ri indicated Moth—"is a risk."

Finn turned to Moth. "He knows you. Why does he know you?"

"I don't remember *him*." Moth glared at Sionnach Ri.

"Oh, but I remember *you*, Alexander Nightshade, formerly of Stratford-on-the-Avon. He stole my heart and doesn't remember."

"*Oh.*" Finn glanced questioningly at Moth, who studied Sionnach Ri with grim suspicion.

Sylvie, gazing at Sionnach Ri, whispered again, "You're not Christie."

"Why didn't Jack come here himself?" Finn didn't bother concealing *her* suspicion.

"He's hurt. I'm sorry." Sionnach Ri lowered his lashes. "Badly hurt."

Finn curled a hand against her stomach, as if a bullet had gone through her.

"He'll live." Sionnach Ri regarded her almost tenderly. "We do need to hurry. Have you eaten? Have your friends? No? And the pretty crow girl—I can smell her blood. She hasn't gotten the elixir?"

"Where can we go to find these things?" As desperate as Finn was to be reunited with Jack, she felt dizzy and knew that human food and elixir were necessary at this point.

"Fortunately for you, there's a place on the way. A dangerous place, but . . ." He shrugged. "So is every environment dealing in contraband."

Finn made her decision. She grabbed her backpack, shouldered it, and tucked Jack's walking stick into the straps. She jammed the ebony box of Jack's mementos into the backpack. "Let's go."

"*Finn* . . ." Moth said her name through gritted teeth.

"*Moth.*" She glared at him. "What choice do we have? Caliban knows we're here."

"How—"

"I don't know, but we need to *go*."

Outside, they were handed helmets by Sionnach and his two companions and Finn swung onto Sionnach's fox-shaped motorcycle while a Fata girl with red ringlets made room for Moth on hers and Sylvie slid behind a boy in a red velvet coat. Despite their pretty manners and sweet faces, Sionnach Ri and his friends shimmered with power and strangeness. As Finn carefully circled her arms around Sionnach, she said, "Did Jack tell you that you resemble one of my best friends?"

"Christopher Hart. Some of us never get to see the true world when our originals remain there. We're not allowed. Also, most of us don't want to see our beauty mirrored in another."

"Originals." Finn thought of Christie's flirty smile and his serious concern and her throat ached. "He might be dead. Your original."

"He's not." Sionnach looked over his shoulder. "He's with Jack."

Her heart jumped as the motorcycle thrummed to life and he began to tell her how they'd found Jack and Christie with the Dragonfly witch.

FINN MUST HAVE DROWSED OFF, because when she raised her head from Sionnach Ri's shoulder, she saw stars spilling across the sky and the dusk had gone. As the night air flowed into the helmet, she thought she tasted snow on her tongue.

The three motorcycles curved down a road lined by giant cypress trees. Sionnach called out, "Goblin Market, coming up!"

He raised an arm to his friends. They steered their bikes onto a highway where the cypresses twined through cement ruins. The roadway soon became an avenue leading toward a gathering of high-rises and dingy storefronts that had fallen prey to Mother Nature. Streets and buildings swarmed with ivy. Emerald moss furred rooftops. Wild grapevines spilled from broken windows. There were cars—rusted and grime-smeared shells filled with shadows. The urban decay was made even more disturbing by wistful objects strung on the trees . . . small clocks, bird skulls, toys, an excess of broken jewelry. Shadowy figures moved like velvet and gossamer in the jellyfish light of the streetlamps. The motorcycles' raucous engines seemed to disturb unseen things, and Finn tried not to look too closely at the phantom city's inhabitants.

The breath left her as the motorcycles cruised down a street toward a tunnel of glowing-white birches, their woven-together branches forming a twisting roof. At the street's end loomed a soot-smudged neoclassical building, its stairway guarded by two gargoyles with lanterns in their mouths. Prehistoric yews surrounded the building, moss-draped branches clawing at the roof, the lit windows. Beyond was the metal dome of a conservatory. Over the entrance, in bas-relief on the triangular pediment, were the words MUSEUM OF NATURAL HISTORY. Spray-painted across the doors in glimmering red were other words Finn couldn't quite make out.

Sionnach and his fox knights halted their motorcycles before the tunnel of glowing birches.

"Goblin Market," Sionnach told Finn as his motorcycle's engine thrummed. "It has everything. True food—there's a changeling who bakes *the* best cupcakes I've ever had. And we'll be able to get the elixir if we're clever. We just need to get past those trees."

"Goblin Market?" Finn said, wary. "And what's wrong with those tree—" Then she noticed tangles of ivory in the roots of the birches and whispered, "Please tell me those aren't *bones*."

"Hold on and don't let anything touch you."

He sped forward. The others followed. As they roared past the birches, Finn, her heart pounding, saw crimson veins glistening in the trees' pale trunks and realized how sharp-edged the silvery leaves were. When something drifted across the back of her neck, she yelped and swatted at a red tendril snaking from one of the branches. She touched her skin, felt a sting, and warmth—blood. The silver leaves drifting around them crackled against her helmet.

Several more tendrils whipped down.

Sionnach's motorcycle shot toward the stairs. Glancing over at Moth and his rider, Finn saw a red vine whip across Moth's hand. Blood spattered—Moth had remembered he was human again, at the worst time. As Sylvie and her rider shot past, Finn ducked her head and held tight to Sionnach.

The motorcycles bumped up the stairs toward the doors spray-painted with the words *Goblin Market*. The doors, their bronze panels engraved with images of knights fighting monsters, opened before them, onto darkness.

The three motorcycles motored down a vast, gloomy corridor lined on either side by hollow-eyed Renaissance statues. Outside light glimmered through the windows. At the hall's end was another set of doors, opened to reveal a cavernous, crumbling atrium with a pterodactyl skeleton hanging on wires from the vaulted ceiling. The first and second floors of the atrium had flickering, jewel-hued lamps above dark alcoves. Moss covered the concrete, as did fields of toadstools. Ivy rustled on the walls, on pillars, around the balustrades of a stairway. An eerie silence folded around them.

"*This* is Goblin Market?" Finn tried not to sound crushed. "It looks like an abandoned museum."

"We're early." Sionnach seemed tense. He raised a hand. "It doesn't wake up until thirteen o'clock."

"Thirteen o'clock?"

It began as whispers, and giant shadows rippling over the walls. Finn's skin iced and her eardrums vibrated with a buzzing sound that shook her brain. She tasted blood in her mouth.

Then the hissing shadows rushed down into the atrium, followed by hundreds of glowing orbs. Dark figures formed. Light slowly melted across the walls, the newly arrived inhabitants, and the fantastical merchandise of Goblin Market.

Sylvie breathed out, "Wow."

Faces flickered. Silver eyes cast back the jeweled lights. The ruin remained, but, now, objects were on display in the alcoves: books and bottles, clocks and taxidermy animals, fanciful jewelry and weapons, bizarre fossils and plants. No one would have mistaken it for a human marketplace, with its denizens that resembled the members of several savage and elegant tribes dressed in clothing from different eras. Despite a lack of dramatic mutations—no pointy ears, hooves, bat wings, or butterfly wings—the Fatas here would never be mistaken for mortals.

Three young men in fedoras and suits strode past, tattoos on their hands. A young woman in gladiator sandals and a red tunic leaned in the inner doorway, smoking a cigarette.

Sionnach halted his motorcycle in the outer hallway. There were other motorcycles there, each forged from an organic metal into the forms of beasts or twining vegetation. As Sionnach and his companions settled their vehicles, Finn hopped off and waited for Moth and Sylvie to join her. She wondered if Sylvie was experiencing the same dreamy acceptance, or if it was just the elixir.

"Christie isn't dead," she told them with conviction. "He's with Jack."

"Why would you think Christie's dead?" Moth was watching the fox knights.

"Caliban called on a phone at Orsini's. He said Christie was dead. He lied."

"Do you really think Christie's all right?" Sylvie sounded so lost and miserable that Finn put an arm around her. She said firmly, "I *know* he is."

Swaggering, Sionnach led them down a corridor to a pair of glass doors, which he flung wide to reveal a lamp-lit courtyard scattered with the metal sculptures of prehistoric plants. There were no Fatas in sight.

"Wait here. I'd rather not lead you through Goblin Market until I've gotten the elixir. Luce and Merriweather will look after you." Sionnach strode back toward the market before anyone could object.

"I told you I don't trust him," Moth muttered.

"Why would he go to all this trouble if he was planning on giving us to Caliban?" Sylvie looked as lost and desperate as Finn felt. And Finn wasn't sure about Sionnach Ri either. They were in another world and clutching at strangers.

As the two fox knights leaned against a sculpture of giant ferns and proceeded to light up cigarettes, Finn sat on a metal toadstool and watched Sylvie wander around. Moth indicated the atrium of Goblin Market, which they could see through the glass doors. "You see that pretty girl, there, the one in pink? That's human blood she's trading in those bottles. The boy with freckles, selling snakes? He lets them bite him and uses their venom in kisses to sicken mortal girls. Those two men in greatcoats and three-cornered hats? They seduce people into doing bad things."

"How do you know all that?"

"I remember their types." He pointed at the ones he'd called out. "*Baobhan sith*, ganconer, elf knights."

"It's the Unseelie stock exchange." Finn wanted out of this nightmare gathering as soon as possible. A hunger pang ripped through her stomach and she winced.

Moth said, "You think it's a coincidence? Sionnach resembling your friend?"

"When we first met, you thought Sylvie and Christie were other people." Her eyes widened. "What if the Dragonfly witch looks like Sylvie?"

"I don't remember a Dragonfly witch or . . . him. Perhaps *I* have a Fata double."

She laid one hand gently over his. "How do you do it, Moth? You were ripped from your life, imprisoned forever in the Wolf's house, changed into a *bug* . . ."

"It's surviving, that's all. Anyone can do it, if they're lucky enough." He had the same feral, striking appeal as Jack, that otherworldly grace. He said, "I fear I've led you to this."

"Well, Seth Lot also threatened me . . ."

"What if I'm a trap?" His hand tightened.

"You're not a trap. I meant to ask . . . did you want to be called Alexander?"

"I'm not Alexander anymore. Do you want to know what she said to me, your sister, the first time I met her? She said, '*He promised to make me his queen.*'"

Finn closed her eyes. "She went with Lot voluntarily." She opened her eyes and regarded him. "You and Lily—"

"I don't love Lily Rose. I *care* about her. Oddly enough, there *was* a girl, a long time ago, named Rose." His smile was crooked. "It was Lily and you who woke that memory."

"What happened to—"

"Seth Lot happened to her. That's when I started blacking out. I had only bits and pieces of my mind left after he murdered Rose."

She watched him as he bowed his head, a muscle twitching in his jaw. She said, "How does he get away with killing humans when it's against Fata law?"

"Why do you think they all want him dead? Lot keeps mortals around so that he might accomplish things. *Aisling*s and changelings are never kept human for good reasons."

Finn said gently, "And the girl called Rose?"

"I dream about her. It was the 1700s, in France." He pronounced "France" as a posh "Fronce." "I remember she was chopping wood, in the forest. She wore a red coat. I introduced myself and told her I was newly arrived . . ."

Finn pictured Moth in a tricornered hat, greatcoat, and cavalier boots, courting a pretty young woman who held a hatchet.

"I didn't know I was being used as a lure." His mouth twisted. Then he flashed that rare smile. "I also didn't know Rose was from a family that had hunted dangerous Fatas for centuries."

"Did she try to kill Seth Lot?"

"She did. And he killed *her*." His face grew hard. "We must find a way to destroy him."

Her heart twisted for Moth, taken out of time and cast adrift with no friends or family. They continued to hold hands for a moment, as if to let go would cause the other to fall. Then she carefully released his fingers.

Sionnach returned with a Fata girl in a short dress of gold silk and golden platform sandals, her hair an auburn mane shot through with more gold, a color also painted around her silver-green eyes. She looked Sylvie over disdainfully and demanded a price that made Sylvie pale.

"My *blood*?"

"It's the only way I'll be able to get the elixir made quickly, little dark thing." The witch didn't smile.

"I don't want a Mean Girl taking any of my blood."

Sionnach said, "We need to make our way through this market. And we'd like to get some coffee, purchase some things, use the restrooms—"

"You're not even *real people*!" Sylvie's outburst was followed by an uncomfortable silence. The Mean Girl witch smirked. Sionnach seemed dismayed. Sionnach's male comrade drawled, "That wasn't very nice."

When Finn calmly offered her own blood, the witch became even more disdainful. "Your blood is chaotic."

"Take mine." Moth flipped a small blade into his hand and sliced the ball of his thumb. Nothing came out of the wound. Sionnach said, almost gently, "Forgotten what you are again, Alexander?"

Moth stared down at the bloodless cut. "But I bled . . ."

"Here." Sylvie held out a hand. "Just get it over with."

SYLVIE TOOK A DROP OF THE WITCH'S ELIXIR—after Moth sampled it to be sure—and the world changed. As she walked with the fox knights, Finn, and Moth through Goblin Market, she gazed around like the blind given sight.

The giant hanging pterodactyl skeleton was singed as if it had been in a fire. There were blackened marks on the walls, too, and, at the top of the colossal stairway, the stained-glass window depicting a forest from a Grimms' fairy tale was veined with red. They passed a stone slab embedded with the vertebrae of some giant creature. Nearby, several girls in denim, their brown hair braided with flowers, spoke with a boy in a kilt and tattoos. He was displaying paper fans on which pictures seemed to move.

Sylvie said, "I can't believe we're here. This is the most amazing—"

"Careful, Sylvie Whitethorn. This is a place of Unseelie things." Moth glanced meaningfully at Sionnach.

Sylvie was drawn toward an alcove of antique weapons, the display piece on the glass counter a small crossbow in the shape of a crow with a woman's head. Seven glinting darts crafted into feathery metal shapes were set beside the crossbow. The dealer, dark haired and sleek in black jeans, smiled at Sylvie, his eyes glinting. His arms and half his bare chest were shadowed with raven tattoos. "Would you like that, little one?"

"No. She wouldn't." Moth gently drew Sylvie back.

"She would." The dealer tilted his head, the beads and feathers moving in his hair. "Wouldn't you? Here. Take it. From one, to another." He slid the crossbow and its bolts into a leather case and held it out to Sylvie.

"We don't accept gifts." Moth set one hand on the case.

"She is a *croi baintreach*." The dealer smiled, and his eyes flickered like a bird's. "She'll find her way to violence eventually. They all do."

"I believe the lady said no." Sionnach leaned forward and smiled, his Christieness accompanied by a flare of rakish sex appeal. "But I'll take it. Thanks."

As they walked away, Sylvie whispered, "What's crow . . . what he said?"

"*Croi baintreach*. Heart widow." Sionnach grinned. "A warrior."

"But I'm not."

"If you say so."

AS THEY WOVE THROUGH GOBLIN MARKET, Moth leaned close to Finn. "Do you remember when we were on that train? When we first arrived?"

"You were a *moth*."

"I still recall, even in that form—isn't that the white-haired Fata Jack threatened?"

Moving through the flickering shadows and light of Goblin Market was a young man in a pale coat, white hair spilling from beneath a bowler hat of ivory velvet.

"Yes." She tensed. "That's him."

Sionnach was purchasing what looked like empanadas from a dark-skinnned Fata with a pink butterfly design painted around her eyes. The fox knights had already bought small cakes, fried chicken, and containers of soup—human food was apparently an addiction here, like crack or meth in the true world.

Finn walked to the dealer with whom the white-haired Fata from the train had been speaking—a purveyor of jewel-colored toadstools in baskets and bottles—and asked, "Who was that white-haired man?"

The slinky dealer replied, "Narcissus Mockingbird. Don't be curious about *him*, pretty thing."

Finn turned away, recognizing that name—*Mockingbird*. Dread clutched her.

Moth moved to her side. "Where is Sylvie?"

Finn frantically scanned the crowds of sleek and bizarre Fatas in their punk-retro clothing. Sionnach and his two fox knights had also disappeared. "Where did they *go*?"

Four figures in fur coats broke from the crowds and Moth whispered, "Wolves."

"Finn!" Sylvie was pushing toward them, her face pale.

Finn grabbed her hand and, following Moth, they raced toward a set of glass doors leading to a hall displaying Egyptian statues and sarcophagi. They fled through it, up a flight of stairs. As they turned into a narrow gallery with shuttered windows on one side and gargoyle statues holding glowing lanterns, something howled in the shadows at the other end.

Two more figures in fur coats appeared, cutting off their only escape route.

Moth shoved one of the windows open. "Climb." He slid over the sill, onto the sloping roof, and Finn and Sylvie clambered after. Far below was a valley of urban decay sprinkled with lights. From somewhere in the distance came the sound of a violin. Moving across the rooftop as if he were a cat, Moth advised, "Don't look down."

Finn saw broken roofs and the steep canyons between them. The museum seemed to be on a mountain of buildings like one of those tiered cities in Europe.

"Oh *hell* no." Sylvie balked. Her eyes were ringed with shadow.

The glass window crashed open behind her, and a young man in a coat of black fur began to climb out. Sylvie whirled and slammed the shutters on the

Fata several times, before kicking the dazed wolf back and pushing the shutters closed. She turned.

Finn and Moth were staring at her. Moth murmured, "Maybe we should have let her have that crossbow."

"Hurry!" Sylvie slid toward them.

Moth led them across the roof. The music from the ruined city below grew louder, a violin solo, eerily isolated.

When Finn recognized the song, she stumbled and steadied herself against a gargoyle.

It was "November Rain," the first song she'd heard after her sister's funeral. Reiko had once taunted her with it. As wind whipped Finn's hair into her face, the night seemed to lighten as clouds tumbled across the stars. Rain began to fall. Moth and Sylvie shouted her name.

"Finn, what are you doing?" Moth strode back to her. "We need to get off this roof."

He led her back to Sylvie, who looked fierce, her dark hair sleeked to her head.

"Finn," she said in a too-calm voice. "How come I don't feel the cold and I can see in the dark? And I'm *strong*—"

"It's the elixir, Sylvie."

"Careful, here." Moth spoke as if they were soldiers. He stepped over a chasm between two peaked roofs. Sylvie leaped first, neat as a leopard. Finn drew a breath, jumped—

—her boot heel slid on the stone.

Moth's grip almost broke bones as he caught her hand and dragged her up. She slammed against him, felt the thrumming of his heart, and noticed the bits of gold in his leaf-green eyes as his face came close to hers.

"Thanks." She quickly drew her hands from his. He nodded and studied her for a moment before turning away.

"Hey," Sylvie said, her breath coming in hiccups. "I think I found the way down."

They clambered after her, onto a ledge over the museum entrance. Moth jumped first and reached up to help each of them down onto the pavement. Their hoods up, they hurried into the hall where they'd left Sionnach Ri's motorcycles.

A few moments later, a grim Sionnach strode toward them, tucking something that looked like a Valentine's Day heart made from black obsidian into his hoodie. "Where have you *been*? Lot's wolves are here."

"We know," Finn said with a bit of an attitude. "We've been on the roof to get away from them."

"Your friends left us," Moth told Sionnach. "Do you know anyone named Narcissus?"

Sionnach shot him a wary look. "Should I?"

When Luce and Merriweather strode into the hall, Sionnach yelled at them in Irish. They yelled back. Merriweather stomped her foot.

A pack of Fatas in jewelry and fur coats broke from the Goblin Market crowds and loped toward them.

"Time to leave." Sionnach spun around and swung onto his motorcycle.

"I'll ride with you this time." Sylvie climbed up behind him and put on her helmet.

Wondering if Sylvie was losing her mind, Finn straddled the bike behind Merriweather.

Sylvie reached out and clasped her hand once, before Sionnach and his knights circled their bikes and shot out the doors.

THEY STOPPED IN A GRASSY GLADE scattered with night-blooming flowers, to eat the human food the fox knights had bought. Finn watched Sylvie and Moth talk with the haughty Merriweather and sly Luce. She felt more alert after the earthly feast and three cans of root beer. Her mind was working now . . .

"Sionnach . . . can I talk to you for a sec?" Finn stood up and walked toward a knot of elder trees. Sionnach ambled after her and leaned against one of the trees, watching her as she gazed into the darkness of the forest and gathered her courage. She said, "You're not taking us to Jack, are you?"

He cocked his head to one side when she looked at him. His eyes didn't glint. He didn't smile. He replied, "No."

"And you haven't seen Jack . . ." She felt grief crest. "Or Christie."

"No. Look, that part was true, me knowing if my original was dead—I'd *know*. And Jack was last seen, with Christopher Hart, heading for the Dragonfly witch."

"Where?" She turned on him. "Where are you taking us?"

"The Mockingbirds."

She nodded, because she'd suspected that. Her heart crashed into her boots. "You were going to give us to the Mockingbirds at Goblin Market, until the wolves interfered."

"They don't want to hurt you, the Mockingbirds. They are Seth Lot's enemies. They want to help you *kill* him. You know that saying—the enemy of my enemy is my friend."

"So they murdered the Blue Lady and hired you to trick me?" Finn glanced back at the others, who were still speaking. When Moth looked up and narrowed his eyes, Finn forced a smile, as if she and Sionnach were talking about—not this. "Okay. Take me. Let Sylvie and Moth go."

"Go where? They are safer with you, Finn Sullivan."

"Please—"

"No." He refused gently. "And if you tell them where we are going, I will make certain Moth is a moth and Sylvie is unconscious."

"And when we get there? I've *betrayed* them."

"The Mockingbirds need Jack. They are searching for Jack. They're superstitious and believe the two who ended Reiko will end Lot—that would be you and Jack."

Her hands curled into fists at her sides as she whispered, "What's wrong with the Mockingbirds? Because I know they're not right. Moth called them *ghouls*."

"More like blood drinkers." Sionnach continued to speak with that gentle ruthlessness. "Reiko Fata and Amaranthus Mockingbird were once like sisters. As impossible as that might seem, some of the older ones were once young. But Amaranthus blames the Wolf, not you, for Reiko's downfall."

Finn turned her back on him and trudged toward her friends.

Moth frowned as she settled beside him. He handed her a cupcake and leaned close to ask, "What's wrong?"

Finn met Sylvie's concerned gaze and said with a calm that felt more like shock, "Plans have changed. We need to go to the Mockingbirds."

Moth reached for one of his daggers, but Finn stopped him. "No. The Mockingbirds might help us kill Lot."

"Is that what *he* said?" Moth indicated Sionnach.

Sionnach sauntered toward them. "Do you know why mortals aren't welcome here, Alexander? Because, when you're here, you *influence* things. You make us *feel* things. You make us *bleed*. It was a fair bargain offered for the queen killer and her companions. Especially since you were one of those companions."

Moth slid to his feet and Luce and Merriweather rose, spiky with weapons. Finn and Sylvie jumped up.

"Moth," Finn said. "The Mockingbirds want to kill Lot . . . and it fits with what goes on here—queens and kings always at each other. And they might find Jack. This is our best chance."

"I told you they are ghouls. They're crazy." Moth didn't take his attention from Sionnach.

"At least they're not backstabbing *traitors*," Sylvie snarled, as she glared at Sionnach.

"Moth. Sylvie." Finn spoke hopelessly. "We don't have a choice."

FINN, HOLDING ON TO MERRIWEATHER as the motorcycle sped down another road, felt as if her blood were freezing. She'd begun to worry about her lack of exhaustion and fear. It wasn't normal to feel zippy all the time, and she'd run out of espresso. She should be falling over by now, or in hysterics—she wasn't; she was calm and focused.

The bikes suddenly curved off the road and onto a forested ridge overlooking a deep ravine tangled with kudzu and obscured in mist. On the other side was a baroque building of pale stone surrounded by yews, their branches scarring the bleached walls as dusk glinted bloodily from the windows. It was a resort from turn-of-the-century Prague, with towers and balconies and fancy statues.

As everyone swung off the bikes, Sionnach stabbed Moth in the arm with a silver pin.

Moth's entire shape blazed into light . . . clothes, backpack, weapons, all shrinking into a shining orb that cascaded into a large luna moth with silver skull markings. As the red-haired Merriweather caught the moth in a wicker cage, Sylvie whirled on Sionnach. "You *snake!*"

"Fox, actually. The snake was the one you burned." Sionnach turned a harrowed gaze on Finn, who watched the bank of mist creeping toward them from the beautiful hotel. Gently, Sionnach told her, "You can change Moth back. He would have gotten himself killed when they came."

She whispered, "You're not like Christie at all. You're a hollow thing wearing his face."

For an instant, something almost like despair flickered in Sionnach's eyes.

Then he took the moth cage and set it at Finn's feet. When he spoke again, the careless mockery had returned. "Say hello to the Mockingbirds for me, Finn Sullivan."

Finn turned from Sionnach as the fox knight strode back to his bike and his hard-eyed companions. As she and Sylvie backed away from the fog crawling up out of the ravine to touch the toes of their boots, Finn said to Sionnach, "Was this all about Moth?"

Sionnach halted without looking back at her. He'd flung up the hood of his jacket. "I grew a heart, for Moth. The Wolf cut it out of me, for kicks. And Moth walked away."

Sionnach got on his bike, and he and his companions spun their motorcycles onto the road, leaving Finn and Sylvie to face whatever came in the mist. Finn whispered, "Sylv, why did you come after me?"

"To give you that sword, to tell you how to kill Lot." Sylvie had picked up the moth cage. With wistful regret, she added, "And I really wanted to see fairy-land."

The mist enshrouded them.

"Finn." Sylvie went very still. "Something is com—"

Then darkness took them.

CHAPTER 14

Just as Little Red Riding Hood entered the wood, a wolf met her. Little Red Riding Hood did not know what a wicked creature he was, and was not at all afraid of him.

—"LITTLE RED RIDING HOOD," THE BROTHERS GRIMM

You want to play with magic, boy? These were the last words mortal Jack heard before Reiko cut out his heart, with Seth Lot crouched beside them, smiling amiably.

Jack had awakened on cold stone stained by his own blood and found Reiko gazing lovingly down at him. He'd screamed as the alchemy of roses Lot had stitched within him stung like hundreds of bees, the thorns stabbing into his bones, venom shimmering through his veins.

Then Finn was kneeling beside him, her soulful eyes wide, her lips moving but no sound emerging. He shook his head, found that he, also, could not speak. As Finn stood and Seth Lot appeared behind her, gathering Finn's hair away from her neck as if he was a lover, Jack tried to warn her, reached for her—

Lot plunged a hand through her and pulled out her heart.

Jack convulsed, watching Finn fall bloodily at Seth Lot's feet.

JACK LAY ON THE FLOOR of the witch's cottage. Night air whispered across his skin. He could hear the wind chimes in Sylph Dragonfly's garden, a flock of starlings sweeping over the roof. He could smell earth and the incense that had soaked into the cottage's wood. He couldn't feel his heartbeat. His brain was splintered by dark, hungry thoughts.

Whatever black magic Sylph had worked upon him had cast a convincing illusion of turning him back into a thing that walked the world solely to cause harm. Worst of all, he could almost feel the phantoms of Reiko Fata's roses snaking through him, thorns scratching at his bones, petals pushing against his internal organs. He could see in the dark once more.

He dragged himself into a crouch and leaned against the wall. His body thrummed with energy. *Finn.*

He hunched over and something slipped out of his mouth, drifting to the floor—a rose petal that looked like blood. The illusion had triggered something else; his mortality was fading fast now, being drained away by the world to which he belonged.

The door opened. Christie, in a fur-lined jacket and tasseled wool hat, peered in. "Jack? Normally, I wouldn't bother you, but Finn and Sylvie are headed toward a bad place. We've got to stop them."

Jack's voice scraped out, "Sylph Dragonfly told you this?"

"Sort of. Are you okay? Because you look like you're not."

"They're together? Sylvie and Finn?" Jack slid to his feet as hope, that fickle fairy thing, hushed through him.

"Together or about to be—Miss Dragonfly says they're both headed toward the same place. You're . . . not really a Jack again, are you?"

"Enough of one." Jack felt the old smile slice across his face.

"THEY'RE HEADED TOWARD A PLACE called Mockingbird Hotel," Christie continued as he and Jack gathered up the satchels Sylph had packed, while she tweaked out the lamps. "There was a Mockingbird Hotel in Virginia. It closed in the '30s because some people were shot to death there."

"And how do you know this bit of macabre trivia?" Jack sheathed his misericorde in his left boot and slid the *kris* Christie had returned to him up one sleeve. Christie had the wooden dagger from Phouka.

"It's just something I read once. What are the Mockingbirds, Jack?"

"The Mockingbirds are crazy. That's all you need to know."

They followed Sylph out of the cottage, through the garden, to a gate camouflaged by bean vines and ivy. She yanked the gate open, revealing a cavern of greenery and two bizarre motorcycles of tarnished metal shaped into reindeer, antlers strung with talismans, bodies engraved with runes.

"The *dyr spokelse* are rusty, but they can still travel a great distance—better than trains." She caressed one of the motorcycles as if it was a living thing and it stirred with a creak, red lights flickering in the eye sockets of the brass reindeer head curving from the handlebars. When the bikes hummed to life with a distinct *tick-tocking* sound from within their brass bodies, Christie stepped back quickly.

Jack moved to the darker beast, peered into one ruby eye. "How do they move?"

Sylph pulled two pairs of antique goggles from her satchel and handed one to Jack, the other to Christie. She swung onto the second bike. As she tugged on an aviator's cap also equipped with goggles, she said, "What energy drives them? Mine. I can put energy back into things, just like I can drain it. I sent one of my dragonflies to Orsini's and it showed me your Finn, Sylvie, and that bastard Alexander—Moth—opening Orsini's door to a fox knight."

Jack's body shook once with overwhelming relief—Finn had escaped Caliban. "How do you know she's headed for the Mockingbirds?"

"The map on the spirit drum—the pointer went right to their lair," Sylph replied.

"And the fox knight?" Jack touched one of the motorcycles as if calming a horse.

"Like all fox knights—not to be trusted."

Christie was pale in the starlight, his eyes glinting from the elixir. "Are we really going to—"

"Get on." Jack threw one leg over the bike. As he familiarized himself with riding again, Christie swung up behind the witch.

"Close your eyes, gentlemen." The Dragonfly leaned forward as Christie slid his arms around her waist. "They move fast."

THE CLOCKWORK BIKES sped down a highway that soon curved into a mountain forest where no light other than that from the stars was visible and night seemed to be a solid thing. They passed through a wall of mist, and the road ended.

They halted the bikes in a forest glade, its trees hung with the feathered and painted skulls of wolves.

"Where are we?" Christie's voice was faint.

"I don't know." Sylph was grim. "We've been waylaid."

From the darkness emerged three masked figures on dead-looking horses with the opal eyes and weed-tangled manes of kelpies. As Jack pushed up his goggles, Christie said, "Please tell me they're friends of yours."

"They're not." Sylph didn't take her attention from the riders as one of the ghastly horses came forward, the Fata in its saddle resembling a Native American in stitched black suede, crow feathers knotted in his long hair. He wore a wooden mask shaped like a raven's face. He said, "Jack Daw. Where is your brother, the crooked dog?"

"I don't have a brother, Blackheart." Jack resisted the instinct to reach for his knives.

The Blackheart's companions remained in the shadows. Both were masked in painted wood. One, in red, wore the horns of a buffalo. The other, in white, had a headdress made from antlers. As the lead Blackheart nudged his kelpie closer to Jack, the water horse's muzzle curled back from carnivore teeth. "The *crom cu* has caused much grief among our nation, Jack Daw. In fact, many of your outlaw kind have been nothing but—"

"Disappointing to you? I agree. The *crom cu* isn't my brother. Feel free to dismember him if he crosses your path. What do you want with us?"

"*The sun will set, the moon will wane.*" As Christie spoke, Jack's irritation level shot sky-high. He narrowed his eyes at the boy.

"*The stars will fall, become our bane,*" Christie continued, his voice steady. "*A tribe will bleed, a nation fade. The spirits will weep and turn away.*"

Silence followed the poem. The lead Blackheart tilted his head and murmured, "Pretty words from a mortal boy—yes, I know he's mortal—I've been told. We won't force you to come with us, but you'll volunteer."

Jack said, "Where exactly are we *volunteering* to go?"

"The *Dearh Cota* wants to speak with you."

"Two friends of mine are about to enter the Mockingbirds' nest. We don't have time."

"You will make time, Jack Daw, because the *Dearh Cota* has the information that will help you take down the Wolf."

Christie said desperately, "*Finn and Sylvie,* Jack."

"Let me explain it this way," the Blackheart continued. "You'll come with us or remain here. Forever."

Jack spoke through gritted teeth. "Ride fast and we'll follow."

The lead Blackheart turned his kelpie. His two comrades followed, the red one idly saying to the white one, "At least the mortal didn't recite 'Hiawatha' at us, like the white folk usually do. The next mortal does that, I'll get someone to cut out his or her tongue."

"Whatever happened to scalping?" The white one looked wistful.

"They don't recite poetic clichés with their *hair*. Removing the tongue makes more of a statement."

"Fantastic," Christie muttered as Sylph and Jack revved up their bikes. "More water monsters *and* a Fata comedy team."

THE BLACKHEARTS LED THEM DOWN a road lined with witchy-looking elms decorated with painted rattles and wooden stick figures. As they passed beneath an arch made of withy and blackberry vines, the trees gave way to a street lined with abandoned brownstone buildings, their balconies strung with colored lights, graffiti on the doors, and talismans hanging in windows of broken glass. The red light muted the sky behind a blackened church at the street's end and made the church's stained-glass windows glimmer like sangria. Citrus trees in urns lined the stair, along with a variety of canine-headed gargoyles. Parked in front was a battered Jeep Cherokee scrawled with silver symbols, a wolf skull attached to the fender.

As the Blackhearts and the clockwork motorcycles halted before the church, the red doors opened and a slender figure in a hooded coat of scarlet, two brindled hounds at its sides, stepped out. Jack got off his stilled motorcycle and murmured, "Jill Scarlet. The *Dearh Cota*."

"Wait . . . that sounds familiar. . . ." Christie stared at the figure as it spoke in a young woman's voice.

"Jack Daw. Do you think you are the Wolf's death?"

"Maybe"—Jack smiled savagely—"I'll be yours if I don't reach the Mockingbirds in time."

The smile in the shadows of the red hood was equally as feral. The *Dearh Cota* didn't look dangerous—she appeared to be a young woman in a ruffled black dress, striped stockings, and button-up boots—but Jack knew better. She receded back into the church, followed by her two hounds. "Come in. I won't keep you long."

Jack ascended the stairs, and Christie and Sylph followed him into the church that now served as a home, bookshelves and paintings on the walls between the windows and the altar area a bedroom with parchment screens. Jill Scarlet gestured with a slim, scarred hand toward an antique sofa and chairs set around a potbellied stove. Jack and Christie sat. Sylph wandered around.

"I'll fetch you something to eat." As Jill Scarlet pushed through a pair of doors that shut behind her, Christie leaned toward Jack. "Who is she?"

Jack replied, "She's Little Red Riding Hood."

Sylph, who still wore the aviator's cap, its goggles pushed up, sat in the chair beside Christie. "The very one."

Jack continued, "The fairy tale didn't originate in Germany, but in the Basque province of France, when there were wolves and things that looked like wolves. She was an innocent girl—"

"Aren't they all?" Sylph tilted her head.

"She was an *innocent* girl"—Jack frowned at Sylph—"who met Seth Lot. When she realized what he was and tried to twist from his grasp—with a hatchet—he killed her and made her into a Jill."

Christie whispered, "I *hate* this place."

Jill Scarlet returned with a basket of tangerines, dark bread, cheese, a bottle of black wine, and a carton of Fig Newtons. She set the basket on the steamer trunk that served as a coffee table. She pushed back her hood and sat opposite them on the altar steps, the hounds settling on either side of her. Mink-brown hair tumbled around her shoulders. Her argent gaze was unsettling; her scarred face seemed familiar . . .

Jack began figuring some things out as Christie said, "*Jill Scarlet*. Sylvie and I were supposed to meet you—"

"And you weren't around when I went to the StarDust Studios. I thought the *Dubh Deamhais* had changed his mind." She studied Christie critically. "I see why he chose you." She turned that reflective gaze on Jack. "Do you want to know how I became a Jill?"

Before Jack could avoid it, she'd reached out and gripped his hand.

. . . a girl in a red gown and cloak fled through a forest dripping with ice and gloom. She held a hatchet in one hand. There was blood on her face, her hands.

She fell, screamed as a massive, spiky shadowy fell over her and a claw as razor-fine and long as a dagger sliced her open as if she were a caught rabbit—

He shook himself out of the vision and edged back to keep her from touching him again. "I know what he did to you. Tell me why you wanted us here."

"You know about the trinity death for the Wolf." Jill Scarlet rose and walked to the painting of a winter forest. She opened the painting as if it were a cabinet door and took a metal box from the alcove behind it. She returned to Jack and lifted the box's lid, revealing a black vial sealed with a tiny pewter dog. "I stole this from Seth Lot, long ago."

Jack stared at the vial but didn't reach for it. "What is it?"

"I suspect it's what will kill him. Do you see the label? *Aconitum lycoctonum.*"

"Wolfsbane?" Jack was skeptical. "Wolfsbane is quite common."

Sylph Dragonfly leaned forward, peering at the vial, not touching it. "Not this. It's not made from the plant. It's an alchemized poison, Jack. Created by a mortal sorcerer with a Fata queen lover."

"They used it to poison her king, a creature of shadows and nightmares." Jill Scarlet watched as Jack studied the label on the vial. When he saw the symbol beneath the label, he said softly, "A pentacle. Solomon? *King Solomon* was the mortal sorcerer?"

"He and the queen of Sheba made it—supposedly from the blood of Cerberus—to destroy the queen of Sheba's king, who was an ancient Fata, as was she. After they pinned her shadow king with holy wood, and poisoned him, they cut off his head."

"The queen of Sheba was a Fata?" Christie leaned forward. "And that wolfsbane came from the three-headed dog in Greek mythology?"

"Probably not. There is no three-headed dog." Jack took the metal box with the vial and slid it into his backpack. "Tell me, Madame Scarlet, why didn't *you* use the wolfsbane on Seth Lot?"

"How was I to get close to Lot? I've only ever been able, with my people, to fight his pack—wolves seduced by Lot's promise of becoming a true king, here, on the new continent."

"That's why the Blackhearts played fetch for you. They don't want Lot lording it over them in their territory."

"They don't want *any* old-world Fata reigning in their territory. The mortal boy may eat and drink, by the way—it's all human food, including the blackberry wine." She turned the bottle, revealing a brand label. "From a friend. Leander Cyrus."

Jack said, "You were the one in the Dead Kings with Cyrus, the night Finn learned what Leander was."

As Christie reached for the Fig Newtons and Sylph poured the blackberry wine into two goblets, Jack continued with his questions, although the urge to go after Finn made him feel as if his skeleton wanted to burst out of his skin. "How did you get the information about the trinity death?"

She shrugged. "The Solomon story. Research. Things I've heard from others. And then we tested it. My people and I have used the wolfsbane against two murderous Fatas as old as the Wolf, Fatas that should only have died by divine fire. Those two Fatas are dead from the *Aconitum lycoctonum*, pinning, and decapitation. One of my best people was killed."

Jack glanced at Christie and Sylph. "I need to speak to Madame Scarlet alone. There's a nice courtyard outside, Dragonfly. Why don't you and Christopher go look at it?"

WHEN THEY WERE ALONE, Jack sat with Jill on the altar steps. "Who are the two big bad Fatas you and your people have ended? It might make my day to know their names."

"The Gray Tinker and the Night Spindle."

"Bloody ridiculous names for two awful things. I recognize their titles—one came from Scotland and the other from Prague. One slaughtered adolescents, correct? And the other terrorized children. Did you do this, like, to impress me?"

She smiled wryly. "No."

"Who, exactly, is in your band of rebels?"

"Changelings and *aisling*s torn from their world and enslaved in this one. I've kept them safe, away from Fata kings and queens. And there are others—Fatas tainted by the true world, friends and lovers to mortals. Where is Serafina Sullivan?"

"On her way to the Mockingbirds. You've kept track of your descendants. You and the Black Scissors have communicated with Lily Rose Sullivan."

"Only the Black Scissors could speak with Lily Rose—they used insects as messengers. I didn't know Serafina and Lily Rose Sullivan were my blood until the Black Scissors and Leander Cyrus came to me for help. The Black Scissors told me about the trinity death, and about the girls."

Jack twisted the ring Finn had given him. "What was your name when you were a real girl?"

"Bronwyn Rose Govannon. I was wed to a man"—her voice cracked with grief—"named Jonathon Sullivan. Seth Lot made me a widow and my two children orphans."

Jack was silent for a moment, acknowledging her grief. "Finn's coworker is named Micah Govannon—"

"My descendant. He works for me."

"You sent him to watch over Finn. You're not the only immortal from their family tree. I knew a Jack named Ambrose Cassandro, their mother's ancestor. Finn came here to get her sister from the Wolf. I was trying to get to Finn before she reached the Mockingbirds."

Jill Scarlet looked down at her boots. Her hands knotted together. "Will you reach her in time?"

"No. And, really, this delay . . . it wouldn't have made a difference. I knew I'd need to snake my way into the Mockingbirds' nest."

"Let me come with—"

"No. I need to do this discreetly. Why do the Mockingbirds want Finn? And me?"

"The Mockingbirds are no friend to the Wolf. He once did away with an entire clan of them in South Carolina. They fear him."

Jack smiled darkly. "Well, then . . . I think I know what they want."

CHRISTIE WALKED WITH SYLPH DRAGONFLY through Jill Scarlet's courtyard. Lights glittered in the citrus trees, and exotic plants cast soothing fragrances into the air. The Dragonfly's bare legs flashed beneath her black gown as it billowed in a honeyed breeze. She said, "What are you afraid of, Christie Hart?"

"I'm afraid that we won't get to Finn and Sylvie in time. I'm afraid we won't get home. I'm afraid that we'll all die here. And I'm so fucking *useless* . . ."

"Christie Hart." She turned, her eyes shining like starlight on water.

Her hair and gown began to swirl. Her lips pulled back from teeth like thorns. Shocked, Christie reeled back and chanted words that came to him in a heartbeat: "*She is darkness, an elemental sprite. Her words mean nothing. I am stone. My heart protects me from this wight. Against her power, I stand alone."*

The dangerous mood fell from Sylph Dragonfly as if she'd discarded knives, and she became herself again. "Do you quote poetry often, Christie Hart? That's a symptom."

Christie couldn't move. *"What the hell . . . ?* A symptom of *what?"*

"In the words of one of your people, *'Red blood out and black blood in, my Nannie says I'm a child of sin. How did I choose me my witchcraft kin?'"*

"That's Walter de la Mare. Or is it Nathaniel Hawthorne? What are you telling me in your spooky, roundabout way?" He felt as if his stomach had dropped into his boots.

"Fear dorchadas are very rare." Sylph Dragonfly drew closer.

"What is a—"

"A male witch."

His heart galloped. "I am not a witch. Sylvie is. Reiko Fata said so."

"My original, Sylvie Whitethorn, is not a witch. I would sense it if she was. Your power must have lingered near her and Reiko mistook it for Sylvie's."

"No. I don't want to be a—"

"Christie Hart, if you ignore this, it will *hurt* you. This world tried to take you once—the fox knight who led Serafina Sullivan away is your double. He was to replace you."

"What?"

She reached out, her brows slanting. "Take my hands."

Grudgingly, he did so, and clenched his teeth against a fierce desire as he remembered last night and what had happened after the kiss, how her bare skin had felt against his as they'd rolled around in the grass. He'd never done it outside before. He'd never been with a Fata girl.

She said, "I'm going to free you from this ridiculous fear. Close your eyes. Repeat my words: *'Light as a feather, my bones made of air. I free myself from all mortal care. Upon the air I gently rise, my breath my power, my soul to fly.'"*

As he reluctantly recited the words, he felt as if a hallucinogenic venom had spilled into his blood. Something dark and old, coiled in his brain, his heart, his spine, woke. Her hands tightened around his. "Open your eyes, Christie Hart."

When he did, he sucked in a breath.

They spun in a slow circle—two feet above the grass. As his heart began its march toward a stroke, the Fata witch laughed softly and twirled him like a child in the air. The waves of shock and dizziness passed. He dared to look down again at the grass far below his feet. The panic began to return—

"Talk to me, Christie. It'll calm you."

He blurted, "The fox knight—who made him to replace me? Who made *you* to replace Sylvie?"

"I've no idea. My first memory is of being a child and playing with dolls made of flowers and bones." When she kissed him, her lips were soft and sweet.

"Goddamn it." The annoyed—and annoying—voice sent them plummeting to the grass. Sylph recovered with a neat twist, and Christie scrambled up to face Jill Scarlet and Jack, who continued, "I might have known you'd turn out to be the woman of darkness."

"The term," Christie said haughtily, "is *fear dorchadas, man* of darkness."

"Man? More like *buachaill dorchadas*."

"That's 'boy of darkness,'" Sylph said helpfully.

"Yes. I guessed that. So, Jack, are we done here? Can we move on and stop Finn and Sylvie from getting to the Mockingbird monsters?"

"I'm going to take the Mockingbirds up on their earlier invitation to tea." Jack's smile made Christie wonder if Sylph's Jack-illusion was becoming a reality. He guiltily hoped it was. Because there was no way they were going to survive the Ghostlands without badass Jack.

JACK'S FIRST WARNING that they were in Mockingbird territory was the sight of a human skull on a pillar, with the skeleton of a bird arrowing out of one eye socket. Standing beside his reindeer motorcycle, Jack regarded the gruesome totem with narrowed eyes as Christie walked to his side and stared up at the skull.

"It's a terror tactic." Sylph Dragonfly was disdainful as she wheeled her motorcycle through the ferns.

"It works." Christie glanced at Jack, the whites showing around his irises. "They've got Finn and Sylvie, don't they? We're too late."

"It's never too late." Jack turned and gazed down the steep ravine, at the fin de siècle–style hotel in the mountain forest wreathed with mist. Even from this distance, he could feel the dark energy of the place buzzing at his eardrums.

It was the same *Go-away-don't-come-here-Bad-Things-will-happen-to-you* glamour Reiko had used to keep people away from Tirnagoth. "Neither of you can come with me."

"I can help—"

"How?" Jack didn't even look at Christie. "Get hurt and distract them by bleeding all over the place?"

"Was that one of your plans?" Christie sounded tired. Sylph was silent beside them, her black hair and gown drifting in a wind that reeked of rust and rotting leaves. Christie continued, "*They're my friends, Jack.* I'm going with you. And I did knife that siren that would have mummified you. And I'm a . . . witch."

Jack studied the boy with the tangled curls and goatlike stubbornness. "I need to go in there alone. This isn't pretend, Christopher."

Sylph's eyes caught the last of the light. "You need to convince the Mockingbirds that you've gone dark. So, Jack, what would make you go dark?"

"I'd rather not say." At Jill Scarlet's, Jack had exchanged his clothes for a black suit and a dark coat lined with fur. His fingers were once again decorated with old rings.

Shadows uncurled from Sylph's black hair, her fingertips, enveloped her, and fell away.

Reiko Fata stood where Sylph Dragonfly had been, her hair writhing, her gown as red as wallpaper in hell. Jack felt as if someone had put an ax into his heart. He didn't move as she glided to him, cupped his face in her hands, and whispered, "Come back to me."

He felt the darkness constrict around the illusion of his fossil heart—then Christie was shouting, "*Let the mask drop and the true spirit rise. Let the mists of deceit fade from our eyes . . .*"

Jack blinked and it was Sylph Dragonfly who stood before him. She cocked her head to one side and looked curious. "Well? Did it work?"

He slid the *kris* blade back into his sleeve. "That was a dangerous thing to do, Dragonfly."

"You needed to remember what you once were."

Jack asked Christie, "How did you know that spell, with those words?"

"I don't know." Christie was staring at the Dragonfly.

Jack stepped back. "You both remember what you need to do?"

"Yes," Sylph said. "Good luck. Is that what you people say at times like this?"

"That's right, Dragonfly." As Jack moved past Christie, he murmured to the boy, "You'd be wise not to kiss the witch again."

And he strode alone toward the grand, ruined nest of the Mockingbirds, the old darkness beginning to fracture the fragile identity given to him by a girl with tawny hair and caramel eyes.

THE MOCKINGBIRDS HADN'T EVEN BOTHERED to conceal the fossilized hotel with glamour; they didn't expect visitors. As Jack pushed through the nettles that had mated with kudzu and overtaken what had once been impressive landscaping, he could smell decay and mildew. He made himself smile as he ascended the massive stairway of moss-slimed marble.

The doors with their patina of old bone opened. From the shadows came a young woman, or something that resembled a young woman. A gossamer cloak billowed like an enormous butterfly around her lily-white gown. Hair the color of moonlight on pewter cascaded to her hips. She was crowned with a wreath of blackthorn and old roses, her lovely face marred by black spirals inked beneath pale eyes lined with red cochineal.

"Jack Daw, as I live and breathe." Her voice was as honeyed as a southern belle's, and venomous. "What brings you all dark and handsome to my doorstep?"

"Have we met before? I've forgotten."

"I am Amaranthus." Her feet were bare and dirty. There was a smear of red on her mouth, and he doubted very much that it was lipstick. "We've met. I visited Reiko once."

He said, remembering, "'Love-Lies-Bleeding.'"

"That's my name. We left an invitation for you and your charming companion at the *Ban Gorm*'s." She took a slithering step down. "And you ignored it."

Grateful for the darkness within him now, he placed a hand glittering with rings on the balustrade. "You should be careful what you invite into your home, Amaranthus." He advanced up one step. "I believe you've got something of mine."

"Are they *all* yours, sugar? You've got fine taste. Two pretty girls and one *lovely* boy. Come on in." Love-Lies-Bleeding turned and moved back toward the entrance. Jack followed. As he passed over the threshold, he felt the dark snake through him.

Leaving footprints on the dusty floor, Amaranthus led Jack into a dingy hall where baroque velvet paper peeled in purple swaths from unhealthy-looking walls. The air was bitter with a smell that reminded him of blood, burned sugar, and the dusty corpses of animals. She pushed open a set of glass doors frosted with the images of lilies and bird skulls, and they entered a large conservatory scattered with Fatas and antique furniture. A creature as gray and insubstantial as cobwebs sat at a grand piano of toad-belly white, fingering a jangling tune from the keys. Some of the Mockingbirds were playing a game similar to croquet, with ivory sticks and a glass ball containing fire.

"Welcome"—Amaranthus looked over her shoulder—"to Mockingbird Court."

A young man, milk-white hair dyed red at the tips, straightened from where he'd been leaning against a headless statue. His gaze was flat. "*You.*"

"Narcissus," Amaranthus chided, "be sociable."

Jack looked at Narcissus and flashed a razor smile. "You were on the train."

Narcissus growled, "You should have put him in chains, instead of letting him run loose. He threatened me."

"Well, he's *Jack Daw.* He threatens a lot of people." Jack heard Amaranthus rustling beside him and sensed, again, that the beautiful girl was merely a cocoon over a thing of contorted bones, moldering feathers, and malice.

Carefully, Jack said, "Finn Sullivan was one of my finest tricks. She was my key to escaping Reiko. I want her back."

"Reiko," Amaranthus said sweetly, "whom you murdered, with your pretty schoolgirl. The girl who made you bleed, who made you mortal. Tell me, sugar: How is it you're a Jack again?"

"Because I prefer it. Now, do you want the Wolf dead or not?"

CHAPTER 15

Her lips were red, her looks were free,
Her locks were yellow as gold,
Her skin was white as leprosy.
The nightmare Life-in-Death was she,
Who thicks men's blood with cold.

—*THE RIME OF THE ANCIENT MARINER*, SAMUEL TAYLOR
COLERIDGE

When Finn opened her eyes and found herself seated at one end of a long table, her head resting against the back of a chair, she was confused. As the nausea and brain fog subsided, she began to focus on an ivory wall stained with mold and hung with a large, peculiar painting of little girls in bonnets, their catlike faces peering at the viewer. Beneath the painting was a hearth filled with flaming candles the color of corpses. Her gaze drifted down.

At the other end of the table, sprawled with one leg draped over the arm of his chair, was Jack.

"Jack." She tried to move, but her limbs felt as if they were tangled in an invisible web. Jack wasn't looking at her, but at the tangerine he was neatly peeling. He wore an elegant, dark suit and his hair was pulled back, emphasizing the sharp bones of his face.

"It's been a great trick," he said, focused on the tangerine as Finn followed the light that gilded his mouth, the pulse in his throat, "to watch you—a shrewd girl, a *smart* girl—fall for a thing like me."

The air hummed slightly—she felt a trickle from her nose and dabbed the back of one hand against her nostrils, looked, and saw blood. Only Fata magic caused such symptoms.

That's not Jack.

Terror gave way to anger. She curled her hands against the table. *"Where are Sylvie and Moth?"*

He set the peeled tangerine on the table and rolled it toward her. She could smell its sweet tartness; her mouth watered. He said, "You freed me. For that, I'm grateful. But I don't want you anymore."

Her nails dug into the wood of the table. For a mad moment, she almost believed him.

"You're bleeding." He slid to his feet and walked to her, crouched beside her chair, and offered her a black handkerchief. She didn't take it. She studied his face for flaws in the mask. "Where is your ring, Jack?"

"I've a lot of rings."

Cold slid through the chamber. Feathers and leaves sticky with cobwebs drifted across the floor as she stared into the eyes of the thing wearing Jack's face. She said, "Why is it you remember what you said to me on Halloween night, *Jack*—what you told Sionnach Ri to tell me, to get me here—but you can't remember which ring I gave you?"

He spoke as if addressing a crazy person, with pity. "The ring wasn't important to me. I'm sorry I used you to be free of Reiko."

"What did you give me before we left, *Jack*?" Leaning toward him, she felt like the predator now. "And what did I give *you*?"

He smiled and sat back on his heels. "You *are* clever."

And Jack's likeness ghosted away from a Fata with the face of a cruel prince and pale hair streaked red at the tips. It was the Fata Jack had threatened on the train, the one called Narcissus, the one she'd seen at Goblin Market.

"I remember you," she whispered.

"Want to know my name?" His voice had a southern lilt. He wore a cream-colored suit with an ivory cameo pinned to his silver tie and he was barefoot. The pupils of his eyes were rectangular, like a goat's.

"It won't be your real name. But I know you're called Narcissus."

"It's Narcissus Mockingbird. Since you refused the invitation we left at the Blue Lady's house, we had to devise another way to bring you and Jack to our doorstep. And dealing with that damn fox knight and giving him his heart back was one of our ways."

"Is *that* what you gave Sionnach Ri?" Finn remembered the black stone Sionnach had pocketed in Goblin Market. She glanced sidelong at the door, white and carved with images of twining lilies. She told herself she'd *chosen* to come here. "You murdered the Blue Lady."

"We left an invitation."

"You left a *piece* of her in a *box*."

"She was going to give you and your Jack to the Wolf, so don't you think she deserved it?"

"Where are Sylvie and Moth?"

"Safe. You should know, child, that Reiko Fata and Amaranthus were practically sisters. I'm just warning you."

"Who is Amaranthus?" Finn didn't believe him—none of the Fatas she'd met had had warm feelings for one another.

"Amaranthus is my sister and the ruler of us. She knows you were the cause of Reiko's death. But she's willing to overlook that, if you'll do her a good turn." He stood and moved to the door. "You did well not to eat the Goblin fruit. It would have made you believe everything I told you."

"What does she *want* from me?"

"A favor only a queen killer can grant her." The door shut behind him.

Finn stared at the tangerine, the Goblin fruit, as it slowly unfurled, puffed out, and became a toadstool shaded a poisonous orange.

She jumped up and ran to the door, grabbed the handle, yanked. She braced herself and pulled with a mighty effort. She slammed herself against the wood, banged her fists against it, kicked it. The room had no windows. She wanted to claw at the walls.

She sank against the door and huddled there. They had taken her coat, her backpack, her friends.

AFTER WHAT SEEMED AN ETERNITY LATER, a girl in a porcelain mask came for Finn and led her down a hallway to another decaying chamber. "There are new clothes on the bed. Make yourself presentable."

Finn brushed past her. "Thanks. Go away."

"Don't you want to know what's going to happen to you—"

Finn turned and slammed the door in her face.

She wandered around what had once been a pretty room. It had the same pale, ancient colors as the rest of the hotel, but kudzu tumbled through the windows and the giant bed was hazed with cobwebs and dust. There was a bird's nest in the fireplace and an electric lamp that flickered unreliably. She grimaced when she saw what had been laid out for her on the bed.

She put on the dress of crumpled, parchment-thin cotton the color of fresh blood, but kept her Doc Martens and tossed the red shoes out the window. She brushed the leaves from her hair in front of a tarnished mirror and scowled at the makeup left for her in a glass case. She grimly applied the lip stain and eye shadow. Her hands shook, but there was a core of ice within her that made her suspect the elixir had done more than change her scent. She would play their game, if only to convince them they'd broken her.

She searched for a weapon, found only a shard of glass. She flung it away and walked to a window, leaned out of it, saw a starlit tangle of garden, far below.

A familiar head stuck out of the window below hers.

"*Sylv!*" Finn gripped the sill. There was no sane way to climb down.

Sylvie leaned farther out, clutching the window frame, her dark hair swirling in the wind. "Are you okay?"

"Yes," Finn lied. "Are you really Sylvie?"

"Oh, Finn. What're they doing to you?"

Moth leaned out beside Sylvie. Finn smiled to see him back in human form. He said, "Are you all right? I'm coming up."

"No—"

But he gripped the window frame below and hauled himself onto a narrow molding that Finn hadn't even considered as a foothold. She watched anxiously as he pushed himself up, as he clambered over the sill. His white, button-down shirt, silver tie, and trousers were smudged with dust. He looked disapprovingly around the room. "I don't know what they're dressing us up for."

"You said they were ghouls."

"Yes." He prowled around, tried the door. "And they're all bat-shit crazy." He held up one wrist banded by what looked like barbed wire. "This keeps me from changing. The witch put it on me."

"The . . . witch?"

"Amaranthus Mockingbird. An old thing." Moth sat on the windowsill and glanced down. "This is my fault. Because I wronged Sionnach Ri. I wonder how many people I've done awful things to?" He looked up with a sudden smile that startled Finn. "I didn't know I was so popular here."

"Do you remember what you did? To Sionnach?"

His smile faded. "Now I do. A while ago, Lot gave me back my mortal shape and sent me after Sionnach Ri and a witch called Dragonfly. He wanted me to steal something from each of them."

Finn waited and he continued softly, "The heart of a fox knight and the heart of a witch are powerful things. Fatas who grow hearts make them into objects of power, which they hide, because such objects can be used to drain a Fata's power, or kill them."

"I know," Finn whispered.

"*I* didn't. When I learned, I tried to steal the hearts back. Lot turned me into a moth until your sister kissed me."

Finn sat on the windowsill beside him. She glanced down at Sylvie, who was perched on the sill below and gazing anxiously up. "It's me the Mockingbirds want, Moth. If you get the chance, take Sylvie and run."

"Now, you know Sylvie won't do that. And your sister sent me to protect you. You've got shadows in your eyes and none at your feet. You need to leave the Ghostlands soon, Finn, or you won't be able to. Don't take any more of that elixir the Goblin Market witch made for Sylvie." One of his hands rested against hers on the sill. "The elixir will change you into something that is not good. You'll be fearless, but . . . not you."

She didn't want to withdraw her hand from beside his. "Moth . . . will Lily be different?"

"She's still your sister." His voice was gentle.

"Has Seth Lot . . . has he . . ." She couldn't finish. Moth gripped her hand and said nothing, which was her answer. She wanted to vomit. She thought of cutting off Seth Lot's handsome head.

"Lily Rose is like you." Moth's gaze held hers. "She is not breakable. She said to me, once, that she would give *them* what they want . . . a queen. And she is a queen in that house of wolves and briars."

Someone rapped at the door. They both flinched.

"I'll see you later, fearless girl." Moth slid out the window to the ledge below, where Sylvie helped pull him back in. She looked up at Finn and winked, before vanishing from view.

A female voice called from behind Finn's door, "Are you decent, sugar?"

"Yes." A primitive terror flashed through Finn. She straightened and pretended to be stone.

The door whispered open, white paint crumbling from its mildewed wood. The air began to hum as darkness ribboned into the room, becoming a young woman in a gown of pale silk, her hair a knee-length cascade of pewter white, her eyes lined with crimson spirals. She looked so much like a real fairy as she moved across the room, bare feet peeking from beneath the ivory gown's dirty hem, that Finn felt her fear become wonder. "Serafina Sullivan, who conquered the white serpent, kissed a Jack back from the dead, and has now come to challenge the Big Bad Wolf."

"Amaranthus?"

"Pleased to make your acquaintance." The girl dropped into a chair and slung her legs over one of its arms as if to imitate Narcissus's earlier pose as Jack. There were scratches on her legs. "That dress you're wearing is Dolce and Gabbana. Do you like it?"

Finn lifted her chin. "Did you buy it? Or did it belong to a *guest*?"

Amaranthus smiled slyly and twisted a finger in her shining hair. "A guest left it. You're prettier than I expected. But, then, Jack Daw always was one for choosing the finer ones of your kind." The girl-thing examined her silvery nails and spoke with idle malice. "He wanted so badly to be a real boy, Jack did."

"Well." Finn felt the cold, distantly. "Now, he is."

"Oh, sugar." Amaranthus's eyes glinted. "Did you ever think that maybe he was sorry he got what he asked for? I mean, he tricked three other girls into loving him just so he could grow one of them whatchamacallits . . . a *heart*. But it seemed he only grew one for you."

Finn became still and tense. "Whatever you think you're doing, you can *stop* it."

"You ever have doubts?" Amaranthus slid into a crouch on the chair. "Ever wonder if he *used* you?"

"Never."

Amaranthus glided to her feet, the fabric of her gown whispering. Her gossamer cloak billowed as she moved toward Finn. "Do you know why Jack Daw is famous in the Ghostlands—or infamous, rather? He was Reiko's assassin. Oh, he might not have killed those three mortal girls with his own hands, but they died *because* of him. Here, in the *Taibhse na Tir*, he killed her enemies, and don't think it wasn't something he enjoyed, slaughtering Fatas."

The Mockingbird queen tucked Finn's hair back from her face in a sisterly gesture. "I had to be sure you weren't easily tricked, little girl. You weren't fooled by my brother. I want you to kill the Wolf. Well, I want your *lover* to kill the Wolf." Amaranthus stepped back and began sauntering around the room. "Seth Lot took Reiko away from me. He murdered my cousins, who were dear to me. I've made it easy for you, Serafina. I've arranged it with Seth Lot. I'm going to give you to him, a sort of peace offering—only not really. Once in the Wolf's house, you'll get Moth in, in his insect shape. He'll be carrying the weapons. Then you let Jack in. Together, the three of you should be able to do the deed."

Finn stared at her. "I'm not a killer. And how do you expect me to get Jack into the Wolf's house? I don't know where he is—"

"He's here."

Finn stopped breathing. Amaranthus resumed speaking, "He's got the poison now. You've got that uncorrupted silver dagger for pinning, and, after those two things strike the Wolf, I suppose that blade hidden in your walking stick will do to cut off the Wolf's head."

Finn sat down. If she were given to Seth Lot . . . the idea made her blood run cold and her stomach twist up. She made her voice hard. "If you just hand me over to him, won't he be suspicious? Tell him to send Lily Rose in exchange. Say you want to hold her here, to keep us apart, to avenge Reiko."

Amaranthus seemed to be considering the idea. "Lot certainly wants you. I suppose I could tell him I'd like to keep your sister as a hostage against your Jack harming me. He doesn't know I have Jack. In truth, I'll keep your sister and the pretty crow girl as insurance against you, your lover, and the moth boy returning here to retaliate. Yes. I like your idea, Serafina."

The Mockingbird swept from the room, leaving Finn to stare at the backpack left on the chair. It was *her* backpack, and set deliberately in front of it was the tiny bottle of elixir Sionnach Ri had gotten at Goblin Market.

This can't work, Finn thought, her hands curling into fists in her dress. *This can't possibly work.*

JACK SAT IN THE MOCKINGBIRDS' COURTYARD, on the rim of a well surrounded by pale, night-blooming plants. Albino bees buzzed past him. An ivory lizard scampered over his boots. When he thought of Finn being so close, he smiled.

Amaranthus slid from the shadows to sit beside him. She said, "Do you want to know why I brought you and your girl here? We want the Wolf dead."

"I believe I told you I know that."

"I've offered to give your Serafina to the Wolf. He accepted."

Jack almost went for her throat. He wound his hands into his coat to keep from doing so as she continued, "In exchange, I've asked for her sister as a hostage. Serafina will go to Seth Lot, willingly, so that her sister might be released. You and the moth boy will follow Serafina to the Wolf. The moth boy will have the poison—you did get it from Jill Scarlet, yes?—and the weapons; Lot would sense such things on *you*, but concealed with Moth, a being riding the shadow, they'll be undetectable. Serafina will let you both into the Wolf's house."

"You're insane."

She leaned close until her lips were only inches from his. He could smell the blood she and her clan drank from the well on which they sat, a well that led down to the river of blood running beneath the Ghostlands. "You'll do what you must because you are Jack Daw, and Serafina is a queen killer. I have faith in you."

He looked out over the night garden as despair strangled any hope left within him. "You expect us to Trojan horse into Lot's house and kill him? Then you'll let Lily Rose and our friends free and we'll all live happily ever after?"

"Lot is an old Fata, older than I am, almost a divine thing. There are only three ways that will end him, if done in succession. And you know what they are now."

One of Jack's hands, knotted in a coat pocket, touched the vial of *Aconitum lycoctotum* Jill Scarlet had given him.

"You have the wolfsbane—I can smell it. Your girl brought a silver dagger that our land hasn't rusted. And there's that elder-wood walking stick with the sword inside that we dare not draw. You'll figure it out, sugar. Once Serafina gets you and Moth into the Wolf's house, you'll figure it all out or you'll die." Her eyes narrowed. "You *are* a Jack again, aren't you? Returning *has* changed you back?"

He wondered what the hell kind of sword the Black Scissors had given them as he leaned close to the Mockingbird queen and whispered, "What's to keep us from returning to give *you* a trinity death?"

She smiled. "Because I'll have Lily Rose Sullivan and Sylvie Whitethorn. Now, would you like to see your Finn?"

A FATA BOY AND GIRL in ivory 1920s clothes escorted Finn to a candlelit conservatory, its chessboard floor tangled with morning glories and the roots of pale plants snaking out of stone urns. Mold furred the tiles and cracks spiderwebbed the grimy, glass dome of the ceiling. Nightshade, and briars dripping livid roses, ran riot. Contained within the cavernous mouth of a hearth hewn into a gorgon face were porcelain hands holding lit candles.

Jack stood before the Medusa hearth. As the glass doors shut behind Finn, she stood very still, afraid that if she moved, he'd disappear like the Fata trick he might be. *"Are you real?"*

"I feel that way." He was half in shadow.

She walked to him, raised her hands to his face. His skin was cooler than usual, and ancient rings decorated his fingers again—but the lions-and-the-heart ring was among them. He bent his head and kissed her as if she were a succulent thing, drawing her onto her toes as his arms slid around her until she was crushed against him and the burning butterflies coursed up from deep inside of her.

She didn't feel his heartbeat. She stumbled back against the sofa. "Jack?"

He stood still, candlelight threading his eyelashes and tied-back hair, the fur of his coat. He said, "I couldn't be weak anymore, Finn."

She kept her voice steady. "You are *not* a Jack. Please tell me you're not a—"

"Finn." He shed his coat and held it out to her. "Aren't you cold in that little dress?"

"I'm not cold, Jack, because I took the elixir."

His gaze was sharp. "How much?"

"Only enough."

He tossed the coat over a chair. "You're all soft skin and delicate bones. Aren't you tired of hurting and bleeding? I know *I* don't want to go back to it again."

Confused and a little defiant, she didn't move as he stepped close and slid those ring-jeweled hands up her bare arms to cup her face. His touch, despite his cool skin, was hot. Gently, he said, "You don't really want a mortal man, Finn, some-one weak and prone to dying. You want a dark and perfect elf knight who can never be harmed, who'll always protect you."

Desire turned to anger and she struck his hands away. "I don't want a dark, cold *thing*. I want someone . . . I want *you* . . . *What did you do to yourself, you idiot?*"

A muscle twitched in his jaw as if he was repressing a smile. "I don't like how the Mockingbirds have dressed you, like some tarted-up Alice in Wonderland."

"*You* look like you just joined the Fata mafia."

"Why do you keep backing away from me?"

"I'm not." But she was, because there was a dangerous look to him now that she remembered from his Jack days. As calmly as she could, she said, "Why do you smell like roses? Please just tell me *what happened to you.*"

His smile was wild. "Remember those westerns you like? Where any man can be saved by the love of a good woman?"

"That never happens in the westerns I like—stop." She held up a hand. He stopped. She'd somehow circled back to the doors.

"I did it for you," he said, his voice rough. "Do you really think I'm going to harm you?"

"I don't know, Jack." It hurt her to say that.

The silver ghosted his eyes and she saw a true Jack, a spirit twisted into the eternal shape of something made to stalk and harm. She turned and yanked the doors open—

He pushed them closed with her against them, imprisoning her with his arms. He whispered in her ear, "You'll need to do more than kiss me to change me back."

She flung herself around. "You were afraid to touch me when you were a Jack before."

He stepped away, and the room's shadows seemed to close over him. He said, "Finn. I need to be like this, to fight Seth Lot."

She heard the click as the doors opened behind her, and she said, *"I love you,"* before sliding out.

The porcelain-masked Fata girl stood in the hallway. "You're to return to your room."

As the doors closed between her and Jack, Finn said, "Tell Amaranthus we'll do it. We'll kill Seth Lot."

FINN DIDN'T KNOW how much time passed while she waited in her prison. Restless, she used the Leica camera to take pictures of the room and regretted it when one of the flashes caught a shadow with a broken doll face crouched in a corner. Finn kept away from *that* corner and didn't take any more pictures.

She studied the vial of elixir. She took another drop.

Then she was summoned. She was allowed to bring her backpack and was led to the conservatory, where Amaranthus sat in a fan-backed chair of white wicker, her court surrounding her. Jazzy music crackled in the background as a man sang about not wanting to set the world on fire. Sylvie, in a little dress of gray gauze and striped stockings, sat tensely in a chair. Narcissus Mockingbird leaned against it. At his feet was a small cage with the moth fluttering inside.

Amaranthus rose to address her people. "Are you all afraid of this little girl?" She sauntered across the floor, her ring-decorated hands holding up the hem of her gown, revealing her scratched legs and dirty feet. "You should be. She's a queen killer . . . and she's going to pay."

She gestured to a set of glass doors frosted with images of birds in flight. The doors opened to admit two figures in hooded coats. The one in the lead flung back its cowl to reveal Caliban Ariel'Pan. He smiled at Finn and said, "I had more teeth and claws than the Jacks and Jills did."

Then his companion drew back her hood and reality crashed to pieces around Finn. *"Lily?"*

The last year had never been. Her sister had never killed herself. The funeral and the numb days afterward, when sleeping had been more of a comfort than living, had been a lie. All of it, all of it, had been a Fata trick. Because Lily Rose, fierce and flushed with life, stood across the room from her, in a black gown beneath a coat shimmering with rain. Finn felt a dazzling rush of relief, joy, shock—and despair that she and her sister would soon be parted again.

"*Finn!*" Lily dashed forward, but Caliban yanked her back.

Amaranthus wound a cold hand around Finn's wrist and said, "*Crom cu.* When the two sisters cross paths, the bargain is made. The queen killer goes to your Wolf and Lily Rose becomes our hostage."

"Seth Lot doesn't trust you, Mockingbird. You tried to take his prey before, at the *Ban Gorm*'s. And where's the Jack?"

"We haven't found the Jack. It was *you* who separated them, sugar. We've only got the girl."

Finn met her sister's wide, blue gaze, saw Lily's lips form her name, the questioning slant of her brows, and knew she couldn't allow herself to believe this was Lily until she could touch her and make sure.

"Seth Lot gave you the fox knight's heart to bargain a betrayal." When Caliban shook Lily Rose, Finn felt snarly. "What I don't understand is why you want *this* girl and not *that* one, the one who killed Reiko. Weren't you and Reiko besties? Or frenemies? Or something similar to that nature?"

"This is the most satisfying revenge, *crom cu.* Seth Lot gets something *he* wants and I get to keep the braveheart's sister from her as long as they both live. They'll never see each other again." Amaranthus shoved Finn forward. "Go on, sugar. Say farewell."

Caliban released Lily. Finn walked slowly across the floor. Lily moved just as cautiously. When they were a few steps away from each other, Finn, her voice breaking, whispered a question she'd been asking far too much lately: "Is it you?"

"It's me." Lily stepped forward and folded Finn into her arms. Her sister smelled the same, of an exotic perfume like fire and flowers. Her skin was cool, her voice angry as she said, "You weren't supposed to come here."

Finn drew back. She gripped Lily's hands and studied her, worried about how pale her sister was, the shadows beneath her eyes. "I still can't believe . . . you were broken and bleeding . . ." Her voice caught.

Lily hugged her again and said into her ear, "Don't let them take you. Don't let them take you to *him*."

"Here." Finn fumbled the bracelet of silver charms from around her wrist and held it out. "Look, it didn't decay."

Lily gazed warily at it. "Where did you get that?"

"Moth—"

"Ladies," Caliban called, "it's time." He dragged Finn back, and the bracelet fell to the floor between them. As Lily's gaze flicked up from the bracelet to Finn, Finn yanked away from Caliban. He held out a hand, his smile so evil it made Finn flinch. He said, "For you, I'll be a gentleman. Would you like my coat? No? Been drinking the elixir, have you? All strong and such?"

He clamped a hand around her wrist, and she had to hurry to keep up with his long strides as he dragged her through the double doors, onto the stairway.

Parked in the hotel's circular driveway was a white Mercedes with tinted windows, its hood ornament a pewter wolf's head. Finn halted, pulling back, and Caliban turned to her. "The brave girl is having an attack of good sense. You've lost, *leannan*, let it go."

His hand vised around her wrist again—she wouldn't let him drag her to the car, so she walked quickly with him down the stair. Despite the monster at her side, she wanted to jump up and down with joy. *Lily's alive.*

"He's got plans for *you*, darling." Caliban opened the passenger-side door of the Mercedes, silver-white hair sweeping across his face. "You might even like some of them."

She almost ran then, but his nails sank into her wrist and he growled, "Don't even think it."

A roaring and a flare of lights from beyond the trees made him snap straight. As Finn stared into the night, wondering what new horror was about to arrive, the glowing orbs shrank to headlights belonging to fox-shaped brass-and-copper motorcycles.

Caliban grabbed her, and a dagger slid from one of his sleeves.

The motorcycles surrounded the Mercedes and halted. The leader removed his helmet, revealing the familiar Christie face of Sionnach Ri the fox knight. "My apologies, Finn Sullivan. I seem to have misplaced something near and dear to me and came to ask if you've seen it—hullo, *crom cu*."

Caliban bared his teeth. "Fox. She's the property of the Wolf."

"Well, we're stealing the property of the Wolf. Do you think you can fight all of us, *crom cu*? Each of us has two knives. There are three of us. That's six knives."

Finn tore away from Caliban, whirled, and dashed back up the stairs.

Caliban moved, quick and light, and his hand knotted in her hair. She twisted free, wincing as strands of hair ripped from her scalp.

As Sionnach's bike roared up the stairway and halted neatly between them, the other two motorcycles ascended and Caliban spun to fight for his life. Finn stumbled back.

Sionnach, his bike humming, told Finn, "Go on. We'll take care of this."

Finn whispered, "Thank you," and lunged past him, toward the entrance of the Mockingbird Hotel.

WHEN JACK NOTICED the single flickering insect dancing above the Mockingbirds, he smiled.

He stood among them in a hooded coat so Caliban wouldn't recognize him. It had taken every bit of self-possession he had not to launch himself at Caliban as the *crom cu* hauled Finn away.

The dragonfly flitted toward Amaranthus. The Mockingbird queen was circling Lily Rose Sullivan, whose stubborn and defiant posture matched Finn's so closely, Jack had no doubt she was Finn's sister.

Amaranthus snatched out and caught the dragonfly by the wing. It whirred. She looked disdainfully at Jack. "*Really*, Jack . . ."

A clicking noise from above made her and everyone else look up.

The glass ceiling was darkening beneath a mass of tiny, glittering shapes. A jagged crack appeared—and became a hundred fissures.

Amaranthus glanced at Jack, her gaze ferocious with hate. There was a sinister, prolonged creaking sound from above.

Jack flung himself at Lily Rose and pushed her to the floor, shouting, "Sylvie!"

Sylvie dove beneath a chair and snatched the moth cage with her.

A thunderous crash was followed by glass shards cascading downward. The Mockingbirds scattered.

As Jack rolled with Lily Rose beneath a table, a giant spear of glass struck the floor where they'd been and minuscule pieces scattered everywhere. When he lifted his head, he saw the bracelet of silver charms Finn had tried to give back to her sister glinting nearby. He grabbed it and put it in his pocket.

"Who *are* you?" Lily Rose stared at him as they crouched beneath the table, watching the Mockingbird court erupt into chaos as the dragonflies descended.

"I'm Jack." He grabbed her hand and pulled her up and they ran toward Sylvie, who scrambled to her feet and raced alongside them, through the storm of insects.

As they pushed open the doors, Jack felt Lily Rose's hand yanked from his. He turned to see Narcissus Mockingbird dragging her back as the dragonflies blackened the room behind him.

"Mockingbird," Jack said carefully. "Let her go."

Narcissus's eyes were slits, his teeth sharp. He began to speak.

Then the dragonflies swarmed over him in a dark, glimmering fog and Lily Rose tore free.

"Go!" Jack told her, backing away with Sylvie, his gaze fixed on Narcissus as the Mockingbird vanished in the storm of dragonflies.

Lily ran. Narcissus lunged. Jack kicked him backward and the Mockingbird reeled toward the roaring fire in the hearth—

The doors slammed shut on the conservatory, revealing the witch runes scratched across them.

Christie stepped out of the shadows, shoving back the hood of his coat. He grinned, but his eyes were dark. "I carved the Dragonfly's spell onto the doors—they would've sensed her getting in. They didn't sense *me*—was that Lily Rose who just ran past?" His eyes widened as he saw Sylvie. "Is that really y—"

He was nearly knocked over by an armful of Sylvie, who, still clutching Moth's cage, threw herself on Christie, wrapping her arms and legs around him. "You're alive!" She pulled back, puzzled. "Why are you covered with words?"

Jack told them, "Time to leave."

AS FINN RACED BACK toward the entrance of the Mockingbird Hotel, the doors burst open, revealing a figure in a black gown racing toward her.

"*Finn!*" Lily flung herself forward, into Finn's arms. Finn held her tightly and closed her eyes.

Then Lily cried out.

Finn felt something sharp against her abdomen. She opened her eyes—

—and met the silvery gaze of Amaranthus Mockingbird as the Fata queen, standing behind Lily, drew back, a blade of blood-streaked bone in one hand.

Horrified, Finn clutched at her sister, who had folded her hands across her midriff. Dark blood was trickling over her fingers. She slowly looked up. "Damn . . ."

Finn caught her as she collapsed.

Amaranthus vanished in a small cyclone of tattered wings, bones, and eyes.

Then Sylvie and Christie—the real Christie, *her* Christie, *alive*—came running down the hall. He and Sylvie helped her haul Lily up and they staggered down the stairs, toward the Mercedes. Sionnach and his two companions were still fighting Caliban.

A Mockingbird with spiky white hair lunged at Finn, a curved dagger in one hand.

A reindeer motorcycle ridden by a black-haired girl in a dark gown knocked the Mockingbird over. Still holding Lily up, Christie met Finn's gaze and said, "That's Sylph Dragonfly. She's a witch. It's quite a story."

"Finn," Sylvie said as they hauled Lily Rose toward the Mercedes, "Jack's still in there."

The Mockingbird Hotel was beginning to flicker with orange flames in the lower windows.

Christie yanked open the Mercedes's rear door. As Sylvie set the moth cage on the floor and helped Lily into the back, he said, "Finn, he'd want you to be safe."

"I'm not leaving him." Finn snatched up the dagger the Mockingbird had dropped and turned toward the hotel now billowing with smoke. "And we need a Fata to drive the damn car—"

A hooded figure strode toward them from the smoke and ashes clouding the stair. The figure pushed the hood away and it was Jack who smiled at her. "Is that the only reason you were coming back for me?"

She rushed to him and flung her arms around him, whispered, "Lily's hurt. How did the fire start?"

"One of the Mockingbirds fell into the fireplace."

The fox knights were circling on their motorcycles, preparing to leave—Caliban was gone. Flame-light cast wild shadows on Sionnach's helmet and bike as he curved to Sylvie's side. As he removed his helmet, Christie whispered, "Holy f—"

"Hullo, Christie." Sionnach winked at him. To Sylvie, he said, "You stole my heart."

Everyone stared at him, then at Sylvie.

Sylvie clarified, "I saw these things for sale at Goblin Market—Fata hearts, I was told. I didn't know they were *real* hearts. Some were glass, some metal, some like keys or jewelry." She took a shiny black stone shaped like a Valentine's Day heart from her pocket. "So when I saw Sionnach with this—I lifted it from his jacket and put another stone in its place. I figured he'd want it back."

"You never trusted me." Sionnach held out a hand, and Sylvie dropped the heart into his palm. He nodded. "My fault, for being so careless with my heart near a crow girl. I should have checked it."

He put his helmet back on and spun away on his bike.

Christie said, "Sylvie, I am mightily impressed. Jack, can we get out of here now?"

As Jack slid behind the wheel of the Mercedes, Sylvie got into the passenger seat while Finn and Christie clambered into the back. Finn gathered her sister against her, glancing over one shoulder.

A hurricane of giant, skeletal wings, eyes, and howling fury swept down the hotel's stairs, toward them.

Finn met Jack's gaze in the rearview mirror. She knew that, here, only Fatas and Fata creatures could give energy to things—if Jack started the Mercedes, he truly was reverting back to what he had been.

He turned the key in the ignition and slammed his foot down on the pedal. The engine roared. The Mercedes shot forward onto the broken road.

Finn pressed her face into Lily's hair and closed her eyes against the inferno reflected in the rearview mirror.

CHAPTER 16

The two sisters loved each other so dearly that they always walked about hand in hand whenever they went out together, and when Snow White said: "We will never desert each other," Rose Red answered: "No, not as long as we live."

—"Snow White and Rose Red," The Brothers Grimm

As the Mercedes sped down the forested road, Finn cradled her sister, who slept now, red-streaked hands cradling her midriff. The smell of blood was sickening. Finn said, as calmly as she could, "Jack . . ."

Jack kept his gaze on the road. "We need to get her back to the true world."

The road seemed to curve forever, the Mercedes's headlights passing over eroding barns, forest walls, a clock tower on a rusting bridge. There was no traffic. There were no lights.

The sound of an escalating siren was almost unrecognizable at first. As lights flashed red and blue in the mirrors, Christie, looking back, said, "Is that a *cop* car?"

Sylvie turned in her seat, eyes wide.

"He shouldn't see us," Jack said tensely. "We're not in the true world."

"That's a real cop?"

Jack squinted into the rearview. "Hell . . . he *is* following us."

"Stop," Finn said calmly. "Pull over—Phouka said there were parts of the true world that crossed into the Ghostlands—well, this is it. We won't need to find the train station to get back—this is the open door. *Pull over.*"

Jack veered the car onto the grass. They waited as the sirens and flashing lights drew closer.

"I never thought I'd be so glad to see a cop in my li . . ." Christie's words faded as the cop car, modern sleek and blazoned with a sheriff's star, flashed past and faded into the night.

No one spoke as Jack steered the car back onto the road.

Lily suddenly raised her head. Her eyes were black. "Finn . . ."

"It's okay. Lily, we're almost home." Finn held her tight and Lily's head dropped onto her shoulder.

Jack swerved the Mercedes beneath an arch formed by two giant oaks with knotted-together branches and continued down a smaller road winding through the forest.

"This is it," Jack said. "This is where we caught our first train."

The Mercedes's power beams blazed past a screen of holly trees and brambles and lit up the quaint train station. He sped down the road, toward it—

—and slammed on the brakes as a nightmare barrier of black metal thorns suddenly materialized from the darkness before them.

The Mercedes screeched and hit the barrier with a metal-shrieking violence that sent everyone inside tumbling. The car shook once, spluttered. A grinding sound emerged from the engine as it died.

Jack looked back at them. "Is everyone all right?"

"Okay." Sylvie's voice was faint.

Finn kicked her door open and helped Lily out with Christie's assistance. Jack bashed the driver's door loose and slid free, reaching back in for Sylvie, who clutched the moth cage as she clambered after him. They stared at the barrier of black metal thorns surrounding the train station.

Jack said softly, "Sylvie, get Moth out of that cage and into his true form. We may need him, and the Mockingbirds armed him for our visit to the Wolf's house."

Sylvie unlatched the wicker cage. The moth drifted up, attempted to pass through the barrier, glided back, and brushed against Finn's lips.

"Everyone. Look away," Jack advised. But Finn watched as the insect lengthened into a spear of white light before becoming a shadow that fell away in tatters from the crouched figure of Moth. The transformation should have hurt her brain—maybe the elixir helped her adjust.

Christie and Sylvie hadn't watched, and Sylvie stepped back as Moth rose, drawing back the hood of his jacket. He had the sword/walking stick slung on a strap over one shoulder. His brows knit when he saw Lily leaning against Jack. "Lily Rose? Is that you?"

Lily didn't respond, her head bowed.

Christie moved toward the barrier. "There's got to be a way inside."

"I just remembered"—Sylvie looked at Jack in panic and dismay—"Christie and I need to return the way we came, or time will have passed in the real world and we might not end up in Fair Hollow."

"We'll have to take that chance. Anywhere in the true world is better than here, at the moment. And you'll end up at one of the Fata gates, which are all near civilization." Jack gently guided Lily to a place beneath a tree.

Finn crouched beside her. "Lily?"

Lily didn't respond, her head down, her breathing faint. Jack settled his coat around her and glanced at Finn. He handed her the bracelet of silver charms. "I don't know why this silver hasn't rotted. It must have something to do with . . . you."

He rose and walked toward the cage of metal thorns around the train station.

As Finn pulled the coat closer around her sister, something clinked from the coat's pocket . . . two tiny vials, one capped with a pewter dog: the other a crystalline bird labeled ELIXIR. She slid both bottles into her coat before Jack could see. She stood up—

The darkness of the forest came to life as big, black shadows materialized to surround them. The shadows—dogs shaped from night—had no features, only jagged muzzles, as if their mouths were filled with piranha teeth. An otherworldly cold followed them. The air crackled with an electrical charge, creating an overwhelming sense of dread.

"Black dogs," Moth whispered.

Jack drew both knives and shouted. "Dead Bird!"

Another silhouette separated itself from the murk beneath the trees and languidly came forward. The Mercedes's headlights illuminated an arch-nosed face and a mane of dark hair spikily knotted with totems. Over stitched, black suede, a coat of raven feathers rustled as if threatening to transform into real birds.

"Mortals and Fatas." Dead Bird looked them over. "You've confused my hounds."

Jack said, "Finn and her sister belong in the true world."

"No, Jack Hawthorn." Dead Bird's voice lacked any warmth. "The *scail amhasge* determine who may return to the true world."

Finn wanted to scream. *No. You will not keep us here.*

Jack took a step toward Dead Bird. "*Marbh ean . . .*"

One of the hounds growled. Then the black dogs paced forward, sniffing, first Sylvie and Christie, moving on to Moth and Finn. Finn kept very still as the creatures came to her, brushing against her legs, snuffling at her hands. Their fur was as prickly as needles of black ice. There were no features in their faces, only solid darkness. They began to circle Jack. Three others slid past Finn, toward Lily Rose.

"No!" Finn turned as one of the dogs began to snarl at her sister. Lily Rose didn't move, her hair veiling her face. Two other hounds made similar noises low in their throats. Finn shouted, "*Get away from her!*"

The rest of the dogs began to slink toward Lily Rose as Dead Bird gently said, "Serafina Sullivan. Come away from there."

Finn stepped between the black dogs and her sister. She drew the silver dagger and slashed out. The hounds bridled, skidding back, barking. One of them began to howl.

Christie and Moth were tensed to fight. Sylvie tried to edge around the dogs, toward Finn. As Jack moved forward, two of the black dogs skirled around and snapped at him, blocking his way.

"Jack! Don't." Dead Bird almost sounded human. "They won't hurt her or any of you."

"*Finn,*" Jack said in a voice that carried across the chaos.

Finn met his gaze and realized it had been too easy.

Lot would never give up his queen this early in the game. Amaranthus's stabbing would have killed a *mortal* girl. Finn remembered the silver bracelet falling between her and Lily. Her sister had not wanted to touch it. The silver.

Her ears filled with a buzzing noise as the thing that had been disguised as her sister unfolded itself, crackling and groaning behind her like a giant, windswept tree. There was a hideous sound, as if someone was choking—*kh . . . kh . . . kh . . .*—and a grotesque, looming shape was reflected in Jack's eyes, in the horror of her friends' gazes.

Jack lunged for Finn with a ragged cry as the black dogs leaped forward.

Finn whispered, "I'm sorry," and closed her eyes and stepped back into the embrace of the thing that would take her to the Wolf and her real sister.

JACK FELL TO HIS KNEES, staring at the place where Finn had vanished in the arms of the white, monstrous treelike thing that had shed her sister's skin like a caul and dragged Finn into the night.

Someone was speaking his name. He looked up, making an effort to focus, and saw Dead Bird standing before him, cold and angry. The black hounds had gone. Stone-faced, Dead Bird said, "Not now. Do not break now."

Christie was swearing brokenly. Sylvie was mute, stunned. Moth strode past Dead Bird and extended a hand to Jack. "We'll get her back."

Jack grasped the *aisling*'s hand and was hauled to his feet. He turned to Dead Bird, who wondered, "Why did I not sense that thing at once?"

"Yes." Jack felt silken menace threading his voice. "Why *didn't* you?"

"It was well hidden behind that girl's form. It was a trickier glamour than I am used to. Are you going to stand here and threaten me or fetch Serafina Sullivan back from the Wolf?"

Moth was snatching up their backpacks and weapons. "Why do you care?"

"Because I am responsible for this Way, and the Wolf has become a menace with that house he stole from the prince of dreams. I'm taking Serafina Sullivan's friends, by train, back to their original entry point and the true world, because, at the moment, that is the least I can do for her without risking my neutrality with the light and the dark." He gestured toward the barrier, which ceased to exist. "Find your brave girl, Jack—but do not take her sister from the Ghostlands. *They* won't allow it."

"Jack." Christie's voice broke. "We need to come with you."

"You can't." Dead Bird spoke gently. "You're not prepared. You and Sylvie Whitethorn would only be detrimental."

Sylvie pleaded, "We can *help*."

Jack accepted the jackal-headed walking stick Moth handed to him and said, to Sylvie and Christie, "If you love her, go back. Tell Phouka and Absalom what has happened."

"Isn't there any way we can—" The hope faded from Sylvie's face as Dead Bird indicated the path to the train station and Moth and Jack stepped away.

"Wait." Christie walked to Moth and held out the wooden knife Jack had given him. Moth took it. Sylvie whispered, "Please, *please* save her."

Christie returned to her and they trudged after Dead Bird, their arms around each other.

Moth said, "I've still got the Grindylow's heart—we can use it to find the Wolf's house."

"Lot *wants* us to find him. He'll make it easy." Jack stalked forward, with Moth, into the night.

LILY SAT ON THE LOWEST BRANCH *of the big myrtle tree in their San Francisco yard. She still wore the filmy lavender gown she'd chosen for the Spring Fling, and her feet, in purple Keds, dangled above Finn, who lay beneath the tree, listening to her sister delete all evidence of Leander Cyrus from her phone.*

"Lily. I like Leander. You better not ditch him for that *guy."*

Lily stopped playing with her phone. Her gown, like a sugarplum fairy's wings, trailed in the breeze. "What guy?"

"The one who looks like a prince and has blue eyes. That *guy."*

Lily tilted her head and smiled dreamily. "You mean the Wolf?"

Finn inhaled and opened her eyes as her body convulsed with the shock of waking.

She lay on a black road shimmering with mist and lined with a stark wood. The night sky was without stars. A birch tree loomed nearby, the hollows in its trunk resembling eye sockets and a gaping mouth. Curling up on the ice, her arms over her head, Finn ached to cry, but that hateful elixir was turning her into a Snow Queen. She didn't even feel exhausted, only lonely and angry and distantly afraid. They had tricked her and she'd naively let them.

Lily! she screamed silently and slammed a hand against the blacktop.

The sudden glare of headlights moved her into a crouch. She fumbled in her pocket and drew out the bottle of elixir from Goblin Market, drank most of what was left, and tucked the second vial labeled ELIXIR into her right boot, the *Tamasgi'po* into her other. She left Jack's mysterious potion in one pocket, along with the bottle containing what remained of the Goblin Market elixir.

She rose to face the ice-blue Rolls-Royce gliding toward her, mist drifting away from a pewter hood ornament that was not a wolf, but a ballerina.

The Rolls-Royce halted, waited.

Finn walked toward the car on rubbery legs. The rear passenger door clicked open. She slid into the dark interior and sat with her hands in her lap and faced the Wolf.

Seth Lot was sprawled in the opposite seat. He wasn't smiling. Shadows and light moved across a face that might have belonged to a young saint, one who had decided that wearing Tom Ford suits and corrupting innocents was more to his liking. As the Rolls-Royce glided forward, the chauffeur a silhouette, Finn defiantly met the Wolf's black-rimmed, blue gaze.

"Well." His voice was gentle, his hands folded on the wolf-head handle of a walking stick. "I apologize, Serafina Sullivan, for that rather elaborate and cruel trick that dumped you here. The revenants are seldom subtle and not very intelligent. Did the bitch hurt you?"

"No," Finn whispered. There was snow in the mahogany-colored hair falling to Seth Lot's shoulders and on his coat's fur collar. There was no weather here, Moth had once told her, no rain or snow—so why did the Wolf smell like winter as well as expensive cologne?

Although she was instinctively afraid, her body sang with adrenaline. She felt as if someone older and calmer and darker was speaking when she said, "Where is my sister?"

"In my house."

"You knew I'd get Lily away from the Mockingbirds. That's why you replaced her with that *thing*."

"You're a resourceful young woman. Tenacious. I wasn't about to take any chances. I see you've taken a stronger dose of the elixir than is recommended." Seth Lot's mouth curved with wry humor. "That's unfortunate." He unfolded one hand and his eyes grew cold. "Give it to me."

She took the nearly empty vial of Goblin Market elixir from her pocket and dropped it into his palm. She gripped the edges of the leather seat. "Why is it unfortunate?"

"Because, Serafina"—he spoke as if he was capable of kindness—"the elixir burning through you is rewriting your—what do your people call it?—your DNA, your very essence. If you don't return to the true world soon, you'll never be able to. You will be one of us. Do you know the penalty for murdering a king or queen of our kind?"

"I didn't murder Reiko." Her voice shook.

"The penalty is stitchery, Serafina. So, I'll ask you, child, what the wolf asked Red Riding Hood: Which path do you prefer—the path of pins or the path of needles?"

That question, with its hint of ancient rituals and primitive evil, stripped away all the false valor the elixir had given her. When one of the Wolf's cool strong hands, heavy with rings, landed atop hers, Finn flinched and her stomach heaved.

"No," Lot gently said, "don't be ill. That's ugly."

"My sister . . ." She could scarcely speak past the bile clogging her throat.

"Don't worry about your sister. She chose her path." His jeweled fingers encircled her wrist and caressed the bracelet of silver charms that had been Lily's. The silver didn't burn him. He smiled and it reminded her of a dark winter road glittering with blood and broken glass. Softly, he said, "And where did you get this pretty charm?"

She pulled her hand from his. "You know."

He settled back into the shadows. She gazed out the window and wondered what it would be like to die.

JACK AND MOTH HAD MANAGED to steal two motorcycles—antlered bikes of green-sheened brass taken from the parking lot of a coffeehouse with an eye of bioluminescent glass as its sign. Jack was able to start his engine, but it took Moth a few attempts to get the ignition working on his. As they roared away, Jack glanced at Moth—whatever Moth was, he was far more than an *aisling*.

As they followed the Grindylow compass toward the house of the Wolf, Jack whispered Finn's name as if it could become a living thing and travel to her upon the air.

SETH LOT HAD CEASED SPEAKING TO HER and sat in the shadows. Finn preferred it when he spoke, because at least, then, he was pretending to be human. She huddled against the door and watched the Ghostlands glide past and thought, *I can't die. Not now.*

As the Rolls swerved around a corner, he called out, "Easy, Hester."

The name sent an icy blade of dread into Finn's heart. When she glimpsed the chauffeur's reflection in the rearview mirror, she thought at first that it was another betrayal.

Hester Kierney, her silver eyes making her an alien thing, met Finn's gaze in the mirror. Her hair had gone diamond white; her skin was alabaster, as if all the blood had been drained from her. *She's one of the dead now,* Finn thought as Hester whispered, "Finn . . . I had to."

Rigid with rage, Finn turned to Seth Lot. "She's one of the *blessed.*"

"She wanted immortality. Didn't you, Hester? She was quite frightened and alone when I found her. Oh, she didn't betray you. She stumbled into the Ghost-lands by accident. She chose the path of needles, so I filled her with her favorite flower and stitched her up. She had to hurt first. But she's not afraid any longer, are you, Hester?"

Watching the back of Hester's head, remembering her as gracious and sweet and *alive,* Finn dug her nails into the seat leather and managed to speak past a violent urge to be sick. "I don't think that's what she meant when you forced her to make that choice."

Hester spoke as if each word were a link to sanity. "He helped me. I didn't want to die, Finn. I was *alone.*"

You're dead now. Finn wanted to scream as Seth Lot placed his beautiful hands on the wolf head of his walking stick and smiled and said, "And that is why you should be careful what you wish for. I could have fed her her own heart, which I used to do with my Jacks and Jills. Or twisted her into a thing that kills. Here we are."

Finn dragged her gaze to the house that appeared as the Rolls-Royce rounded a forested curve in the road. The Wolf's mansion was as forbidding as she'd imagined it, a Gothic chateau, spiny and crooked, a deformed creature looming in caverns of briars and cradled by black alders like the broken bones of giants. Two stone wolves guarded a cracked stair leading up to a pair of medieval-looking doors. The house's leprous-white marble and blanched stone were stained nearly black by a sludge of dead leaves and moss.

The Rolls-Royce halted in the weed-choked driveway. Hester got out and opened the back door. Seth Lot exited the car and began strolling up the lane.

Standing with Hester, Finn studied the ruined house. Her vision was suddenly blurred by tears she furiously blinked back. "Why aren't there guards?"

"He doesn't need any. Who'd be crazy enough to break in?"

"*Hester.*" Finn turned to her, but Hester looked away.

"No worries, Finn. The number-one law of nature is adapt or die. Give me your backpack."

With a shaking hand, Finn held the backpack out to Hester, who took it and began moving down the lane, the heels of her boots clicking against a pavement clotted with toadstools and lined at intervals with rusty metal poles holding empty birdcages. Finn followed. The house was worse close up, decrepit and dark, its windows shattered. The exterior walls were streaked with reddish stains. The miasma of rot and mold drifted in a clammy vapor from the shadows beyond the gaping windows. As they walked through an evil-looking garden scattered with headless statues and debris that seemed to have come from the destruction of other houses, Finn stepped over a porcelain sink and avoided a broken rocking chair.

Lily was in that awful place.

Whatever alchemy the elixir was working on Finn's body, heightening her adrenaline, alerting her to any movement around her, it also kept her from breaking.

Seth Lot moved up the split stairs and touched the doors. As they opened, the house shimmered into a gorgeous, lamp-lit mansion of snowy marble and pale granite with friezes of briar roses around stained-glass windows and a garden that bloomed around Finn into a winter-touched fairyland of white roses and statues with the beautiful faces of remorseless angels.

"Come along, Serafina." The Wolf, a shadow now, turned in the light from the house and extended one hand.

HE LED HER, WITH HESTER, down a starkly elegant hall and paused in front of a scarlet door. He took a key from his pocket. Finn scarcely noticed the key, waiting for that door to open and reveal her sister.

The door clicked inward. He gestured to her. "The house wants to welcome you."

She stepped past him—

—and into a birch forest. She staggered. There was snow beneath her boots. A road. The sky was gray. The elixir hummed through her like thousands of dragonfly wings.

A twitching, girlish shadow stood at the road's end. It was . . . *wrong.*

Finn whirled, to run—

—and came face-to-face with her silver-eyed double.

It was an alabaster creature wearing the same ruffled dress, only in black. Her—its—hair was tangled with tiny bones and red berries. Black spirals were painted beneath eyes as inhuman as moonlight on mirrors. It exuded harm and *malice*.

Finn stepped back, clutching at a tree for balance. She whispered, "Don't—"

"*Don't*." It mimicked her voice exactly.

Finn choked out, "What are you?"

"*What are you?*" The thing smiled at her, its teeth small and sharp.

"I'm not afraid of you," Finn lied. "*What are you?*"

"Your future."

Finn shook her head. In folk tales, meeting one's double was *never* a good thing. Carefully, she said, "I'm Finn Sullivan. *You* are nothing."

The creature hissed and vanished.

Finn now stood in an enormous hall, its stone walls hung with threadbare tapestries and ancient weapons. A black velvet chair was draped with a fur-lined coat. Before her was a door of gray wood carved with images of snarling wolves. She strode forward and gripped the doorknob, tried to twist it. When it didn't turn, she slammed both fists against the wood. "Stop playing games! I don't like your damn house and *where is Lily*?"

The door opened.

Finn peered into a girly, Victorian bedroom that was all creams and ivories, the large bed veiled by gossamer curtains patterned with butterflies, the open windows revealing a Ghostlands night. A girl sat on a sofa of white velvet, her head bowed, long dark hair concealing her face.

"*Lily?*" Finn stepped in, hope tearing at her.

The girl raised her head—and it was Reiko Fata who smiled at her.

The door slammed shut behind Finn. She backed against it, slid down. Reiko laughed, rising with serpentine grace. "Oh, he *said* it would be entertaining, your reaction. Who do you think I am?"

Finn wanted to push herself through the door's wood as Reiko sauntered toward her, speaking. "You're the queen killer, a little thing like you . . . He won't tell me which queen you've slain. Did you do it alone, little mayfly?"

Finn couldn't believe how vivid this trick was. "You can't . . . *be* here . . ."

Reiko leaned close. "Seth said you did it to save a lover. A *Jack*."

As the Fata queen stepped back, Finn understood what was happening . . . Absalom had said Seth Lot had stolen this house from a creature of dreams, so it held memories, phantoms. This was a Reiko from *the past*, a memory, trapped here . . . This Reiko wouldn't remember the child Finn she'd nearly drowned, because they hadn't met. This Reiko hadn't yet decided to sacrifice eighteen-year-old Finn at the Teind.

"*I* have a Jack." Reiko fixed Finn with a playful look. "And I would murder kings and queens for *him*. You do seem familiar." Reiko approached again. Her green eyes glinted as she reached out—

—and gently pulled Finn away from the door to open it. "I don't know what you are, little mayfly, but you belong to the Wolf now. You may roam the house. But you will never leave it."

As the door closed, Finn sank down onto the sofa and began to scheme.

JACK AND MOTH LEFT THEIR MOTORCYCLES in the forest surrounding Lot's house, a looming, hollowed wreck that stank of toadstools and the iron taint of blood that meant mortals had died there. As they slipped closer to the house, reaching the border of the sinister garden, a figure in a grimy, white suit moved from the darkness.

Although Jack had his *kris* at Leander Cyrus's throat in a heartbeat and Moth had drawn a dagger, Leander calmly said, "You can't take Lily Rose out of the Ghostlands."

"And why is that, Leander?"

"This house, Jack . . . the Wolf's house . . . it once belonged to someone else. This house is a tomb for memories and parts of the past. Ghosts."

A cold despair cut through Jack. "I know that."

"Do you understand why Lily can leave the Wolf's house, but not the Ghostlands?"

"What is he saying?" Moth demanded of Jack. "Lily isn't a *ghost*. She's real—"

"Listen," Leander's voice broke. "Lily isn't ali—"

"Stop." Jack felt as if everything was collapsing around him. What they had *risked* to come here . . . He stepped close to Leander. "You are not to tell Finn.

And if you betray us, I'll rip out your flower stuffing. Do you understand?"

"I understand"—Leander was somber—"that you are truly Jack Daw again."

"Jack," Moth said quietly, "shall we stick to the plan?"

Jack sheathed his *kris* and said to Leander, "So Jill Scarlet got my message to you, did she?"

Leander nodded, his eyes silvery and rimmed with shadows. "I've been waiting . . . I saw Finn . . . she's in there now."

Jack's black heart pulsed and he almost snarled. "Get us in, Cyrus."

Leander turned and led them down a tunnel of briars that clung to their skin and hair. Jack, silent as the night itself, felt a predator thriving within him. They pushed through a decaying door into a courtyard where a tower rose at the back of the mansion over which a lavish glamour had fallen. The tower's stained-glass windows glowed with light, its walls covered with wickedly thorned briars and roses as pale and perfumed as a Fata queen's false skin.

"That's Lot's room"—Leander indicated—"at the top. It's the last place he'll expect anyone to attempt."

"Grab a vine. We're going up."

"Jack?"

The voice caused Moth and Leander to whirl around, but Jack turned slowly, ready to kill the girl in her white chauffeur's uniform.

The familiar face, despite the white hair and Fata eyes, made him pause. He took a step forward. "*Hest*—"

Moth slid past him, grabbed her, and kissed her on the mouth.

As Moth cascaded into light and shadow, Hester backed away from the insect that emerged and glided away. She looked at Jack. "You can't help me."

"*Hester.*" Jack held out a hand. "Come with us."

"Just . . . help *her*. I'll try to distract him." She turned and ran.

Leander cursed. Jack gazed at the tower, rage coursing through him. "Let's climb."

"Jack—"

"She won't give us away, and Moth is doing his part."

The briars made them bleed, but Jack and Leander climbed quickly. Reaching a ledge, Jack hauled himself up. He broke the window with his elbow, unlatched it, and swung it open, then slid over the sill into an elegant chamber of black,

green, and gold. A fire burned in a hearth. The deceptive debris of books and masculine ornaments was scattered everywhere.

The strength left him as Sylph Dragonfly's illusion was stripped away from him. He collapsed to his knees, retching, and began to choke up wet, red petals. He heard Leander speaking frantically, but the buzzing in his ears kept him from understanding. His heart slammed to true life and he tasted blood in his mouth. *No. Not now.* He couldn't become mortal *now* . . .

The horror of returning to being a Jack had been a price he'd been willing to pay, to save Finn. When he saw his shadow stretching across the floor, he began to shake.

"Well done, Leander." The velvety voice hit Jack like a train. "You've earned your reward for bringing him to me. Go on."

"Jack." Leander moved past Jack, who was on all fours now and feeling every injury he'd recently received. "I'm sorry, Jack. He *knew*. He knew you were coming."

Struggling not to fall, Jack raised his head and managed to rasp out, "You've killed all of us."

As Leander fled, Jack focused on Seth Lot. The Wolf lounged against a bedpost as the room slowly faded into a dark, stone chamber, the bed becoming pillars strung with rusted chains and gruesome totems of bones and teeth. There were stains on the floor. The windows had metal grilles. "Can you hear me, Jack?"

A shudder racked Jack's body as he gasped out, "Where is Finn?"

The booted foot that slammed into his side sent him flat to the floor. He coughed, spat blood as Seth Lot circled him, the rings of the Fata kings and queens he'd murdered shining on his fingers. "Are you hurting, Jack?"

Through sheer force of will, Jack dragged himself into a crouch.

"It's what you wanted, wasn't it?" Seth Lot's foot shoved him down again. "To be a *real* boy. After all the trouble Reiko and I went through to make you invincible."

Jack clenched his teeth and grabbed a chain on one of the pillars, pulling himself up, wincing as the bits of bone on the chain bit into his fingers. Seth Lot continued to circle. "Serafina is such a fine, brave girl. I think Reiko made a mistake, calling her a mayfly. *Underestimating* her."

Jack whispered, "*I* caused Reiko's death, not—"

Seth Lot slammed his walking stick against Jack's chest. Jack cried out and clutched at the pillar to keep from falling. He retched. "Don't dissemble, my Jack." Lot threw an arm around his shoulders, smiled, and, with false, threatening intimacy, said, "Did you know I once thought of you as one of the best of your kind? When Reiko botched the Teind for you one hundred years ago, I realized that was what made you dangerous. To her. And now you've slain her, you and that fine, brave girl."

Jack could feel the grinding of a broken collarbone. He said in a low voice, "I think a Fata who murders mortals and other Fatas shouldn't toss around accusations."

"Maybe I'll let you live long enough to watch me cut her open and stitch her full of flowers. What flower should it be? Something innocent but exotic."

Jack used the last of his strength to twist free and kick at Lot's throat. The Wolf disdainfully struck him across the face with his walking stick and Jack fell, blood filling his broken nose. Exhaustion crept over him, worse than the pain.

"Rest now, my Jack." Seth Lot crouched down and gently pushed the sweat-damp hair from Jack's eyes. "Tonight, you're going to dine with your beloved for the last time."

As Jack struggled desperately against the mortality that he'd wanted for so long, the mortality that was now killing him, the Wolf rose and swaggered away.

CHAPTER 17

Out of this wood do not desire to go
Thou shalt remain here whether thou wilt or no.
I am a spirit of no common rate;
The summer still doth tend upon my state;
And I do love thee;
Therefore go with me.

—*A Midsummer Night's Dream*, William Shakespeare

Finn discovered that the door to the ivory bedroom was unlocked.

As she fled down a corridor, the tiny vials of elixir and *Tamasgi'po* hidden in her Doc Martens chafed against her ankles. She pushed through another door, into a walled courtyard where dwarfish apple trees clustered, their branches hung with rusting birdcages. Moving forward, she found that each cage contained a portrait or a photograph in a fancy frame. The pictures, torn and stained, were of young people from different eras. Lot's victims . . .

The path took her to a pair of glass-paned doors that shed light onto a hunched yew tree. The doors opened when she pushed at them and she entered a large chamber, its black floor reflecting lit lamps on pillars shaped like birch trees. The leaf-green walls and the ceiling—a mass of green marble vines—gave the chamber the appearance of an otherworldly forest. It was so quiet she could hear her own breathing. *Lily . . . where are you?*

From the unlit places in the chamber figures emerged, their modern clothing trimmed with fur. Jewels glowed at their throats, on their fingers. Their faces hidden by wolf masks of painted wood, they watched her make her way through the forest of pillars until she stopped before a door carved with brutal images of people fleeing wild animals. She drew in a breath and opened the door.

The Wolf king sat in a luxurious parlor, on a divan in front of a fireplace crackling with flames. Leander Cyrus was crouched at his feet, facing her.

"Leander." Dismay crushed Finn's voice.

"Leander," Lot said pleasantly. "Take Serafina to her sister."

Leander rose, his face bleak. Without speaking, he walked past her. She followed, feeling as if the shadows of this place were dirtying her skin. He led her up a winding tower stair and spoke softly as they climbed. "She looks different, but she is still your sister. This place . . . it affects mortals."

"*Infects* them, you mean." She had to stop moving as everything around her began to spin. She bent her head, trying to keep that poisonous sleep from returning to trap her here, in the enemy's house. *No.* She fought it with her hands and teeth clenched.

"Finn." Leander spoke with gentle insistence. "You need to keep moving."

She nodded and, feeling as if her equilibrium had returned, continued following him up the stairs.

He halted before a pair of stained-glass doors ghosted with the images of lilies. It was dark, beyond. He turned to Finn. "Never forget she's your sister."

"You're not coming with me?"

Bitterness dulled his voice. "She doesn't want to see me."

He left her standing before the doors and she thought: *This house . . . all it is is doors . . .*

She stepped into a chamber lit only by the glow of winter through the surrounding windows. On the walls between the windows were shadow boxes filled with pinned butterflies. Cabinets and tables were neatly cluttered with books—leather-bound tomes and paperbacks—and objects: a little wax mannequin in a bell jar, a skull of white marble with antlers that looked like red coral, bottles that held luminous feathers, fantastical insects, unusual stones. Several music boxes were displayed in another cabinet. Hanging on one wall were four gowns that looked as if they'd been sewn from fabrics stained with the purest hues of night, winter, moss, and blood.

She approached an arch curtained with glittering black beads. She could see someone standing beyond. Was that her sister, her sister whom she'd seen dance through a window, whom she'd cradled in broken glass and blood, who had wasted away in a hospital bed? Her sister, who was supposed to be dead?

"Lily?" Tears blurred the room. "Lily . . . it's me."

The beaded curtain parted. A figure in a dark gown, shadowy hair spilling around her cold, white face, appeared. Her eyes were framed in black butterfly designs. She clutched a dagger made of glass.

"Lily," Finn whispered.

Her sister's remote expression became ferocious. "You *thing*. You think you can fool me?"

She lunged, slashing out with the knife. Finn yelled. She fell over an ottoman, scrambled back as the girl who resembled her sister came after her, barefoot and lithe.

"*Lily!*" Finn pushed up and hit a wall, held out a hand. "Lily. If it's really you . . . *please* . . . just stop! It's me!"

The young woman drew back. She stared at the bracelet of silver charms glinting on Finn's wrist. The hand with the dagger fell to her side, and Lily slowly looked at Finn. Her voice torn, she whispered, "Finn?"

"*Lily.*" Finn flung her arms around the sister she'd worshipped and envied since childhood. *This* was her true sister, as tough and fiery as ever, her skin pale, as if she'd been kept in the dark for months.

Lily, holding Finn unbearably tight, said faintly, "*Why did you come?*"

"Why do you think?" Finn drew back, gripping Lily's hands. The tears began then, and she blinked them away, forced words through her closed throat. "I came to take you *home*. Moth found me."

"Moth was supposed to keep you *safe*." Lily led Finn to the other room, where they sat on a large bed draped with night-blue gauze. "Not bring you to . . . *this*."

"Why did you go with the Wolf, Lil?"

Lily's lashes flickered down and she became almost sullen—it was a typical Lily emotion and, this time, it delighted Finn. "It wasn't like meeting Leander. I thought Leander was just an ordinary boy. It never occurred to me that I only saw him after sunset. He went to a different school, he said. He had a job on the weekends. Seth Lot was hunting in Muir Woods when he saw me. When I saw him. One day, Leander told me . . . he told me what he really was, and, when he found out I'd spoken with the Wolf, what *Seth Lot* was. He warned me. I didn't listen. Mom was dead. I hated everything. I didn't love this world enough, Finn. So I went with Seth Lot because he offered an invitation I couldn't resist. Look at you." She laughed a little, her eyes shining. "You're not my little sister anymore. *How long have I been gone?*"

"Over a year. And your new friends"—Finn couldn't keep the fury from her voice—"made it look like you'd killed yourself."

Lily went still. "Dad . . . ?"

"Thinks you're dead."

Lily put her hands over her face. Finn hugged her again and said, "I'm going to get you out of here. I just need to find Jack."

"Jack," Lily whispered.

Then the wolves came and dragged them apart.

THEY TOOK FINN AND LILY TO SETH LOT. The Wolf still sat before the huge fireplace that reminded Finn of a dragon's mouth. Leander crouched nearby, his head bowed, his bruised hands loose on his knees. When he looked up at Lily, pain and yearning crossed his face.

Ignoring him, Lily moved to stand before Seth Lot. "*Let her go.* You don't need her. You have me."

Seth Lot smiled, but his face was hard. "But I don't want you anymore, my Lily."

"Bastard!" Lily went for him, but Leander rose and caught her hand.

"It doesn't matter, Lil," Finn said hoarsely. "We're going home."

"And how," Seth Lot gently interrupted, "do you plan on accomplishing that extraordinary feat, Serafina?"

Finn said her voice low, "Every story written about your kind is in our favor."

The Wolf rose. Firelight reflected in his eyes. He breathed out, "Is that so? How do *traitors* end in your stories? Shall we see how they end in mine?"

Lily reached for Leander, who looked haggard and resigned.

Seth Lot stalked out of the room and the masked wolves, bracketing Finn and Lily, escorted them into the tree-pillared hall. *Jack*, Finn thought with gut-wrenching fear.

Between two pillars stood the Rooks: Trip, Hip Hop, and Bottle; Victor,

Emily, and Eammon Tirnagoth. They weren't in their raven finery now, only casual clothes, which somehow made them seem vulnerable. Seth Lot folded his hands on the snarling wolf head that topped his walking stick and gazed at the Rooks. Softly, he said, "They promised me loyalty, these three. One of them told Phouka Banríon about me."

"It wasn't us." Trip stood with his dark hair in his eyes. "We would never do that, *Madadh aillaid*."

"We were loyal to Reiko Fata. She gave us immortality." Hip Hop glared at Leander and pointed. "*He* knew you were here, your girl's *lover*. He's been hunting you—"

"No, Emily." Seth Lot stepped toward her and cupped a hand beneath her chin. "Leander has been working for me to keep his Lily from being gutted."

Finn and Lily both turned to stare at Leander, who bowed his head, his hands clutched tightly together.

"And you, Eammon?" Seth Lot sauntered to stand before Bottle, the youngest, who glared ahead like a soldier about to be interrogated.

"Bottle." Hip Hop nudged him, rhinestone pins glinting in her ropes of black-and-blond hair.

Bottle raised his head. His expression was defiant as he said, "*Down with the Wolf.*"

"No," Hip Hop breathed out. "*Eammon.*"

Seth Lot smiled. He stepped back and turned away. Gracefully, he plucked one of the rhinestone pins from Hip Hop's hair, whirled—and jabbed it into Bottle's right eye. Bottle—Eammon—screamed.

Lot slid the pin back out. As the Rook fell to his knees, clutching one hand over his damaged eye, the Wolf returned the pin to Hip Hop's hair.

Hip Hop shrieked curses at Seth Lot, who walked away from her. As Trip grabbed his brother and hauled him up, the wolves surrounded the Rooks.

Finn let go of Lily's hand and started forward.

Seth Lot seized Finn's hand. As Trip and Hip Hop, cradling their wounded brother, were escorted away, Finn saw blood drops on the floor.

Seth Lot pulled Finn toward the first drop, crouched down, touched it, and raised his fingertip. The blood faded on his skin. He said, "The *memory* of blood—that's all changelings have. Isn't that right, my Lily?"

Finn thought of Moth, who sometimes *forgot* to bleed. She glanced at her sister, who gazed at Seth Lot as if she'd like to murder him.

"We do have teeth when we need them, and claws." Lot rose and stepped close to Finn. "Do you think you are my death, Serafina Sullivan? You and that twisted-up Jack now locked in my tower? You are not."

Lot's revelation of Jack's capture stunned Finn, who couldn't move as the Wolf slipped a hand into her pocket and removed the pewter-dog-capped vial—the one that had fallen from Jack's coat. He turned the bottle in his fingers. "*Aconitum lycoctonum.* Wolfsbane. The real stuff. This could kill me. Shame on you."

He dropped the vial on the floor and crushed it beneath his boot. Glad she'd tucked Jack's elixir and the *Tamasgi'po* into her Doc Martens, she said, "If you hurt him, I *will* kill you."

Lot only looked at her as if he pitied her.

Lily broke away from the two Fatas holding her. She put herself between the Wolf and Finn, but the Wolf only strode away, signaling to his pack, two of whom dragged Leander with them. Lot said, "I do admire courage, however. Lily, come with me. Antoinette, return Serafina to her room."

Lily looked back at Finn, her eyes dark, before the doors shut between them.

"THIS SNOW IS YOUR FAULT, LITTLE MAYFLY."

Finn frowned at the young female Fata who stood in the doorway to Finn's prison, a windowless stone chamber with fancy furniture. A lamp of pink glass glowed on the nightstand, and books and old board games had been considerately left in a mahogany cabinet. They'd taken her coat, her backpack, the silver dagger. "What snow?"

The Fata girl was aristocratic despite her shaven head, the skin around her silver eyes painted with crimson designs. She was smiling and her teeth were sharp. "The snow falling around this house. There's not supposed to be snow." She polished her pointy nails on the fur vest she wore over an emerald gown. She indicated the dress folded on the bed. Next to it was a black wooden half mask carved into the face of a deer. "He wants you to wear that, queen killer."

"I will not." Finn was still absorbing the idea that the snow following the Wolf king around was *her* doing. But, then, why should anything like that surprise her?

The wolf girl was annoyed, as if this task had been forced upon her. "Put the dress on or my brother—outside in the hall—puts it on *for* you."

"I don't think he'd look good in that dress."

The Fata's mouth curled, and genuine amusement flickered in her ghost eyes. "Be a smart girl. You want to see your Jack, don't you?"

SO FINN WORE THE DRESS—a small thing of gray silk and filmy gossamer—and a choker of tiny rubies that felt like a slave collar. She placed the mask over her face, but kept her Doc Martens, disdaining the high-heeled shoes as she'd done at the Mockingbirds. Shoes were capricious things in fairy tales.

She was led to a chamber where flames roared in a black hearth, glossing furniture carved from ebony wood into dragons, bears, lions, and wolves. A massive mirror in a gold frame of wolf skulls, briars, and grotesque imps dominated one wall. Beneath a chandelier of green glass was a table set with a feast of almost obscene splendor.

Seth Lot stood near the window, its view a landscape of crooked trees and snow. He looked like a Brontë hero in an expensive suit, his ring-decorated fingers resting on the handle of his walking stick as the firelight brushed his profile and the high cheekbone with its romantic scar. His hair was pulled back.

Finn was glad she wore the deer mask—it concealed her fear. Defiantly, she extended one hand. Her sister's silver charm bracelet glittered. "Why did your people let me keep this? And these?" She touched the lionheart locket Jack had given her and Jack's phoenix pendant.

"To remind you of what you have to lose." The Wolf moved toward her. "And silver does me no harm." When he was close, he gazed down at her almost tenderly. "You have forfeited the game, Serafina. What shall I do with you now?"

"Don't hurt Lily or Jack. Are they all right?"

"I thought we would have a proper dinner." He turned without answering and pulled out a chair. She walked to it, sat down, and wondered what he would do if she threw up on the plate. She wasn't hungry and the last thing she'd eaten had been a cupcake Sionnach Ri had bought her. "Where is Jack?"

"Jack is on his way."

"Where is my sister?"

There were three chairs. He chose the chair in the center and stabbed a knife into what looked like a roast pig with wings. "Your sister came with me willingly, Serafina."

"You faked her *death*."

"Actually"—he smiled and Finn thought that the Fatas smiled too much, especially when their intentions were bad—"Reiko accomplished the masterpiece of Lily Rose's demise, a bizarre death fitting a ballerina, and a suicide no less."

There was a steak knife near her plate. She crazily thought of using it. "It didn't matter to you, did it, that it would break her family?"

"Serafina. Your sister will remain beautiful and young forever. No sickness will touch her. No senility will splinter her intelligence. And you never would have met Jack if it hadn't been for us. He would have been dust and rot in a grave."

"You *destroyed* Jack."

"You don't understand what those times were like. Jack was lost, hungry, bitter." His smile was gorgeous. "Those sorts of boys and girls . . . they're the easiest."

"Living forever isn't what most people want."

"It's what your sister wanted. It's what Hester wanted. It's what Jack wanted."

She said, with quiet precision, "It must be horrible, not having a soul. All that emptiness inside. Being nothing."

Something flashed in his eyes, something like terror, which could also have been a trick of the light. He casually set Eve Avaline's silver dagger in the middle of the table and said, "What did you intend to do with *this*, Serafina? I shall leave it here, and when Jack arrives, I'll show you what *I* intend to do with it."

She stared at the dagger shining within reach on the polished table. It had not begun to corrode at all, despite being taken from its wooden scabbard days ago.

The doors opened again and Jack, in a rabbit half mask of white wood, wrists wrapped in chains, was escorted into the room by two wolf Fatas in fur and leather.

He was shoved into the third chair. Beneath the mask, she could see that his jaw was bruised, one corner of his mouth caked with blood—somehow, the otherworldliness that had made him infallible had been taken from him, and that terrified her. His masked gaze met hers. "Are you all right?"

"Yes." She realized Seth Lot had put them in the masks to keep them from seeing each other properly.

"She's not all right, Jack. The elixir has poisoned her. If she returns to the true world, slivers of it will remain within her until she becomes something strange."

Jack made a sound that was almost a snarl. The chains around his wrists tightened.

Seth Lot continued, "Shall I make her my new queen? I'm afraid Lily and I have had a bit of a falling-out."

Finn glanced at the silver dagger Lot had set on the table to taunt them. Jack looked at it and went very still.

"Lot." Jack sounded peeled to the bone. "Don't. She wasn't responsible for Reiko—"

Leaning forward, Lot took up the silver dagger and traced the tip of it across Jack's throat. Finn stopped breathing. "Jack, the two of you killed Reiko and decimated the Mockingbirds. The Mockingbirds I don't mind, but Reiko . . . you'll both have to pay for that."

Finn met Jack's gaze as despair splintered through her.

The flames in the hearth burst outward, flowering into black-and-orange butterflies, an impossible storm of them. Finn screamed Jack's name as she was flung backward by thousands of parchment wings that beat against her with delicate, bruising force, pushing her toward the mirror—

—through it.

FINN LIFTED HER HEAD. She lay in a night lit only by snow. Not far from her, a monstrous, spiky shadow crouched, surrounded by bones and blood, silently screaming horses, and mutilated men—

Then she stood in a black room before a painting of a Fata man with russet hair knotted with leaves, his bare face and chest tattooed with spirals, his eyes those of a beast.

"See how I play this game, Serafina?" Lot circled her where they now stood in a cathedral-like hall with wooden pillars looming around them and immense arches curving toward a groined ceiling. Leaves and snow crackled beneath Finn's boots. Candles flickered. Primitive music accompanied a banshee voice singing softly as figures masked with ornate representations of animal skulls—birds, bears, stags—waltzed around them, candlelight caressing luxurious fabrics.

Turning her head, Finn frowned into a tarnished mirror in a knot of black briars. She saw a pale girl with jewels on her fingers, her silver eyes framed by dark ink. Her gray dress had become a gown, its sleeves nothing but ribbons of silver silk. There was a wreath of fresh roses on her brow.

"That was your sister's doing." Lot stood behind her. "The monarchs. She's learned some new tricks. It used to keep our relationship exciting. Lately, it's just become annoying."

Finn stepped back, frantically scanning the feral costume ball that surrounded her. She said, "This isn't real."

He slid a hand over her shoulder, turning her as music blazed through the dead air. Too disoriented to rebel, she allowed him to take her hands. "It is real if I wish it so."

"I thought only mortals could make wishes here." She wouldn't let his tricks or his distressing beauty throw her.

"I've told you, Serafina, you're not quite mortal anymore." He spoke as she concentrated on the dancers around them. A woman in a horned headdress inclined her head. A man whose face was concealed by a beaked mask bowed to her. There were cobwebs and splotches of mold and blood on their beautiful costumes.

"Did you ever wonder"—Seth Lot's hair fell forward to brush her cheek as his scent of expensive cologne and musk made her dizzy and sick—"what would happen if Jack had the chance to meet Reiko again?"

She thought of the Reiko *before* the Teind, the one haunting Lot's house, and ripped her hands from Lot's. Shadows crept through the forestlike ballroom, beyond the animal-masked Fatas moving languidly across the floor littered with debris, dying monarch butterflies, and snowflakes that didn't melt.

"Reiko is *dead* and gone." She thought she saw a crack in the Wolf's perfect façade and relentlessly continued, "Take me back to your house. *Now.*"

He gestured. As if instinctively connected to him, the dancers drifted apart, forming an aisle. At the end of the aisle were two doors in a wall tangled with thorn-starred vines.

"Go on." He indicated the doors. "Pick one."

The dancers stood still in their beast masks as Finn walked toward the doors, snow and crimson leaves fluttering past her. She heard whispers, *"The path of pins or the path of needles . . . the path of needles or the path of pins . . ."*

When she reached the doors, she halted, hands clenched in her gown. One door was white, carved into images of lilies. The other door, black, was hewn into the forms of loping jackals.

Seth Lot's voice carried to her as he moved down the aisle, toward her. "You'll remain here no matter which you choose, Serafina. But I'll give you a companion. Select which of your loved ones will leave my house—your sister or your Jack—and I'll allow it. The other will remain."

"I won't choose."

He said, tenderly, "Then, Serafina, I will kill both."

WHEN THE BUTTERFLIES SWEPT FINN through the mirror, Jack shot to his feet, the chains biting into his wrists as he lunged forward. Lot had also vanished in the storm of orange-and-black wings.

"Jack." The soft voice sent a razor pain through Jack, who raised his head, saw *her* reflection in the mirror, and didn't believe it. Even though her face was shadowed, he knew it was her. *Another of Lot's tricks.*

He closed his eyes against her, opened them to see if she'd gone.

Reiko came forward, her slip dress and gladiator sandals blood red against the chamber's darkness, her long black hair stranded with pearls. He yearned for her with an almost voluptuous shame, but he refused to turn and face her. The rabbit mask was his only shield against her. "Reiko."

"Why are you in that ridiculous disguise?" Cool fingers settled on his face to lift the mask. He thought of Finn, her warm skin and fragrant hair, her good heart. She was the opposite of this heartless young woman—Circean, lavish, nomadic—who had drawn him, smiling all the while, into the dark.

"Jack." Reiko's hands slid along his wrists, to the chains. "Who has done this to you? Was it Lot?"

The Wolf's house, Absalom and Leander had told him, *is filled with memories.*

When he'd been here with Reiko, long ago, he'd been a new Jack. This Reiko from the past, before Finn, before the Teind, the Reiko he had once loved, this Reiko had sheltered him from Seth Lot. He almost broke as her lips touched his. His body leaned toward hers. She spoke against his mouth. "You still love me, don't you?" She kissed him again. He was shaking by the time she drew back. She said, "You're different."

As he remembered her burning, he whispered, "Reiko."

She pressed a hand over his slamming heart. Her green eyes glowed. "A *heart*, Jack?"

"I'm not your Jack."

Her eyes silvered as fury curled her lips. "Then what *are* you?"

"I'm what caused you to die. As you caused those girls to die. And the boys. And all the innocents whose lives you sucked away like the parasite you are."

He saw the true Reiko then, beneath her skin, a scaled, thorn-toothed thing of blood and darkness. Then she was just a girl, turning away from him and walking from the room, heels clicking on the floor like a devil's cloven hooves. She said, over one shoulder, "I'll forgive you, Jack. I always do."

When she'd gone, he sank to a crouch, chained hands between his knees, and stared at the giant mirror framed by its grotesque and golden dance of imps, wolf skulls, and briars.

A reflective glint drew his attention to the silver dagger in the center of the table.

FINN STOOD BEFORE THE TWO DOORS. This time, there would be no tricking a Fata. Behind her, Seth Lot patiently waited as his court whispered among themselves.

"*. . . pins . . . path of needles . . .*"

She couldn't choose and Lily and Jack would die because of it. Here, she had no weapons with which to fight the Wolf, magical or otherwise.

She remembered Absalom Askew saying, *Rules keep us in shape*, and an idea cut through her hopelessness. She slowly turned to face Seth Lot. "You invited Lily here. You invited *me* here, and Jack, when you told us to come find you."

The whispering, skull-masked court went silent. Seth Lot's eyes narrowed, and shadows made his face hard as she continued, "By the invitation from thee to me, I invoke the law of hospitalit—"

"No." The word was more snarl than voice. "*You will not—*"

"*Your* laws." Finn pointed at him. "Laws that keep you from returning to night and nothing. What will happen if you break that law of not harming invited guests, Seth Lot?"

His smile was ugly, and she saw the old, hungry thing hiding beneath his skin. "I have broken many laws, Serafina. Don't you know? And this is *such* a little one . . ."

Glass shattered behind her. She whirled.

The two doors shimmered as if the air was a reel of melting film—and faded.

Then she was gazing at her reflection in a large mirror. There were only shadows behind her and a larger shadow among them, spiky and bestial, with silver eyes: Seth Lot.

The mirror glass began to crack. The point of a dagger emerged.

Lot stepped between her and the mirror and closed one hand around her throat. Softly, he said, "I see Jack has made *his* choice."

Someone came up behind Finn. A wooden knife carved with runes slid over her right shoulder, aimed unwaveringly at Lot's left eye. A familiar voice said, "Let her go."

"You can't kill me with that." Seth Lot didn't move.

"No. But it would ruin that mask you wear for a while, and you wouldn't want the pretty things to see what you *really* look like, would you?"

Seth Lot met the gaze of the knife bearer and released Finn, who twisted around. The knife bearer tore his beaked mask away, revealing Moth. He backed toward the enormous mirror, pulling Finn with him.

"Go." Moth gently shoved her. She turned to face the glass, saw the shadows behind Lot surging forward—

She leaped at the mirror. Moth followed—

She slammed into Jack in the dining hall and he reeled back. She flung her arms around him and kissed him once as Moth strode toward them, saying, "I was invited in by Leander Cyrus and Lily." He stripped off the fur-lined coat he'd worn to disguise himself and revealed a small arsenal of weapons, including the jackal-headed walking stick strapped across his back. "They're waiting for us."

Jack set his chained hands on the table. "You have anything to cut through these?"

Finn looked at the mirror, at Eve Avaline's silver dagger quivering in the glass. When something dark loomed behind the dagger in the mirror, she whispered, "*He's coming.*"

As Moth stabbed a bronze knife into the lock of Jack's chains, Finn searched for something to smash the chains with. Moth, unsuccessful, backed away, then turned to face the mirror and said, "We need to leave. You'll have to run in the chains—"

The silver dagger hurtled out of the mirror and clattered at Moth's feet as a dark figure began to emerge from the reflective glass—

Moth snatched up the silver blade and leaped forward.

The figure appearing in the mirror lunged—onto Eve's silver dagger.

Hester Kierney slid from the blade, clutching her bloody midsection and staring at a horrified Moth. Magnolia blossoms spilled from her mouth.

Finn ran to her as Moth dropped the dagger and caught Hester in his arms. Finn cried out, "Why is she bleeding if she's a Jill?"

"Because," Jack said, "she's fresh-made. She's still mostly mortal."

Moth, like death in his black clothes and black hoodie, bowed his head as Hester clutched at Finn, who laid trembling hands over the other girl's midriff and sought to stop the blood. She didn't want to look at the other girl, to see her pain, watch her . . . "Hester . . ."

Hester fumbled with something on a chain around her neck. She pressed a metal object into Finn's hand, and her breathing became a terrible, wet rasp. Her eyes widened as bloody petals frothed from her mouth.

Moth cried out, holding her. Finn brought the back of her own blood-streaked hand against her mouth as Hester convulsed, her breathing becoming a liquid gasping that seemed to rattle her bones. She wanted to end Hester's pain . . . didn't know how . . .

Moth reached down. "Look away," he told Finn softly, and she closed her eyes. She didn't see him snap Hester's neck. But she heard it. And felt as if Hester's pain had moved into her as silent sobs shuddered through her body.

Jack bowed his head.

Hester's skin, glazed like porcelain, cracked apart. White magnolia blossoms drifted away from her bones. Finn could hear Moth and Jack speaking, but she could only stare at Hester's remains. Then she hunched over and was sick on the floor.

Seth Lot stepped out of the mirror.

Moth rose to meet him with two blades in his hands. Lot came at him, swinging his walking stick as serenely as if he was strolling through a park.

"*Finn!*" Jack's voice was urgent.

Finn snatched up the silver dagger and ran to Jack. She stabbed the blade into the lock holding his chains together. As the horror of Hester's death began to cut through her shock, crippling her ability to think clearly, she heard Moth and Lot fighting, the blades and the walking stick shrieking and clanging against one another.

"The lock won't break," Jack grimly said. "Run."

She uncurled her other hand and raised what Hester had given her—a key shaped like a dragonfly. Jack whispered, *"Where did you—"*

She shoved the key into the lock of his chains. The lock clicked.

Moth slid across the floor on his back. Seth Lot was striding toward them, his face cold.

As his chains fell away, Jack grabbed Eve's silver knife from Finn, twirled it, and strode to meet Seth Lot, who slashed at him with his walking stick. Jack dodged. The Wolf grabbed him by the throat and flung him at the mirror. As Jack hit the glass, which shattered spectacularly all around him, a rain of silver, Lot stalked toward him, unsheathing a blade from his walking stick.

Jack had dropped the silver dagger and was painfully climbing to his feet. Finn, backing toward the door, felt her heel strike something and looked down at the jackal walking stick. She shouted to Moth, who dragged himself into a crouch. She shoved the walking stick across the floor. He caught it.

As Jack pushed himself up from the shards of glass, Moth, gripping the walking stick, rose unsteadily and ran at Lot, who turned.

Moth swung the walking stick and hit the Wolf in the skull. Lot dropped to one knee, hair falling over his face.

Finn turned to the door, still holding the dragonfly key, knowing it was the key the Black Scissors had given Sylvie to get her and Christie here. She wondered if that sly and dangerous enemy of the Fatas had suspected they'd end up with his key.

"Please work," she murmured as she heard Jack and Moth running toward her. She pushed the key into the lock.

Lot flung his sword. It slammed into Jack's shoulder, pinning him to the wall. Finn dropped the key with a cry.

Jack, bleeding from the mirror glass, looked as if he'd collapse any second. Moth grabbed the sword's hilt and frantically attempted to free him as Finn ducked down for the key. She glanced over her shoulder to see Lot had risen to his feet. As she straightened with the key, the Wolf said, "You won't get out."

Moth yanked the blade from Jack's shoulder—there was more blood—and held him up as Finn turned the dragonfly key in the lock.

As shadows began to swarm around the Wolf, the door opened.

Finn, Jack, and Moth raced down the hall. Darkness howled past them. It clotted before them, sweeping into the shape of Seth Lot, who ran at them with the sword.

Moth stepped between Lot and Finn. He blocked Lot's blade with the jackal walking stick and the force of the blow nearly bent him backward. Then Lot hooked a leg beneath one of his and Moth fell.

Jack had retrieved the silver dagger. As he strode forward, Finn leaped after him and wound one hand around his, around the dagger's hilt. When Lot writhed into darkness, they launched themselves at him, and, together, plunged the dagger toward the Wolf. *For Lily*, Finn thought.

The dagger stabbed into the shadows that had swallowed Seth Lot. The Wolf collapsed in his mortal form, clutching at the hole in his chest as darkness spilled from his mouth, his eyes.

Jack pulled Finn back. They swung around and hauled Moth to his feet and fled down the hall.

A storm of shadows massed behind them.

They pushed through the doors into the courtyard where Leander and Lily waited, looking as if they'd just come from a cocktail party, he in his white suit and she in her black gown. Leander carried Finn's backpack.

Finn flung herself forward and fiercely embraced Lily. "That thing with the butterflies . . . where'd you learn it?"

"Someday I'll tell you." Lily's attention switched to Moth and she said, "Hey, you."

Moth smiled. "Lily Rose."

"We need to fly." Jack gestured to a door in the wall.

"*That* was your plan?" Finn whispered to Jack as she took her backpack from Leander. "Get caught?"

"As long as Lot believed Leander would betray me." Jack handed Finn a wooden dagger. "Elder wood. We need to pin this damn house down so we can get out. Would you do the honors?"

As a howl came from within the mansion, Finn gripped the dagger. Then Lily's hands settled over hers and, together, they pushed the wood into the ground. The world shook.

They ran to the door in the courtyard wall. As Jack shoved it open, Moth and Leander swept out first to make sure nothing waited on the other side.

"Jack."

Finn and Jack slowly turned.

Reiko Fata, in a blood-red dress, stood near the wooden blade in the ground. The courtyard had become a creeper-snarled mess of neglect, the mansion once again a hulking ruin. Black hair whipping across her face, Reiko said, "Do you think another girl is going to free you, Jack? You are mine. Not *hers*. Not *his*. So, run, my Jack, from the Wolf. But *I* will find you."

With one foot, she shoved the wooden blade all the way into the soil.

A howling, inky void descended upon the Wolf's house.

Finn grabbed Jack's hand and they fled through the door in the wall. They turned to look back as the mansion and the grounds around it disappeared in that whirlwind of darkness and snow until all that remained was an empty clearing in a forest of mammoth oaks and towering yews.

"She pinned it." Jack sounded stunned.

Finn remembered Hester and felt her legs go wobbly. Jack gripped her elbow to keep her from falling and told her, "We're almost home, beloved."

Shadows seemed to stir in the forest that surrounded them. Caverns of darkness gaped. Mist crept around trees like monstrous figures, adding to the forest's baneful aspect. Close by, something howled.

Jack said, "He let some of his wolves out."

They ran, following Moth's, Leander's, and Lily's noisy flight through the black-and-gray world of the forest. Finn heard Lily shout her name, saw Moth racing ahead, leading the way. A strange barking sound echoed in the night around them.

When Jack halted, Finn nearly crashed into him.

"Where are they?" Finn cried. "Lily! Moth!"

"Finn." Jack's voice silenced her. "He's sent something else after us."

His fingers lost their grasp on hers.

She yelled as he was dragged away, through the leaves, into the dark. Lunging, she almost fell. She tore after him, into a deeper darkness, where the trees seemed bigger and older, their roots forming bridges and caves. Tiny lights danced in blackberry bushes and crimson toadstools scabbed the trunks. She flinched when she broke through a glistening spiderweb the size of her torso.

"Ja—" She bit down on his name.

To her right, a dark shape slinked through the forest. The shape was too narrow to be a wolf, its head sleek, with big, pointed ears. As it lifted its head to sniff the air, she fell to her knees in the snow.

She knew what it was.

She scrabbled up and began to run again, crashing through walls of ferns, avoiding low-hanging branches. The forest, a labyrinth of dire shapes and sounds, was now her enemy. Despite the elixir gifting her with litheness and an athlete's lungs, she knew she could not run forever.

When the heavy, muscled shape of the beast collided with her, she fell hard into the leaves.

Then the weight was gone. She sobbed and slid around in the dirt and snow. She kicked out, but couldn't see what had slammed her to the ground.

When a low laugh came from close by, she climbed to her feet.

Jack stepped from the shadows, a black greatcoat sweeping around him, his hair over his face. His eyes were icy silver. She stared at his hands glittering with rings.

This Jack wasn't her Jack or a trick . . . this was a *memory* released from Seth Lot's house with the wolves, before the house had been pinned into a void. This was a Jack of the past.

"You know what I am?" His voice was the hoarse, velvety one she recognized from when he'd hated himself. As he moved toward her with savage grace, she thought of the jackal she'd glimpsed, the beast that had knocked her to the ground. She backed away until she came up against a tree.

"Yes."

He circled her, his ghost gaze fixed upon her. He halted and moved his head as if scenting something. His brows slashed down. He drew closer and his fingers caressed her cheek. "You don't smell like a mortal girl. Why is that?"

She whispered, "Jack, listen—"

"Yes. I'm a Jack. But what are *you?* Why does Lot want *you?*" His fingers slid along the line of her jaw. "You look familiar, pretty little human."

"My name is Finn."

"You should never give your name to anyone." His eyes darkened. For a second, despite the bitter curl to his mouth, the ragged edge to his voice, she saw *her* Jack—and she wondered how much longer this version would have to suffer before being freed from Reiko and Lot.

She tilted her head up and tenderly brushed her lips against his, felt the mocking curve of his mouth soften as he returned the kiss until it became something lush and desperate—still, a stranger's kiss. His skin was cool, but familiar. She laid one hand over the place where his heart should be, felt nothing.

He tore back as if she'd bitten him. She reached out as if coaxing a skittish animal. "Jack . . . you'll know me again when you see me. But now you have to let me go. And you have to lead the wolves away."

"I know you, yet I don't." He turned and vanished into the forest. Finn ran in the opposite direction.

Something large swept down, rattling the branches. She caught herself against the nearest oak and almost collapsed, wondering what new monstrosity was about to descend upon her.

A girl emerged from the gloom between the trees, her coat billowing around a black gown. She carried a staff that resembled an antique hobbyhorse, but the toy horse's head had been replaced with a reindeer skull. She had Sylvie's face, but she wasn't Sylvie. Her eyes glimmered Fata silver. "Do you know who I am, Finn Sullivan?"

"You're Sylph Dragonfly. The witch." Finn felt unbalanced.

"I do wish your kind would stop using that word. Come along. We'll have to walk because you can't fly. Your friends aren't far." The Dragonfly twirled her staff.

"Jack . . ."

"He's with them. He was dragged away by a wolf. *Jack's* in fine shape. The wolf is not." Sylph Dragonfly began moving gracefully away. Finn followed, noticing that the witch's heeled boots didn't leave prints in the earth. "You are quite the firecracker, Finn Sullivan—or rather, an atomic bomb." She grabbed Finn's wrist and pulled her close. "Hush. Don't move."

Finn followed her gaze to an upright shadow loping through the trees to their left. She glimpsed a white, ghastly face above a mouthful of teeth.

As the wolf Fata loped away, Sylph Dragonfly jerked her head. She and Finn continued on. When Finn felt safe enough, she whispered, "Why weren't Sylvie and Christie, as kids, taken by your people and replaced by you and Sionnach Ri?"

"Our originals were flawed and protected. My people don't like flaws and they don't like being exorcised. So."

"Flawed and protected." Finn wondered what that meant.

"Could you lose that backpack? You're too encumbered."

"There are things in it that I need."

"Like what?"

"Stuff." Finn hoped they were getting closer to Jack and Lily and the others. This replica of Sylvie was making her nervous.

"Stuff to slay a wolf? You dropped this." Sylph Dragonfly tossed something to Finn, who caught it and stared down at the tiny sphinx bottle labeled *Tamasgi'po*. She'd forgotten about it. It must have fallen from her boot as she ran.

"Spirit in a kiss." Finn quickly reached down to check that the elixir was still in her other boot.

"*Tamasgi'po*. Where"—Sylph gracefully turned—"did you get such a thing?"

"From the Blue Lady. What is it?"

"Hellaciously dangerous." The Dragonfly began walking again. "What is memory, Finn Sullivan?"

"A storage of life events."

"It is conscious spirit. It is being *something* over being *nothing*. Therefore, memory for us is a tricky thing. Here we are."

"*Finn!*" Lily ran from the trees and embraced her. When she stepped back, she gripped Finn's shoulders and shrewdly looked her over. "You okay?"

"I'm fine." She wasn't.

Lily nodded once to the Dragonfly, who curtsied as if Lily was a queen. Behind Moth and Leander stood two girls dressed in fashionable black, Egyptian designs painted around their eyes. Each girl held a staff adorned with ribbons and topped with animal skulls.

"Finn." Jack walked toward her. He had a bloody scratch on his face, but he smiled like his old, wild self, and his eyes were the beautiful gray and blue. He touched her face and said, "I knew I hadn't lost you."

Finn glimpsed a shadow in her sister's gaze when Lily looked at Jack.

A howl broke the quiet. Sylph Dragonfly glanced at the other two girls. "We counted twenty wolves. Half went in another direction, as if led that way. The other ten—"

A huge, spiky shadow launched itself from the trees.

The humanity sloughed from Jack like a shed skin. He moved with feral grace, flinging Eve's silver dagger into the shadow, which became a Fata man, who fell to the forest floor.

Lily looked impressed as Jack put one booted foot on the Fata's shoulder and pulled out the dagger. The Fata blackened and bled until all that was left was a fur coat and some fossilized bones that didn't seem human at all.

"He had teeth." Lily gazed down at the monstrous skull that remained. Again, something dark passed behind her eyes. She raised one foot—she wore black Converses—and smashed it down, shattering part of the wolf's skull. Everyone stared at her.

The howling came from all sides now, growing closer. More big shadows were moving through the trees. Finn said, "They've found us."

Sylph strode to Moth. She grabbed him by his hoodie and kissed him as everyone stared. He flinched back from her but didn't change. Then she and her witches walked to three points around Finn and her companions, facing outward. The air began to hum. Finn heard another sound in the distance, like roaring, and whispered, "What—"

Lights danced through the trees. The roaring grew louder.

The wolves howled, circling closer. Feral eyes glowed in the dark.

The bright lights and thunder of the motorcycles that sped from the night to surround them seemed like the descent of battle angels. As the lead rider glided up to Finn, she counted a dozen riders.

Removing his helmet and handing it to her, Sionnach Ri smiled. "Nick of time?"

She grinned and put the helmet on. "You do that on purpose, don't you?"

CHAPTER 18

This maiden had scarcely these words spoken,
Till in at her window the elf knight has leaped . . .
"Seven kings' daughters have I slain.
And you shall be the eighth of them."

—"LADY ISABEL AND THE ELF-KNIGHT"

Sylph Dragonfly and her sisters vanished into the night as Finn, on the back of Sionnach's speeding bike, glanced over one shoulder and saw a pack of silver-eyed Fatas in fur coats emerging from the forest darkness behind them.

The wolves had lost their prey.

As the fox knights sped onto a highway with Finn and her companions, Finn yelled into Sionnach's ear. "Where are you taking us?"

"To Thomas the Rhymer."

The name belonged to a character in a ballad about fairies. Finn sighed. "You're not going to betray us again, are you?"

"Sylph Dragonfly threatened to turn me into a fur coat for her next lover if I did. So, no—also, I'm scared of your boyfriend. The Rhymer is a friend of yours, isn't he?"

"I don't know." Finn looked over at Jack, who rode with a leggy fox knight. When his eyes flashed silver, Finn's heart ached; now that they had left the Wolf's house, Jack's mortality had fallen away and the Dragonfly's spell was taking root again and becoming a reality.

AS DUSK CRIMSONED THE SKY, the fox knights' motorcycles curved onto a street of deserted-looking mansions untouched by age or neglect—a Ghostlands suburbs, as silent and perfect as a painting. They halted in front of a large oak door set in one of the ten-foot-high hedges lining the avenue, and Sionnach said, "You've got a key, Finn Sullivan. Don't you? I saw it."

She lifted the dragonfly key on its chain around her neck and gazed at it doubtfully. "Will it work here?"

"I'm sure it will. It has the *Dubh Deamhais*'s scent all over it."

"My friend died," Finn told him, her voice tight. "The one who gave this to me."

"I know." Sionnach Ri was somber. "I scented the death on it as well."

Jack glanced at the fox knight. "Don't think this makes up for you and your tribe handing Finn over to the Mockingbirds."

Sionnach nervously tugged at a gold hoop in his ear.

Finn climbed from the motorcycle, stepped forward, and jammed the dragonfly key into the lock of the door in the hedge. When the door swung open, she breathed out and felt like crying.

Beyond was a Mediterranean garden of fig and olive trees, with a townhouse of pale stone rising in the center, its large windows depicting stained-glass scenes of fairy-tale menace: a knight in thorns; a girl in a red coat, with a beast's shadow; two lovers, heads bowed, holding a bleeding apple between them.

"Go on in." Sionnach nodded to Finn. "The house door's open."

With a little shiver of apprehension and relief, she handed him the helmet he'd let her borrow. "Thanks."

Sionnach glanced at Moth, who was frowning, his face shadowed by the hood of his jacket. Then Sionnach smiled at Finn. "Any girl who can make Jack Daw grow a heart deserves my undying loyalty."

"That so? And how is *your* heart doing?"

"Fine." He put the helmet on. "Now that you've got time to breathe, maybe you and your man can go madly for the zippers, eh?"

"Good-*bye*, Sionnach." She waited until he and his knights had sped away, before turning and entering the garden with her companions. She said to Jack, "Thomas the Rhymer?"

"You know him as the dean of HallowHeart." Jack opened the townhouse door.

They stepped into a modern parlor illuminated by a chandelier of orange crystal. A wall of shelves held books with true-world titles. Antique furniture circled a fireplace carved with the image of an oak tree. Another wall was hung with green man masks spouting leaves and ivy.

"Welcome. At last." Rowan Cruithnear entered the parlor and he looked as aristocratic as ever in a Brooks Brothers suit, his hair seeming more silver than before. "Miss Sullivan, Christopher Hart and Sylvia Whitethorn have returned safely to the true world. Hopefully, you'll not be more than an hour later."

"But we can't go all the way back to that station—"

"You won't. I've arranged another way. It'll be a bit tricky."

Of course. Finn straightened when what she really wanted to do was fall onto the sofa. "Who are you, really?"

Jack answered, "This is Thomas the Rhymer, Thomas Learmont, whom I'm sure you've read about, your father being what he is. He's the only true love of the biggest, baddest fairy queen who ever lived—Titania—who gifted him with immortality."

"'Gifted,'" Rowan Cruithnear said wryly, "is a matter of opinion."

"You're like the Black Scissors?"

"Not quite, Miss Sullivan. I don't hate the Fatas as he does. And I have a conscience." Rowan Cruithnear turned to Moth and Leander. His gaze fell upon Lily and his smile faded. He whispered, "Lily Rose."

Lily stood silently, looking as if she'd stepped out of a Rackham illustration. She frowned at Cruithnear. Jack moved to stand in front of her, as if to protect her from Cruithnear's shocked gaze. "We're taking her home."

"Jack"—Cruithnear seemed about to voice an objection, then apparently changed his mind. He glanced at Leander and Moth. "This is Leander Cyrus, I presume? I've met . . . Moth."

Jack said, with that dangerous calm, "We need to get home before the Wolf figures out a way to come back at us out of the shadows."

"I think you first need to rest and replenish—I've real food. Afterwards, you'll be heading home."

"How did *you* get here?" Moth spoke coldly.

"Our key is working again—the Ghostlands, young man, is my second home." Rowan Cruithnear's response was stern. "I arrived the way Finn and Jack were supposed to. The key we gave you was set to bring you to the Green Road Station, not far from here. And I fear it was one of my people, not Phouka's, who hexed the key. It certainly wasn't Lulu."

"Then one of the professors is a traitor," Finn said grimly, "who sent us to the Wolf."

THE BOYS DIDN'T SEEM TO MIND being grungy and sweaty, but Lily and Finn headed for the bathroom on the second floor after Rowan Cruithnear gave them clothes that belonged to occasional guests of his. Finn wondered what kind of lady friend wore cocktail dresses and elegant coats.

Waiting for her sister outside the bathroom, seated on the floor in the hall, Finn shattered.

Quiet sobs racked her. Jack was suddenly crouched before her, pulling her against him. She pressed her face into his bloody shirt as he stroked her back, whispering, "Finn. Your sister is *safe*—"

"Don't leave me." She knotted her fingers in his shirt. "Okay? Just don't."

He didn't say anything. He didn't reassure her. And that should have warned her.

WHILE JACK SPOKE with Rowan Cruithnear in the parlor and Moth brooded in the kitchen over a cup of tea, Finn went to check on her sister, who had left to take a nap. When she knocked on the bedroom door, Leander called out, "Come in," and she stepped into a room where lilacs in a vase cast a soothing fragrance into the air and curtains drifted around an open window through which could be seen a picturesque view of the hedge maze.

Leander sat in a chair, his head in his hands. Lily was curled on the bed, asleep. Jack's coat and her Converses were neatly set on an ivory trunk.

"She was crying out before, in her sleep." Leander didn't look up as Finn sat on the bed, gently lifting the dark hair from her sister's face.

"Tell me how you met her."

Leander gazed at Lily with such longing, it made Finn ache for him. "I had just joined Lot's court, ten years ago, because I was alone and desperate. I didn't know what Lot was. He seemed solid. I saw Lily in Golden Gate Park. She was sitting on a fountain and she was in sneakers and a hoodie and a black ballet costume, like some delinquent ballerina."

"She *is* a delinquent ballerina."

"Her hair was in her face and she was smoking." He sat back, and a smile tugged at a corner of his mouth. "She told me to fuck off when I tried to talk to her. I wanted to take her picture."

"When did she find out what you were?"

"Well, pretty soon afterwards. I mean, she only saw me between dusk and dawn and I didn't have a heartbeat. She asked me, point-blank, if I was a vampire. She told me, if I was, she'd stake me with a wooden spear your dad owned. I wondered what kind of girl has a dad who owns spears."

"That's my sister. No sense of romance whatsoever. The ballet thing was eccentric." She hesitated. "How did . . . why did Seth Lot want her?"

"The Wolf"—Leander's voice shook—"found the darkness in her, the part that raged because of your mom's accident. Lily had always seen things when she was a kid. It's my fault for opening that door, for revealing myself. All the Wolf had to do was promise her a place at his side as a queen of shadows."

Finn had known her sister hadn't been happy—all those late nights and sneaking out and coming home through the window with the bite of alcohol on her breath. Finn knew her sister's flaws; Lily was not some brave, adventurous hero—but rather selfish, reckless, and angry with the world.

But in Lot's house, Finn suspected with a glimmering of unease, Lily had become something else.

Leander said quietly, "Finn, Lily can't leave the Ghostlands."

Although she'd heard it before, the shock of this statement made her cold. She told him, "I know you're worried Seth Lot will follow her. But we've got friends back home, people who can protect us. We'll be safe." She changed the subject. "How did *you* become a Jack?"

The rosy light haloed his tangled hair. His short fingernails were grimed and his suit was still grubby. He looked so beaten, she regretted the cruelty of her question.

Then he answered it: "It was in 1987. In San Francisco. I found one of *their* places. I met a girl. Her name . . . can you believe I've forgotten it? She was a Jill." He hesitated as if trying to find his way around gruesome details. "She didn't understand what she was doing. The Fatas . . . they're drawn to the lost and lonely like sharks to blood."

"She fell in love with you. The Jill."

"I loved *her*. But the Fata who made her—*that* name I remember—it was Amphitrite. She was a sea witch and she wasn't happy that I was taking away her Jill. As twisted as she was, Amphitrite saw her Jacks and Jills as her children. So I made a deal with Amphitrite. My girl was returned to almost human, enough to forget what she'd been and go home. And I drowned."

"Returned her to *almost* human?" Finn didn't want to comment on his drowning.

He nodded. "A spell. She was still a Jill, physically, but the illusion of being human would keep anyone, even physicians, from noticing. And *she* believed it." He continued, gently, "Like what happened to Jack after the Teind. He *believed* he was mortal."

"But"—Finn spoke with bitter realization—"he wasn't."

Lily twisted in her sleep, cried out, and pushed at the air with one hand. Finn curled beside her and put her arms around her.

Leander came and stretched out on Lily's other side and, together, they cradled the stolen-away girl they both loved.

ROWAN CRUITHNEAR WOULD LEND THEM his car in the morning. He'd given Jack directions to a train station not used by the Fatas anymore—one unknown to Seth Lot.

"Then we're almost home." In the second-floor room Cruithnear had given her and Jack for the night, Finn sat on the bed. Outside was a deep forest of evergreens—a completely different view from the hedge maze in the front of the house. She'd changed into the summer dress of silver silk Cruithnear had given her. She'd put on a fur hunter's cap and wrapped herself in a fur jacket because she wanted the terrace doors open. Jack had started a fire in the hearth, but the cold air felt good—it cleared her head. "It's beginning to snow."

Jack sat beside her. He'd changed out of his bloody clothes into a black jersey and jeans—Cruithnear apparently had many visitors who left clothing.

Finn thought of Lily Rose in the house of the Wolf and pictured Leander drowning to give a girl back her life. She thought of Hester disintegrating, never to be seen again. She curled her fingers in the fur coat. Her jaw clenched.

"Do you see those lights flickering through the trees?" Jack's voice soothed the prickly sorrow of her thoughts.

"Are they pixies? Will-o'-the-wisps?"

"Those are the souls of the dead passing through the Ghostlands. Don't ask me where they're going, but that's what they are."

"They're beautiful." She watched them and wondered if she knew any of them.

"You wouldn't think a river of human blood ran beneath that beautiful world out there, would you? Or that a beast disguised as a man stitches up the young with magic. Finn, the train we're going to take . . . to get back to the true world, we'll be passing along the border."

"What border?"

"The one between the land of the living and the land of the dead."

"Oh." She didn't say anything else because she figured the two of them had been walking that border for some time now.

As Jack kept his gaze on the forest outside the window, she studied his profile and felt a shiver of fear for him, the uncertainty of his place in her world. His fingers tightened around hers as he said, "A few days ago, I wondered if I'd lost you forever. There is silver in your eyes, Finn Sullivan, and your shadow hasn't returned. What's with the outfit?"

He flicked the fur hunter's cap she wore, and she snugged the flaps over her ears. "It was a gift from Rowan Cruithnear. My ears were cold. The dress belonged to a lady friend of his. And what about you, rocking the gangster look at the Mockingbirds?"

"I was trying to play the role." He sprawled back on the bed, propped up on his elbows. "You know, that dress kind of looks like something Phouka would wear."

"You think Cruithnear and Phouka . . . ?" She raised her eyebrows. "How scandalous. What about the young menswear he has on hand?"

"To each his own. You look very fetching."

"Oh. Here." She unclasped the phoenix pendant from around her neck.

He sat up and tugged her onto his lap and she fastened the pendant's leather thong around his neck. She twined her fingers in his hair as her lips sought his in a sensual, openmouthed kiss. He twisted and she was beneath him, cradled by him, protected by him.

"I'm a Jack again, Finn." His eyes were dark, troubled.

But his skin was warm. She drew him down against her, and his sinewy strength and the softness of the bed became the safest place in the world. He slid the coat from her, his beautiful eyes hidden by his lashes. She arched, pressed her face between his neck and shoulder, tasted his skin. His mouth found hers again, hungrily. For a moment, her existence was only skin and heat and tangled limbs and breath. He groaned as she slipped her hands beneath his black jersey. When she touched his shoulder where Lot's sword had gone through, she felt only a rough seam. *It's safer for him this way*, she thought sadly. *Not being like me.*

He yanked the jersey off over his head and curved above her with a vinelike grace, the golden phoenix brushing against her lips as he whispered, "I *missed* you—"

She dragged him down against her again, sighing as his skin kissed hers, as his mouth touched her throat, as his fingertips drifted across her thigh. She felt as fragile as glass containing fiery butterflies. He reminded her of what he'd been transformed into at the Teind: an eagle, a python, fire, water—

Her foot knocked her backpack from the bed. Things clattered across the floor. Remembering one object in particular, she scrambled up in a panic.

Jack saw it before she could lunge for it. He moved with inhuman grace as she jumped to her feet. He was already crouched at the foot of the bed, holding the wooden box gilded with the shapes of jackals, staring at its contents strewn across the floor. He said, his voice ragged, "I remember this . . ."

"*Don't.*" She knelt helplessly amid the scattered contents of the box.

"*Where did you find this?*"

"Orsini's Books."

He dropped the box, shoved his hands through his hair. "Did you think that these were *innocent* things I had collected? Finn?"

"Some of them." Her voice was faint.

"The box was my mother's." He reached out and traced the golden jackals on the lid. "She was Romany before she was Irish. And it was brought, by her ancestors, from Egypt. She gave it to my father, so that he could keep his amulets and talismans in it."

His father had been a coachman from Hungary, but also an exorcist. She watched as Jack picked up a ring shaped like a serpent. He said, "Most of these are trophies."

"Were they Fatas?" She carefully coaxed him back from the past. "The ones you took these things from?"

"Seven." He closed his fist over the ring. "I got away with each kill here.

They were Reiko's enemies. Some were Lot's. Not all of them were bad."

Finn watched him set the serpent ring on the floor.

"This ring belonged to a Fata named Evan-on-the-Hill. He was a Redcap but hadn't yet begun to turn poisonous. I prevented him from becoming anything."

She reluctantly lifted a fan of ivory parchment painted with images that seemed to move. "And this?"

"She was called *Ban Beache*, the White Bee. She fed on mortals as they dreamed."

Finn lifted another object, and another, and, in this way, lanced an infection that had been festering within him for far too long. He told the story of each trophy. As he spoke each Fata name, Finn flung the objects into the fire. When it was done, she handed the jackal box back to him. Silently, they watched the flames. He said in a raw, quiet way, "Have you thought of finding someone real?"

"Real? What the hell is that supposed to mean?"

His gaze didn't leave the fire. "I'm old, Finn."

"Two hundred years of arrested development isn't old."

"Bloody *Peter Pan*. It's influenced all you bookish girls."

"I'm not book—well, a little. Anyway, this conversation is over, because it's a waste of time." She pushed to her feet and walked to stand before the open terrace doors.

He came to her side, settling her fur jacket back over her shoulders, and she whispered, "I don't see your shadow anymore."

"That's the least of our worries, beloved."

"No, Jack. Not the least of mine."

"Finn . . . Lot knew the Mockingbirds would try for us, to recruit us. He *expected* us to do to the Mockingbirds what we did to Reiko. He used you and me to eliminate an enemy. He isn't underestimating us."

"He'll come after us."

"Yes. I had to tell Rowan about Hester Kierney. He says that'll end it between the Fatas and the blessed—it'll leak out, to other places where the Fatas have lodged themselves. It's not good for either side."

"They won't even have a body to bury. Her family." Finn felt fatigue creeping up on her. *Hester* . . .

"What are the odds," Jack said darkly, "that that key would end up just where we needed it, in Lot's house? In Hester's hand?"

Finn closed her eyes.

"Christie said he and Sylvie were swept through the Way when they came here, that the key was left behind in StarDust Studios. What made Hester find it and step through into the arms of Seth Lot? Someone set her up, Finn."

Finn pressed a fist against her midriff. "Someone sacrificed Hester, to save us."

"Yes."

They were quiet then, watching the snow and the shimmering orbs of the dead drift over the forest.

JACK SLID FROM THE BED where he and Finn had fallen asleep—regretfully, their passion had been somewhat subdued by the realization that Hester's death might have been the result of an ally's manipulations. He moved out into the hall, down the stairs. With the exception of a grandfather clock ticking, the house was silent.

As he slipped out the back door and into the garden, he heard a voice. "What are you doing, Jack?"

He turned. Moth was hunched forward in a chair on the back veranda, his face shadowed.

A chill swept through the garden, which had transformed from Mediterranean Zen to a wintery, English courtyard of red roses and blackberry bushes. Jack said, "I'm making certain Lily Rose is able to accompany us back to the world."

Moth's voice was hard. "I know what you're going to do. I *know* what Lily Rose is. You can't. It'll *break* Finn."

Jack looked toward the darkest part of the garden. "There's no other way. And you've got to admit"—he smiled as his heart began to beat faster—"it's a perfect way to set things right."

Moth said nothing.

Jack walked deeper into the garden, toward the dark figure waiting for him, the one Rowan Cruithnear had reluctantly summoned, the one whose shadow stilled the air around it and withered any living thing close by.

FINN WOKE IN DARKNESS, an image from her last dream still vivid in her head—a white umbrella planted in the snowy ground, its stem blossoming with mistletoe.

Jack was gone.

She rose from the bed, then grabbed her coat and Doc Martens. Hopping into the hall while pulling them on, she glanced at Lily and Leander's door, heard them talking, and was reassured.

Finn hurried down the stairs. A blue lamp glowed in the parlor redolent of leather-bound books and burnt wood. Their backpacks and equipment had been placed against a wall. She knelt down and carefully sorted some of their belongings: the jackal-handled walking stick with the sword; the Grindylow's compass heart; the dragonfly key; the *Tamasgi'po* in its vial shaped like a sphinx; Eve Avaline's silver dagger.

Poisoning, pinning, and decapitation.

"What," she whispered to the air, "will really kill the Wolf?"

She rose as Moth entered the parlor. When he saw her, he halted, looking as if he'd been caught at something. "Finn."

"Have you seen Jack?"

"He's in the garden, I believe."

"What's he doing in the garden?" She began to move past him, but Moth gently caught her arm and said, "Don't go out there . . . he needs to put his mind together."

The grave look in Moth's eyes made her sink onto the sofa instead. Finn said, "He knows he's turning back. Into a Jack."

He sat beside her. "He does."

She'd rescued her sister from the Wolf, but she was helpless against Jack's transformation. "If we hadn't come here—"

"You wouldn't have your sister."

"He'll hate himself again."

"He has you."

What can I do? she thought. *Love him enough to keep him with blood, heart, and breath?*

"Finn, I want to show you something."

He rose. She watched as he closed his eyes. He began to shimmer. "Moth—"

When he burst into sheets of gossamer light, she gasped and scrambled back. A luna moth spiraled from the glow. She jumped up.

The moth shimmered again, changing into a mass of light and shadow, and

Moth crouched in the middle of the room. He raised his head, triumphant. "I've been practicing."

It hadn't shaken her, what had just transpired. It should have. She smiled. "You might be our best chance against the Wolf."

DUSK BLED ACROSS THE SKY as Jack drove Cruithnear's Lincoln town car down a crooked road lined with graffiti-painted warehouses and giant, lightning-blasted oaks. Finn sat in the back with Lily, who had her head on Leander's shoulder. Moth was in the passenger seat up front, glaring out the window as if expecting an army to descend.

Jack had been suspiciously optimistic at the breakfast Cruithnear had made for them. As they'd sat in the blue-and-white kitchen, surrounded by porcelain painted with ethereal blue shepherdesses and windmills, Cruithnear, pouring coffee, had informed them he'd soon return to Fair Hollow after he cleared up some things here.

Finn, watching the Ghostlands pass by, realized that she was going to miss it. Maybe it was the elixir. Maybe it was Stockholm syndrome.

"So what's wrong with this station?" Finn could tell Moth was scowling even though she could only see the back of him.

"The MossHeart Station. It's old. It's broken. Something bad happened there a long time ago." It was Lily who spoke.

Warily, Finn asked, "What bad something?"

"A love story." Lily gazed out the window.

"And how did you learn about this story?" Jack sounded interested.

"I had my sources. People wanted favors in Lot's court—I took information in exchange."

Finn stared at her sister. So did Leander. Moth slowly turned his head to regard Lily with wary respect. Jack didn't take his attention from the road. Lily straightened. "The guardian of MossHeart Station was a *Lham Dearg*, a Bloody Hand—a Fata who feeds off murders."

"So far, I *don't* like this story." Finn's brows pinched.

"He fell in love with a mortal girl, a girl who could speak with the dead. She came close to his territory in the true world and he noticed her. He became curious and began following her. She was in love with a mortal boy. So he sent his spies to watch them, to *learn*. He began to neglect his duties as a spirit who shadowed murderers. He worked for Seth Lot."

Lily continued blithely, "The Bloody Hand, BatSong, appeared to the mortal girl, spoke to her, pretended to be harmless. But she saw what he was—she was an oracle. And she wasn't afraid. She felt sorry for him. That was her downfall. One evening, as she and her boy were kissing in a field filled with dragonflies, they were set upon by bats, who became the *Lham Dearg*. He ordered the girl to come with him or he would kill her lover. But her mortal lover was from one of the blessed families, and this caused a conflict between Seth Lot and the Fata queen who looked after the boy's family. Seth Lot didn't like that the girl *knew* things. He gave the *Lham Dearg* a choice: murder the mortal girl or Lot would do it himself—and you can imagine how *that* fucking bastard would have done it. BatSong couldn't do it, so, instead, he turned the girl into a tree, because he had Redcap blood and he thought that was the only way to keep her safe . . . until he could find a way to destroy Seth Lot."

"So they're both there now, at the station?" Finn glanced out the window as if she could glimpse MossHeart Station through the forest. "BatSong and the tree girl?"

"They're both there now," Lily finished.

Finn felt the elixir like cold electricity within her, glimpsed her eyes silvering slightly in the rearview mirror.

JACK TURNED OFF THE ROAD and stopped in front of an octagonal building of green marble scrawled with more graffiti and nestled in creepers and giant ferns. Rusting railroad tracks snaked around it into a wilderness of redwoods and fir trees. The station's stained-glass windows were grimed with so much lichen, they looked black. Scarlet fungus streaked the walls like an infection.

As they stepped out of the car, Lily reached out and gripped Finn's hand. Jack began walking toward the building. Leander and Moth flanked the sisters as Jack led the way up the stairs to the metal door engraved with stylized images of bats. He tried the handle, brushed his fingertips across the rusting lock.

"We don't need to get in, do we? All we need to do is wait for the train." Finn's voice faded when Jack shook his head and stepped back.

"At this little-used place, we'll need to summon the guardian. You have a key."

Finn lifted the dragonfly key Hester Kierney had given her from its chain around her neck. She studied it and uneasily remembered that the Black Scissors created keys from living things. She moved to Jack's side, inserted the key into the lock. Apprehension swept over her as the door opened.

They stepped into a high-ceilinged lobby littered with leaf wrack and the bones of tiny animals. Wooden benches sagged beneath colonies of toadstools. Lamps of black metal rusted on walls painted with faded murals of Victorian advertisements for soap and bicycles and typewriters. In the center grew a tree, black even to its leaves, its roots cracking the marble floor, its branches strung with hundreds of red and green glass beads that glowed in the dusky light.

"That's it?" Finn breathed. "An elder tree . . ."

As she and Jack approached the tree, the glass beads became incandescent. Finn curled her hands to keep from reaching out and touching one of the beads. Her skin began to warm in the glow from the tree as threads of light ebbed outward. Jack, studying the tree with concern, said, "She's become a guardian between the lands of the living and the dead."

"We are caught between mortal and not." Lily moved forward. "And getting back is not as easy as arriving."

In Finn's hand, the dragonfly key whirred to life, a silvery thing that shot forward into the darkness beyond the tree. In that dark, Finn thought she glimpsed a young man's white face and long black hair—she remembered the photo of Thomas Luneht on Sylvie's wall.

The tree continued to exude tendrils of ruby and emerald light, but the only sound was the *whirr* of the dragonfly's wings in the dark. Watching the jeweled tree shimmer to life, Finn became aware of a thundering pulse beneath their feet and remembered Jack telling her about the river of blood that ran beneath this land, blood from all the mortal battles on earth.

A voice whispered: *You are not welcome here.*

A sudden vacuum of hostile cold struck Finn down to her bones. *No,* she thought. *Not when we're so close.*

"*Ialtag Amrhan.*" Jack spoke the guardian's name. "We are here to return to the true world."

The shadows birthed a statuesque young man in a sleeveless robe of inky fur, his hair a mane of tangled black, his eyes an acid green. His arms were gloved to the elbow in red.

"And what does that have to do with me?" The guardian bared curved teeth. "Why do any of you want to enter the mortal world?" His gaze slid over each of them. "Is there a mortal among you that I can't scent?"

Moth idly reached for the knives hidden in his hoodie. Jack rubbed the back of his neck, his hand in close proximity to the grip of the jackal walking stick/sword strapped across his back.

When Finn stepped forward, Lily grabbed for her hand and Moth swore beneath his breath. Finn said, "What was her name?"

No one moved. The guardian was as still as a statue. He slowly looked at the tree. His voice scraped out, "Miriam."

"We're going to kill Seth Lot," Finn told him. "Let us back to the true world. The Wolf will follow, eventually, and we'll kill him there." She glanced at the whispering tree. "And you'll be able to free *her*."

She returned her attention to the guardian and flinched—his bloody hands were cupping an object made out of twigs, moss, and red creepers.

"Take it," he whispered. "My heart. Break it, and you'll summon the train that runs between the borders."

She moved toward the Fata and placed her hands over his bloody ones. Carefully, she accepted the fragile object, stepped back. She didn't take her gaze from him as she snapped the Fata heart in two.

There was a sound like a glacier cracking. The air became sweet with ivy, clover, and berries. The tree's black leaves lightened to emerald and the beads of glass began to tremble.

As a sigh drifted through the air, the guardian vanished and the dragonfly whirred from the shadows and out the door.

The whistle of a train shattered the silence. They ran onto the platform.

A train as derelict as the station, laced with rust, forged from black metal tinged with ivy-green and streaked with the red light of a Ghostlands day, was thundering down the tracks. It was the most gorgeous thing Finn had ever seen.

"The dragonfly," she said faintly. "*Thomas Luneht* was the lover of BatSong's mortal girl."

Jack, watching the train approach, reached out and clasped one of her hands. "I always wondered why Reiko and Lot split in the '70s. Lot ordered Caliban to murder Thomas Luneht, one of her blessed."

Finn pictured a smiling Thomas Luneht and a black-haired girl kissing in a field dancing with dragonflies. She felt snarly.

The train creaked and groaned and halted with a terrible screech like a dying dragon. The singed air stung her nostrils. The doors slammed open and a few bolts and screws clattered to the tracks.

Lily whispered, "We're going home."

Finn gripped one of Lily's hands. "Yes."

Moth was the first to step up into the train. He reached down for Lily.

When Leander shouted, Finn glanced over her shoulder. A large white shape was running toward them, its muzzle curled back from a cage of teeth. She spoke the name like a curse, "*Crom cu.*"

"Hurry!" Moth held the doors open as Jack and Leander pushed Finn and Lily up the steps.

Caliban materialized from the pale hyena as if he'd shed white shadows. His gray coat billowing, he loped toward the station.

"Go! *Go!*" Jack yelled. Leander leaped up into the train. Jack followed.

Caliban halted, raised an arm, and aimed a revolver of white metal. A shot cracked out.

Finn and Leander grabbed Jack as the doors began to close. As Jack dove in and the doors hissed shut behind him, a second bullet struck the metal. The train lurched forward.

Jack pushed to his feet. "It seems the *crom cu* has left old school behind."

"Jack." Moth was somber. "You're bleeding."

Finn pushed aside Jack's coat and saw the hole in his shirt and the fresh blood. But the bullet wound was already closing. He lifted a bloody projectile between two fingers and she winced—it was a human molar. She met his gaze as relief mixed with dismay in her head and heart.

Moth said to Jack, "We need to make sure whoever else is on this train isn't going to be a problem."

"And if they are?" Lily was watching Jack.

"Then they're getting off this train." Jack stepped back. "Finn. Lily. We won't be long." As Moth and Leander strode down the aisle, Jack said to Finn, "Do you still have the silver dagger?"

"Yes."

"Use it if you need to, on anything that enters." He turned to follow Leander and Moth.

Finn dropped into the seat beside Lily, her mind blank, her body numb. Desperately, she said, "You're real, Lily, aren't you?"

Lily took the silver dagger from Finn. Before Finn could stop her, she'd sliced the ball of her thumb. As red blood welled, she met Finn's gaze. "I'm real. I had to tell myself that, every day, in that house. And if it weren't for Leander and Moth, I would have lost my mind. Time is different there. I feel like I've been away for *years*. I can't wait to get home"—she huddled in the seat, her knees drawn up beneath her chin as she looked out of the window—"and see Dad, and walk on the beach and go to the park and Fisherman's Wharf . . ."

Finn had forgotten to tell Lily that they'd moved. "Um . . . do you remember Gran Rose? She died, after you . . . Well, Da and I moved into her house in New York."

"That big old place?" Lily turned in her seat to face Finn. "In Fair Hollow? Huh. Gran Rose died . . . I barely remember her." Her eyes were dark, and Finn, who couldn't imagine what terrible memories might be slivered into her sister's brain, curled her hands into fists in her lap. Lily let her head fall back against the seat and said, "We didn't have a chance, did we? Leander smiled at me and pretended to be normal—even when I began to suspect. And Seth . . . all he had to do was look at me." She hung her head and her long hair veiled her face. "And promise to make me a queen of night and nothing."

Gently, Finn said, "Leander loves you, Lily."

"They're so good at pretending, Finn."

"Do you remember what you said . . . that night . . . 'They call us things with teeth.'"

Lily's mouth curved. "I got that from the first Fata I ever met. *Norn*."

"I've met her."

"You have?"

"She was part of Reiko's . . . family."

"It's the first thing Norn said when I saw her. It was in the woods in Vermont and the sun was setting and she came walking toward me like some kind of rebel angel, in jeans, tattooed and barefoot. And she said, 'Hello, little thing with teeth.'"

Finn shivered, imagining the Viking Fata girl approaching the child version of her sister.

"Mom told me once"—Lily's voice was soft as she gazed out the window—"that the first life-forms on earth to grow teeth were, technically, going to become the first humans. And Fatas, well, they were probably the first life-forms, right, but they're all spirit. But they can make themselves solid. And some use their teeth to—"

Lily went silent.

"Tickets, misses?" A figure dropped into the seat opposite them and Finn almost stabbed him with the silver dagger.

The Black Scissors smiled. He looked as if he'd just stepped from a neo-western in his black duster and wide-brimmed hat banded with bird skulls. He said, "Good evening, Misses Sullivan. I see you've broken all the rules to achieve your desires, as usual."

Gripping the arms of her seat, Lily straightened. "*You.*"

"You know him . . ." Finn glanced at her sister.

The Black Scissors touched his hat brim. "We're acquainted. Has the Wolf stopped howling?"

"Why don't you go check?" Finn scowled. "And how did you get on this train? Cruithnear told us it's a ghost train between the Ghostlands and the realm of the dead."

"The realm of the dead"—his mouth twisted—"doesn't bother me. I walk the borders. The dead and I have an *understanding.*"

"Finn, don't be rude." Lily Rose tucked her hair behind her ears and leaned slightly forward. "Did you really expect my sister and her gorgeous boyfriend to kill the Wolf? We barely escaped. Why don't you grow a pair and kill him yourself?"

Finn looked from Lily to the Black Scissors. The Black Scissors said lightly, "I couldn't get near him. Believe me, I've tried. I gave your sister and Jack the *means* to kill him, but I didn't expect them to be assassins."

"Sylvie and Christie could have *died,*" Finn said.

"They could die in the true world, too, Finn Sullivan. Now, they'll be helpful comrades to you and Jack when the time comes."

"Finn," Lily said. "Don't hit him."

"A girl named Hester Kierney found your key. She's *dead*. You used Moth and turned *him* into a key—and Thomas Luneht—what did you do to *him*?"

"I'm sorry about Hester Kierney—that was not my doing. However much that dragonfly key would have helped you, *I* didn't lure Miss Kierney into the Ghostlands. But someone did . . . someone who knew what that key was and wanted it in the possession of a girl who could only get it to you at the very moment you needed it. As for Moth, he was without memory or any sense of what he was when I found him, shimmering with the remnants of Fata enchantment. He was a void, as if someone had sculpted a persona around nothing. And Thomas . . . well, he's still fighting. He agreed to become an object of power for you . . ."

"So you turned him into a *key*?"

"To *help* you, Miss Sullivan. I've done these things to *help* you."

"You did them to help *yourself*."

"Miss Sullivan . . . what do you think your chances are against the Wolf when he comes to the true world?"

"Home team advantage." She felt everything go quiet inside of her. "Are you going to be here when the menfolk return? I wouldn't advise it."

The Black Scissors and Lily exchanged a look that send a chill through Finn, as if she'd just discovered a dark secret between them. How well *did* they know each other?

"Why, exactly, are you here?" Finn spoke softly.

"To make sure you get through this safely." He unfolded one hand and the dragonfly key glimmered on his palm. "And to retrieve Thomas Luneht. You don't need him anymore, but I still do." He rose gracefully. "Before your capricious and prosaic paramour returns, I'll go to another car. Oh, and, Miss Sullivan." He leaned down to whisper, "Don't look at your sister when this train passes through the darkness into the true world."

Finn sucked in a breath and glanced at Lily. Her sister was gazing broodingly out the window. Finn didn't think she'd heard.

The Black Scissors was already striding away, his coat swirling as he opened the rusting door to another car and stepped through.

Lily murmured, "What did that slinky socio just whisper in your ear?"

Finn breathed out. "Lily. Just how do you know the Black—"

The light outside the windows became darkness.

A gut-wrenching pain doubled Finn over, as if the elixir was rebelling inside of her. She reached out and grasped Lily's hand as night swept through the train. Lily's grip was painful, but Finn didn't dare let go, even as she hunched over and retched so violently she slid to her knees. She realized she could no longer see in the dark—the elixir was fading from her, which meant the train was leaving the Ghostlands behind. Closing her eyes and still clutching her sister's hand, she whispered, "Lily, are you still there?"

Her sister didn't answer. Her grip on Finn's hand was still painfully tight, and the blackness around Finn had become suffocating. As the train sped onward in the dark, and the hand clenching hers began to dig nails into her flesh, it became harder to resist looking.

She *had* to look, to see that Lily was still with her, or all the horror and risk, the death, had been for nothing. Her voice left her in shivers, "*Lily* . . . you need to answer me. Please. *Please* say something."

The temperature in the car dropped. A funereal fragrance of lilies drifted through the air and she was convinced that whatever sat there, holding her hand, was only *pretending* to be her sister and had become a *thing* now that they had left the Ghostlands. Had she been tricked again? Slowly, she lifted her gaze to what sat there, glimpsed white skin, the curl of a mouth—

"Finn." Jack slid from the darkness. He carried a small lantern that glowed with electric light. "We're almost there."

Still holding the cold, clenching hand of whatever sat next to her, Finn whispered, "Jack, is Lily there? Please make sure it's her . . ."

"Finn—"

"Finn?"

Finn heard Lily's voice before the pain churning through her sent her plummeting into the dark.

THE CLATTERING MOTION OF THE TRAIN WOKE FINN. She opened her eyes, winced at the sunlight, and found herself in the seat beside Lily, who slept, her sneakered feet tucked beneath her, her hair pulled away from her face. Opposite, Moth also napped. Finn turned her head and gazed out the window at the snowy landscape dappled with the brilliant light of day. She saw cars and restaurants, power lines and concrete . . .

"Coffee?"

She looked up at Jack and smiled. "Thanks." She accepted the paper cup of coffee, inhaled its fragrance. "We're not on a Fata train anymore, are we?"

"No." He stepped back as a businessman brushed past. Across the aisle, a kid with a nose ring was listening to an iPod. A woman behind them was talking on a red cell phone. "Our phantom train kind of blended with a real one."

"Jack. It's *day*. We left at midnight—"

"It's eight thirty, Saturday, the morning after. We'll get you home in forty minutes and sneak you back in your room before your dad even wakes up."

She reached out to brush the hair from her sleeping sister's face, reassuring herself once again that Lily was real. She smiled and savored the sunlight on her skin. "That'll have to do. Where's Leander?"

Jack sank into the seat opposite her, next to Moth, and hunched forward. "Unlike me, Leander's still all Jack. He's not here anymore. It's daylight." He smiled ruefully. "It's a good thing Sylph Dragonfly's spell remained with me for all those wounds in the Ghostlands, because my body is a bit confused. If I suddenly blink out of existence, don't be alarmed."

She didn't understand at first. Her eyes widened when she did. "Leander's not here? You mean, he doesn't exist in the day? That can't . . . that's . . ." She frowned. "So, as Jacks, you and Leander, in the day, become . . . nothing?"

"That's right. Finn, Leander will find himself wherever he wished to be before he went away. We've gotten Lily Rose back and we'll deal with what comes afterwards, just as we've dealt with everything before that."

"Together," she whispered fiercely. She didn't want to ask any more about Leander. She'd never really thought of Jack *not-existing*, even when he'd once vanished in her arms as dawn cascaded into her room.

She sank back in her seat, drank bad coffee, and watched the magic of sunlight touch everything around her, including Jack.

CHAPTER 19

Their life stood full at blessed noon;
I, only I, had passed away:
"Tomorrow and today," they cried;
I was of yesterday.

—"At Home," Christina Rossetti

Lily didn't ask about Leander's disappearance. When she woke, she stared around in amazement. As they stepped from the train into the crowded terminal, Finn watched her sister move hesitantly, avoiding pools of sunlight.

"Finn!"

Finn laughed breathlessly when she saw Christie and Sylvie, accompanied by Jane Emory, pushing through the crowds. Her eyes burned with tears as she met them in a big, jumbled hug.

Jane stepped back—and saw Lily. Christie and Sylvie slowly turned from Finn and also stared. Jane whispered, "Is that—"

"I'm Lily." Lily jutted her chin.

"You're just like Finn said." Sylvie was wide-eyed, as if meeting a celebrity. "I'm Sylvie. This is Christie. That's Jane."

As Jane and Lily gazed warily at each other, Jack spoke. "We need to separate. Jane, if you'll take me, Moth, and Lily, Finn can go home with Sylvie and Christopher."

"Like hell—" Lily began.

"You can't go home," Jack gently told her. "It's too dangerous. We need to keep you away from the obvious places."

"It won't be for long." Finn glanced at Jane. "How did you know we were coming here?"

"The Black Scissors told me." Jane was watching Lily. "I was leaving Lulu's Emporium after we got that damn key unhexed and Rowan had gone through to the Ghostlands, when the Black Scissors appeared and told me you'd be here today, that he was going to meet you on the train. He's damn unnerving—where is he?"

Jack leveled one of those stern looks on Finn that always made her feel like young King Arthur being scolded by Merlin. Finn shrugged. "The Black Scissors was just checking up on us. I don't know where he is."

Moth tilted his head back in annoyance. Jack frowned at Lily as if he knew she had secrets. Sylvie spoke up: "Where's Leander?"

As Jack explained, Lily moved to Finn and embraced her with willowy strength. Finn gripped her older sister, her best friend, as if letting go would cause her to evaporate. "You were always the brave one," Lily whispered. Then she stepped back and addressed Jack and Moth. "Let's go, boys."

"You girls might need these." Jane handed a pair of sunglasses to Finn, one to Lily.

"Perfect." Lily put them on against the sun she hadn't seen for a year. She walked into a pool of light and spun.

Jane turned to Jack. "Where, exactly, am I taking you, Jack?"

"My place," he told her. "Thank you, Jane." He moved to Finn and bent his head, spoke gently. "Go home. Rest. I'll be the only one who knows where Lily is. I'll be the only one taking her to where we agreed she should stay. Meet me and Moth at Max's Diner at five, with Christopher and Sylvie, and we'll go to Tirnagoth together. Hopefully, Leander will show up when the sun sets."

He kissed her as if she was the last bit of warmth in the world and he was slowly freezing to death. She resisted clutching at him as if she were a child. When he drew back, he lifted the phoenix pendant from beneath his shirt. "I still have this and your ring. My talismans."

She tugged the lionheart locket he'd given her from beneath the neckline of her dress. "I still have this."

"That's my girl." He kissed her one more time, stealing her breath, before striding after Moth and Lily.

Finn found Jane watching her with bright eyes. "You want to hug me again, don't you?"

Jane stepped forward and did just that, and Finn, who had thought it would be awkward, closed her eyes and, for an instant, guiltily remembered her mother.

When Jane stepped away and followed Jack, Finn, repressing a giddy urge to linger in the sunlight, looked around. She loved the sight of so many people. She savored the stray aromas of fast food and car exhaust and coffee. She said to Sylvie and Christie, "It doesn't feel real."

"Finn . . ." Sylvie looked as if she was going to cry. "Jack didn't have a shadow."

"I know. Take me home."

AS CHRISTIE DROVE HIS MUSTANG down the oak-lined road to Finn's home, Finn bit down on her bottom lip and felt her eyes sting. This was the house where she and Lily would be sisters again. All the horrors of the Ghost-lands began to dim . . . the terrible deaths of Atheno and Hester . . . phantom Reiko . . . Seth Lot's savage and seductive promises . . .

Then Finn saw the sporty red car parked behind her da's SUV and her stomach twisted up. Christie clenched his hands on the steering wheel. "Is that Professor Avaline's car?"

Finn pulled her backpack into her lap. "It's not what you think. She's not my da's type."

"*Call* me." Sylvie and Christie said at the same time, as Finn slid from the Mustang, her boots stomping on ice-crusted snow.

"I'll tell you everything when we meet at Max's Diner." She strode up the shoveled path to the front porch.

She slipped into the hall, sloughed her coat, and set her backpack down quietly. She could hear voices in the parlor—her father's and Sophia Avaline's. She stood a moment, absorbing the idea that she was home. With a wrenching pang, she suddenly craved pot roast, a strawberry milk shake, chocolate. What had Lily eaten in that otherworld? Fairy cakes and Goblin fruit and the meat of fantastical beasts?

She moved down the hall and peered into the parlor, where she saw her father hunched on the sectional, hands clasped. Seated on the love seat opposite was Professor Avaline in a little black coat and high-heeled boots. She looked up, directly at Finn, who stepped in with a forced smile. "Da. I stayed at Sylvie's—Oh, hello, Professor Avaline."

"Finn. We need to talk." Her da seemed weary, and afraid. Finn frowned at Avaline, who moved to her feet as Finn's father stood and said, "Thank you, Sophia."

"I'm sorry, Sean." Avaline walked toward Finn.

"What did you tell him?" Finn whispered as she passed.

Professor Avaline spoke so that only Finn could hear. "You should never have been allowed to go where you went. I think it's Jane Emory you should be wary of, Miss Sullivan."

"Did you tell him everyth—"

"Speak to your father, Serafina." Avaline walked to the door. As it closed behind her, Sean Sullivan said, "The power went out last night. I went to check on you." He lifted a folded piece of paper from the coffee table. "I found your letter. And this." He held up Lily Rose's journal. The desperation in his voice scared her. "What is this, Finn? Fairies and boggarts and Lily *being stolen away?*"

"Da, it's not what you think."

"I thought it was just college, the move . . . I'm *losing* you, Finn, and I feel there's nothing I can do—"

"Da. The Fatas—"

He blinked as if he'd been struck and said, "What?"

"The Fatas—"

"Finn." Almost distractedly, he set down Lily's journal and the folded letter. "I'm sorry. I'm working so much." He ruffled a hand through his hair and sat, scanning the other papers on the coffee table before shoving aside his open laptop. "I've completely blanked—what were we talking about?"

Finn said faintly, "The letter?"

"I'm sorry. What letter?" He began rummaging among the papers and books. "Damn. I lost my train of thought."

She approached the coffee table and picked up her letter and Lily's journal. "You were saying how I'd left some of my stuff with yours—are you *writing* again?"

"I am." He smiled ruefully. "You're up early on a Saturday."

Clutching Lily's journal and the letter she'd left her da, Finn watched her father succumb, unawares, to a spell—most adults never acknowledged the Fatas' existence because they couldn't. It was a disturbing thing to witness. "Da—why was Professor Avaline here?"

"She was telling me about Jack. She disapproves of Jack. I told her it was none of her business."

"Okay. Well." Finn backed out of the parlor even though she wanted to hug him—that would seem odd, as, to him, she hadn't been away for a week, only a few hours. "Thanks for trusting me."

She turned, grabbed her backpack, and loped up the stairs.

Her room was cold and dusty despite the sunlight drifting through the gossamer curtains. All her things—the butterflies and moths in shadow boxes, her mother's watercolors of strange and whimsical figures, the Leonor Fini print, the Cheshire Cat clock—none of it seemed to belong to *her* anymore, but to an entirely different girl.

She sank to the floor, pressing a hand over her mouth. Everything was falling apart: her father's memory; Jack becoming less human; the Wolf ready to break into this world for revenge. But Lily was alive. Lily had stood in the sunlight and hadn't faded away.

A book slid from the shelves, flew across the room, and struck a shadow box on the wall. She flinched. Both book and box fell, the shadow box's glass breaking over the white moth inside. As the pages of the book rustled, Finn reached for it, pulled it toward her. She squinted down at Lewis Carroll's *Through the Looking-Glass*, at an illustration of Alice sitting between the Red Queen and the White Queen, each of them crowned like a chess piece. She glanced at the shattered glass, the moth, the book. What was the mysterious entity trying to tell her? Just knowing it wasn't Lily made the hair rise on the back of her neck. Who else could it be . . . ?

"Oh," she breathed, looking up. "*Gran Rose?*"

CHRISTIE ARRIVED IN THE LATE AFTERNOON, ten minutes after she called. When she flung the glass doors open, he hugged her like a kid. She obligingly put her arms around him, patted his back. "There, there. We already did this."

He stepped back, worry shadowing his eyes. "The Wolf isn't dead, is he?"

"No." She snatched up a coat and put on Jane Emory's sunglasses; the light was still bothering her. She tucked the vials of *Tamasgi'po* and elixir in one pocket. "Avaline told my da that Jack is bad news. My da found Lily Rose's journal and a letter I left in case I didn't return. He thought I was going crazy."

"*What?*"

"The minute I mentioned the Fatas, my da forgot what we were talking about." She grabbed her backpack.

Christie followed her onto the terrace and shut the doors behind them. "Why would Avaline tell your dad bad things about Jack? And aren't you *tired*?"

She shrugged and stomped down the snow-crusted stairs. "Not really. I'm worried about my da's brain being rewired every time the word *Fata* is brought up. Weren't you covered with ink scrawls last time I saw you?"

He looked rueful. "They faded. *Will* you slow down?" He strode quickly to keep up with her. "I understand your dad's memory loss is distressing, but I'm a little more concerned about when the Big Bad Wolf is coming back to town."

"I think Phouka and the Black Scissors expected Jack and me to murder the Wolf. Their plan didn't work."

"Well, of course it didn't. That wasn't the reason you went there—you went to get your sister. Don't you think it's *their* turn to fight the bad guy? Let them do it. Finn, before Sylv and I got out of fairyland, you were being dragged away by a monster tree-ghoul that had been pretending to be your sister. You know how messed up we were? At least Phouka had the decency to tell us you were safe after you got to Cruithnear's."

"I'm sorry. I really am."

"*Are* they going to help?"

"It's daylight, so Phouka doesn't exist at the moment. And I don't know where the Black Scissors is. Rowan Cruithnear is still in the Ghostlands, and Avaline just stabbed me in the back."

"Oh. So nothing new." He hesitated, then asked, "Why do you think Sylv and I weren't replaced by our doubles?"

"I was told you and Sylvie weren't taken because you were flawed and protected."

"Flaw—oh. I was born hearing impaired. They would think that was a flaw. Jerks."

Her eyes widened. "You're so—"

"Eloquent? What can I say? I was a fast learner." He continued with a shrug, "So *I* was the flawed part. Sylv must be the protected part. She's got a Finnish Laplander dad and a mom who was raised Shinto. Knowing that our doubles exist, though—that's a door that I could have happily kept closed. When I saw that guy . . . it was like someone walked over my grave."

"His name was Sionnach Ri, your other. But he was treacherous and not really into girls."

"Exactly what do you mean by 'treacherous'?"

"Remember? He betrayed me and Sylvie to a family of psychopaths called Mockingbirds? Then changed his mind because Sylvie pickpocketed the heart he grew for Moth—"

"Got it. My replica and Moth. *That's* a door I'll happily keep closed." He became quiet as they continued walking, Finn absorbing every beautiful, ordinary thing around her, from the slush in the roads, to the mailboxes like sentries on the sidewalk, to the colonial houses decked out with wreaths and tacky holiday decorations. When Christie started talking again, she was almost annoyed. "Sylph Dragonfly, Sylvie's twin . . . she wasn't much like Sylvie."

Given Christie's reputation, Finn did *not* like where this was going. She turned to him and gravely said, "You *didn't*."

"I had no *choice*." He pressed his hands against his chest. "Jack and I needed her help and she wanted more than a kiss."

"So Sylph Dragonfly *ravished* you." She folded her arms.

"Not really." Ruefully, he continued, "Did I tell you I'm a witch?"

"*A wit—*"

"The Dragonfly showed me."

"Can you do . . . tricks?" Finn's eyes widened.

"I'm not a Las Vegas magician, Finn. This is different. It's dark. And slithery." He took a deep breath. "I don't want it."

"Okay." She had a bad feeling he'd have no choice in the matter. She said, "Sylvie's some kind of warrior soul called a heart widow. Did she tell you? I probably should have let her tell you. Don't tell her I told you."

"I won't. I'm not surprised she's a knight in shining armor." He clenched his knit hat, pulled it down in anguish. "Do you know how hard—I mean, difficult—it is to look at Sylvie now? And now I know she can kick my ass . . ."

"You absolute idiot."

"What do I do? She's my best friend—"

"You made your bed with the Dragonfly . . . you know how the rest of *that* goes." She stalked away from him, toward the retro building that was Max's Diner. He caught up to her and said, "I just need a little advice."

"What do you want me to say? 'You should inform Sylvie you slept with her double'? I wouldn't do that if I were you." She tucked a stray strand of hair behind one ear and smiled. "Oh, look—Sylvie's here already. Should I tell her how cool Sylph Dragonfly was?"

"You've got a sadistic streak in you, Finn Sullivan. I *don't* like it."

"FINN, I CAN'T SPEAK TO YOU while you're wearing those sunglasses." Sylvie looked up from her waffles. "I mean, we're inside now."

"There are lots of windows and I told you why the sun was bothering me." Finn primly adjusted the sunglasses that had gone askew when Sylvie had hugged her again. She wished Lily could be here. But Lily was in a safe place now, a location known only to Finn and Jack.

"So where's the prince of darkness?" Christie glanced around. Sylvie, pouring syrup over her waffles, scowled at him and said, "Stop calling him that. Jack saved your life."

"And I saved his. The way I see it, we're even."

Sylvie told Finn: "Christie killed some kind of skull-headed screaming woman."

"It was a *siren*, a very dangerous creature."

"Really?" Finn was startled. "You never told me."

"There wasn't time."

There were a lot of things he hadn't told her about his journey with Jack. When Finn thought of Jack and the Ghostlands, she felt a breathless yearning that shocked her. With the elixir sizzling though her and the alchemy of roses blossoming within *him*, they had, for once, been a match.

She told Christie and Sylvie about her and Jack's harrowing escape from Lot's house, leaving out the bits about Reiko's and Jack's phantom replicas and Hester's death. They didn't need to know about that terrible thing yet.

Sylvie had little silver clovers pinned in her dark hair, which was knotted spikily on top of her head. "What if *Professor Avaline*'s the traitor Cruithnear suspects among the professors?"

"I don't know." Finn knotted her hands on the table as she studied her friends from behind the shield of the sunglasses. Their unexpected journey to the Ghostlands may have strengthened unsettling, innate qualities within them, but all Finn saw was their fragility and the precarious disruption of their lives. For a mad moment, she actually thought of asking Phouka to cast a forgetfulness spell over the two of them. But that would only leave them more vulnerable. And if it wore off, they'd never forgive her. She watched Christie nibble around a piece of omelet and Sylvie check her phone, her tongue between her teeth. If they were killed . . .

Finn said, in a very faint voice, "Please . . . leave me."

Christie looked up. Sylvie blinked at her distractedly. "Did you say something, Finn? I'm checking when the sun sets."

The moment was past. They wouldn't leave her anyway. Finn sighed. "Reiko killed Sophia Avaline's sister, but I think Avaline blames Jack."

"Avaline didn't like the idea of an eighteen-year-old girl being sent into a world of monsters. She didn't want you to go, Finn. Jane Emory did," Christie pointed out.

"Christie, Jane gave me the Ghostlands key with Rowan Cruithnear's permission. She knew I'd get there somehow—and she cared that Lily was a captive of Seth Lot. I trust her. Unless she's an award-winning actress, she's for real. How was your trip home?"

"Marvin—Dead Bird—took us onto the train and informed the three Fatas in the car that he would turn them inside out if we didn't reach our destination. He told us what botched Sylvie's and my entrance into the Spooklands—there was interference, he said, from the dead. He didn't say the Black Scissors was an asshole, but I think we all silently reached that conclusion. Then Sylvie asked him if he was really a . . . Tengu?—and he got an attitude. With his help, we found our way back to StarDust Studios. We stepped through the door—and here we are."

Sylvie's eyes were shadowy. "Are the Fatas going to slay the Wolf?"

"They tried, once." Jack sat down in the booth next to Finn. "It didn't work. I believe Lot recruited some of the Fatas to his side and ate the rest."

Finn finally set aside her sunglasses to look at Jack. He was all in black, the fake fur that lined his coat making his skin even paler. In the sunlight, his eyes ghosting silver, he scarcely looked human.

"Finn." Christie's voice sounded shaky and Sylvie was staring at her, a glass of milk halfway to her mouth. Jack somberly said, "Your eyes, Finn."

Finn fumbled in her small backpack, pulled out the compact mirror Sylvie had given her, and opened it. Her brown eyes were sheened with silver.

Jack was calm. "It's just more obvious in the daylight. It'll fade."

"If you say so." Finn closed the compact and put the sunglasses back on. There was a slight tremor in her hands. "Where's Moth?"

"At the counter, there—he seems to have developed an addiction to coffee."

"Is that the walking stick strapped over his shoulder?" Christie tilted his head. "The sword the Black Scissors gave us? Who's going to cut off the Wolf's head—"

Crack! Something hit the window with such force it made all of them, except Jack, jump.

"A bird?" Sylvie rose to peer out.

"That's not a bird." Jack slid to his feet. "That's a bat."

When Finn saw the dark cloud of flying creatures descending from the sky, she whispered, "*What—*"

The bats began smashing into the window. Christie scrambled up as the glass cobwebbed beneath spatters of jellied blood. Someone screamed.

Jack and Finn ran out the door with Sylvie and Christie following. Moth strode after.

Outside, Finn looked away from the dead and dying bats in the snow. Sylvie knelt and whispered, "Poor things."

Jack crouched down and, from the blood-speckled snow, lifted a ring of green metal set with rubies. "This was *Ialtag Amhran*."

"BatSong?" Her heart slamming, Finn gazed around at the snowy street, expecting more horrors. Other people were coming out of the diner.

Jack rose. "Lot's back. We need to get to Tirnagoth before the sun sets."

IN THE LATE AFTERNOON, Tirnagoth was a menacing silhouette rising from a wilderness of neglected landscaping. Even though she was now acquainted with what lived there, the sight of the boarded-up hotel still made Finn's skin crawl.

Sylvie and Christie followed Jack, Moth, and Finn, as they approached the gates to the inner courtyard. The gates opened and Jack loped up the stairs to the entrance. He took a key—a regular, old-fashioned one—from his pocket.

"Lily Rose is mortal." Sylvie spoke in a hushed voice as Tirnagoth's doors swung inward and they stepped into the mildewed lobby. "How is she here, among the Fatas?"

"Lily Rose isn't here." Jack strode across the lobby to a wall of dusty shelves, where he twisted something. The wall slid open to reveal a hall and a stairway.

Christie walked forward. "A secret passage—so awesome, yet so cliché. Isn't this the first place the Wolf is going to visit?"

"It's the safest place for us to be." Jack led them up the secret stairs to a mahogany door carved into the shapes of peacocks. "This is where we kept guests."

"Guests?" Finn was wary.

"Guests." Jack shoved open the door to reveal a long, windowed gallery stark with winter sunlight. At the far end was a chamber scattered with old furniture. There was a wall of books, a fireplace stacked with logs, and a wine rack filled with dusty bottles. Despite the rich hues of the drapes and oriental rugs, the room was dreary and artificial, as if someone unfamiliar with creature comforts had attempted to imitate them.

As Sylvie and Christie wandered around, and Moth stood vigilant near a window, Finn said to Jack, "He'll still find us."

"Most likely. But we have allies here."

Finn peered out at the wintery grounds and wondered what stolen or enchanted boys and girls had been in this deceptively harmless-looking room, awaiting their fates. "It's so cold in here."

"That it is, beloved." He walked to the hearth. Squatting down, he stuffed paper from a basket beneath the logs and took a butane wand from the mantelpiece.

Finn ducked back into the hall and halfway shut the door. She took out Lily's recharged phone and pushed the number. When her sister answered, Finn said, "Lily . . . the Wolf's back."

Lily's voice was clipped. "Where are you?"

"In a Fata place, a safe place."

"Anna was telling me some things. She's kinda mature for a kid—"

Finn heard Anna Weaver's voice in the background. "I'm not a kid!"

"Tell Anna I'm sorry I had to drag her into this." A cold draft brushed the back of Finn's neck.

Lily continued, "We're in her attic. She's made quite the little hideaway up here. Lots of books and a mini fridge. Her mom and dad are down in the shop and don't know I'm here. I feel like a stowaway—how is Dad?"

"I haven't told him."

"Good. Don't. Finn . . . I think it's *you* Seth Lot wants. Be careful."

"Lily . . . I love you."

"I can do this alone. Finn, you don't need to—"

Finn ended the call and slumped against a pillar. She looked down the dark hallway with its mahogany nymphs and flower lamps and thought how the Fatas reminded her of these art nouveau objects that mimicked nature in such a poisonously beautiful fashion. She straightened and walked to a pair of glass doors and shoved them open.

A second later, Jack was leaning against the door frame. "Finn . . ."

Finn gazed out at the winter landscape barred with pink and said softly, "When we were running from the Wolf's house, I saw you. The you from before we met."

He didn't seem surprised. "You saw my past self."

"You saw Reiko too, didn't you?"

There was pain in his voice. "She was only a memory."

"Lily was in that house . . ."

"That is your *sister*, Finn. That is Lily. She won't fade away or become a monster."

Finn sank down because the world had begun to spin. Jack squatted before her, the phoenix medallion flashing between his collarbones. "She's *more* than a memory. She's flesh and blood."

She could believe him, or let doubt cripple her. *Lily.* She breathed out, "Lily's alive and here."

He stood and pulled her to her feet. Snow began to drift past the glass doors she'd opened.

When a girl screamed in the woods below, he walked swiftly to the stone railing and peered down. He said, "Stay here."

"*Jack—*"

There was another scream.

"I can't ignore it, Finn." He leaped over the railing to the snow below and vanished into the trees. She wanted to shout at him to not be so gallant, but she heard the scream again and her heart smashed into a hectic panic when she thought it was someone calling *her* name. She thought of Anna, of Claudette Tredescant, of any girl who might be encountering something that prowled Tirnagoth's grounds. "Jack!"

The Fatas don't exist right now, she thought. *It's still daylight.*

But there were the Grindylow.

When she looked out over the snowy landscape again, she gasped. Nathan Clare stood at the border of trees. He was bleeding from the chest. Incredulous, she whispered, "*Nathan . . .*"

She had the silver dagger in her coat. She jumped down and hurried toward him, but he ran into the woods.

There were drops of blood in the snow. She followed them, gripping the silver dagger. In places where the branches twined thickly above, the snow had drawn away from patches of crimson toadstools and unnaturally green moss. She avoided these patches as if walking through a minefield. She called Nathan's name again and winced as her voice echoed. She knew the warehouse district was close by, but she couldn't hear any city sounds, only an occasional branch cracking.

She glanced at the sky. She still had time before the sun set. She took from her pocket the vial of elixir she'd smuggled into the true world, the one she'd found in Jack's coat. It wasn't supposed to work here, but she uncapped it, tilted it, and let one drop fall onto her tongue.

An old road appeared before her, its blacktop broken by the roots of ancient birches. The sky beyond the leaves was still red, streaked with clouds. The air burned with a honey glow.

She followed the road to a birdcage-shaped glass building surrounded by brambles and drifts of deadfall. The building looked like an old conservatory, but she couldn't see what was beyond the glass walls because they were so filthy with dead foliage and lichen. The metal doors were partially open, engraved with images of stylized eyes, hands, and feet twined in ivy and stars. An arch of letters above the doors formed the words STARDUST STUDIOS.

Malcolm Tirnagoth, who had built the Tirnagoth Hotel, had given his wife this film studio in the 1920s. Jack had starred in the silent movies created here. He'd told her that none of the other actors had come to a good end. Tirnagoth's wife had died from illness. It was a place with bad mojo and it was a Way into the Ghostlands.

The blood drops led right to its doors.

Finn was backing away when a light blinked on inside of StarDust Studios and Jack called her name from within.

CHAPTER 20

This time, she found a little bottle on it . . . and tied round the neck of the bottle was a
paper label, with the words DRINK ME beautifully printed on it in large letters.
—ALICE'S ADVENTURES IN WONDERLAND, LEWIS CARROLL

Where did they *go*?" Sylvie strode with Christie and Moth down the Tirnagoth hall to the glass doors swinging in a wind that carried with it a sparkle of snow. The sky was streaked with clouds and the orange of the setting sun.

Christie stepped onto the terrace with Moth and gazed desperately at the plot of wild land, black trees on white snow, and the places where shadows seemed to clot. Moving out beside them, Sylvie said, "Finn's backpack." She lifted it and rummaged through it. "And her phone." She shouted, "Finn! Jack!"

"*Don't.*" Moth stared down at the trees. "Something else might hear you."

Christie turned on him. "We need to go look for them."

"And what will that do? Aside from getting us lost? No. We wait here. When this place wakes up, we tell Phouka. Finn will be safe with Jack."

"No." Christie looked bitter. "She'll *never* be safe with Jack."

IN THE WOODS, Finn drew back as the doors to StarDust Studios opened farther, revealing a chandelier of thorny black metal spilling light over abandoned film equipment and Egyptian-sleek furniture that cast crooked shadows between pillars with lotus-and papyrus-styled capitals. The raised stage was strung with creepers, bits of colored glass, and antique toys. Lilies, their roots clinging to the wet floor, grew from broken urns. Velvety white, black, and lava red, the preternatural lilies' scent only enhanced the atmosphere of Egyptian Revival decay.

A figure stood on the stage. It whispered, "Finn? Is that you?"

Stepping to the threshold, Finn drew the silver dagger from her coat. "Where is Jack? And Nathan?"

The shadowy figure raised its head, and the vague light glanced from red hair and white skin. "*Help me.*"

Finn spoke carefully. "Are you the one who screamed?"

The shadow sobbed once, raising hands over its face. " . . . *murdered* me."

Finn began to back away—

Crypt-cold air swept through the studio. Something shoved her forward. The metal doors crashed shut behind her. She whirled and kicked at them. *Idiot*, she thought angrily. *Falling for* this.

Behind her, the shadow girl laughed. Gripping Eve Avaline's dagger, Finn turned—

—and inhaled a scream, because a girl's corpse stood before her, one spiteful, milky eye glaring at her from a bloated face. Its voice was blurry with rot. "*Jack* murdered me."

"Leave her alone." Another figure was crouched on the stage, darkness dripping from his wrists. "I want her. I brought her."

The red-haired girl's corpse vanished, and Finn sagged against the doors. "*Nathan . . .*"

The shadow on the stage rose and moved down the stairs, the gloom drifting away from a familiar young man who wore jeans and a crown of hyacinths. Around his right arm were black tattoos—wolfish shapes that made Finn queasy. His eyes glinted metallic as he came closer. Then he became a shadow again and a voice taut with anguish drifted from the silhouette, "*I can't remember.*"

"*Nathan.*" Finn's fear paled into grief. "You are Nathan Clare."

He stepped forward. "You're Finn."

She slid the dagger into her coat. "What happened to you?" Although she knew, she needed to hear him say it, to believe it.

He lifted one hand as if to touch her face. Then his eyes went black.

He lunged at her, lips parting to reveal sharp teeth.

"Don't," she said, only that, and he halted, his head down. She clenched the silver dagger's hilt. "Nathan, you're *not* a love-talker, a ganconer . . . whatever they've made you."

His eyes were brown again. "The Lily Girls are here . . ."

Abigail, Beatrice, Eve—three of Reiko's victims, for whom Jack had been used as a lure. Finn realized the red-haired specter had been Beatrice, who had died in the 1920s. She knew Beatrice and Abigail were vengeful spirits and had probably been the ones to botch Christie and Sylvie's arrival in the Ghostlands. "Nathan—did Beatrice lead Jack somewhere?"

"They're dangerous, Finn . . ."

The doors to the studio slammed open. Finn spun around.

The sun had set, and Caliban Ariel'Pan, silver hair drifting around his shoulders, swaggered in.

CHRISTIE STOOD BETWEEN TIRNAGOTH'S FRONT DOORS, anxiously surveying the landscape for any signs of Finn and Jack in the dying light. When he saw a figure staggering across the snowy grounds beyond the courtyard gates, his heartbeat spiked with alarm. "Moth, Sylvie, get over here."

They moved to his side. Moth growled, "That's not Jack."

As the figure approached, clutching one arm, blood drops spattered the snow. The courtyard gates opened.

Then Christie recognized the young man in a fur-lined coat and jeans. "*Micah? Micah Govannon . . . ?*"

The last of the sun faded in a streak behind the clouds. As if a protective bubble had burst, chaos broke out around them.

Shouting Fatas pushed past Moth, Christie, and Sylvie, loping across the snow toward Christie's friend, to help him. Christie turned in the midst of the mayhem to see the lobby filling with more grim-faced Fatas and Phouka Banríon striding toward him.

"Get inside," she said. "The wolves are coming."

NATHAN'S REVENANT HAD VANISHED when Caliban appeared. Kitted out in black leather that resembled armor, and a long coat, the crooked dog stood on the threshold, his eyes a malefic silver. He said, "Jack's busy with a wolf at the moment."

Finn retreated as he sauntered toward her. "Who were you talking to, darling?"

She sneaked one hand into her coat and gripped the hilt of Eve's silver knife. He halted, cocked his head to one side. "Are you going to do it? Go on. See if you can get past me after putting that knife in me. If you fail, I get to make the next move."

She tensed to make a run for it. He braced himself like a goalie in front of the doors and curled one hand at her. She took a deep breath—

She spun and raced for the glass doors in the back.

But he had a Fata's predatory speed—he caught her and shoved her against a wall. She cried out as the dagger clattered to the floor. He let her go. She backed away.

As if pushed by an invisible hand, a dusty bottle of wine scraped across a table near her—she saw it out of the corner of one eye. *Nathan?* She wondered how a bottle of wine would save her—

She grabbed the bottle. She swung it at Caliban's head. He clamped a hand around her wrist and pried the bottle from her, studied the label. He shoved her back into a chair and hooked a table leg with one foot, dragged the table between them. "Nineteen twenty-three. Shame to waste this—don't run, Finn. If I have to chase you, I'll be angry."

He wiped the dust from two wineglasses, set the glasses between them, and sprawled in another chair. He uncorked the wine. As he poured it, Finn carefully reached for one of the vials in her pocket and loosened the cap with her thumb.

Then she went for the dagger on the floor.

"Oh, Finn." He seized her by her coat collar and yanked her back. She hit the table, wincing as he pressed her against it. "What an exciting girl you are. *Sit down.*"

"How old are you?"

He stepped back, confused, a predator who didn't understand a weird reaction from his prey. He decided to play along. "Older than most of your ancestors, *leannan.* Why this sudden desire to be sociable?" His eyes became glittering slits. "Stalling until your lover finds you? He doesn't even know *where you are.*"

"What were you like when you were human?"

He stared at her. He bared his teeth. "Say that again and I'll slice a bit off you with your pretty knife."

"Well, you'll need it, won't you? Because I'm going to say it again: *What were you when you were human?*"

Caliban spun to snatch up Eve's silver dagger by its ebony hilt.

Finn dumped the contents of the vial from her pocket into both glasses before he whirled back around.

"Think you're clever, do you?" He backed her up against the table and she flinched as his body contacted hers. He whispered into her ear, "You're braver than most. I'm almost beginning to feel a bit romantically inclined toward you."

After this nauseating statement, he picked up his glass. "Drink, *leannan*."

She reached for her own glass.

"Ah, no." He snatched it from her and forced *his* glass against her lips. "You drink from *this* one."

She met his gaze and drank. If she'd dumped the *elixir* into the wine—well, it didn't work in this world and she'd already taken a few drops. If it had been the *Tamasgi'po*—*that* only had something to do with restoring memory. She didn't know if either would have any effect on the *crom cu*. She was gambling.

Caliban stepped back and drank from the same glass, emptying it. He flung *her* glass across the room. It smashed against a mirror as his hungry gaze slid to her. "So, Miss Clever, what kind of poison did you drop into the glass we *didn't* drink from?"

SYLVIE AND CHRISTIE STOOD IN TIRNAGOTH'S LOBBY, surrounded by Fatas preparing for war. Sylvie could now identify with the people on the *Titanic*—the ship was going down; the crew was in a panic; and she couldn't see any way out.

Christie turned to Phouka. "Finn and Jack are out there."

The doors were still open, revealing the snow-patched grounds and Phouka's Fatas, young women and men in black suits, waiting, armed with small crossbows and beautiful, engraved pistols. Phouka said, "If Finn is with Jack, I believe she'll be safe."

Christie spoke through clenched teeth. "Why does everyone keep *saying* that?"

Sylvie reached into her backpack and drew out the two knives she'd bought from a real blacksmith at a medieval fair. She handed one to Christie, who sighed. "Have you ever killed anyone, Sylv?"

"No."

"Well, I have." He scowled when she, Phouka, and Moth glanced at him in surprise. "A Green Lady. A *siren*. I told you."

Sylvie wondered if he'd killed the siren by accident.

"It was traumatic and not something I'm proud of." He lowered his voice. "It's not like picking things off in a video game, Sylv. It's really disturbing and messy."

"But you get used to it." Moth tugged the jackal-hilted sword from the walking stick strapped over one shoulder and stalked toward the open doors.

Christie said sourly, "Well, *he's* come a long way from being the confused innocent he once was."

"Christie. Sylvie." Leander Cyrus, still resembling a golden-haired bridegroom in his grubby white suit, came striding toward them. He held a pistol of ornate metal. He glanced at Phouka. "Banríon, isn't there a safe place for them?"

"Too late." Sylvie's gaze was on the night beyond the doors, where tall, glowing-eyed shadows had begun moving across the snow. Tirnagoth's light glistened on jewels and fur, teeth and nails.

The wolves had arrived.

FINN BACKED AWAY as Caliban prowled toward her. He grinned, revealing unnervingly perfect teeth. "Don't be shy, darling. Let me see what's in your pockets."

She snatched up a lamp and swung it toward his head. He knocked it from her hand and it flew across the room, smashing to pieces against one of the pillars. She fell back over a table, kicked out as he lunged at her. She grabbed a crystal sphere paperweight and flung it. He caught it and gazed into it as if he could see his future.

Then he staggered. The crystal orb fell, rolled away. Finn, bruised and aching, straightened, watching as his eyes darkened. He stumbled toward her, caught himself against a moldering chaise. He croaked out, "What . . . the *wine* . . . ?"

His snarl shouldn't have come from a human throat. He leaped at her, his teeth sharp—

He was wrenched back by a force that slammed him against a rusting spotlight and Eve's dagger fell from his hand.

As the *crom cu* straightened awkwardly, Finn took a breath and looked at Jack, who watched Caliban. Defensively, she said, "I had it."

Jack cast a disbelieving glance at her. "You *had* it?"

"Charming." Caliban stepped back, almost drunkenly. "Having defeated the villain, they think, the hero and heroine embrace before the cameras."

"We're not embracing." Jack's voice was flat.

"Jack." Finn frowned at him. "Are the wolves at Tirnagoth?"

"Phouka and her people will be there, too." Jack didn't take his attention from Caliban as the crooked dog reeled, hunched over, and spat out black liquid. Jack said, "Finn? What did you do?"

She fumbled the vial out of her pocket. "I dumped this into his wine."

"The *elixir*?"

" . . . *poisoned* me." Caliban's eyes had darkened. He hunched over and coughed up a slimy knot of black petals. He took a halting step forward, before falling to one knee.

"It shouldn't be effective in this world." Jack drew Finn away. "Not to mortals . . . I don't know what it'll do to a Fata."

Without taking their gazes from Caliban, Finn and Jack backed toward the doors. Caliban rasped out, "*What did you do to me?*"

Jack raised a revolver—Finn realized he must have gotten it out of Caliban's coat, because Caliban had had it in the Ghostlands. *Let him do it*, something savage inside of her urged.

"Jack . . ." She remembered how, together, they had stabbed Seth Lot with the wooden dagger, an act of desperate self-defense. This was different—

"Remember the ones he's slaughtered." Jack aimed at Caliban and fired.

AFTER FINN AND JACK LEFT STARDUST STUDIOS, a voice drifted from the dark, saying, "It's *him*."

"The crooked dog."

"Hyena. Killer."

"Poor little doggie. Is he dying?"

Two shadowy girl figures crouched beside the body of Caliban Ariel'Pan, which had begun to bleed from a wound in the head. A third shadow girl stood watching. "Beatrice. Abigail. Leave him."

"Oh no, Evie. He doesn't deserve to go on so easily. Ooh, look . . . is that real blood?"

"This is a border place and he drank a border potion."

One of the girls smiled, and it was a slash of white in her shadow face. "We'll fix him. We'll fix him good."

FINN AND JACK SPRINTED THROUGH THE WOODS.

Tirnagoth's windows radiated saffron, crimson, and viridian light. The snow on the ground in front of the stairs was trampled and a trail of red led through the slush, up the stairs, to the closed doors. The silence was worse than the blood.

Thinking only of Christie and Sylvie, Finn raced up the stairs, Jack at her side as the doors swept open and two Fatas in dark suits appeared, one armed with a handheld crossbow, the other with a dragon-shaped brass revolver.

"Come in." Phouka stepped into view. Sleek in leather and a fur-lined aviator's jacket, she looked at Jack. "You missed the wolves, but your friends are mostly safe."

"What do you mean 'mostly'?" Finn frantically surveyed the wrecked lobby. She skirted a pool of water and shied away from a pile of ichor-streaked leaves, glimpsing a fossilized animal skull that had rolled beneath one table. The lobby desk was splintered. The floor was littered with bits of stained glass. "Whose blood is on the steps?"

"They took Leander."

Shocked, Finn glanced at Jack, who said to Phouka, "Took him alive?"

"Finn!" Sylvie appeared and ran to Finn and hugged her, hard. Then she turned and threw her arms around Jack. When Sylvie faced Finn again, her eyes were rimmed with red, as if she'd been crying. "They took Leander."

"I know." Finn's voice shook. She watched a black-haired Fata in a dark suit stride past, his eyes flashing. A girl in brown velvet knelt mournfully beside a pile of ivory wands and pearls wound with red seaweed.

"Fatas." Sylvie followed Finn's gaze. "Some of them died."

Moth strode toward them, Christie at his side. Christie had a black eye and there were scratches across Moth's face.

"Finn, where *were* you?" Christie looked as if he wanted to shake her.

"With Jack. Are you all right?"

"Moth saved Christie." Sylvie threw a comradely arm around Christie's shoulders.

Christie, who also had a rip in his T-shirt, forced a smile, but his gaze was harrowed as he said, "I didn't get to kill anyone though."

"Why would they take Leander?" Jack asked Phouka, who shrugged.

"Because they thought Leander knew where you hid Lily Rose Sullivan. Yes, Serafina, I know that your sister is in the world. You shouldn't have brought her back here."

Finn felt something snap. "Jack and I were supposed to play assassin for you and get rid of Lot. My sister was the lure you used to get me into the Ghostlands. And now Leander is in the hands of that monster and some of your people are dead. Happy?"

"That's what happens in war." Phouka turned and moved away. "There is someone I want you to listen to."

As they followed Phouka, Finn wound a hand around one of Jack's and whispered, "Lily."

"She's safe where she is. How could the Wolf know?"

THE SNOW HAD TURNED TO FREEZING RAIN, a dreary and relentless veil of it drenching Fair Hollow. Across the street from Hecate's Attic, the New Age shop owned by the Weavers, two figures stood. The tall one, his jeweled hand resting on a wolf-headed walking stick, didn't seem to mind the rain that scarcely touched his hair or fur-lined coat. The other figure stood beneath an orange umbrella that sheltered his slim body and citrus-bright mane.

"I know how Jack thinks," the slight figure said. "He brought your queen of briars here. Oh, and look, there's a light on in the attic. I bet that's where she's hiding. The oracle is mine, so let her be."

"I don't trust you, Fool, considering your habit of switching sides." Seth Lot sauntered toward Hecate's Attic. "So I'll be taking your oracle girl as insurance."

"I wouldn't do that if I were you," Absalom called out as the Wolf moved across the street, followed by three shadowy shapes from his pack. Seth Lot ignored him and Absalom turned, twirling his umbrella and humming softly. Walking away, he lightly said, "It's your funeral."

❖ ❖ ❖

AS FINN AND JACK FOLLOWED Phouka, Moth, Christie, and Sylvie down a hall in Tirnagoth, Jack said to Finn, his voice low, "I need you to give me the elixir."

She tried not to flinch. "It's all gone."

"Your eyes are silver, you're pale as the dead, and you're not casting a shadow—and you kept up with me as I ran. The elixir shouldn't affect you in the true world. That stuff was supposed to leave you and it hasn't. Which means *you're still taking it.*"

"I dumped all of it into Caliban's glass."

Jack gazed at her with despair ghosting his silver eyes. "Do you think it's going to make you invulnerable? It won't. It will *kill* you."

"I'm not dead. I won't let him take Lily again. I don't have any more of it."

"Are you even aware of what a terrible liar you are?"

They reached the parlor where Phouka's guest waited.

"I'm not dead—" Finn halted. "*Micah?*"

Micah Govannon, her coworker from BrambleBerry Books, sat on the sofa, a large bruise on his face, bandages white beneath his bloody, ripped T-shirt.

"So"—Christie dropped into a chair and stared at his friend—"it turns out Micah, here, is secretly a wolf slayer."

"I haven't actually slain any—"

Christie continued, "He works for Jill Scarlet."

Finn sat down, because she needed to. "Who is Jill Scarlet?"

"Red Riding Hood," Jack told her, perfectly serious.

"Sit. All of you." Phouka gestured. "Micah has a story to tell."

THE MICAH SEATED ON THE RED VELVET SOFA across from Finn was not the shy, harmless boy Finn worked with at BrambleBerry Books. This was a warrior, graceful and strong, and he didn't wear his glasses; his scars were explained now. There were talismans braided into his brown hair, on a leather thong around his neck.

"Seth Lot declared war when his house found its way back to the Ghostlands from whatever void you sent it to. He has more allies than we thought. He went after the guardians first, the ones *you*, my lady"—Micah inclined his head to Phouka—"set up at the border stations."

Phouka swore in something that sounded like Latin. Finn said faintly, "Did he kill them all? The guardians?"

"Most of them are dead. He can do damage with his Grindylow, his Jacks and Jills."

Finn looked at Phouka. "Do you do that?"

"There are no Jacks or Jills in my court, other than what has already been. I don't practice stitchery." Phouka studied Micah. "What about Rowan Cruithnear and the *Dearh Cota*?"

"I think Rowan Cruithnear and Jill Scarlet are still in the Ghostlands. For now, no one can come in or out—I got away. The *crom cu* found me." He shuddered.

"We've encountered the *crom cu*," Jack said, "in the woods. He's dead."

There was a moment of disbelieving silence. Then Christie hunched forward. "If the Wolf is searching for Finn and Lily, won't he go to Finn's house? Her dad—"

Finn said, "My da's with Sylvie's dad, playing poker at the Antlered Moon."

"No, he isn't," Sylvie breathed. "Poker night was canceled."

Finn snatched Lily's phone from her backpack and hit Home, standing as the phone buzzed. She strode out of the parlor. Jack followed with Christie and Sylvie hurrying after.

Outside, in the driveway, Finn felt as if she was falling to pieces. The phone went to her da's voice mail.

Moth strode toward them. He had the jackal walking stick over one shoulder and held a set of jangling keys in one hand. "Phouka gave me the keys to her vehicle—it'll apparently be faster than yours, Jack. She and some of the others will follow."

Jack guided Finn to Phouka's Cadillac as Finn said, into the phone, "Da. Da? When you get this message, get out of the house. Just drive somewhere. *Please*..."

Jack turned to Christie and Sylvie. "You two stay here. You're safe here. The Wolf has already made his move on Tirnagoth."

"Don't argue," Sylvie said to Christie, who shut his mouth. "We'll stay. Finn, call me the *minute* you know your dad's okay."

❖ ❖ ❖

AS THE CADILLAC TORE AWAY DOWN THE DRIVE, Sylvie drew Christie back up the stairs. He said forlornly, "She's always leaving us."

"Remember what happened the last time we followed her? We both, individually, almost got eaten?"

"Point taken." He looked determined suddenly. "But we're her backup. Let's make sure Phouka follows."

JACK DROVE LIKE A MADMAN as Finn attempted again and again to reach her father by phone. Moth said, "What if the Wolf's waiting for us there?"

"Moth." Jack spoke lightly, which meant he was in a dangerous mood. "You need to be the strong, silent type now."

"Have you told her about the sword?"

"The one the Black Scissors gave us? Sylvie told me." Finn looked over her shoulder at Moth.

Moth pulled the jackal-hilted blade from the walking stick, horizontally, revealing that the sword was razor-sharp steel. He said, "Iron, beneath the steel."

Jack said, "For decapitating the Wolf. That's what I had it made for, way back when. I remember it now. And it's sheathed in enchanted elder wood so the Ghostlands wouldn't ruin the iron."

Finn breathed out and faced the front window. Even with the sword, she didn't know how they'd kill Seth Lot.

When the Cadillac swerved around a corner, onto her street, she wanted, irrationally, to scream at Jack to hurry. Then they were pulling into the driveway of her house. Before Jack could hit the brakes, she was out.

Jack caught up to her on the veranda and grabbed her wrist. "He's not here."

"There's no car in the garage." Moth strode toward them.

Headlights glowed down the street and Finn turned, thinking *Phouka*.

But it was a dark limousine that appeared.

Moth vanished into a shimmering light. His form diminished. As the insect he'd become fluttered into the collar of Finn's coat, she whispered, "Phouka isn't coming, is she?"

Jack gripped her hand as the limousine halted at the curb.

"Did we break a rule"—Finn didn't look away from the limousine—"when we brought Lily back?"

"Well, there've been so many rules broken, it's a bit late to start worrying about them now."

The passenger door opened and Finn whispered, "*No . . .*"

Anna Weaver emerged from the limousine. Dressed in a pale coat, white dress, and boots, the fifteen-year-old opened her Alice in Wonderland umbrella and held it over her head against the rain as she said solemnly, "The Wolf has Lily Rose. He sent me for you."

CHAPTER 21

Black the town yonder,
Black those that are in it;
I am the White Swan,
Queen of them all.

—*Carmina Gadelica*, Alexander Carmichael

Finn had known this confrontation was inevitable. It had lain like a shadow over the brightness of her first day back in the world. Now, in the limousine, she felt naked, defenseless, almost unbearably afraid for Jack, Lily, and Anna. Only horror awaited them, and it came at her in such a thorny rush, she found herself slipping into a dreamlike stillness.

"Finn." Jack's voice, calm and velvety, made her turn her head to gaze at him. His eyes were dark as he said, *"Remember what you are."*

And what am I? she thought. *Just a girl about to face down a monster.*

As the limousine Lot had sent for them coasted up the road into the Blackbird Mountains, Anna whispered to Finn and Jack, "The Wolf came in through the attic window. Lily tried to hurt him. He got hold of her. He made me follow. There were others with him."

Finn began, "Anna, I didn't mean to—"

"It's okay." Anna folded her hands over the painted umbrella Absalom had given her. "This was meant to be. Just like Christie and Sylvie were supposed to go with you to the Ghostlands, I was meant to be here with you."

She was trembling. Finn said to the two wolves in front, "*Let her go.* She's only—"

"—an oracle who knows too much." The shaven-headed Fata girl seated next to the driver smiled—Finn recognized her as the one from the Wolf's house, Antoinette, glamorous and sinister in a silver silk gown and fur coat. "Naughty children."

The rakish wolf driving didn't look back at them, but the rearview mirror revealed his smile, the gold of one tooth. Beneath his hair, gold hoops glinted in his earlobes.

Finn took the vial of *Tamasgi'po* from her pocket, opened it, and traced the liquid over her lips. The Fata girl, watching in the rearview, smirked. "Our little mayfly is making herself lovely for the *Madadh aillaid.* How charming. What kind of lip gloss is that, sweetmeat?"

Jack said, idly, to the wolves, "You can stop smiling."

"Is that a threat?" the male wolf mocked. "What can you do, pretty boy? You've still got a mortal taint."

"*I* won't do anything." Jack indicated Finn with a tilt of his head. "*She* might, being the queen killer."

The male Fata muttered something in French.

Antoinette turned and held out a hand to Finn. "Give it to me. Your bottle."

Finn dropped the vial of *Tamasgi'po* on the floor.

"Clumsy child. *You're* a threat?" Antoinette's lips curled.

Finn, pretending to scrabble for the fallen vial—which was clearly labeled *Tamasgi'po*—furtively switched it under the seat with the nearly empty vial of elixir in her other hand.

"Got it." She straightened and set the elixir vial into the wolf girl's palm. She didn't dare look at Jack as he wound one of his hands with her other.

"Elixir, girl? It won't help you." Antoinette opened her window and tossed the bottle out.

The limousine detoured into the woods, down a road that had appeared out of nowhere. The rain was coming down in sheets by now, and the sound of it battering the car was accompanied by the hiss of the windshield wipers and the crunch of tires on gravel. The headlights illuminated nothing but endless corridors of trees. Finn whispered to Jack, *"We're not going to die tonight."*

"I know."

Anna, to Finn's dismay, remained silent.

The limousine broke from the giant trees, its headlights blazing over what seemed to be a medieval cathedral that resembled one of those Gothic ruins from a Turner painting. The stone walls were barbed with briars. Roses as crimson as though they'd been dipped in blood bloomed as if winter had no hold here. Graceful angel figures carved from obsidian framed the arched entrance, but the angels had the faces of wolves.

The limousine halted. The female Fata exited the car, opened the back door, and bowed mockingly. Jack slid out. He turned, extending a hand to assist Finn, then Anna. Anna handed him her umbrella and he opened it and held it over their heads.

As they approached the massive ruin of stained glass and mottled stone, its more sinister aspects became apparent. A chiaroscuro of candlelight and shadows flickered beyond a screen of spiky briars draped over the entrance. A large pale snake moved among the briars as if it was some true-world embodiment of a guardian dragon. Living eyeballs nestled in the centers of the roses—Finn didn't flinch from the snake, but she winced when she saw the eyeballs. A skull-headed gargoyle with a female body turned its head to regard them with malice. This was the true shape of the Wolf's house, a piece of the Ghostlands wrecked on the shores of reality, now infecting the world around it.

Finn and Jack moved forward, hands clasped, with Anna following. As they passed beneath the arch, pollen swept over them, whirling around Finn and falling away. She looked down at herself and inhaled sharply—she now wore a summer dress of silver silk and gossamer, but she still had the lionheart pendant and her Doc Martens. She could smell the roses that had appeared in her hair and touched them to make sure they didn't have eyes. She checked to see that Moth was still fluttering against her neck, hidden by her hair.

Jack and Anna hadn't been changed.

"It's psychological warfare," Jack said gently.

"I know." She ducked as he lifted the curtain of briars for her and Anna to pass beneath.

They stepped into the cavernous nave, where a cracked ceiling failed to prevent flecks of rain from entering and a rectangular table of old oak was set with a grotesque feast of roasted meats, tiered cakes, and goblets of black glass. Morning glories tumbled from vases of dark crystal. Seated at the table was Seth Lot's pack in their modern finery of fur, velvet, and leather, their faces concealed by elaborate half masks. The Rooks were there, in the beaked visages of medieval plague doctors. Hip Hop wore a cowled coat of crimson crushed velvet.

Lot sat at the other end of the table behind a roasted, skinned swan with a gilt crown on its skull. The candles' glow highlighted the ivory scar snaking along his cheekbone and shone in the glass eyes of the jawless wolf's head he wore as a headdress. One jeweled hand rested on his walking stick. His fur-lined coat was open, revealing a bare, muscled torso decorated with a golden torque and tribal-looking tattoos.

"Well, Serafina Sullivan. Here we are." The gentleman Wolf's black-rimmed eyes glittered with amusement. "And Jack. Thank you, Anna."

Anna looked warily around at the wolves. Finn felt the elixir shimmering coldly through her blood and slid an arm around Anna's shoulders as Jack snapped shut the umbrella and handed it back to Anna.

"You see, Finn, Anna," Jack said, his voice sultry, "the *Madadh aillaid* doesn't like to play with his victims unless he has an audience."

"Jack knows me well." Seth Lot didn't smile. "Once, we were very alike."

"We were *never*"—Jack watched Seth Lot from beneath lowered lashes—"alike."

"You were a killer, Jack." Seth Lot spoke gently. "You enjoyed it—sending those Fatas to their deaths . . . White Bee and Mr. Bones and that idiot carnival giant."

The wind drifted Jack's rain-glittering hair over his face as he said quietly, "I never killed innocents."

Lot continued, "And what about the Lily Girls?"

There was a bitter twist to Jack's mouth. "They were *tricked*—"

"But you *knew*, Jack, that by making those three girls fall in love with you you'd be putting them in danger. You grew a heart for each, but they were selfish hearts—especially the last one, seeded by the girl who would have taken your place as a sacrifice, the girl standing beside you right now."

Finn, who did not care that Jack had once loved the three Lily Girls, and who reasonably knew she hadn't been Jack's only love—he'd been around for nearly two hundred years, after all—withdrew her hand from Jack's and took a step back, pretending that the news hurt her, when it did not. She turned and walked to one of the empty chairs. Tracking her with his gaze, Jack moved along the other side of the table.

As Anna sat beside Finn, the masked wolves began talking among themselves, reaching for wine goblets, slicing meat from the ornately posed roadkill on the table.

Finn spoke as if the words were shards of glass in her throat. "*Where is Lily?*"

Lot curled his fingers. "Here."

Two female Fatas glided from the shadows with Lily between them like a young queen in a gown of sleeveless black with a high, ruffled collar. Lily lurched toward Finn, was yanked back by one of the wolf girls.

Finn began to rise, but Lot's jeweled fingers closed over hers and she sat back, watching as her sister was escorted to the chair next to Jack. The wolves continued to revel as if mortal pain and fear were exquisite appetizers. Seth Lot said to Finn, in a voice luxurious with hate, "You stole her from me. With me, she was a *queen*. Now she is *nothing*."

Lily's eyes, inked around with elaborate designs, widened as she leaned toward Lot and smiled fiercely. "I faked *all* of it. Every *minute* with you."

He stared at her and the beast flickered beneath his skin but was swiftly concealed. Civility returned to his manner. "Here is my offer, Serafina Sullivan. You take your sister's place at my side and I'll allow your loved ones to leave. Alive."

It was a deal meant to cause the most harm, to leave Finn's family and friends—and Jack—forever not knowing what had become of her.

"Don't you *touch* her!" Lily leaped to her feet, was slammed back into her chair by Antoinette. The Rooks stirred. Bottle looked up, his injured eye obscured by the beaked mask.

When Jack met Anna's gaze, Finn glanced at Anna and saw a flickering sorrow there. Doubt began to shadow her—Jack had a plan, one he had not told her about.

"Anna," Finn whispered, "what do you know?"

Anna bowed her head. "I see a death that should have been and never was."

A death that should have been . . . Finn lifted her gaze to Lot's blue one. "You invited Jack and me. *You can't hurt us.*"

"Not *that* again. I didn't invite your sister or the oracle. I *took* them." Lot twirled a bone-handled knife between his fingers, his expression disdainful. "Stop trying to be clever." He pushed a plate of little white cakes oozing red toward her. "Have a cake. Someone put their heart into them."

Finn saw the killer in Jack's eyes when he turned his head to regard Seth Lot, who reached out to pluck one of the morning glories from a vase. "Do you like the morning glories, Lily, my love? And the utensils—the handles are made from real bone."

He flung the bone-handled knife and the morning glory at Lily. Both landed before her, the knife pinning the flower to the table. As Lily stared down at the knife and the flower, Anna murmured, "Morning glories and bones, from the boy taken by the sea, the boy who wanted to make stories with pictures."

Finn looked at the bleeding cakes, the forks and knives, the wet purple flowers that now reminded her of internal organs. Sour bile filled her throat. Horror shook her. *Leander. . .*

"And this is especially for you, my Lily." Lot sat back as Antoinette set a large bronze platter with a lid in front of Lily, who was now arched as far from the table as her chair would allow.

"No . . . Lily—" Finn slid to her feet as her sister reached for the handle on the lid and tilted it up so that only she could see what was beneath.

As Lily's voice broke in a lament that caused the wolves to cease their carousing, Seth Lot smiled and Antoinette, the shaven-headed Fata girl, touched a band of teeth around her throat. Jack swore with vicious fury. Anna curled up in her chair, her arms over her head.

Lily's eyes were black holes in her face.

As she lunged, screaming, across the table, the bone-handled steak knife in one hand, a legion of black butterflies streaked with neon red descended on the wolves, who leaped from their chairs, shouting.

Finn jumped up, reaching for her sister.

Lily was dragged back by Antoinette. Jack snatched up two knives and flung them—one at Lot, the other at Antoinette. Antoinette received hers in the left eye and fell back, howling. Lot caught the blade meant for him in midair and whipped it back at Jack. Jack fell into his chair, the knife sunk in the middle of his chest.

Lot went for Finn.

Jack, all Jack now, pulled the knife from his chest and leaped over the table. Cake and shards of porcelain scattered. The wolves caught him. He snarled as they wrestled him to the ground.

And as Finn tried to reach her sister, Lot seized Finn by the nape of her neck. "And what is this?"

She cried out as he drew from her hair the fragile form of the moth. He began to close his fingers around the frantically fluttering insect. "This was your secret weapon? How predic—"

"*Don't*," Finn said, desperate to keep him from killing Moth. "I'll *stay with you—*"

"Too late." His smile was all teeth.

She cried out as he crushed the moth. Glittering dust spiraled from his fingers, drifting above their heads. Anna pushed to her feet, reaching up. "He's still here."

Before Lot could get hold of her again, Finn leaped onto the table, scattering goblets and plates as she ran, following the shimmering cloud of moth wing fragments. She stood on tiptoe, felt the fragments drift across her lips like electric pollen, shivered as a current ran through her, leaving her breathless. She whispered, "Alexander Nightshade . . . *come back to me*."

As she was hauled, kicking, down from the table by two female Fatas, she saw the cloudy night sky through the crack in the ceiling. Then the world righted itself.

The tiny cloud of moth remnants ignited, speared down—and Moth crashed into existence, crouched amid the devastated feast, the hem of his coat sweeping over the table. As he yanked the jackal-hilted sword from the strap across his back, candlelight glistened along its blade of silvered iron. Seth Lot shouted as the young man rose and ran toward him down the length of the table, porcelain and glass crunching beneath his boots.

In the chaos that followed, Jack broke free of the wolves and Finn struggled against the Fatas hauling her away. Jack vaulted across the table, swung Anna to Lily's side, and went after the wolves holding Finn. Two big Fatas in fur coats stepped in his way.

Twisting in the grip of her captors, Finn saw shadows begin to writhe around

Seth Lot, until he was completely obscured. She glimpsed something monstrous moving in that darkness and screamed a warning to Moth as he made his way through the wolves, toward Lot.

While Jack and Moth fought the wolves, Finn clawed and kicked at the two who held her.

One of the wolves was torn from her. She wrenched free of the other and turned to see Hip Hop in her cowled coat aiming an ivory pistol at the remaining wolf. As Finn backed away with Hip Hop, the Rook's hood fell back—revealing, not Hip Hop, but the scarred face of a young woman who resembled . . . Finn whispered, "Who . . . ?"

"I'm Jill Scarlet. Go!"

Finn turned and ran—

A black mass so cold it stopped her breath fell over her, entangling her limbs with an icy grip, lifting her. She couldn't even scream as she was flung—

—she hit the ground and uncurled in a gloomy corridor. She lay there, shaking and glazed with cold sweat. Nausea and fear wrenched through her in a convulsive shiver.

The tentacled darkness churned back into the shape of Seth Lot. He strode to her and dragged her to her feet.

"*Lot.*" Looking like a prince of hell, Jack stepped into the corridor.

Lot hooked an arm around Finn's throat and yanked her back against him. She felt the fur of his coat prick against her neck, flinched as sharp nails caressed the pulse beneath her left ear. Lot said, "Let's see if you can get to her before I tear her open."

Jack raised the ivory pistol the young woman called Jill Scarlet had carried, a Fata weapon shaped into a leaping hound. "Silver bullets coated with wolfsbane, Lot. They'll hurt."

"Jack." Lot sounded disapproving. "You're cheating."

Finn slammed a heel into Lot's right foot. He growled and tightened his grip, but she braced her other foot against the wall and pushed with all her might. She slid down, felt a sharp burn across her cheek from his nails, heard the crack of a gunshot. Lot released her.

Jack shouted her name as she launched herself toward him.

Lot, bleeding darkness from where the bullet had grazed the left side of his face, seized her wrist. She shouted as she felt a bone snap, and fell to one knee in agony.

Lot whipped the sword from his walking stick and speared it at Jack.

The blade struck Jack in the chest, exactly where his heart still beat, but it was Finn who made a faint, wounded sound as Jack collapsed, the pistol clattering across the floor. Lot said, in a voice rich with satisfaction, "I thought I'd taught you better, Jack—never bring a gun to a swordfight."

Jack clutched the sword in his chest. Blood trickled from a corner of his mouth.

Lot smiled down at Finn. Then he walked away, snatching up the ivory pistol and snapping it in half, scattering the bullets, before leaving them. When she heard him call, "*Li . . . ly . . .*" she staggered to her feet, cradling her wrist.

Jack raised his head. "Go. Moth will help . . . I'll follow in a sec—"

"Jack . . ."

"Go!"

Torn, she rushed to him, but he pushed her away. "He'll kill your sister. Go to Moth!"

She stumbled back, turned, and ran.

THE SWORD HAD PIERCED HIS HEART.

Jack clutched the hilt, cried out as he pulled the blade from him and felt the mortal blood leaving him in hot, pulsing streams. *No. I'm not human. I am already dead. This can't kill me.*

There was a shadow beneath him. His heart had stopped pumping. He was as cold as night and nothing.

"Not yet," he gasped as his shadow rose before him, saturating the air with cold. Eyes as burning and bright as the sun glowed in the shadow's jackal head. Dozens of wings seemed to flutter and thump and rustle behind it. What he had made a deal with in Rowan Cruithnear's garden had come for him. At last.

He raised his head. "Not yet. Let me save her first. And then you'll have me."

SETH LOT HAD FOUND LILY and was dragging her up a flight of stairs, away from the mayhem around the feast table. Finn raced after them with only a steak knife in her good hand—her other wrist still hurt with a jagged, grinding pain. Lot was heading for an arch shaped like a face with a gaping mouth. Beyond, she saw an otherworldly forest cast in the violet glow of a primeval night, the leaves of the trees flickering with orbs—the Ghostlands.

"*Finn!*" Lily tore away from Lot. He slammed her against a stone pillar and she crumpled to the floor.

Then he strode toward Finn. "I will make you fear me every moment of your life, Serafina Sullivan, for what you did to my Reiko."

"I didn't kill Reiko."

"You caused a beautiful, divine girl who had walked the earth for ages to *burn*. You snuffed out the life of a *goddess*."

"She wasn't a goddess. She was a *monster*." Finn backed away, hit a wall. She slashed at him with the steak knife, gripping the handle made from Leander's bones. *Get up, Lily. Just get up.*

He knocked the knife from her grip. One of his hands slowly closed around her throat as he said, "You think *we* are monsters?"

"You kill people and stitch them up filled with magic flowers." She continued to speak despite those cruel, squeezing fingers, buying time. "You've *eaten* people."

His grip on her throat lessened. He shrugged, his blue gaze holding hers as if he were curious. "I was a madman, back then." He stepped back. The coldness seemed to leave his eyes for a moment. Finn didn't antagonize him further, her gaze flickering to her sister, who was beginning to stir. "We were not always nothing, Serafina. Or things of the dark. There are moments"—he reached out and she flinched as his fingertips caressed her brow—"when we are good."

Her vision was replaced by a field of heather, where a tower rose against a twilit sky. A girl in a green gown was standing in front of the tower, her dark hair knotted with white roses. As she moved forward, she became Reiko—a younger Reiko, without the shadows. She smiled and held out a hand and masculine fingers free of rings clasped hers. Seth Lot, in armor of organic metal, stepped close to her, bowed his head to kiss her.

Finn blinked and met the Wolf's gaze as he continued, "The elixir is changing you, Serafina. Soon, you'll understand."

She thought of Jack bleeding for her. She wondered if the Wolf had ever bled for anyone. "What were you, before?"

"I was good. I was noble." He circled, never taking his gaze from her. "I was like you."

"So you know you're not good and noble now, right? Not the hero of your own story?"

His mouth twitched in what might have been a smile or a snarl.

A slender shadow slid up behind him.

He must have seen it mirrored in her gaze, because he spun, vicious and quick, and slammed a blade that snapped from his sleeve, into the breast of the hooded figure.

Jill Scarlet slid to the floor, a sword clattering from her hands. As Finn whispered, "*No*," Lot casually drew his blade from the Jill's heart and snatched up her sword. As bloody, black petals drifted from the wound in Jill Scarlet's breast, his blue eyes shadowed. "Wolfsbane. You fool. I used *mistletoe* on that blade that went into you."

He slid to one knee beside Jill Scarlet, gripping her sword, its point balanced on the ground. He bowed his head like a knight about to receive a blessing and whispered, "Did you really think you could win?" He folded one hand over Jill Scarlet's scarred face, tightening his grip as if planning to crush her skull.

Finn edged toward Lily.

Lot snapped up and shoved Finn against a pillar. The beast, for an instant, made his beautiful face hideous. "Where are you going, my dear?"

She whispered, "*'A wilder'd being from my birth, my spirit spurned control.'*"

His eyes narrowed. "What are you doing?"

She continued with the words of a poet haunted by darkness, "*'But now, abroad on the wide earth, where wand'rest thou my soul?'*"

"What"—his teeth clenched as his hand returned to her throat, fingers tightening—"*are you doing?*"

She laughed breathlessly and wondered if the elixir or the fear was making her crazy—behind him, Lily was pushing to her feet. Finn said, "Don't you like poetry?"

"Hekas don't work on me either. Dangerous girl. What a *waste*." His fingers gouged into her throat.

Something burst through his chest.

He collapsed to one knee, staring down at the point of the umbrella that had speared him. The Mad Hatter painted on its vinyl folds gazed madly back at him as the umbrella's handle protruded from his back.

Finn lifted her gaze to Lily, who stood behind him, breathing hard and looking ferocious. Anna—whose umbrella Lily had used to impale the Wolf—was backed up against a wall, her eyes wide. Lily whispered, "That's for Leander, you fucking monst—"

Seth Lot spat out a dark liquid, laughed, reached around, and yanked the umbrella out. Black ichor spattered Lily's gown. She slowly retreated from the shadows that had begun rippling around him.

"Anna," Finn whispered, "*run!*"

There was a tearing roar, as if reality itself had been damaged, and the darkness grew around Seth Lot, who vanished, warping, towering. Ice cracked the glass in the windows. Frost furred the walls. As violent, guttural sounds came from within the dark cyclone, Anna backed away, one nostril trickling blood. She looked at Jill Scarlet's body and flinched.

A monstrous shape began forming in the darkness and Finn whispered, "That's one death for you—only two more."

Lily, on the other side of the black mass, met Finn's gaze. Anna was staring at the writhing shadow as if it contained all her childhood fears—the beast snarling in that spinning darkness exuded glacial cold and decay. Whatever emerged from that, whatever toothy, ripping horror . . . Finn wanted it to come at her, not Lily and Anna.

The cold vanished. The shadows fell away. Seth Lot stood before Finn in his beautiful form. As if recovering from a loss of control, he tucked his tangled hair behind his ears, the jewels flashing on his fingers. The ragged wound in his chest spilled more darkness as he bent down and picked up Anna's smashed umbrella. Turning it over in his hands, he sauntered toward Finn.

"The Fool," he said softly, running his fingers across the umbrella's wooden handle. "Wolfsbane poison on the tip and the rest puzzled together from sacred winter plants—mistletoe, holly, poinsettias, and black hellebore . . . made to kill a winter king. So, it was planned, was it? To bring the little oracle and her umbrella."

He looked up at Finn with a weariness that frightened her as much as the monster in the shadows had. Then he whirled and flung the shattered umbrella across the room, at Anna. Lily cried out and pulled Anna against her. The umbrella struck the wall and splintered.

Seth Lot spoke to Lily like a lover, but his blue gaze returned to Finn. "You were a fine queen, my love, but I have found a better one."

He gracefully extended a hand toward Finn, who didn't move.

"It's only because you don't want to die," she whispered. "And I can kill you."

He staggered a little, dropped his outstretched hand, and braced himself against a pillar. He laughed again, softly. "I'm not dead yet." As he pushed away from the pillar, malice in his gaze, she felt a swift terror of a different sort. He moved closer, leaned in. "Your Jack is dying of mistletoe poisoning. Aside from you, I see only two frightened girls." He raised his voice as Lily stepped toward something glittering on the floor—the steak knife that Finn had held. "And if those girls move, they will cause your death."

Lily stopped moving. Anna reached out and drew Lily back.

Seth Lot lifted one hand and laid it against Finn's face. She felt the rings on his fingers bite into her skin. "Think of what you could do as a queen. You could *change* me. You could make me a *good* man."

She said, her voice cracking, "I think it's too late for you."

"Then see," he breathed, "what *I* shall make *you*."

Her body shuddered against his as she slid toward darkness.

She stood in a forest, perhaps the first forest ever, branches arching above and before her in massive tangles over emerald gloom. Dusk stained the sky a nuclear crimson. Leaves of a red and orange so bright they seemed toxic fell around her. Her bare feet, jeweled with rings and tiny gems, crushed trilobites and prehistoric ferns. She saw her reflection in a pool of silver water suspended between two trees—she was a white-skinned creature in a black gown that trailed ribbons shimmering with spiderwebs, her brown hair dusted with pollen, braided with acorns and berries. She was crowned with briars and antlers. Her eyes were silvered, framed by black spirals, her smile a curve of malice. She felt strong, fearless. She could see every detail of the dark, fairy-tale forest around her: a striped spider in its web, its poison sac luminous; a cluster of crimson toadstools in the roots of an alder; the bones of what had once been a beautiful boy beneath her feet.

She could *rule* the dark.

Lot was walking toward her, his fur coat billowing, the wolf headdress a savage crown. His fingers, strong enough to crush bone, drifted like an electrical current across her collarbones, curved against one breast, over her heart. He began to unknot the ribbons on her gown. His autumn hair was tangled with thin braids and he smelled of sun-warmed fur, musk, and green things. A sleepy desire coursed through her.

He raised his head, his eyes radiant. "Why do you think you were drawn to those grand, ruined mansions, Serafina? To *our* places?" He leaned close, a darkness blotting out the world, and whispered in her ear, "Because you've always been seeking us."

And his mask slipped a little, revealing, for an instant, something shadowy and ancient and grinning. Smashing down her terror, Finn curled her fingers in the fur of his coat. "*Show me.*"

He kissed her as if intent on killing the mortal girl who remained. Biting and ruthless, it was not a sweet kiss; it was a devouring one, of lust and pain and power. Her blood began to ice, stinging her insides. An expanse of empty tundra filled her.

When Seth Lot snapped back from her, she tasted blood. He raised the edge of one hand to his mouth. He shook his head, once, like an animal trying to orient itself. When he lifted his blue gaze to her, the Wolf moved behind his eyes. "*What did you do to me?*"

"*Tamasgi'po,*" she whispered. "Spirit in a kiss. Second death."

The true world returned as he lunged at her, his nails curved claws meant for her eyes.

A knife arrowed through the clawed hand reaching for her.

The Wolf twisted around, pulling out the knife, staring at Lily. He still gripped Jill Scarlet's sword in his other hand. He pointed the sword at Lily and lovingly said, "I'm done with *you.*"

"You're dying." Finn's voice was faint. He turned on her and she thought she saw a flicker there, of horror, of someone trapped who had witnessed things that should never be. *It's a trick*, she told herself.

Then the Wolf smiled before whirling and lunging at Lily Rose, the sword's point aimed at her throat.

Another sword, the silvery-blue of new steel and engraved with runes, deflected his blade from Lily with an earsplitting shriek . . . and Jack, lithe and deadly, drove Lot back, moving as if the mistletoe hadn't done him any harm. He attacked Lot with quicksilver ferocity, his blade scything at the Wolf's neck, his torso, his legs. Seth Lot dodged, on the defensive.

Finn edged along the wall, toward Lily and Anna.

She saw Jack stagger—the wound in his chest dripped rose petals. Lot drove forward, effortlessly, relentlessly, bashing him into a defensive position, the ringing and clanging of their blades echoing from the stone walls.

"Finn!" Lily, shielding Anna from the whirlwind of Jack and Lot's battle, was edging with the young girl toward the exit.

Lot suddenly spun and lunged toward Finn, stabbing the point of his blade toward Finn's left eye.

Jack slid between them.

Lot twisted the blade to plunge it through Jack's chest.

As Lot dragged the sword out of Jack, who crumpled to the floor, hemorrhaging rose petals and blood, Finn dropped to her knees. The world went still.

"Jack . . ." Clutching one hand over the wound in his chest, she pushed the hair back from his face as he coughed blood and closed his eyes. Angrily, irrationally, she said, "Jack, don't you *dare* leave me now . . ."

Seth Lot crouched beside her. Gently, he said, "You see how this sort of thing concludes? This childish belief in happy endings?"

Jack's hand moved beneath hers. His fingers clasped hers around the hilt of the sword—she recognized the jackal hilt. She couldn't do it. She *couldn't* . . .

Jack took her hand from his chest and smiled. His lips moved: *You can.*

She rose and slammed back against the wall, gripping the sword's hilt with both hands. Her broken wrist still *hurt.*

Lot stood at the same time, gazing searchingly at her. Kindly, he said, "No. You're not a killer." He hefted the blade he held and looked at Jack. "So, now, *he* dies, and if he is in pieces, he won't be brought back again."

"Don't." Her voice scraped out of her. She still gripped the sword.

Lot stepped forward. He set a booted foot on one of Jack's hands, to hold him in place.

Jack's eyes opened. He twisted from beneath Lot, shouted, *"Now!"*

Moth slid from the shadows. Finn flung the sword to him. As Moth caught the sword by its hilt, Lot met Finn's gaze. And it came into his eyes, then, the soul with which the *Tamasgi'po* had begun to poison him.

He lunged toward her, his form as jittery as an old film as he sought to ride the shadow—

Moth swung the iron blade with two-handed strength. She wanted to look away, but she needed to see the monster end.

Before the flash of metal sliced through Lot's neck, the Wolf's eyes turned summer blue, the memories surging back, a *human* soul, long dead, waking up.

She closed her eyes, heard a whisper of breath, then silence.

"It's over, Finn." Jack spoke. "It's done."

She opened her eyes to see Moth standing above the body of a man, the head at his feet, the hair mercifully flung over its face. There was blood. She could hear Anna sobbing softly and Lily's hushed words of comfort. She lifted her gaze to her sister's and decided never to tell Lily what she'd seen at the last moment in Lot's eyes—the gratefulness of someone released from hell.

Jack rose from his false death to draw Finn into his arms. She was shaking, with anger, fear, and an immense relief.

"He died as a man," Lily whispered. "*How?*"

"*Tamasgi'po.*" Finn watched Moth, his face shadowed by the hood of his jacket, his hands blood spattered. "Spirit in a kiss. Memories. A soul sealed him into that body."

Moth said, his voice hoarse, "When you kissed me, Finn, when I was in pieces, you had the *Tamasgi'po* on your lips."

"Yes, Moth."

Moth walked to Jill Scarlet's body, crouched beside her, and laid one hand over her face. Without looking up, he said, "I'm remembering things. Do you recall the girl I told you about? The one in France? This was her. Rose Govannon, who wed a man named Sullivan. She was your ancestor, Finn. And Micah Govannon is of your blood."

Finn took a step forward, staring at Jill Scarlet's body, but Jack clasped her hand and said quietly, "Moth."

"Go," Moth said without looking up. "I barricaded the wolves in their atrocious banquet hall. Go before they get out."

"Moth—"

"*Go.*" Moth laid the jackal-hilted sword across his knees. "I'll take care of the Wolf's bloody house. I'll send it and his pack to hell."

"No, you will not." Finn pulled away from Jack.

Distant howling came from within the ruins.

"Finn," Lily said urgently as Anna glanced around in alarm.

"Finn, he's right, we need to go." Jack wrapped his coat close. "Moth—we'll see you again."

Moth didn't move. "Maybe you will. Finn, take your sister home."

"*Moth,*" Finn pleaded. Then Jack was pulling her away and she was running with him and Lily and Anna, down the hall, toward the stairs, as the Wolf's house began to shudder.

CHAPTER 22

I took her hand in mine, and we went out of the ruined place.
—*Great Expectations*, Charles Dickens

They staggered into a rainy night where Phouka Banríon and a small gathering of Fatas armed with beautifully crafted weapons had just arrived. Micah Govannon was with them, a silver crossbow shaped like a mermaid in one hand. Phouka, in her aviator's leather, looked ferocious.

"We followed you, but there was a glamour on that limo." Phouka lifted her gaze to the Gothic ruin. The air vibrated as if after a sonic boom.

The Wolf's house vanished. Finn whispered Moth's name.

"You did it," Phouka said, as her Fatas backed away toward a gypsy assortment of cars on the dirt road. "You killed the Wolf."

"Jack." Finn reached for him, pushing back his coat, revealing the bloody holes from Lot's sword.

"I'll stop bleeding, eventually." He smiled, but his voice was ragged with pain.

"But the mistletoe. Lot said it was on his blade—"

"Don't worry about it. You knew he'd find Lily at Anna's. And did you tell Anna to bring that umbrella? How did you know it was made of winter wood?"

"It was just a guess," Finn murmured. "I figured Absalom would know where Lily was because he seemed to be guarding Anna—he'd see you take Lily there, And he'd given Anna that weird umbrella . . . It was Absalom's chance to bargain for Anna's safety by handing my sister over to Lot. I don't know that he expected Lot to take Anna too. I thought Lot would just take Lily. I told her to bring Anna's umbrella." Putting her sister in danger again had made Finn a raw nerve, but it had been their last chance to be free of the Wolf. "I knew Absalom had made that umbrella as a weapon of some sort. And I knew Lot would get hold of us somehow."

"I'm a bit scared of you now." Jack swayed a little and Finn put an arm around him. Phouka slid a shoulder beneath Jack's other arm.

"*Help him.*" Her voice savage, Lily moved forward. "He nearly died fighting a monster *you* people wouldn't."

"He's a Jack now." Phouka was somber. "We can't—"

"Finn!" Christie and Sylvie were running toward them and Finn felt her fear lessen as the strength inside of her became steel.

Then Anna said, in a hushed voice, "They're coming."

Sylvie halted. "Who's coming?"

Jack said quietly, "Finn. Listen to me . . ."

She felt a breath of chill air against her skin as she gazed down at their entwined fingers, his ring with the lions and the heart glowing like a tiny sun. She was aware of the others withdrawing as he gently told her: "I've set things right."

"No." She was insanely calm even though she sensed a crackling in the air. "Not if you leave." Her eyes stung. She raised a hand to brush fingers across her cheek, felt grit on her skin. When she looked at her fingertips, they shimmered as if with diamond dust.

"Tears," Jack explained softly. "But the elixir changed them, is changing you. I can't let my world take you, Finn."

"*What did you do?*"

"What should have been done a long time ago."

The air began to rumble as if with the onset of a violent thunderstorm. The cold of a tomb, not a winter's evening, settled around them as a silvery mist curled from the forest, orbs of light dancing within it.

Finn met Jack's gaze as if they were the only two in the world and she spoke the poem they had chosen for their secret code, because, although it sounded like a love sonnet, it was really about a demon and a warrior. "'*I am thine, and thou art mine. 'Til the ending of the world.*'"

He bowed his head until his brow touched hers. "Let me go."

346   *Katherine Harbour*

"You idiot." And, because she couldn't cry, she kissed him as if that would cast out all the dark that made him want to die. For a moment, there was nothing in her world but the scent of his damp hair, his cool skin against hers, the tang of blood, the spirit burning in him. With grief like a high-tension wire all through her, she held him as she'd done the night of the Teind, when death had nearly taken him.

They turned, hands clasped, to face what had come for him.

The rumbling sounded like dozens of hooves striking the ground at a gallop, before transforming into the roaring of engines. The glowing orbs in the mist became headlights. The headlights and the swift shadows became black motorcycles shaped into sleek, animal forms. The motorcycles were otherworldly enough, but the riders, in soot-black suede or ash-white leather, were stranger still, in helmets representing the faces of things that scavenged the dead: a coyote, a hyena, a vulture, a raven, a fly, a wasp. A jackal.

The jackal's bike glided to a halt in front of Finn and Jack. His helmet looked almost Egyptian. His pale coat billowed as a fragrance of lilies, frankincense, and earth drifted from him. The rest of the motorcycles formed a crescent behind him, becoming nothing more than silhouettes. Terror hummed in the air, the terror of the unknown, of alien things without human feeling.

Finn tightened her grip on Jack's hand. She knew what the Wild Hunt, the *Fian Fiaghi*, was—a host of the dead, spirits led by death's general, collectors of lost souls. And this . . . this seemed to be one of their less horrifying aspects.

Lily moved to Finn's other side and clutched her hand as the leader spoke in a youthful and sexless voice, "A divine law has been broken: One of the true dead has entered the world."

It was Phouka who said angrily, "I might have known *you* were more than you seemed."

The jackal head tilted. Behind the seven riders, a whirlwind of inky darkness and cold began to form, branching out, solidifying into an arch of black stone hewn into writhing figures wreathed in nettles and thorns. Beyond the arch was a hole in the world, the void of night and nothing. Finn felt her courage shatter. She whispered, "No."

The jackal continued, "One must come or one be taken."

Jack turned to Finn, rain shimmering on his lashes. He kissed her again as the grief blinded and choked her. *The path of pins or the path of needles.* When he stepped back from her, she didn't move, as if, by keeping still, she could stop this from happening.

As Jack walked toward the leader of the Wild Hunt, the leader removed the helmet to reveal the snow-gold hair and haughty face of a Fata girl.

"*Norn?*" Lily whispered.

Jack halted.

"Jack." Norn inclined her head.

"No!" Lily strode forward. "Take me!"

"Lily!" Finn reached for her. She looked at the Wild Hunt. "It's *me* you want! *I* broke the rules!"

Jack, without turning or breaking stride, said, "Phouka."

When Phouka gently took hold of Lily's arm and grasped Finn's hand, Finn felt as if those nettles around the arch into the land of the dead were tearing into her. She watched Jack walk past the riders. The Wild Hunt turned their motorcycles.

"*Jack!*" Not even the elixir could tear Finn from Phouka's grip. As Lily sank to her knees, her head bowed, Christie and Sylvie moved to either side of Finn. They, too, were grimly prepared to hold her here.

Finn said, her voice raw, "*I'll find you!*"

Beneath the arch, Jack halted. He looked back at her, dark hair drifting over his face.

Then he turned and walked into the shadows with the Wild Hunt on either side of him. The nettles closed over him. The arch shrank into a black orb and winked out. The rain became snow, falling silently.

Christie and Sylvie were speaking to her. Anna was sobbing softly. She heard Phouka's voice, but she couldn't understand what anyone was saying as Lily wrapped her arms around Finn and, together, they gazed at the place where Jack had vanished.

CHAPTER 23

Jill Scarlet, who had been Rose Govannon Sullivan before the Wolf; Leander Cyrus, who had met an ancient mermaid; Hester Kierney, who had been tricked; Moth, who had been Alexander Nightshade before a curse; Jack, who had only wanted to be human. Each loss was more unbearable than the last.

As Finn rode in the back of Phouka's Mercedes with Lily, Anna, Christie, and Sylvie, she watched the snow fall over the holiday lights and decorations of Main Street. She couldn't cry. Her tears hurt, because, due to the elixir, they were like diamond dust now. No one spoke.

She would not let go of Lily's hand.

As Phouka drove the Mercedes down Finn's street and Finn glimpsed her da shoveling snow on the front path, she wanted to cry again.

The car stopped. Finn, her voice hoarse, said, "Lily, wait—"

Lily shoved open the car door. Finn slid out with her, trying to catch her, but Lily was already running up the path, her black gown fluttering around her legs. "Dad! *Dad!*"

He turned. The shovel dropped from his hands. He looked as if he'd been struck by some invisible force.

Lily halted with Finn beside her.

Then their father was striding toward them. He pulled Lily into his arms, whispering her name over and over, his eyes bright with tears. "Is it really you? *Is it really you?*"

And as Sean Sullivan dragged Finn into the embrace, Finn closed her eyes and held on to the family Jack had returned to her.

JACK FELT THE WILD HUNT on either side of him as he walked the path of pins and needles, of briars and thorns. He wasn't afraid of ending.

He glanced back over one shoulder, thought he saw a spark of light, caught a fragrance of the spring that would soon reach the true world, overwhelming, for a moment, the scents of nightshade and dust around him.

She was safe.

He turned and smiled and continued on, into the dark.

Lily told me there's a word in their language that sounds like the Irish one for "butterfly"—elvaude—and it means "one of us, becoming one of them." There is no word in their language for one of them becoming one of us.

Finn set down her journal, a book of scarlet leather embossed with a golden butterfly, similar to the book of maps she'd found in the Black House haunted by Ellen and Roland and once the home of Jack and Reiko. Perched on the window seat in her room, she gazed out at Christmas Eve, the dazzle of holiday lights on snow. She heard her sister and her da talking downstairs in the kitchen as if Lily had never been stolen away.

It was Lily who had told the story, about her death having been faked by a nomadic cult who had kidnapped her in California. When their father decided to call the police, Lily had told him she wouldn't be able to identify anyone because they'd drugged her. And that had resulted in their father setting down the phone and taking Lily to the emergency room—where Lily had had to speak, perfectly poised, with two police officers.

That night, huddled in Finn's bed, Lily had cried softly for Leander, and Finn, who still wasn't able to shed tears for Jack, or anyone, had held her and whispered something she remembered from Shakespeare's *The Tempest*, "'Nothing of him *that doth fade, but doth suffer a sea-change, into something rich and strange.'"*

There had been a lot of midnight talks between them since then.

Her da called her for dinner and Lily echoed him. Finn smiled. She walked out of her bedroom and closed the door.

A DRAFT SWEPT THROUGH THE ROOM, riffling the pictures on the bulletin board—the Leica photographs of glowing orbs: of a ghostly young man and woman in antique clothes; of Finn and Moth seated on a giant, metal toadstool; of Finn and Jack on the train that had brought them back to the true world.

The photograph of Finn and Jack glided from the bulletin board and fell on top of her last journal entry:

Jack saved me twice. He saved Lily. Now it's my turn to save him.

EPILOGUE

Phouka Banrión sauntered along the path in Tirnagoth's garden, her hands in the pockets of her coat. Snow and chrysanthemums glimmered in her copper-dark hair. She wore white, the Fata color for sorrow, although she didn't know how to mourn anymore, only how to perform the motions.

She bowed her head. *Jack.* She owed him and Finn Sullivan.

"Was that not a clever trick?" A voice spoke from above. "You see how she uses their natures against them?"

Phouka looked up at the figure crouched on a branch of the holly tree near which she stood. "Absalom. Why did you give Anna Weaver that umbrella of winter wood?"

"Anna wasn't targeted or suspected. Unlike Finn or her comrades." Absalom grinned. "You think Lot saw that coming?"

"I don't think he saw the umbrella coming, or the *Tamasgi'po*, or the sword that took off his head. How you orchestrated Serafina Sullivan obtaining those things . . . you are a devil."

He shrugged with false modesty. "Honestly, it was only because our heroine did what she was supposed to."

"And if it hadn't rained? You don't think Lot would have found Anna's insistence on bringing her deadly umbrella a little suspect?"

He shrugged.

"And there is the matter of her sister," Phouka continued. "Whom Serafina believes you betrayed to Lot."

Lithe and careless as a cat, Absalom jumped down before her. In his fur-lined jacket and worn denim, his orange hair falling over his face, he looked like any teenage boy—except for the eyes. He could never get those quite right. "It was part of my master plan. You do realize Lily Rose doesn't remember her death? Funny thing about memory . . . it can be so inconvenient at times."

"What"—Phouka took a step toward him—"have you *inconveniently* remembered?"

The devil light flickered in his golden gaze. "I've remembered who Moth really is."

She shut her eyes for a moment, thought better of it. Carefully, she said, "Go on."

"I first met Moth before I cursed him in your time, Lizzie."

"Don't call me that."

"Long ago, Moth was born among the Laplander tribes, a creature who could pretend to be anyone he wished. A mortal witch. A human freak of nature. Some believed his father hadn't been human. Then one of us made him into a Jack."

"Which one of us and how long ago?"

"You recall Hans Christian Andersen's poignant tale 'The Snow Queen'? Well, the cold bitch was real—she's the one who taught Seth Lot stitchery. Anyhow, later on, Moth the Jack stole something from me—that was during the Renaissance, and I was quite peeved."

"What did he steal?"

"I'd rather not say. It's embarrassing. So, when I met Moth as a Jack—Alexander Nightshade—pretending to be an actor in Shakespeare's theater—and plotting against you, by the way—I took his memory and cursed him so that, whenever he kissed someone, he turned into a bug."

"So you just left a dangerous creature like that around like a discarded toy all chock-full of magic, for the Black Scissors and Seth Lot to find?"

Absalom looked glum. "I didn't expect Lot to find Moth and what Moth stole from me. I didn't expect the Black Scissors to turn him into a key."

"Absalom. *What is Moth?*"

"Our first mistake." Absalom's mischief vanished and the age returned to his eyes. "Our first Jack."

Fear was a rare experience for Phouka. "Where is Moth now?"

"When our cracking-clever Finn kissed Moth, her lips were glossed with the *Tamasgi'po*. I'm afraid the terror we came here to watch for has been under our noses all this time—and he's just woken up and remembered what he is."

Phouka whispered a name that shivered the unfamiliar element of dread through her. "Harahkte."

IN THE NIGHT RADIANT WITH SNOW FALL, a lean figure in a black hoodie and jeans stood outside of Tirangoth's gates, gazing at the hotel. He raised a hand to idly caress the roses blossoming unnaturally around him. The roses blackened, flaked away, drifted over a birch tree where an insect that should not exist in winter hovered like an eye.

As a smile glinted in the shadows beneath the figure's hood, the brass dragonfly, unseen, flickered urgently away into the dark.

CHARACTERS

THE PROFESSORS
Finn Sullivan
Jack Hawthorn
Christie Hart
Sylvie Whitethorn
Sean Sullivan
Caliban Ariel'Pan
Leander Cyrus
Anna Weaver

James Wyatt
Edmund Fairchild
Sophia Avaline
Charlotte Perangelo
Patrick Hobson
Jane Emory

THE BLESSED
Seth Lot
Sionnach Ri
Sylph Dragonfly
Amaranthus Mockingbird
Moth (Alexander Nightshade)
Micah Govannon

Ijio Valentine
Nick Tudor
Victoria Tudor
Hester Kierney
Claudette Tredescant
Aubrey Drake

OTHERS
THE FATAS
The Black Scissors (William Harrow)
Jill Scarlet (Rose Govannon Sullivan)
Murray
Lulu

Atheno
Aurora Sae
Darling Ivy
DogRose

Devon Valentine
Trip (Victor Tirnagoth)
Hip Hop (Emily Tirnagoth)
Bottle (Eammon Tirnagoth)
Thomas Luneht
Eve Avaline
Beatrice Amory
Abigail Cwyndyr
Norn
Rowan Cruithnear
Ellen Byrd
Roland Childe
Lily Rose Sullivan
Jill (David Ryder's)

Farouche
Black Apple
Wren's Knot
Narcissus Mockingbird
The Blackhearts
BatSong
Dead Bird
Antoinette
Luce and Merriweather

If You Liked the Book, Here's the Sound Track

"I Know Places"—Lykke Li

"White Winter Hymnal" and **"Terrible Love"**—Birdy

"King and Lionheart"—Of Monsters and Men

"For You"—Passenger

"Team"—Lorde

"Northern Lights" and **"Depuis Le Debut"**—30 Seconds to Mars

"Tomorrow"—Daughter

"Keep the Streets Empty for Me"—Fever Ray

"The High Road"—Joss Stone

"Human"—Christina Perri

"House on a Hill"—The Pretty Reckless

"By the Evening"—Benjamin Booker

"Darkness, Darkness"—Robert Plant

"Silhouette"—Owl City

Glossary of Names and Fata Words

aisling (AH sleen)—immortal changeling

ban dorchadas (baan doruk HUDus)—female witch

ban nathair—white serpent

Ban Gorm (baan GORim)—Blue Lady

baobhan sith (baan SHEE)—vampire

Banríon (baan nREEN)—queen

Bean Beache (baan makh)—White Bee

Cailleach Oidche (kah lee ahk ee YEE)—owl girl

croi baintreach (KREE banch rukh)—heart widow

crom cu (krom KOO)—crooked dog

Damh Ridire (daav ree JEER)—Stag Knight

Dearh Cota (jarv KOHtu)—red coat/hood

Dubh Deamhais (doov DEE amayus)—Black Scissors

elvaude (AYL vawd)—a mortal become Fata

Fata (FAY dah)

fear dorchadas (fahr doruk HUDus)—male witch

Fian Fiaghi (fee in fee AH gee)—Wild Hunt

Ialtag Amhran (ee OO tag oe rahn)—BatSong

leannan (lah NAAN)—sweetheart

Lham Dearg (laam jarOO)—Red Hand

Madadh aillaid (maDOO ahlah)—Wolf king

Marbh ean (maROO ae en)—Dead Bird

muirneach (mor NUKH)—beloved

Phouka (FUU ah)

Reiko (RAY koh)

scail amhasge (skaal oe OSK)—black dogs

sluagh (es LOO ah)—the dead

Taibhse na Tir (tahvs na TEER)—Ghostlands

Tamasgi'po (tamus GEE poh)—spirit in a kiss

Tarbh-naith irach (tahr naath EERahk)—dragonfly